ellen c. maze

BEYOND THE RABBIT

Anomaly: Beyond the Rabbit
By Ellen C. Maze Sallas
First Edition
©2018 by Ellen C. Maze Sallas

ISBN-13: 978-0692098493
ISBN-10: 0692098496
Also available in eBook

Little Roni Publishers
Byhalia, MS
www.littleronipublishers.com
v.11.14.2019
Cover Art & Design: Hyliian Graphics, http://hyliian.deviantart.com
Creative Consultant: Jill Potts Jones,
www.IAmBelievingGod.wordpress.com
Authors Links: www.ellencmaze.com ellenmaze@aol.com

Twitter: @authorellenmaze
Facebook: www.facebook.com/ellencmaze

Ages 13+, Language, Sexual Situations, Vampire Violence

PUBLISHED IN THE UNITED STATES OF AMERICA

From the Publisher:
Ages 13+, Language, Sexual Situations, Vampire Violence

Concerning the *Rabbit Trilogy / Rabbit Saga*, Books 1 & 2 are written largely from a "mortal" perspective, with limited peeks into the mindset of the demonically-spawned Rakum. Although still written with a Biblical worldview, *Anomaly,* and its upcoming sequel, *Conundrum*, deal primarily with the Rakum mindset. Because of this, caution is extended to sensitive and/or young readers, mainly in the areas of the sexual themes and somewhat harsher profanity which is presented within the confines of what you might experience with a PG-13 feature film.

NOTE: The strongest expletives have been redacted, but not entirely obscured.

Christian Fiction / Fantasy / Paranormal
by Ellen C. Maze

Rabbit: Chasing Beth Rider *(Book One)*
Rabbit Legacy *(Book Two)*
Rabbit Redemption *(Book Three)*
Anomaly *(Book Four)*
Conundrum *(Book Five)*
The Vestige *(Final Chapter)*

The Judging:
The Corescu Chronicles Book One
Damascus Road:
The Corescu Chronicles Book Two

Vampires are fiction;
The Rakum are real...

Rakum (RAH'-kum) – a.k.a **Wraith**, from Heb. *raca*; "vain thing." Def: From Semitic mythology; a race of vampire-like beings thought to be descended from fallen angels.

MAIN CHARACTERS
(In Order of Seniority)

Kilmeade – b.1633, apparent age ~40, Rakum Elder, Roman's fraternal twin

Canaan – b.1652, apparent age ~35; Rakum Elder, recently split from human mate **Marcy Haddle** after 40 years

Roman – b.1633, apparent age ~50; *former Rakum Elder*, now human

Javier – b.1877, apparent age ~35; *former Rakum grunt*, now human

Beryl – b.1901, apparent age ~19; transforming Rakum captain, of the infamous Rakum twins

David Walker – b.1935, apparent age ~25; *former Rakum grunt*, now human

Chloe Mina Bushman – 20, human, student at the University of Alabama, Elder Rufus's victim in *Rabbit Legacy*

Rafael – b.1772, apparent age ~30, transforming Rakum grunt

Simon Miller – 27, human, former Cow to Javier

ANOMALY: BEYOND THE RABBIT
PICKS UP WHERE THE RABBIT TRILOGY LEAVES OFF...

Rabbit: Chasing Beth Rider / Book One

1 The decimation of the Rakum began with Beth Rider seven years back at what became known as "Last Assembly," when a woman marked as a Rabbit brought down their leaders with an amazing power, of which the Rakum previously knew nothing about. After that night, the 100,000-strong Rakum population had been reduced to half.

Rabbit Legacy / Book Two

2 Picking up seven years later, insane and bloodthirsty Elder Rufus has taken it upon himself to lead, destroying the brethren who refused to bend the knee to his psychotic agenda. By the time Isaac "The Last" joins with Elder Canaan and the Rabbit posse to destroy him, a mere twenty thousand brethren remain.

Rabbit Redemption / Book Three

3 When the dust clears and Rufus is dead, childlike Father Isaac Akaron has the power to return his brethren to their former glory and when the secret that slumbers in his spirit awakens, no flesh on Earth can match him. Serving under duress, Elder Canaan seeks assistance from Javier who struggles with a bizarre and bloodthirsty secret of his own. The ensuing conflict on November 13th, spans dimensions and affects the Rakum in a surprising and life-altering way.

And here we are... The survivors must go *beyond* the Rabbit. Elders Kilmeade and Canaan remain intact, their power and glory only increasing. But, for how long? The time has come to choose sides. The spiritual forces that propel all flesh demand allegiance, commanding each cognizant being to *choose:* darkness or light? One end of the spiritual spectrum promises limitless pleasure for as long as they live; the other, eternal peace in the presence of the Creator who loves them. Kilmeade knows which choice best serves; the challenge is convincing his flesh—and that of his brother—to agree...

"Anomaly. That's you now..."
~Javier to Canaan in the aftermath of 11/13
(Rabbit Redemption)

PROLOGUE

1899 Montreal, Quebec

Elder Kilmeade was hungry and bored, but mostly, he was hungry. Under a gloriously full moon, Canaan raced Kilmeade into town, his thoroughbred outpacing his cohort's warmblood by four strides. When the bend in the road straightened, Canaan kicked the leggy gelding into high gear, leaving Kilmeade eating dust in his wake.

Tonight marked the end of the senior Elder's punishment for taking the Dying Buzz[1] at his hospital assignment in Manhattan. The Ten Fathers quarantined Kilmeade for two years, during which he endured a strict diet of only Elder-Candidate Canaan's blood. Tonight's celebratory gallop also marked Canaan's graduation to Elder, earned by seeing his brother succeed to the Fathers' satisfaction. The Rakum were ruled by the Ten Fathers, all of whom dated back two millennia. Under their wise and sometimes brutal guidance sat the One Hundred Elders, who each held responsibility for 1,000 brethren, breaking up their packs with captains and lieutenants at the Elder's discretion. Canaan had been Jack Dawn's lieutenant for decades before being called up for promotion. Canaan's spirit soared over the accomplishment after more than twenty years of harsh training. With the difficult tests behind him, he need only see Kilmeade through this night.

"Elder Canaan!" Kilmeade called, winking when Canaan peeked over his shoulder at the sound of his new title spoken aloud. "Slow down or I will end that nag right out from under you!"

Canaan smirked and sat upright to bring the horse to a canter. A dozen meters ahead, the brothel-inn-pub came into view, the only such business in the tiny Montreal village. Canaan's horse broke to a trot and he posted past the sundries establishment and a one-room building that served as a schoolhouse and church, both unlit at this hour. The brothel, however, teemed with life, attracting patrons from many kilometers away. When he reached the pub, Canaan dismounted and flipped the reins over the rail alongside a shaggy saddled mule. Kilmeade was seconds behind him and soon, they stood on the establishment's plank porch prepared to

---

[1] The Dying Buzz is the practice of drinking a mortal to death. It brings various side effects (euphoria, increased mystical and physical power, altered physicality of teeth, hair, nails, etc.), all short-lived unless the infraction is frequently repeated.

1

enter. Kilmeade inhaled deeply and sent Canaan an eager glance. In two years, he had not once left their tiny compound, while Canaan had been free to come and go as he pleased.

"Good thing you're an Elder," Canaan sent telepathically. *"A lesser Rakum would go insane with such a sentence."*

With a grin, Kilmeade inclined his head to the door. *"Enough small talk, pup. Let us enter!"*

Not offended at the demeaning moniker, Canaan pressed the door handle's thumb latch and the cacophony of humanity heard from the dark street poured forth with substance. He grinned wide at the sight of Kilmeade barely containing his exuberance. Taking the lead to make way for his superior, Canaan stepped through the bodies toward the bar. Teems of locals and travelers jostled between the scattered tables and working women in long skirts and tight, scooped blouses peppered the crowd. When a stranger bumped against Canaan, he ignored the incident and moved on. When the same man collided with Kilmeade, the Elder took him by the shoulders and kissed both cheeks.

"Bonjour!" he said too loudly in his excitement.

"Bonjour!" the man replied with a drunken grin and shuffled away.

Canaan waved Kilmeade to his side. The mortals wouldn't notice he and his brother weren't human. They wore the correct fashions and groomed within the parameters for men their apparent age. Slender and strong with bright gray eyes and a five-o'clock shadow he never grew into a proper beard, Kilmeade stood 6'3" and wore his auburn hair to his shoulders. Canaan topped his height by one inch and had grown thick with muscle. He maintained his bright blonde curls above his ears and he preferred to be clean-shaven. Also, the humans would never know each had seen two centuries pass, neither of them appearing out of their thirties.

Kilmeade elbowed Canaan to bring him out of his thoughts. With a furtive heads-up, he caught the eye of the barkeep who ambled close on bowed legs.

"Monsieur Canaan, the regular?" the man asked, his tiny eyes dwarfed by enormous pink jowls.

Canaan gestured to Kilmeade. "Add Rebekah for my friend."

Kilmeade flattened his palms on the bar top. "Rebekah..." he muttered to no one, his eyes dancing about.

"The Fathers insist I go with you," Canaan sent telepathically.

Aware of the stipulation, Kilmeade offered a tiny nod. The barkeep delivered two frothy beers in heavy pewter steins and by the time Canaan downed half, his favorite girl and the one she recommended entered from the rear of the boisterous space.

"Master Canaan!" the woman said reaching his side, hands behind her back. A seasoned Cow,[2] Keri understood the tenets regarding proper behavior around the Rakum. A slender brunette Canaan recognized as Rebekah nodded to them both.

Canaan inclined his head toward Kilmeade and instructed the younger prostitute, "Call him *Master.*" When she understood, Canaan smiled. "Lead the way, my beauties!"

Rebekah lifted her long skirts from the floor and swished by with Kilmeade directly behind. Canaan put out his arm to Keri who took it.

"Beka knows the ropes, Master," Keri said so low only a Rakum would hear. "She is not a Cow, but she will consent."

"Excellent," Canaan grinned; Kilmeade would want the woman's blood and her consent made the draw worthwhile.

When they had reached the small windowless inner room that the women used for business, Canaan closed the door with the four of them inside. Hearing the lock flip, the women instinctively grouped side-by-side. Canaan remained with his back to the door and Kilmeade stood beside the small table bearing an oil lamp, its wick providing light for the women. Sparsely appointed, the room supplied a straw-stuffed mattress in one corner and a spindly wooden stool beside the lamp table.

Canaan raised his brow when Kilmeade met his eye. *"It's your night, Master,"* he sent with respect.

Kilmeade clasped his hands at chest-level, bottling his titillation.

Rebekah broke the stillness, taking two steps toward Kilmeade. "I am at your service, Master," she said with her eyes to the floor.

With no hesitation, Kilmeade pulled the woman close. He brushed his lips against her throat, sending the woman telepathic suggestions that Canaan monitored; Kilmeade would be a Rakum in *control,* not one whose need for visceral thrill overshadowed his desire to please the Fathers.

"Be still, shh..." Canaan overheard followed by, *"That goes for you, too, pup,"* and Canaan smirked at Kilmeade's mischievous tone.

The girl gasped and strained as Kilmeade gathered her tight to his body. The Elder's physical malformations caused by his transgression had returned to normal, except for his teeth. Still sharp enough to serve as fangs, he surprised the youngster with the sudden stab at her throat.

---

[2] Rakum Cow: a human with a visceral need to let blood to the Rakum.

When Canaan discerned Kilmeade had taken enough, he expected his superior to withdraw. Another two seconds passed, and then four, and then ten. The young woman had a level her heart could bear and Kilmeade had near exceeded it. When Canaan tensed to act, his partner broke free and covered the wound with his palm. He turned his face to Canaan and grinned—no evidence of a Dying Buzz; a normal and extremely satisfied Kilmeade looked back at him, drunk with blood he had waited two years to enjoy.

Reading the Elder's movements, Keri closed in and caught Rebekah as Kilmeade handed her off. He slumped onto the stool, placed both palms to his thighs, and leaned over as the buzz tickled him deep within. Canaan stood against the door, a half-grin reaching his face. No one spoke and Keri gently laid her friend on the lumpy mattress, her eyes on her master. Within another minute, Kilmeade chortled deep in his chest and straightened his spine to catch Canaan's eye.

"Now, I will have yours," he said for the woman to hear. Canaan's grin completed and he nodded. Keri gulped and whispered the coached phrase. Kilmeade yanked her close. As a Cow he needn't be as gentle, and he wasn't. Again, he took her several seconds past ideal, but Canaan remained still. His superior had been an Elder for a century; he knew what he was doing and had no desire to return to the prison of the Fathers. When Keri fell unconscious, Kilmeade placed her against her friend. Their hearts beat strong in their chests and he had erased their wounds with his touch. Canaan unlatched the door.

"Pay them triple. They won't be able to work anymore tonight."

"*Merde,* I'll leave it all." Kilmeade emptied his pocket. "Worth every ounce." Enough silver for a week's wage tumbled onto the table and Canaan collected it into his palm to shove beneath Keri's body. As they reentered the main room, Kilmeade asked, "What about you?"

"Wait for me at the bar," Canaan said with a wry grin and then followed Kilmeade with his gaze until he leaned in and ordered a beer. When the barkeep shoved it to him, he met Canaan's eye. With a nod he removed his apron and came around.

"Two Cows in this tiny village?" Kilmeade asked as Canaan and the barman disappeared into his cluttered quarters. *"Oh, you've been spoiled!"*

Canaan smiled; it was his turn to buzz and he needed no chaperone.

1, NOV 14, TUSCALOOSA, AL

Present Day

"BACK THE HELL UP! I'LL KILL HER!" Boris shouted to the mortals crowding him outside the emergency room entrance. Unable to help him without drawing attention, Kilmeade and Canaan melted into the crowd surrounding the wide-eyed maniac holding a knife to a nurse's neck. Fifteen minutes ago, damp and smelly, Kilmeade had led them safely out of the storm-drain.[3] Unfortunately, Boris had lost his grip on reality. Leaving him behind, the Elders reached the Caddy and Rafael hastily got them on the road. Beryl occupied the front passenger seat, leaving Canaan and Kilmeade in the back, sliding crazily on the slick leather when their chauffeur took the first turn too excitedly.

Canaan chuckled, "Slow down, Mario. No one's chasing us."

Kilmeade said nothing and watched the back of Rafael's head. Only five days ago the appealing pup had arrived at his California home seeking healing for his Cow. Kilmeade came alive in his presence after seven years alone, hiding from a homicidal Elder Rufus.

But look at him now...

Like all remaining Rakum, Rafael was transforming into a mortal. Beryl had further yet to go and Kilmeade determined he might even need to stay out of the sun a few more days. On top of his thoughts, Canaan kicked the back of Beryl's seat.

"B, stay out of the sun a little longer, got it?" Canaan waited for a nod and returned his gaze to the night.

"Take us to Simon Miller's house," Kilmeade directed in a low voice and he leaned back, happy to be out of the sewer. As predicted, he had tumped into the inch-high liquid during his sleep and all four of them were foul. At Simon's, they could clean up, formulate a plan, and head out. Kilmeade sent a test telepathic directive to Beryl: *"Text Javier."*

Beryl's face whipped around to his, a sad sparkle in his bright fawn-colored eyes, and then he faced front, cell phone in hand. Beryl had been taking the news hard, yet there was nothing to be done about it but keep

---

[3] *Anomaly* Chapter 1 picks up directly where *Rabbit Redemption: Book Three of the Rabbit Trilogy* ends.

5

moving forward. Kilmeade closed his eyes and imagined arriving at Miller's home. He and Rafael had never met the man Javier held as a Cow before his change. Kilmeade frowned. *I'm not looking forward to this,* he thought, not truly speaking to Canaan, who did not respond.

What now? Javier and Roman greeting them with their concerns when they arrived; their Cows, Santiago and Jimmy, seeking comfort and reassurance; the affable Rakum Bankers, Guap and Polly, masking their despair with humor and false joviality. *So many mortals and almost-mortals depending on their Elders to make everything right...*

"Look at me."

Kilmeade reluctantly met Canaan's gaze. For several seconds nothing happened, just two Elders in a blinking contest. Then Canaan sent him a half-grin.

"Hang in there. One more hour, then the two of us head to Nashville. Alone."

Kilmeade offered a tiny nod and leaned back, preparing to close his eyes and shut everything out, but Canaan wasn't finished. He slid to the center of the leather seat.

"Cheer up," he sent silently, pushing up his right sleeve. Kilmeade stared at his arm, his mind a million miles away. So many changes upon them, so many details to sort out, and the structure of the way he had lived his life the past four centuries had been altered in one fell blow. Yet the blood remained vital. Kilmeade pulled Canaan's offering to his lips.

"You cheer me, Canaan. You always have," Kilmeade replied silently and sank his un-Rakum-like fangs into the Elder's inner arm. Would he lose his precious anomaly: the fangs developed many years ago by drinking the blood of the dying? Besides Isaac, no other Rakum had them and as the last Rakum ever bred, Isaac had been an anomaly unto himself.

Their group had been forced to destroy the legendary youth last night, but if they hadn't, he would have eventually murdered them all in his budding insanity. High Father Abroghia dubbed him Yitzhak Akaron, loosely translated *He Laughs Last*.[4] The legends of The Last did not come close to preparing any of them for the boy's ruthless and cannibalistic nature. Yes, Isaac had sported fangs, but he manifested them with power not even the Fathers possessed.

Kilmeade sighed as Canaan's blood coursed down his throat as smoothly as he remembered. Every cell in his body awoke, chastising him for going so long without an Elder's blood. But he and Canaan had been apart for decades, only reconnecting during the current emergency

---

[4] Isaac was the central antagonist in *Rabbit Redemption: Book Three of the Rabbit Trilogy*.

regarding The Last. He ceased his feast and the punctures healed in seconds. Canaan leaned against him, two powerful Rakum Elders against a planet of six billion non-Rakum. It was going to be lonely.

"It's going to be fine," Canaan sent over and Kilmeade noted Rafa watching them from the rearview mirror. How would he manage? For two hundred and forty-five years, the beautiful Spanish Rakum had lived in the world of the night, one of the brethren, of a race of walking gods.

They reached Miller's newly-inherited estate and Kilmeade focused on the present, determined to stay only as long as necessary. When the car came to a halt, he assumed his game face and Canaan escorted him to the house.

Precisely one hour later, Kilmeade dropped into the passenger side of one of Miller's extra cars, borrowed due to the sewer-tainted condition of Canaan's Cadillac. Javier D'Millier, Canaan's long-time Rakum chum, presented the four arrivals each with a personalized bag of toiletries, plus one set of clothing, to replace the putrid rags in which they arrived. Kilmeade had been impressed, but now? He was bored. Canaan's young friend glanced his way. Javier had been a superb proselyte and companion to his twin Roman for many years. His Gypsy-like swarthy appearance brought a sense of drama to an otherwise even-tempered personality. Canaan took a liking to him a century ago and their bond had only strengthened over the last few months.

Kilmeade drummed his fingers on his thigh and watched the farewells continue. *"Kiss him goodbye, you fairy,"* Kilmeade teased.

Canaan grinned in response, only his profile visible at the current angle. The two men continued their conversation and Kilmeade exhaled; patience had never been his strong-point.

"Beryl isn't taking it well," Canaan was saying to Javier a dozen yards away. "Keep an eye on him. I'll come back for him if necessary."

Kilmeade agreed with the sentiment. Beryl had been one of the most celebrated Rakum captains in their history. Along with his identical twin Meryl, their reputation was a ruthless, bloodthirsty, and power-hungry pair, their closeness manifesting as two in one brain. When Meryl was killed mere weeks ago by the Rakum spirit Ta'avah, part of Beryl went with him. Now the passionate Rakum was transforming and did not lean on Javier's God for peace.

God: the common denominator among the grunts he'd witnessed change so far—those who listened to the God of the humans found comfort in Him. Beryl still refused to acknowledge His help even though

Javier's God had healed a horrible curse eating half his face.

"Guap and Polly will put him to work," Javier replied.

Kilmeade didn't look over, sensing another handshake and shoulder-bump occurring between the two. *Canaan and his friends...* Largely considered to be an irascible and pugilistic loner, Canaan had allowed a scant few into his circle; Beryl and Javier being the main two and of course, Marcy Haddle, a female he held as a mate the past four decades.

"Don't forget Kilmeade, who I selflessly rescued with my precious blood," Canaan said entering the driver's seat. "Come on, sexy, Marcy's waiting."

"I hope she gives you some release. You're very full of yourself."

Canaan chuckled. "Leave off the crap about my little collection of friends and point to yourself. Latching onto Rafael the way you did? Putting your neck on the line for Roman..." Canaan switched on the car. "...a *human.*" He said the last word in a conspiratorial whisper and then giggled like a maniac.

Kilmeade smiled. "I am what I am, and I always have been."

Canaan laughed aloud, having heard his cohort's personal mantra many times over the course of their history. "That's my favorite thing about you, Kilmeade. You yam what you yam!"

"Drive on, pup." Kilmeade closed his eyes to ponder what lay ahead.

"Yes, Master!" Canaan replied grinning and left him to his thoughts.

《回》

Waking Marcy hadn't been difficult; she'd lived as a Rakum's mate for decades and had long given up sleeping through the night. She met them at the door, irritable because of the hell Canaan's people once again subjected her to. Kilmeade graciously took the car out for a spin to afford the couple their privacy. Now, deliciously alone, lying on crisp white linens, Canaan cradled Marcy's head with one huge hand and used the other to brush a strand of her frizzy red hair aside.

Earlier when he arrived, something was different. The love was there, but an unfamiliar hardness lingered deep. They had embraced, they had kissed, but before the ignition sequence could begin in earnest, she steered them to the dinette instead of the bedroom and informed him she was moving in with her mother.

"Cee," Canaan began and stopped. Everything he would counter would be something for which she had an argument. Her eyes told him she had moved on and there would be no changing her mind.

"Canaan," she said softly and touched his hand, "I just want to be a

ellen c. maze

normal person. I'm done with the Rakum."

"There are only two of us left," Canaan said and held up his hand before her follow-up correction. "I know what you meant." The abuse she suffered at the hands of his people had finally broken the bridge between them. Marcy gave him a gentle smile.

"Honey, let me plant flowers. I want to ride horses, train little dogs, maybe raise some rabbits. Let me live in the sun. Be happy for me."

"I am, baby," Canaan nodded, studying his knuckles on the tabletop.

"Hey," she said and squeezed his forearm, "you're going to live hundreds of years. Take another mate. You have my blessing."

"Shew," Canaan exhaled. "Not gonna happen." She would read the rest in his eyes; *there is only one Marcy Haddle.* He met her by chance and chose her because his heart wouldn't allow him *not* to. Before and after, other women meant less than nothing.

"You will be happy. Take care of Kilmeade," she said softly.

"I will," he mumbled aware that the wall she began grew steadily between them moment by moment.

"Oh," she said and rose to grab a package off the counter. "Take these. It's two copies of *The Rabbit* by Beth Rider-Stone. Give one to Kilmeade. You told me you wished you had read it."

Canaan peeled back the butcher paper and stared at the glossy cover. Under the embossed title a white rabbit rushed through a hellish and rainy night. A bright beam of light stabbed the grey clouds in the top right corner and Canaan recognized the symbolism as the author's hope for his people.

"This book explains a lot about God, hon," she said waiting for him to raise his eyes. "You wanted to know how Jesus fits in. Read it. The Rakum may be over, but you're not." Marcy touched his cheek and leaned forward. Canaan met her halfway so their lips would touch. "God spared you and Kilmeade for a purpose, I know it."

"Okay, hon," Canaan told her, dismissing most of the last. "We will shelter here and depart at sunset."

"Good," she whispered, a familiar smolder now in her hazel eyes. She leaned in and when she rose from her seat, he did, too. Marcy folded into him as she always had.

Canaan maneuvered her to the bed, covering her neck with kisses. Telepathically, he called Kilmeade back and loved his mate one last time.

2, JAN 2, Tuscaloosa, AL

Six Weeks Later

"They're calling it *eleven-thirteen*," Canaan said in a horror-movie voice piloting the car back to Tuscaloosa after their six-week Biloxi Casino Resort getaway.

"Appropriate," Kilmeade replied in a low voice aware his cohort was forcing his humor.

"Appropriate," Canaan mimicked in Kilmeade's inflection. "Judas Priest! If our guys cry about it to me, they'll regret it for days."

In lieu of a verbal response, Kilmeade exhaled and returned his gaze to the night. Appropriate or not, the melodramatic and ominous moniker fit. From *Last Assembly* seven years ago to the previous November 12, the 100,000-strong Rakum population had been reduced to twenty thousand. Then 11/13 *happened* to them all. On November 13th, the very spirit that empowered their people for millennia was erased by the God of the mortals. That instant, all their brethren began the transformation to mortal flesh. *Only Canaan and myself remain intact. Why?*

"What a whiner," Canaan teased. "You're pouting because you didn't get a Dying Buzz on our vacation." He reached over to bump Kilmeade's arm. "You're going to lose those fantastic teeth if you don't kill someone soon, you evil bastard."

Kilmeade humphed; Canaan did not disdain his practice of drinking a dissident or otherwise unpleasant human to death. A Rakum with superior self-control could handle it; next opportunity, he'd provoke someone nasty to attack him—those were the ones he enjoyed ending.

"We'll find you someone, brother." Canaan patted his near shoulder.

"The next rest area you see, pull in. I'll show you some teeth."

Canaan grunted a response and Kilmeade closed his eyes still pondering the past month. Their resort stay had been a great diversion, but the time had arrived to attend their suffering brethren and help if such a thing were possible.

Canaan groaned, overhearing Kilmeade's stream of consciousness more and more since they left the storm drain. "They're just... *so... pitiful...*"

Canaan stressed the last two words and rolled his eyes. "If I was transforming, I'd own that bitch, guaranteed."

Kilmeade lowered his chin. "Seriously? You'd be in a puddle crying your little human eyes out."

"*Fffftt,*" Canaan disagreed with a raspberry. "I'd do better than you, that's for damn sure."

Kilmeade raised his eyebrows. "My dear sweet baby Elder, there is nothing you can do better than I can do."

Canaan humphed and smoothly steered the car onto the Rest Area exit ramp. Kilmeade looked out the windshield and sent his brother a grin. In another minute, they were parked in a dark corner of the lot.

"We're two hours from Tuscaloosa," Canaan said and rubbed his chin. "Tell brother Canaan what you want to do."

Kilmeade steepled his fingers and watched the patrons milling about the building housing the toilets. There was no armed security, but cameras peppered the eaves surrounding the roof.

"I'll let you chase me. I could get out and start running," Canaan joked unbuttoning his sleeve.

Kilmeade grinned and focused on a group of men leaning on motorcycles in the glow of a streetlamp. "What do you think? In the very least, I get myself a reluctant buzz? One of those men will follow me to the restroom and get the surprise of his life."

Canaan nodded. "Pick a big one. He's gotta support that appetite you're so famous for."

"I am what I am," Kilmeade said as he shoved open his door to stroll toward the group. Twenty minutes later, a dazed man stumbled out of the men's room as Kilmeade settled in the passenger side.

"At least he's alive," Canaan joked and started the ignition.

"I know what I'm doing." Kilmeade released a satisfied sigh.

"True. Let's go see our boys," Canaan said with a grin and pulled away from the rest area. In the rearview mirror, the biker reached his friends and Kilmeade vaguely wondered what story he would tell.

In another two hours, they approached Javier and David's address.

"We put our condo on the market and Roman found a house we can share for now," David was saying to Canaan on the BMW's Bluetooth moments before they pulled into Javier's neighborhood.

David Walker had transformed voluntarily at Last Assembly and Kilmeade chuckled at Canaan's sideways telepathic lob: *this one is the softest moron I've ever met, shiiiit..."*

"Makes sense," Canaan replied and rolled his eyes for Kilmeade. "Everything cool with the place Roman bought for us?" For practicality, they had used Kilmeade's money and alias, since over the years, he had accumulated millions on the Stock Market.

"Yes, sir," David replied with respect. "You'll love it."

Canaan grunted thanks and ended the call. He turned to his partner. "I'm going to end up drinking that idiot."

Kilmeade didn't react and only stared at Javier's front door.

"You're thinking about the last time you were here," Canaan said and then snorted. "Wait, you saw Father Damien as a mortal. *Shew.* That must have blown your mind."

"And then I watched Isaac choke him to death."

"Da-a-mn!" Canaan joked. Kilmeade remained in his thoughts and Canaan added, "The world has turned upside down since then."

"I had my pet, Rafael," Kilmeade reflected quietly. "And I was going to revert Roman to his birthright..."

"If you hadn't traveled here from California..." Canaan whispered.

Kilmeade sighed. He had wearied of his California groupies, so when the dashing Rafael showed up out of nowhere, his entire plan changed. Without delay Kilmeade left the West Coast to seek out Roman. Who put that urgent desire in his heart? Kilmeade didn't need to ask; Javier's God did it to make them come together for His purposes.

"We truly are puppets," Canaan said in a faraway voice.

"Yes, we are," Kilmeade replied quietly and opened his door.

The Elders walked to the stoop in silence, both unwilling to contemplate the broader implications. Once inside, Roman nodded to Canaan, but Kilmeade grabbed him into his embrace.

"Brother!" he said, his cheer returning in the proximity of his twin. Despite his transmutation into a human, what used to be Elder Roman held sway in Kilmeade's heart as he had since they were young. Only during the last two hundred years, did their Elder duties pull them apart. And then of course, Roman fell in love with Javier's God and left the Rakum race entirely. Ending the hug, Kilmeade shook his thoughts away.

"I gather your vacation was restful?" Roman asked.

Because of the shock they had only just overcome, neither he nor Canaan wished to yet discuss their activities in Biloxi. Kilmeade mussed Roman's hair and redirected with a question about their house.

"It's ready to move in," Roman replied and led Kilmeade to the small desk in the corner where he dropped into the chair.

"Excellent," Kilmeade remarked and placed his palms on Roman's shoulders. Before Last Assembly, Roman had been a powerful and influential Elder, but now? *How soft and small he is...* The reality of it disturbed Kilmeade still. Canaan read him from across the room and commiserated with a tight-lipped nod.

"You saw this virtual tour," Roman said absently as he scrolled. "The documents are ready to sign," his brother continued and typed a few lines before closing the webpage. He sighed with finality and Kilmeade patted Roman's back.

"I'm sorry to tell you that Boris was killed resisting arrest the night you left the storm drain," Roman said apologizing with his gaze.

"That is unfortunate," Kilmeade replied before turning to Canaan, who needn't hear his voice to know he'd been summoned.

The hulky Elder crossed to their position, hands in his pockets, his constant grin in place. "Boris flipped his shit. Not our fault," Canaan stated. "You ready?"

Kilmeade nodded. Javier had warned them that the Bushman girl was coming over and neither Elder wanted to discover firsthand if her infatuation with the Rakum stood. The young woman hadn't truly been a Cow, but like many in her generation, Chloe Bushman lived in awe of the supernatural. She had dated former Rakum David Walker before being abducted and held prisoner by a violent and unstable Elder two months ago. Kilmeade met her briefly days before 11/13 and thought her charming, but he had no such inclinations now.

"Come," he said softly to Canaan who stood ready to follow. At the front door, Javier put his hand to the knob to see them out and Canaan grunted. They were too late; both Elders heard her on the stoop.

"Let's run out the back door," Canaan joked. Kilmeade sighed and they returned to the living room.

"What?" Javier asked, unaware. He pulled open the door and Chloe Bushman grinned up at him, fist raised to knock.

"Hey! What did I miss?"

"Oh," Javier said and held up his hand. "Stay right here."

Kilmeade's eyes must have shown his surprise for when Javier closed the door in the girl's face and turned to them, he grinned.

"I don't need telepathy to know you don't want to see Chloe." Javier's palm remained flat against the door. "Ya'll go out the back. She's never met Canaan and she might flip out seeing two Elders at once."

Kilmeade agreed and turned for the rear exit, but Canaan stepped toward Javier.

"Let her in," he said. To Kilmeade he sent, *"I want to see her flip out. I am especially gorgeous, you know."* He offered Kilmeade his toothiest smile.

Javier waited for Kilmeade's order. Every person in their group looked to Kilmeade for leadership and he approved of their choice, having seniority in every way that counted. He gave Javier a small nod and remained by the back door. If Chloe still loved Rakum, at least she'd see Canaan first. Let him absorb her parasitic energy.

"Ouch! Damn!" Canaan sent, his tone echoing with humor.

Javier opened the door. "Hey, Chloe, before you come in..."

"Is everybody here? I have so many questions," she said, peering around him and not able to see inside. "Why aren't you letting me in? I'm cold!"

"Wait, listen," he said beginning his short lecture. "Elder Kilmeade and Elder Canaan are both here so be normal. If you act freaky, I'm kicking you out." His tone teased, but she nodded with wide eyes.

"*Geesh,* Javier. I'm not crazy," she said bobbing her head to see over Javier.

Javier and Chloe had almost been intimate; he shared with the Elders that when he suffered the bloodthirsty effects of ingesting Isaac's blood, Chloe came on assertively and he nearly bedded her. Watching them interact, her relentless determination only proved Javier's account.

"You're still too agitated," Javier said blocking the door.

"Okay, I'm sorry," she replied and Kilmeade noted an immediate slowing of her heart rate.

"Whoa—did you hear that?" Canaan sent with a quick glance.

Kilmeade nodded. It was unusual for a mortal to have such control of her autonomic systems. Whatever it meant, Kilmeade tucked it away; Javier was letting her in.

Chloe entered meekly, her hands clasped behind her, meeting eyes as she entered the living room. She greeted David and gave Roman a generous amount of respect. She met Kilmeade's eyes next and he maintained his blank expression while sending her a miniscule wink.

Javier gestured toward her and said, "Meet Elder Canaan."

Chloe stepped to Canaan and put out her hand. "Nice to meet you."

Canaan grinned like a buffoon and shook with his thumb and pointer finger. His silliness broke the tension of the room and the others exhaled with relief.

Chloe turned away to face the others. "See? I'm normal." She cracked a grin and trained her eyes back to Kilmeade.

"Sure, you are," Javier said teasing. "Have a seat and we'll fill you in on what happened in Athens. Kilmeade and Canaan are headed out."

"Wait—you're leaving?" she asked and stepped around Canaan to Kilmeade.

"Is she blind? Somebody check her eyesight," Canaan sent, still grinning.

Kilmeade didn't respond to his telepathic jibe and watched with interest as the girl approached. As females went, she was flawless—petite, pretty, she smelled nice, and her long brown hair reached her waist in flattering curls. But Kilmeade hadn't pursued women in a century. Maybe she wanted to give him her blood. His eyebrows went up; a woman who consents...

"How is your friend, Rafael? Is he okay?" she asked.

Kilmeade discerned that she was genuinely concerned and not making small talk. Chloe had been alone at Javier's condo when Kilmeade arrived with Rafa and their Cows. He gave her a half-smile, standing back and away, his hands folded at chest level.

"He is well. I will tell him you asked about him."

"That was an awesome and very human response, brother," Canaan sent over, still sore he hadn't made her swoon.

Kilmeade had an evil idea; blocking Canaan, he bent and whispered in Chloe's ear, *"You should give Canaan more attention. You've made him feel ugly and unwanted."* When he regained his stiff posture, Chloe smiled and turned to face his counterpart. She played along automatically and for a reason he wasn't yet sure of, this pleased Kilmeade a great deal. Canaan noticed the short mental block and he protested with a quick inhale, but Chloe walked nearer to him and put her hand to her forehead.

"Oh, God! I'm going to swoon! You are so amazing! You take my breath away!" she said her voice dramatic and accented like the Southern Belle she was. Canaan grinned and caught Kilmeade's eye.

"Ass," he whispered and then watched Chloe pretend to faint into Javier's arms. "This one's funny," he said about Chloe, meeting Javier's gaze. "She's a riot. Okay, we're outta here." Grinning he stepped toward the front door.

"Wait!" Chloe responded following after him.

Kilmeade said goodbye to Javier, Roman, and David and listened to Canaan and Chloe at the same time.

"I was only joking," she said, breathless from her sudden acting debut. "You *are* amazing. Totally. I'm playing it cool so Javier doesn't kick me out." Then she stepped closer. "I have a crush on Kilmeade," she whispered. "Trust me, you take my breath away, for real."

Canaan grinned down on her and patted her head like a good doggie. "You look yummy to me, too," he said and looked up as Kilmeade approached. Chloe was sandwiched between the Elders with mere feet on either side.

"She likes you," Canaan said over her head.

"I heard," Kilmeade replied.

Chloe's cheeks flushed red and she scooted away, her back rubbing the wall, and disappeared into the living room.

Canaan laughed. "That one is really funny."

"Hilarious. Let's get out of here," Kilmeade said, but took one last olfactory sample of Chloe's feminine scent. It was pleasant and it made him smile. Canaan jibed him about it and led the way to the car. As females go, she wasn't horrible.

3, JAN 5

Roman's text said it was time to move in and he had generously stocked their new home with groceries and basic furniture, which they could replace and customize later. When the sun set, Canaan drove them in Simon's BMW to their new address, arriving as Roman prepared to leave. A shiny black pick-up sat in the driveway beside Roman's car and Canaan shot Kilmeade a grin.

"Is that for me?" he asked as they exited the car. Roman stepped up to greet them and Canaan pointed at the truck, asking again with smiling eyes, "Is that for me?"

Roman handed him a set of keys. "My brother asked me to buy you the manliest truck I could find."

"Oh, he knows me too well!" Canaan laughed boisterously and jabbed his arm, remembering to withhold his Rakum strength.

"Look at our son, he's so happy," Kilmeade joked and grabbed Roman's neck to place a kiss on his forehead.

"Enough," Roman grumbled hiding his smile and handed the housekey to his brother. "Before I forget, Rafael is coming into town soon and will want to see you."

Kilmeade exhaled with drama at the news and Canaan pat his back as he passed him for the house. Kilmeade remained outdoors a few more minutes and Canaan looked over the new house. He barely reached the finished basement when his cell rang.

"Elder Canaan!" a cheery voice called from the speaker. "Had any good buzzes lately?"

"Polly! Come to Poppa. We'll see how you taste," Canaan chuckled, recalling him fondly. Just before 11/13, the jovial duo of Polly and Guap re-entered his life bringing with them the revelation that they had managed the wealth of the Fathers—funds no doubt greater than the GNP of a small country. Plus, for Rakum, they were unusually likeable.

"I wish I could—I'm sure I'm delicious," he teased. "Guap's there, though. He is running Beryl-the-Sad directly to you."

"You're shittin' me." Canaan dropped his grin.

"I hate to say it, Boss, but being pretty isn't enough for that one,"

Polly said also more somber. "Gotta split; Guap's calling you. Kazak[5]!"

Canaan grumbled and stared at the quiet phone as he trudged up the stairs to the main floor. *"Kazak, my ass,"* he said under his breath and met Kilmeade entering the hall. When he opened his mouth to speak, the phone rang and Canaan answered it frowning.

"What the hell's going on with Beryl?" he shouted into the phone.

"Ow, Boss, you hurt my sensitive human ear," Guap snickered.

"Get to the point! What happened?"

"Our man swallowed an entire bottle of Ambien," Guap answered, suddenly all business due to Canaan's tone. "I found him unconscious and squeezed him until he vomited. If he wasn't still transforming, I think he would have died."

Canaan barely contained his anger. "Bring him," Canaan said and disconnected the call. He turned to Kilmeade. "He's suicidal."

Kilmeade shook his head. "Not necessarily."

"Dammit, Beryl!" Canaan growled under his breath and then shouted, "DAMMIT!" and cursed his way to the front of the house. Kilmeade followed him with concern evident in his expression.

"Calm yourself," Kilmeade said filtering angry thoughts Canaan accidentally transmitted in his elevated emotional state.

"Trust me," Canaan growled. "I know this man better than anyone alive. When he arrives, back me up."

Kilmeade showed his palms. "You know I will. I'm seeing it now— Beryl is your Rafael."

"What?" Canaan asked, truly wondering what he meant. He never drew blood off Beryl as Kilmeade did his Rakum pet. In fact, he had buzzed off Beryl three times in a hundred years.

Kilmeade shook his head. "It's all about the blood to you," Kilmeade said now in teaching mode. "I meant you are genuinely concerned for him. We are the last Rakum on the planet and you're as human about that man as I was for Rafa."

Canaan processed his logic. "Whatever. It's a bunch of tricky bullshit that we develop these hearts *now*, with no parameters and no Fathers. No one to rein us in... UGHHH!" he bellowed to the ceiling.

"That's attractive," Kilmeade returned. "You're losing it."

Canaan wanted to smile at the playful teasing but couldn't. Guap had been nearby when he called so the doorbell rang moments later. Canaan took a deep breath and snarled at Kilmeade when he whispered for him to

---

[5] "Kazak!" – (Hebrew) literally, "Be strong", the common hello / good-bye for the Rakum race.

be nice. He opened the door with telekinesis and crossed his arms.

Let him come to me, the little Nancy...

"I said, be nice..." Kilmeade sent.

Canaan ignored him; he hadn't been addressing anyone but himself anyway. Beryl entered the room at a careful walk, warily meeting each Elder's eye before returning his gaze to the floor. He looked fine. Had his mind cracked?

"Go away, Guap," Canaan barked when the banker poked in his head. Unoffended, Guap nodded like a Rakum, offered Kilmeade a bow, and turned away. *Guap and Polly assimilated—what makes it so hard for Beryl?* When the front door closed, Canaan cleared his throat.

"Are you trying to die?" Canaan asked with his hands in his pockets. He wanted to appear calm, but was angry with the guy for being so weak. Beryl met Canaan's eye a moment and then Kilmeade's before shaking his head with a sigh. He parted his lips but said nothing.

"Did you try to kill yourself, pup?" Canaan asked, aware that referring to the kid the Rakum way might encourage him to answer more readily. It worked.

"I think so," Beryl said and scratched his head.

Canaan steadied his response, still incredibly incensed. "How do you feel now? Do you still want to die?"

"Why should I go on?" he asked and looked at Kilmeade. "If you have any idea why I should go on, please share."

"Canaan loves you," Kilmeade said playing light. "He thinks about you all the time and can hardly sleep when you're not around."

"Kilmeade, goddammit!" Canaan barked and stepped into Beryl's space. "Come here," he said and grasped the man behind the neck with one big hand. "I'm not the guy to give you reasons to live, I'm just not. But I'll tell you one thing. If you try to kill yourself again and fail, I'm going to finish you off. I will suck you dry and leave you for dead. Then I will chop off your head and piss down your neck!" Furious, Canaan meant every word, but Beryl didn't think so. His face remained the same and behind them, Kilmeade laughed.

"I will drink him to death, brother. That is my specialty. You stick to pissing," Kilmeade said with a soft snicker. Canaan shot him a glare and retracted it immediately in respect to his partner's status.

Beryl shrugged. "I know what you're trying to do and I appreciate it," he said and hung his hand on Canaan's forearm.

Canaan squeezed his neck briefly leaving his hand in place. "Damn-it-all, B, I'm pissed at you. You pitiful, wearisome..." Canaan's voice had softened and he realized he was no longer enraged. "...beautiful, almost-human person."

"I was being stupid," Beryl said finally registering regret.

Canaan released his neck to ruffle his hair. "Move in with us," he said and looked to Kilmeade who shrugged. "I insist."

"You guys don't need me around," Beryl said in a low voice.

"No, I want you here," Canaan said, "to make sure you fly straight." Before the man could deflect again, Canaan grasped his shoulder. "You will stay with us and leave when I say so. *Comprende?*"

Beryl sighed. "I'll bring my bags over."

"Good boy." Canaan pulled him into a half-hug and put a heavy noogie in his hair until he yelped to be freed. "Choose a room. The two on the right are available."

"You're the boss," Beryl said and walked for the stairs.

His affect was cool, but Canaan read relief in his countenance, glad to stay a little longer with his former Elders. Canaan was surprised it meant so much to him.

"I'm becoming so sweet!" he joked to Kilmeade. "It'll be fun."

Kilmeade nodded with suspicion. "Fun to drink when you're thirsty?"

"No," Canaan refuted and then shrugged. "Maybe."

"Ah," Kilmeade said with a chuckle.

"I'm running to Javier's. Gonna brag on my new truck. Join?" he asked Kilmeade who declined.

"I'll visit with Beryl, dig around in his head. That will amuse me."

Canaan laughed. "Don't hurt him. He's a wittle fwagile."

Kilmeade grinned. "I promise not to harm your sad little baby."

With a thumbs-up to his cohort, Canaan headed out and hoped Kilmeade didn't find anything unpleasant in Beryl's brain. Kilmeade's strength had always been sussing out a Rakum's mental state. Beryl possessed a famously sharp and eager mind and hopefully his partner would find everything intact.

4

He had to come out eventually. At sundown, like a stalker, Chloe parked herself a block away to see if the Elders returned to visit Javier. She watched Canaan enter and wasn't leaving until she asked him about Kilmeade. To pass the time, she studied for her Psych quiz with one eye on Javier's front door.

The day she met Kilmeade, the Rakum cornered her in Javier's hallway and mesmerized her with no effort. He wasn't like those depicted in Beth Rider's book, nor the monsters that abducted and terrorized her in November. Just then, Canaan exited at a brisk walk and did not look at Chloe when she popped out and trotted his way.

"Canaan! Wait!" she called, and didn't he grin? Still, he walked on. Unlike the slender athleticism she noticed in Kilmeade, Canaan was beefy with muscle and a dramatic tattoo snaked out of his collar and left sleeve. His curly blond hair fluttered in the cold wind and he didn't acknowledge her even when she reached his side. "I need to see Kilmeade," she said, breathing hard. "Since you guys live together you can get him to call me."

The Elder climbed into the truck and closed the door. Only after he switched on the vehicle and lowered the window, did he turn. Grinning, he met her eye and Chloe looked away, unnerved by his ice-blue gaze. Catching on, Canaan did not speak until she braved to look up.

"Did you just call us *you guys?*" he asked with a toothy grin. "Together, we're 746 years old. How old are you again? Twelve?"

"I'm twenty," she replied gauging his seriousness.

"Like I said, *twelve,*" he huffed. "Here's some advice; you'll catch more flies with a little sucking up."

Ignoring his false indignation, Chloe asked, "How can I reach him?"

The man shook his head, still faking offense. "Can't hear you."

Chloe furrowed her brow in frustration. "Please, um, Master Canaan? The Amazing Canaan?" Chloe's eyes widened as she thought of more grandiose titles. "Your Highness? Oh-Mighty-Handsome-One?"

"Any of those will bend an Elder's ear." He grinned, propped his chin on his palm and gave her an adoring gaze. "Now, what did it want?"

"Your Wonderfulness, will you please tell Elder Kilmeade I want to speak to him?" Chloe said with exaggerated respect. It was a game for this one and she didn't mind playing.

"Like to, but honey, Kilmeade doesn't like humans."

"He likes *me,*" she said defiantly and Canaan's grin widened.

"Ooh, it is *sassy!*" Canaan chuckled. "Look, tiny, I gotta look after my brother. Do you know what you're asking? Rakum Elders don't make *friends.*" His gaze remained playful, but Chloe's mind went blank. Canaan held up three fingers. "Blood, sex, violence," he said, his opposite hand manually lowering a digit with each word. "That is the limit of our interest and not always in that order."

"I just wanted to talk to him..." Chloe sighed, growing perturbed. Kilmeade had come on strong when they met; it never occurred to her their interaction may have been meaningless.

"What a lip. Look at it," the Elder teased regarding her with a tight grin. "Don't pout, tiny. Kilmeade has spoken of you." Canaan checked his mirrors. "I'll tell you how to reach him, but you've been warned; he doesn't want to bake cookies, gossip, and paint toenails. *Comprende?*"

Chloe nodded slowly. "Okay."

Canaan fluttered his eyebrows. "Do this..." He put a finger to his temple. "Picture his face, look for his thread, and grab it." Chloe's mouth must have dropped, because he added, "That's all there is to it. *Easy.*" Without another word, he abruptly drove away.

Chloe watched him go, her mind racing. *Can I really speak to Kilmeade telepathically?* She walked to her car, planning what she would say in case she attempted and he answered.

When she was home again, Chloe had the house to herself. As teaching physicians at the University, her parents had gone on a medical missions trip. In the three months since she was kidnapped by a devil and rescued by God, she'd attended class and kept up a happy face. Her parents didn't know she'd been abducted; how could she tell them when those involved were of supernatural ilk? Her mother already thought she was a wild child, so Chloe depended on her coping skills and advice from Roman to keep her mind and spirit strong. The now-human Elder helped her understand her infatuation with Javier when he was under the influence of Isaac's blood. He also helped her and David remain friends after their awkward break-up, telling them all that God probably orchestrated her puppy loves with David and Javier as part of His plan to bring the Rakum race to a complete end.

Complete, except for two Elders...

Chloe switched on the lamp beside the sofa and furrowed her brow. Did God play matchmaker to bring about His purposes? Roman had tried to give her examples from the Bible, but Chloe had been distracted thinking about Kilmeade. *And Canaan thinks I can contact him telepathically...*

Chloe collapsed in a pile on the sofa and pondered the possibility. When in the horrible Rufus's clutches, he spoke in her mind. It terrified her knowing that one who wanted to kill her could communicate with her so intimately. Then when Javier showed up as the Anomaly, he heard her thoughts. So why not this Elder?

Chloe dimmed the lamp to the lowest wattage and closed her eyes. Only for the tiniest second did her conscience whisper to her to think twice. Blocking her inner voice, she brought up Elder Kilmeade's face from the other night. He hadn't given her much attention, but the first time they met, he'd been brazenly flirtatious.

"Elder Kilmeade," she thought, not realizing until the words flowed that she might be beginning their conversation. *"Please come see me..."*

Chloe experienced a peculiar lightness in her middle. Had it to do with telepathy? She hadn't felt it before, so she experimented more.

"I have questions only you can answer," she thought, picturing his face and the way his gray eyes twinkled when he shot her each daring compliment upon their first meeting. The floaty feeling resumed and she exhaled; if she could only fall quiet enough, even to the extent of holding her breath, she might hear a reply. She counted to ten not breathing and definitely heard a soft chuckle in the very back of her ear. Without opening her eyes, she sat up.

"Did I do it? Did I reach you?"

"Breathe, Miss Bushman, breeeeeeeathe..." the voice teased.

Kilmeade! She grinned. *"Why won't you come see me?"* she sent as goose pimples covered her arms.

"You live at 220 Poplar?" the voice asked.

"Yes," Chloe said aloud and opened her eyes. The connection remained, and she sensed a tether to the voice on the other end. Then with an almost audible pop, the string snapped, and she was alone. Suddenly anxious, Chloe got to her feet. Was he really coming over? A full-blooded Rakum Elder at her house while she was all alone? Chloe looked at her watch, checked the locks and the alarm on the doors, and hoped she'd done the right thing.

Nearly four hours later, Chloe lounged on the leather recliner in her dad's den; the voice never came by. She flicked off the television and the room slumped into the brownish glow of an amber desk lamp. Chloe grumbled about the late hour, stretched her arms to the ceiling, and turned for the hallway.

"How scandalous!" Elder Kilmeade said from the doorway. "Inviting me over when you're all alone..."

"Oh, god!" Chloe hissed with her hand over her heart.

Leaning casually against the threshold, Kilmeade grinned. "You rang?"

"Oh, god," Chloe said again softer. "You... You just came in?"

He shrugged. "You invited me. I'm here. What do you want?"

Chloe paused, thrown off by his sudden appearance. "But that was..." She glanced at the wall clock. "...three-and-a-half hours ago."

"I am not a dog. I go where I want, when I want." He held her gaze, his chin lowered. "Come close," he said and held out his hand.

Chloe's throat tightened and she hugged herself. She was still dressed, thank God, although her sweater was tattered and her sweatpants too loose. When the voice hadn't shown within an hour, she'd dressed down for no one's eyes but her own.

"You look delightful. Is that cashmere?" Kilmeade asked, hand still waiting for her to reach out. "Give us a feel."

Chloe unwrapped her arms and looked at her front. It *was* cashmere, but it wasn't likely the Elder wanted to touch it; he wanted her closer. While she wrestled with what to do, he closed the distance between them. Inserting his fingers underneath to caress the soft weave, the back of his hand brushed her skin. Chloe gasped and stood frozen in place.

"I knew it," he said inches away. He waited for her to look into his face and he smiled on her. "Would you like to tell me why I'm here?"

"I... I wanted..." Chloe began and stopped.

"I'm not very patient," Kilmeade said and moved his hand from her sweater to touch her face. He ran his fingers down her cheek and then over her lips. "Your mind is bloated with conflict. Shall I choose?"

"I wanted..."

"You want...?" Kilmeade sent her a tiny smile. "Tick-tock."

Chloe swallowed and sought the right words.

Kilmeade's thumb brushed her bottom lip when she hadn't replied. "Allow me to help. You want to let your blood. Right now."

"Oh, no, I..." Chloe stuttered. Part of her indeed wondered what it would be like if he took her blood as Javier had in November. But hadn't she just wanted to talk?

"I no longer prefer human blood, Miss Bushman. Haven't for decades," Kilmeade said absently, his eyes trained to her neck. He pushed her long brown curls aside. "But a female that consents? I would make an exception."

"Umm," Chloe moaned wishing he wouldn't rush her.

"Do you?" Kilmeade's two fingers touched her chin and he turned her face to his. "Consent? I have to hear it."

She found her voice. "I don't think I'm supposed to..." The Elder rolled his eyes and began to pull away. "No! I mean, yes! I mean, it's okay," Chloe said in a rush, clutching his thick biceps through his burgundy sweater. "Yes."

Kilmeade drew her close in an instant and pushed elongated teeth through her skin. One arm embraced her gently, but the one at the back of her throat pressed their contact together too firmly and she reflexively struggled to be free.

"Be still," she heard in her mind as she began to panic. Then it was over. The punctures stung only a moment before the sensation of his tongue pressing against the wound melted the discomfort away. Then he backed completely and leaned against the threshold across the room.

Chloe dropped to the sofa, and with her mind numb, she watched him savor the aftereffects. When the clock noisily rang the quarter hour, Kilmeade met her eye and smiled.

"That was a treat," he said with quiet reverence. He seemed to be waiting for her to speak or move, but she did neither. When she still hadn't reacted, Kilmeade stood off the doorframe and thrust his hands into his slacks pockets. "Three, two, one. Bye," he said out of patience.

She wanted him to stay. She wanted him to leave. And she wanted him to do it again. All of this was moot, for the Elder turned on his heel, waved his fingers from behind, and disappeared down the hall. Chloe didn't hear him exit the front door, but she hadn't heard him earlier, either. She turned the dimmer to full-light and relaxed into the couch.

Rufus took her blood when she was terrified, Javier when she was unaware, and Kilmeade took it by consent where she recalled 100% of the experience. And she was, well, *fine.* Tired, sleepy, but no worse for wear. Chloe allowed the moment-by-moment recollection to return and pondered it until she fell asleep where she sat.

5, JAN 8

The sun had been down an hour when Kilmeade and Canaan rose from the light-tight basement to lounge and reflect in the ridiculously comfortable living room recliners Roman had chosen. After Kilmeade shared highlights of his visit with Miss Bushman the night before, Canaan launched into his recollection of when he shot Beryl with Marcy's Glock. Afterward, both Elders fell into their own thoughts. Beryl knocked on the living room threshold five minutes later and neither of them paid him any mind. Sensing they purposefully ignored him, Beryl cleared his throat. When they still hadn't acknowledged him, Beryl finally spoke.

"Javier asked me to come by. Either of you want to go?"

Canaan rolled his eyes to Kilmeade and raised his eyebrows. In response, Kilmeade only exhaled. "Go on, B. Take my truck," Canaan said and fell quiet.

Beryl regarded them in silence a few moments before he was heard exiting the front and Kilmeade snickered.

"What so funny?" Canaan asked with eyes closed.

"Your little Beryl," Kilmeade said softly.

"You told me his brain was fine, so what's funny?" Canaan asked again, obviously too relaxed to open his eyes.

"I shouldn't have laughed," Kilmeade said and pushed his recliner back further. "We're supposed to be *nice* now. Our transformed brethren can't take the ribbing like they used to."

"Oh, Beryl's funny because he's pitiful," Canaan agreed with a chuckle and nodding with his own statement.

"Not only that, but he's so *self-accusatory*. Everything is his fault." Kilmeade shivered. "It's disgusting. Javier isn't like that."

"He's smart. He'll get used to it." Canaan then lowered his voice and cleared his throat waiting for Kilmeade to look over. "You realize we can't compare Beryl to Javier. Between Roman and Jack Dawn?" Canaan regarded Kilmeade with one eye. "Javier had it easy with your brother."

Kilmeade agreed with a chuckle.

"Damn straight," Canaan huffed. "We all wanted to be like Jack.

Meryl and Beryl especially; they worked hard at it." Canaan grinned as his memories rolled in. "Jack Dawn—he was a powerhouse..."

Kilmeade scoffed. Jack was ruthless and he was old—1200 when he died—yet he had no class. "Your master did not impress me," he replied. "As for the twins, Meryl had the personality. Him, I enjoyed."

Canaan chuckled and Kilmeade glanced his way. "Assembly 1969," he stated and peeked sideways. "Meryl came to me about you."

Kilmeade grinned, chortled once, and looked to the ceiling. "Petulant squirt."

"Indeed!" Canaan laughed more boisterously. "Always searching for a pet, weren't you? *Shiiiiit...*"

"I only asked him to travel with me," Kilmeade said with a sideways grin. "Anything else was of his creative imagination."

Canaan shook his head still smiling. "Jack would never have released either of them, you know he wouldn't."

Kilmeade said nothing, his mind playing on memories of better times when his brethren were intact and they loved, loved, *loved* their Elders. Every grunt *served* and Elders were allowed their whims. If an inferior's appearance pleased Kilmeade before Last Assembly, he exercised his will in any way he chose. Some grunts took it better than others, but any that expressed disdain of Kilmeade's attentions were manhandled all the more. Add to that, Meryl had been very young, so gullible and eager to impress his masters. Kilmeade chuckled anew and Canaan looked over, after catching a glimpse of what he'd been thinking.

"Judas Priest, you were relentless."

"What?" Kilmeade shrugged innocently. "I sent his brother to see you. I heard no objections."

"Hah," Canaan huffed softly and then exhaled, deep in their conjoined memories. "Jack was very possessive. I'm surprised he didn't strike you back. He was vindictive."

"What could he do? Jack Dawn was no match for Kilmeade. I am the greatest Elder that ever lived. Everyone knows that."

"Yes, they do," Canaan said with a curt nod.

Kilmeade allowed the silence to stretch as he stared at the ceiling. Canaan sighed when he did and he looked over. "Brother, the Old Way is over. The *New* Way will be foreign and challenging." He took a deep breath before continuing in a soft voice. "No matter what we do, over time, you and I will grow more human. It is inevitable."

Canaan didn't disagree. He exhaled thoughtfully and stared off.

Kilmeade picked up his internal ramblings and smiled. *Javier and Roman will help us make sense of it. And the Bushman girl...if Kilmeade continues to see her, her presence will soften things up...*

"I like the way our minds are melding. It's very—" Kilmeade began without looking over.

"Comforting," Canaan said finishing his thought.

"Precisely," Kilmeade sighed. "I'm too comfortable to move. I might order pizza, watch TV, and sit here all night."

Canaan agreed with a grunt as his phone rang. He answered it and hissed at Kilmeade when he saw the caller ID. Kilmeade overheard their exchange: Rafa wanted to drop by. Kilmeade shook his head, no.

Canaan grinned mischievously. "Your master doesn't like mortals."

"Elder Canaan, please..." Rafael's telephone voice was plaintive. *"...I'm down the street. It'll only take a minute."*

Kilmeade grimaced when Canaan met his eye. "I won't see Iago," Kilmeade grumbled. "Tell him."

"Come on," Canaan told him. "But don't bring that Cow. Just you." Canaan ended the call. "I was nice to Beryl. You be nice to Rafael."

Kilmeade groaned histrionically and sat up without closing the footrest. "I miss my freaking pet!"

"You and your pets," Canaan said under his breath.

Kilmeade shook his head. "You have no idea what he was like—what it was like having him with me—and our time was much too short."

Canaan nodded. "I'll take your word for it."

"You are not above it, my brother. Take Javier—when you reconnected last year, you wanted him with you." Kilmeade stared at Canaan's face.

"Yeah," Canaan said noncommittally. "Maybe..."

"No, *for certain,*" Kilmeade countered with more vigor. "If there had been no Rufus to destroy and you came upon little Javier all human and mixed up, you would have carried him home with you." Kilmeade laughed at Canaan's impertinence. "Do not pretend with me. I see all."

"I wasn't alone. I had Marcy."

"Psshhhh. Another Rakum is what an Elder needs. A mate has her place, but she can't know you like a brother." Kilmeade nodded to himself. "Rafael was perfect. I had a very nice life ahead of me with that one by my side." Kilmeade's voice tapered off, deep in thought.

"It's not all shit. You've got me." Canaan reached across the distance between their recliners and held out his forearm. "Pet it. You can pet my arm..."

Kilmeade chuckled and slapped it down. "I'll pet you..."

"*You* want to pet Miss Bushman," Canaan teased. "I warned her how tough it is to please an Elder as great as Kilmeade."

Kilmeade grinned despite his disconcert regarding Rafael. *She already pleases me a great deal.* Kilmeade rubbed his face.

Canaan exhaled, having overheard his unspoken sentiment. "She's tiny," Canaan mused aloud. "Makes me think of those little birds— chickadees. Marcy loved those silly things."

"Little bird...that's what she is," Kilmeade said softly, his mind on her face, her scent, her laugh.

Beside him, Canaan grew still, scheming an attack. Before Kilmeade could warn him of the futility, his partner surged forward and took a swipe at his feet, hard enough to knock his legs off the footrest.

"Are we bored?" Kilmeade asked and finished sitting upright. He made an effort to stand and Canaan reached forward in a blur to grab his shirt into his fists. Kilmeade returned the grasp on Canaan's thick sweater and pushed into him as he found his feet. "Now I'll pet you!" Kilmeade said in an urgent grunt as Canaan shoved him backward.

"All this talk of pets has me thinking. It's time I made you my bitch," Canaan said, grinning now with exertion, putting every ounce of his strength into pushing his friend off balance.

In the Rakum heyday, Elders pummeled each other on a regular basis. Pulsing with adrenaline, Kilmeade shoved Canaan hard enough to surprise him and break free.

"Old man's still got it!" Canaan barked and leapt in to reestablish his hold on Kilmeade's clothing.

"You've gotten so flabby!" Kilmeade barked and advanced into Canaan until he was forced to leap out of his grasp or be pushed into the side table. "Come here, you big baby!" Kilmeade called and chased him to the back of the couch.

Canaan turned, ducked behind Kilmeade's reach, and came up behind him to yank one arm up hard against his own back. "I'll show you flabby!" he said and surged forward until he'd pressed the Elder's cheek into the drywall. "If you cry uncle, I won't snap it off..."

That's adorable. You fight like a pup just out of First Ritual," Kilmeade sent and concentrated on his next move. When he had built the appropriate energy, he pushed them both off the wall with his free arm and sent Canaan sprawling. His partner's body struck the back of the couch at hip-level and flipped head over heels. He crashed into the glass coffee table, which disappeared into a thousand harmless chunks. Canaan lay on his back in the shattered mess and laughed.

"You surprise me, old man!" he said and laughed again. The doorbell sounded and the bolts clanked as Canaan opened them with his mind. *"Be sweet, Kilmeade. He's had a shock."*

"Never instruct your Elders, Flabby," Kilmeade replied telepathically and turned to see Rafael enter as tall and devastatingly handsome as ever, but with a new aroma that revealed his rapid and unwelcome transformation.

"Elder Kilmeade," Rafa said without entering fully. He didn't know how to behave and Kilmeade didn't know how to receive him.

"Rafa," Kilmeade said and remained as he was, standing over Canaan littered with glass. When neither spoke for a few seconds, Canaan stuck his hand out to Kilmeade.

"Rafael, you look great," Canaan said as Kilmeade yanked him to his feet. "Not all the way there?" he asked and reached the man in a few strides. Rafa consented to Canaan pulling him close to sniff his head.

"Almost, Master," Rafael whispered and cut his eyes to Kilmeade. With one hand on his shoulder, Canaan held the man in place at the living room threshold.

"Tell us what's happening," Canaan instructed on Kilmeade's behalf.

"The sun pains me at high noon. Other than that," he said in a low voice, "very soon, maybe tomorrow, I will be completely human."

Kilmeade groaned and dramatically turned away to the kitchen.

"I'm moving Iago to Las Vegas," Rafa said quietly and Kilmeade stopped his forward motion. "He has family there. He wants to run an art gallery," Rafa continued. "His cancer returned; *es malo.*"

Kilmeade slowly faced him, still a room away. Canaan moved Rafael forward by the contact on his shoulder and stopped a few feet from where Kilmeade stood with his hands in his pockets.

"Iago has been a good companion," Kilmeade offered.

Rafael nodded with sad eyes. "I will leave information with Javier so you will know where we are."

"Be gentle," Canaan sent and Kilmeade sighed with a miniscule nod.

"May I speak with you privately, Master?" he asked in a whisper.

"I'm not your master any longer, Rafa, but yes. *Yes,*" Kilmeade said exasperated, "Canaan, go away."

Kilmeade crossed the kitchen without turning on the overhead light. The only illumination came from a nightlight set in the door of the stainless-steel fridge. He exhaled and leaned against the counter. Crossing his arms, he sighed again. "What in the world do you want?"

"I have a couple of messages," Rafael said and leaned on the island across from Kilmeade in the dimly-lit space. "Elder Canaan, you can hear, too," Rafael said to the side aware Canaan was listening from wherever he waited out of sight. "A moment alone is all I request."

Kilmeade looked down. "Okay, he heard you. Go ahead."

"First, Guap and Polly are dispersing the Father's funds to the Brethren. They deposited mine today allotting me twenty million dollars. Javier asked me to tell you since you don't use a phone. The Elders are also entitled to a portion so contact him to make arrangements."

"HOT DAMN!" Canaan's voice resounded through the house with gusto. Kilmeade shook his head, but smiled at his enthusiasm. Rafael grinned, too, and Kilmeade's heart melted a fraction at the sight.

"Second, I am sorry to say that James DuPont killed himself over the weekend."

Rafa waited for Kilmeade to meet his eye. On the one hand, DuPont had been a good Cow for many years. On the other, all Cows were emotionally unbalanced. Kilmeade gave Rafael an end-of-topic nod.

"Also, I intend to dispose of the contents of Locker 1191."

Kilmeade's eyebrows went up. "My babies?"

For the Rakum race, only the Ten Fathers were fertile. Nonetheless, in 1901, Kilmeade's keen inquisitive nature led him to experiment on his own seed after acquiring a Cow who was also a pioneer in the field of genetics. Using Black Magic, Dr. Penny succeeded in fertilizing her eggs with his seed. Thinking ahead, he stored the preserved materials to await the future technology. But now? With no Rakum spirit to embody the progeny, who was to say one of the horrible demons they fought in November wouldn't enter them as the one called Zahdone had the infant Isaac? No, it was better to destroy the cells than risk it.

"I will alert you when it is done," Rafa added.

Kilmeade tipped his chin once, morose at saying goodbye to his fantasy of fathering children.

"Last, I know you don't prefer to drink from mortals, but still, whatever I have is yours." Spoken like a Rakum grunt to his master.

Kilmeade watched his dark eyes; the Rakum he had been was gone, but a sincere and intelligent man remained. Kilmeade stepped off the counter and cupped the back of Rafa's neck and pulled him into a warm embrace.

"I will check on you from time to time," Kilmeade whispered.

Rafael returned the gesture, standing slightly taller, his chin tucked in beside Kilmeade's ear. "Please do," Rafa whispered. "I will miss you."

Kilmeade held onto him another long minute and then pushed him away to arm's length. "Now go make your offer to Canaan."

"OH, YEAH, BABY!" Canaan again shouted from the other room. Kilmeade and Rafa both grinned at his antics and Kilmeade watched him leave. He had lost his pet, but Rafa wasn't at fault.

Kilmeade exited the kitchen the back way and headed up the stairs to his bedroom. The aroma of blood hit the air and he shook his head. It was human. Rafa was human.

A colossal cluster.

6, JAN 9, DALLAS, TX

The Rakum language remained unknowable to mortals, thus navigation of their exclusive website prevented nosy human intrusion. Tonight, Dae Kim scrolled through the sad entries seeking his perfect match: a brother whose transformation was taking its sweet time. He was on month three and had been able to force much of his Rakum identity to adhere with a combination of sheer will and copious amounts of human blood. In three months, ten mewling cattle were murdered in his care, yet because of their sacrifice, he remained Rakum enough to do what needed to be done.

Dae Kim turned his gaze to Lonnie shivering in the corner chair, barely holding it together. Before November 13th, Lonnie had been a loyal and dedicated Cow serving Dae Kim the past five years. But as the Rakum lost their mojo over time, Lonnie lost his in minutes; one second, he's adoring his Rakum master and the next trying to run away. Dae Kim waved at him with his fingers. He didn't run anywhere now. Shackled and bound, Dae Kim was reeducating Lonnie to be useful, even if he no longer loved his master.

Ping! Dae Kim's email box alerted and he clicked it open.

"Screw the cattle! I'm in Corinth. Where are you? *A vér az élet?* "

Dae Kim grinned and typed a quick reply, arranging a meet-up in two hours. *"Dallas, sundown, Hooters on Gentry."*

He winked at Lonnie. "Wanna go for a ride?" Finally getting with the program, the Cow nodded and grinned, missing two teeth for his earlier insolence. "Good," Dae Kim said and stood from his chair to approach. "Real good."

Two hours later at the local Hooters, Lonnie led the way, moving the sloth types aside for his master. The Cow had played pro ball for the Cowboys and only when he met Dae Kim in a Dallas nightclub five years ago did he discover there were things in life that meant more than *Team* and *Money*. Six-foot-seven, three-hundred and fifty pounds, Lonnie created a path for Dae Kim all the way to the crowded bar. When he gestured to

---

[6] (Rakum-Hungarian, a bastardized version for their use alone.) "The blood is the life!"

an empty seat, Dae Kim took it.

"Wait by the door," he instructed. Well trained, the man did exactly as commanded and warily eyed Dae Kim from across the space.

After ordering whiskey, Dae Kim turned to watch the entrance. After downing a second shot, the Rakum walked in. Unbidden, a rush of relief flooded Dae Kim's system; although loathe to admit it, he had been stressing the loneliness.

"Kazak," the Rakum said under his breath when he reached his barstool. He was taller than Dae Kim and movie star handsome with pale green eyes, a luscious mane of black hair, and a neatly-trimmed beard. This one groomed for the ladies and judging by the way the buxom servers gave him double and triple takes, it worked.

"Come with me," Dae Kim said softly and even though the bar was full and the restaurant hopping with cattle, the transforming Rakum heard him. Dae Kim led him out the front of the establishment and Lonnie fell in behind. Once to the edge of the parking lot, the Rakum stopped walking and waited for Dae Kim to notice.

"This Cow is way too big for shit." The Rakum looked Lonnie up and down and shoved his hands in his pockets. "Name's Pete."

"Dae Kim," he replied and matched the Rakum's posture. "So you've stopped the transformation. What are you doing?"

Pete gave him a hard look. "Had to accept a new master, and damn, is he awful. Did you read that shitty Rabbit book?" Dae Kim shook his head. "You have to read it or there's no hope," Pete said, his eyes flashing with a mixture of emotions. "How much do you know about what happened to High Father Abroghia?"

"I don't know anything, and my telepathy is worthless." Dae Kim shook his head. "I'm getting all sorts of images from you; I can't understand any of it."

Pete smirked. "Apparently, we can't have that anymore; gives us too much leverage."

"Over who?"

"The cattle, moron." Pete huffed with disgust. "You won't understand any of it until you comprehend what we're up against. The High Father's spirit is gone. He alone allowed us our mystical powers."

"His spirit? Why do you care about stupid fairy tales?"

Pete chuckled a little and then tossed back his head to laugh louder.

"What? What?" Dae Kim asked, not at all offended. This Rakum had answers and he would get them one way or another.

"Do you live near here?" the Rakum asked.

"I do, want a ride?" Dae Kim gestured for his old Trans Am.

"In that? Hell, no." Pete clicked his key fob and nearby, a late model Lamborghini chirped. "You obviously haven't spoken to the Bankers."

Dae Kim paused and then said, "I guess not."

"We have a lot to discuss. Lead the way."

Dae Kim nodded and piled into his car. When Lonnie stuffed his body into the passenger side, he wove his way out of the parking lot to the highway. Very soon, Pete was going to teach him some wonderful new things.

A short drive later at the apartment complex, Dae Kim waited while Pete parked his luxury sports car and joined him on the curb.

"Oh, baby," he whispered and looked up at the crumbling edifice, "you're gonna kiss my feet when I finish telling you the good news." He whistled in disbelief and shook his head.

"Get inside," Dae Kim said as Lonnie opened the door. Dae Kim entered first, then Lonnie stood back respectfully and watched Pete. Once in, Lonnie closed the door of the two-bedroom apartment and remained in the tiny foyer, his bulk dwarfing the space.

Pete chuckled. "That giant is hilarious," he said and looked around. "First things first. Did you investigate all the tabs on the website?"

"I thought so."

"If you had, you wouldn't still live here," Pete said flatly.

Dae Kim didn't follow. "What?"

Pete shook his head with his eyes closed. "You're a millionaire, asshole. Twenty million dollars awaits you as soon as you claim it."

Dae Kim shook his head.

"Open the site now," Pete said and crossed his arms standing in the middle of the small living room. Dae Kim did as he said and opened the website on his iPhone. "Click the tab that reads 'claims.'"

Puzzled and intrigued, Dae Kim did as directed and once clicked, a new screen opened with a simple message in the center.

"Is this next screen for you? Answer this question and find out."

Dae Kim set down his phone and jogged to his laptop. After a few seconds, he reached the same place on the site.

"Kedvenc első rituálé?" it read.

Dae Kim grinned and looked at Pete.

"Broken Bones. That's my favorite," Pete said laughing, referring to

---

[7] (Rakum-Hungarian) "Name your favorite stage of First Ritual."

the stage of First Ritual where the guardian, proctor, or Elder broke certain bones in succession over a period of months to teach the young Rakum's body how to heal.

Dae Kim nodded and typed, *"töröt zontok."* Once he hit *send,* the website changed to a black screen with yellow letters across the middle. *"Your Bankers are holding a disbursement for you. Call us to have it deposited to your account today. Signed, Guap and Polly, Bankers for the Ten."*

"You have GOT to be shitting me!" Dae Kim exclaimed and sought Pete's eye.

"Nope. Got mine a month ago. Call them. Go ahead."

Dae Kim dialed the number, his eyes glued to the amazing statement on the screen. A man answered on the second ring. "Kazak!"

"Kazak! This is Dae Kim—what's this about money from the Ten?"

"Dae Kim," the man said and conferred with someone on his side before returning. "Your Elder?"

"Jack Dawn," Dae Kim replied excitedly.

"Your Father?"

"Johann."

A guffaw sounded on the other end. "FOUND ANOTHER! Hello, brother! My name is Polly. How goes the change?"

"It's slow. This money will help," Dae Kim said truthfully.

"Got a pen? Here are your numbers."

His Rakum memory diminishing daily, Dae Kim jotted the account info on a sheet of scrap paper.

"Caribbean accounts, you'll get checks and a bank card in the mail. Give me your current numbers for an advance while you wait."

Pete held up all ten fingers and mouthed, *"Ten thousand dollars."* Dae Kim grinned, eyes wide. As a Rakum, only the Elders enjoyed true financial success. He knew a few grunts making half a mil a year, but they were rare.

"Allllllllllrighty, Dae Kim," the banker said jovially. "If you run into any of our brethren, give them the news. There's plenty to go around. In three years, we will initiate another disbursement."

Dae Kim's pitiful Wells Fargo account carried a balance of five hundred dollars. He grinned, a new joy overtaking his spirit. "This is friggin' awesome!"

"Dae Kim," Banker Polly said in a serious tone, "many of our brethren are perishing from the gluttony of sudden funds. If you eat, drink, or drug too much, you will die. Be careful."

"Don't worry about me, brother," Dae Kim said with respect. "I have a partner—we'll watch out for each other." He winked and Pete gave him a nod.

"Excellent," the banker said. "Can I answer any questions for you?"

Dae Kim looked to Pete who shrugged. He looked at Lonnie looming in the doorway. "Polly, November 13th, what happened?"

"On the website, click Javier d'Millier; he will fill you in. What else?"

"I dreamed Elder Canaan is intact. Is he?" Dae Kim asked. Pete's eyes widened and he listened in, apparently interested in the answer.

Banker Polly paused, conferred on his end and returned to the phone as chipper as before. "Two Elders remain Rakum and they prefer you not seek them out. Elders Kilmeade and Canaan. If you have banking issues, call us. We never sleep!"

The banker disconnected the call and Dae Kim grinned, but Pete's expression had turned sour. "What? The Elders?" he asked, taking a stab at the man's problem. Pete's frown deepened. "Kilmeade or Canaan?" Dae Kim pressed narrowing his eyes. He'd served them both at different times and they were equally self-absorbed assholes. When Pete sucked his teeth, Dae Kim read the signals—*Kilmeade,* the one Elder known to manhandle grunts with eye-appeal, which Pete possessed in spades.

"Drop it," Pete said when he realized Dae Kim had caught on. He cut his eyes to Lonnie, "we gotta talk about that giant."

Not interested enough in Pete's past to care, Dae Kim let it drop and called his Cow in. Before 11/13, Lonnie had been happy and good-looking, grinning most of the time. Now fear filled his face and because of his hulking stature, it made him appear young and simple-minded.

"Yes, Master," he said in a wavering voice.

"Go stand outside."

Dae Kim watched him shrug on his coat and exit the apartment. He turned to Pete, eyebrows raised.

"I really can't say much until you read the book, so download it right now and don't show it to your Cow." Pete crossed his arms. When Dae Kim did nothing, he said, "Now."

With a nod, Dae Kim returned to his laptop at the chipped dinette table and pulled up the Amazon site. Once *The Rabbit* by Beth Rider-Stone had been downloaded, Pete nodded.

"Read it now and you'll be done in a few hours. Tomorrow night around nine, come to my house and we'll get started with the next phase of your salvation." Pete moved toward the door.

"You can stay here," Dae Kim said and Pete chuckled.

"I'll head home, thanks," Pete whistled. "Oh, and Lonnie's coming with us tomorrow. If he has any belongings, gather them up."

"Lonnie's a goner, isn't he?" Dae Kim asked.

Pete opened the door. "Bring him."

Dae Kim nodded and watched his new friend stroll to his car in the dark lot. When he called Lonnie inside, he resisted looking at the oaf. Pete was going to kill him and Dae Kim was in no position to argue.

《回》

When the sun had sufficiently set, Dae Kim loaded Lonnie into his car and headed for Pete's address. The sun barely bothered him now, but to maintain a Rakum body, he figured it best to maintain his Rakum mind. Was it working? Dae Kim was afraid to examine himself for details. Hopefully, tonight Pete would show him precisely what he was doing wrong.

Pete didn't exactly live in Corinth, but his five-acre spread lay close enough to the city line that conveniences were only a stone's throw away. Dae Kim sat in the Rakum's large den, gawking at the shelving full of trophies and sports memorabilia Pete had been collecting. Not a book in sight, which was fine with Dae Kim—he wasn't much of a reader, either.

The Beth Rider novel confounded him more than anything he'd ever read in his life. Now in Pete's domain, he hoped the guy would explain everything to him in crayon. Lonnie had been given permission to peruse the knick-knacks and he stood with his back to Dae Kim, reading the trinket labels and team awards situated around the room.

"Okay, I'm back!" Pete said carrying two cold beers. "Tell your Cow to follow us downstairs." Pete turned and left the room and Dae Kim hopped up to follow. He didn't need to say anything to Lonnie, who fell in behind them, looking around with wide eyes.

Pete led them down a hallway, which ended in a solid door to the basement. He threw on the light, possibly for Lonnie's benefit, but Dae Kim wasn't sure—he'd lost his night vision already, so Pete may have done it for them both. Once on the basement's smooth cement floor, Pete pointed to a room off to his right.

"Tell Lonnie to wait in there."

Dae Kim glanced at the Cow who then crossed to the room and opened the door. He stepped inside and sat in the tiny space's only chair. A light bulb hung above his head with a chain and Pete stepped up to yank it once.

"You'll wait here until we get back." Pete handed Lonnie both beers and closed the door.

"Master? I'm sorry… Master?"

Lonnie's voice through the door almost made Dae Kim turn, but Pete grabbed his bicep with firm fingers.

"Do you want to be friends with that Cow or be a Rakum? Make your mind up right now, because either you're my partner or my dinner."

"Damn, Pete, chill the hell out," Dae Kim said on the defensive. He yanked his arm out of Pete's hand and walked away from Lonnie's tiny room. "Let's get started."

"Yes," Pete said and passed to lead him up the steps. "I didn't want Chinese food tonight anyway."

"Screw you," Dae Kim said without venom and trotted up behind him. The flare in aggression was a welcome thing and had been missing from Dae Kim's life several months. His existence as a Rakum made sense, had order, but the new way, with no Fathers or Elders to direct their way brought with it only misery.

At the landing, Pete turned. "It may just be you and me, DaeDae. My master sent me a dream last night and there were only two heroes for our cause." Pete resumed walking to the den and Dae Kim followed. "I sure hope to hell you're up to it, because I know I am."

"Are you going to call me DaeDae, now?" Dae Kim said with a sardonic grin. "Because if you do, I'm going to call you PeePee. How's that grab you?"

"So long as you don't call me human," Pete said with a laugh. In the den, he stood in the center. "Ask me a question."

"In the basement, you flipped on the light. Have you lost your night vision?"

"No, but it's different than before. Once I accepted the new terms, I can still see in the dark, but it's hazy. No crystal-clear luminescence like I had before. We're not allowed telepathy, which I mentioned already, and all of our mystical skills are outlawed—no healing, no rejuvenation, which means no mental force period." Pete crossed his arms at his chest. "But don't despair. We keep our super-human strength."

"Why? I still don't understand. The book said the spirit of High Father Abroghia abandoned us. All that happened seven years ago. I still had my Cow during that time and all I lacked was telepathy…"

"Let me draw you a picture," Pete said, much less condescending than Dae Kim expected. "The spirit that empowered Abroghia left to his dimension seven years ago, but the portion he'd given every Rakum remained because he remained—in his own dimension." Pete waited for Dae Kim to nod. "November 13th, the spirit of Abroghia was erased."

Dae Kim parted his lips, but Pete interrupted him.

"I don't know how, and I can't get the story from the Unseen. Just accept it as fact. When he was erased from existence, he was erased in all of us."

"The Unseen?"

"Just what I said—the Unseen. You'll hear them, but not see them. They are the new Brethren, I guess."

"Okay, tell me how to submit to this master and avoid becoming human."

"The Master is a spirit, or rather, a collection of spirits, that seem to enjoy being called, *The Master*." Pete shrugged. "I discovered them by accident very soon after November 13th."

"How?" Dae Kim asked, still working to comprehend how the spirit foolishness worked.

Pete sighed at his own weariness, not at Dae Kim's question. "I reached out for Ta'avah's kind," he said simply. "Once I learned High Father Abroghia was embodied by a powerful god—and that's what Ta'avah was, don't you doubt it. Anyway, the Rabbit book said Ta'avah had three spirit equals, so I prayed to them." Pete chuckled then and rubbed his face hard.

Dae Kim only nodded, his mind reeling.

"Because of all the movies I've seen about evil spirits, I figured some blood would help. I brought a prostitute here and sacrificed her to these spirits. I made vows and waved my arms about..." Pete laughed again and looked at the ceiling. "Shit, I was desperate. Anyway, I must have eventually done the right combination of magic tricks because The Master introduced himself in my mind."

"*Judas Priest*," Dae Kim whispered.

"Yep," Pete said with a whole-body-shake. "Now listen, The Master absolutely *hates* humans. That means he hates the human part in you and me. He hates our brethren who are *turning* human. He especially hates anything associated with the Rabbit and her God. I learned all of this after I submitted to him, but you can choose with more knowledge than I had."

"And?" Dae Kim prodded.

"If you join up, you'll be a slave to the Unseen. Also, you can never leave. It's a lifetime commitment."

"Well," Dae Kim began and paused. "Why are you spooked?"

Pete grinned and lowered his chin. "Because the Ten Fathers were interested in our well-being, if only for the continuation of the race. The Master only wants to kill, maim, and destroy mortals, and he will use our flesh toward that end. He won't look out for us. He will be *using* us."

"But we won't be mortal." Pete nodded. "Then count me in. What do I do?" Dae Kim put his hands on his hips and expected the worst.

Pete nodded, rolled dramatically away, and shuffled back down the hallway toward the basement. He trotted the last few steps and shouted, "WE'RE COMING, LONNIE!"

Dae Kim sucked his teeth. In another minute, they were before the small room's door and Pete gave Dae Kim one last word of advice.

"I'll instruct you on accepting The Master. Do exactly what I say without question. You'll hesitate, I know I would have, but go through with it. I think The Master can kill us pretty easily. Don't make him mad."

"I will do precisely what you tell me to do."

Pete put his hand on the doorknob and paused. "You're still strong enough to manhandle that giant?" Dae Kim nodded. "Good. I won't help. The Master will be impressed." With that he opened the door.

"Take the Cow and put him over your knee like this," Pete said going down on one knee and miming a man draped over his leg.

Dae Kim only caught the tiniest glance of Lonnie's eyes and was sorry he had; the man was crying real tears. Dae Kim reached up—Lonnie stood more than six inches taller—and wrapped strong fingers around the back of his thick neck. With practiced pressure, he squeezed enough that the Cow's knees buckled, and he went down. Dae Kim timed it so the man's torso landed heavily on his bent leg as he dropped to one knee.

"Like a Cow," Pete said simultaneously drawing a thumb across the front of his neck and handing Dae Kim a long carving knife. Lonnie bucked, but was unable to escape Dae Kim's grip. He received the knife from Pete's hand and drew it deep into the Cow's throat, dragging it toward himself from the outside. Lonnie's blood issued forth in a splatter at first, and then a steady stream. Dae Kim looked to Pete for his next instruction, feeling nothing whatsoever for the dead man—which surprised and pleased him.

"Copy me," Pete said, and he dipped his right palm into the blood pooling on the cemented floor. He wiped his entire face twice and licked the blood off his hand. He paused and watched until Dae Kim mimicked him perfectly. Then Pete wrote in the blood three symbols Dae Kim had never seen before and placed both palms in the circle he'd drawn around

41

it all. Dae Kim copied him, allowing Lonnie's corpse to fall off to the right.

"Swear allegiance to The Master and invite him into your body."

Dae Kim hesitated only a moment, recalling snippets of the Rider book and then did as he said. Immediately, his flesh rippled head to toe with a palpable chill, forcing him to cough several times in succession.

"Took you long enough, idiot," a raspy voice said in his mind. Dae Kim looked at Pete who only shook his head. *"Clean this mess up and let's get to work!"*

Dae Kim stood and looked down at his hands. He had no interest in the blood—no desire to drink it, no desire to seek it. "We don't drink blood anymore?"

Pete bent down to drag Lonnie away and answered, "Yeah, but not because we want to." Dae Kim puzzled too long and Pete cleared his throat. "We'll lye-melt him, I'll show you how. Then we have to get up top. The Master showed me something big is coming and it has to do with the Elders."

Dae Kim nodded and wondered about Elder Canaan. Dae Kim had honed his fighting skills under the Elder's expert tutelage. But the blood... What shit was this? Now he would drink it for The Master and not derive any pleasure for himself? What had he agreed to?

"We see seven other slow-changing Rakum out in the world that we could initiate. We think we will kill you, stupid one..."

Dae Kim dropped to his knees. "No! Wait! I want to serve you! I will serve you! I will!"

"At least he didn't apologize."

"Idiots have smarts, too."

"Carry on, idiot."

Dae Kim began swabbing up Lonnie's blood with the towels Pete tossed him and he pondered the amazing yet ruthless nature of his multi-voiced new Master. At least he hadn't turned mortal.

7, JAN 15

Kilmeade leaned against the doorframe awaiting Roman's arrival. He had asked his brother to lend a hand with the Bushman girl's infatuation; now that she learned to call him telepathically, she did so frequently. Ignoring her longing was not without discomfort and every time their minds touched, he wanted to know her better and in more familiar ways. Now he desired Roman's approval, or in the least, acquiescence. Dealing with a myriad of mortal mindsets in his new circle, it was as if he needed *permission* to be a Rakum. Making an effort to deflect the girl justified pursuing her when that failed.

Kilmeade snickered as Roman pulled up, his eyes wide and serious. He slowed and stopped, worry covering his face. Kilmeade fell into the passenger side and nodded. "Brother, thank you for your time."

"You're welcome," he answered tersely. "Do I need to say out loud that seeing that girl or even communicating with her in any fashion is an extremely bad idea?"

Kilmeade lifted both palms. "What do I do? She calls me nonstop."

"You don't have a phone," he said as if afraid of what was coming.

"She's picked up the invisible line, brother." Kilmeade placed both hands on the dash and studied his knuckles. "I guess she spent too much time around David Walker and your little Javier."

Roman pressed the ignition, frowning. "That blasted Rufus. He started this—he opened her mind to it."

"Maybe so..." Kilmeade hummed. "If you witness that I attempted to dissuade her, I will get less strife later when this goes south." Kilmeade lowered his chin and finished with, "Because it will go south."

"Don't do it," Roman said, gritting his teeth. "Ignore her."

"You know that's not an option."

Roman shook his head. "You have no intention of stopping her. You want me to be your excuse."

Kilmeade leaned back into his seat. "Elder Roman," Kilmeade said purposefully calling his brother by his former identity before he became soft and fluffy, "a delightful and youthful female worships the ground you walk on and you would ignore her? Think about that and there's only one correct answer." Roman didn't reply. "Are you trying to make me into something I'm not?" When Roman still didn't reply, he added, "Am I a man or a Rakum?"

Roman waved his hand. "Yeah, yeah, yeah. You're a Rakum."

"Yes, and an Elder."

They drove in silence a few minutes and Roman said, "I'll do what I can, although I know precisely how this is going to end."

Kilmeade squeezed his near shoulder. "Give her some of that mortal wisdom you're so full of."

Roman nodded. "Trust me; I'm going to give it my best shot."

Kilmeade pressed a handwritten sticky note to the dashboard, the script flowery, revealing the Bushman girl's address.

Roman scowled. "When did she give you that?" Kilmeade smiled and didn't answer. "You saw her already?"

Kilmeade looked out the window, mischievous grin in place.

"How many times?" Roman grumbled.

"Twice," Kilmeade said and sucked his teeth. "She consents, brother. You know what that means."

"Please, stop." Roman held up one hand and steered with the other. "I'm sorry I asked."

"She's chaste," Kilmeade chuckled. "Alas, she never asks for *that*."

"Yet," Roman replied with a huff.

"Yet," Kilmeade mimicked and laughed facing away.

By the time they reached Chloe's house, both men had returned to a more serious mood. Because Roman was with him, Kilmeade rang the doorbell instead of gaining entry the Rakum way. The Bushman girl's parents were out of town, so he didn't mind meeting her there. It was private, and well-appointed in the ways of luxury to which he was accustomed. Chloe answered in short order with a noise of surprise when she realized Kilmeade brought a chaperone.

She greeted them both and asked them in. Kilmeade sent her a wink and she blushed. He liked looking at her, smelling her, imagining trysts with her. This was why he wanted his even-minded brother along. It was Kilmeade's way to take whatever he thought was his. Upon his first visit to her house, he had begun to feel she belonged to him. She wasn't a Cow and she wasn't his mate, so Roman needed to help him break loose of her pull. After tonight, if Roman didn't dissuade her, he would respond to her affections like the Rakum Elder he was.

"Hi, Miss Bushman," Roman said following her to the sitting room.

"Well, this room is awful," Kilmeade said, looking around. It wasn't as comfortable or casual as the room he'd met her in twice already. This room had shelves of brass kitsch, a short embroidered couch flanked by matching wood-trimmed Queen Anne chairs and harsh track lighting.

"This room is not fit for anyone but blue-haired old Cows," he sent silently to Chloe who grinned and asked them to be seated. Roman sat on the couch between them once she found her spot. Kilmeade gestured to Chloe's jeans. "I like those." He didn't say more, but she blushed then at a few additional compliments he slipped to her telepathically.

"Miss Bushman," Roman began after shooting an irritated glare at Kilmeade. "Let me get straight to the point. You need to stop calling my brother. There is absolutely no place in his life for you." Chloe objected, but Roman barreled on. "There is no way to have a happy ending with a Rakum Elder." Roman leaned forward. "You know that God doesn't approve of the Rakum and is trying desperately to save these last two. I'm afraid you're being a problem instead of a help."

"Wait, that's not fair," Chloe said and sought Kilmeade's eye. He sent her a grin but said nothing. "You told me that God matches people up for His purposes. What if He's doing this?"

Chloe sat forward and Kilmeade watched Roman's eyes widen, unaccustomed to having his words thrown back at him.

"Kilmeade asked me to dissuade you," Roman said. "You know I want what's best for you and Kilmeade both."

"I'm not hurting him," she pouted. "Am I hurting you, Kilmeade?"

"Very badly," he joked, "in a very special place."

"Kilmeade!" Roman barked. Chloe giggled and Kilmeade watched her with a tight grin.

"I got in trouble there," he sent her telepathically and she giggled again.

"Miss Bushman," Roman continued, turning his back to Kilmeade. "My brother's way is unabashed truth. He doesn't lie because he has the power to back up his every whim with extreme prejudice. Because of this, I am going to make you ask him some hard questions."

"I'm not scared of the truth," Chloe said with a glint in her eye.

"Good. Kilmeade is 381 years old—look at me, Miss Bushman," Roman said when her gaze wandered back to Kilmeade.

"I know. He's a Rakum Elder and old as dirt."

Roman took a deep breath. "I said that to precursor this: Kilmeade only wants you around because you make him feel good. It has nothing to do with you being magical soulmates who will live together forever in perfect harmony."

His brother had her dead to rights and Chloe made no reply. Roman turned center and looked at Kilmeade.

"Brother, tell Chloe what you think about her."

Kilmeade smiled. "Chloe Bushman, you *consent*. This is of the utmost importance. I wouldn't waste a single moment of my life taking blood from a female who resisted or even had second thoughts. You consented, so I gave it a try."

"That's good, brother. Add to that the answer to this: if another sweet-smelling young woman approached you this very night and offered you her blood, would you accept?"

"Oh, yes," Kilmeade admitted. Chloe hardened her gaze but didn't back down.

"What if she also wanted sex?" Roman said his voice edgy.

"Without question," Kilmeade answered holding Chloe's gaze.

"You're not making me mad," Chloe said to them both her expression unwavering.

Roman changed tracks. "Brother, tell her the blood you prefer above all others."

Kilmeade licked his lips. "My favorite is Elder Canaan's blood," he said with a hungry grin. He hadn't had a blood meal of any sort for several days and his stomach rumbled at the thought. Canaan left for a week to settle property with Marcy so if tonight went sour, presumably Kilmeade would remain hungry and the thought turned his mood.

"And?" Roman prompted bringing him back to task.

"My next favorite is the blood of a strong, willing—or unwilling— human male that I can drink to death."

"Did you get that, Miss Bushman?" Roman pressed. "A person dies when Kilmeade fancies a Dying Buzz."

Kilmeade grinned at Roman's back. His brother hadn't sounded the least bit judgmental, which was a surprise since he had become the preacher for the family.

"And I will keep that up as long as I like. I don't want to lose my edge," Kilmeade said and flashed his anomalous fangs for Chloe alone. She blushed and then shook her head at Roman.

"It's not like I approve of murder," Chloe said seriously, "but I'm not here to control an Elder who's three hundred and eighty years old."

"Three hundred and eighty-one," Kilmeade sent over with another wink.

"Kilmeade," Roman said with a sigh, "please continue."

"My third favorite is a consenting Chloe Bushman. That's the order of it."

"You're lying about the order," Chloe said silently.

"Maybe," he teased, not revealing to Roman the communication.

"See, Miss Bushman," Roman continued, "you are food. Think about it. You're a hamburger. A self-replenishing hamburger."

"You're not a hamburger," Kilmeade said to her silently.

"Tell him, not me!" Chloe yelped pointing at Roman. Roman caught his eye.

"She's more than food, brother," he said with a small shrug.

Roman frowned. "Continue with the reasons you like her."

"You are fun to look at—"

"And expound on that," Roman prompted.

"You're fun to look at because I long to touch you," Kilmeade said and looked to Roman for approval. When his brother nodded, he continued smiling. "The skin on my palms..." Kilmeade held up his hand and Chloe trained her eyes to it. "...burns for you. Tingling, painful, delightful." He closed his hand into a fist and lowered it to his lap. Chloe looked away. "Knowing I can't touch you because of my devotion to these mortals..." he looked down his nose at Roman and winked, "...causes immense pain and you may have noticed, Rakum enjoy pain nearly as much as pleasure."

"Well, that's just weird," Chloe whispered looking away again, her arms crossed.

"Go on," Roman said softly, approving his performance so far.

"You smell nice—not only of soap, but of the blood you will offer me..." Kilmeade paused and inhaled deeply. Chloe turned to see his face as he continued. "...and a feminine essence you would call pheromones."

"Eww," Chloe said, "Don't be gross."

Roman latched onto her objection. "Right there—this is one of those deeper ones you could have saved us from talking about."

Chloe huffed. "What? So, he wants to touch me and smell me."

"He is a fully functional sexual being," Roman said lowering his chin to look at her over his glasses. "How long until you consent to that? How long before you move your relationship to that place? He can't be a husband to you. If he doesn't start falling for God as I did, presumably he'll live on. You'll grow old and gray and he'll look just like this."

"My brother is right," Kilmeade said. "How long will you be nice to look at and fun to touch?"

"But Marcy and Canaan—" Chloe began.

"Marcy released him. It's over. Because of this very thing," Roman said softly.

Chloe was quiet a long time and then she said, frowning, "*One day* of happiness is priceless as far as I am concerned."

Now it was Roman's turn to be quiet. He shot Kilmeade an unreadable expression and Chloe sighed clasping her hands in her lap. Kilmeade's stomach grumbled loud enough for all three to hear and he cleared his throat.

"Brother, Chloe, we have all suffered greatly in recent weeks. All of my brethren are gone, save one. All the Cows are gone. Your God has left me this flesh and is patiently waiting for me to wake up to His truth..."

Roman turned his head to Kilmeade as he spoke and his eyes grew wide with sincere surprise.

Kilmeade gave him a smug smile. "But..." he stressed and then grabbed Chloe's gaze, "tonight, right now, I hunger." He watched Chloe's face drain, her consent not erasing her trepidation.

Roman got to his feet. "Miss Bushman, are you going to continue to call on my brother?" Chloe nodded, her eyes locked to Kilmeade's. Roman sighed and began his walk from the room. "I did my part, Kilmeade. I'm sorry I didn't get a different outcome."

Kilmeade did not respond and rose from his chair to approach Chloe.

Roman paused, watching them both. "God help us. I'll wait for you in the car," he said and was gone.

Kilmeade kneeled on the rug before Chloe and put his hand to her inner shoulder. "Roman's visit was a fun diversion, but I *am* hurting. Would you like me to hurt or shall I enjoy the ecstasy your blood provides?"

"I don't agree with all that stuff Roman said about you and me," Chloe said in a whisper. "And I don't want you to hurt."

"Do you consent?" he whispered and scooted closer.

"Yes, Kilmeade. I consent," Chloe said softly.

Kilmeade needed no other prompting. Humans were an odd lot, females even odder. At least this one was crazy for him and not crazy in general.

8, JAN 23, DALLAS

"Now we wait," Pete said, looking straight ahead and leaning forward, arms draped over the steering wheel.

"Did the Master say what we're looking for?" Dae Kim asked, looking out the windshield. From the lot, parked in the shadowy place between the sodium lights, they watched the door. The Unseen had led Pete to Baylor-Dallas Research Hospital, but that's all Dae Kim knew. Did Pete know more and wasn't telling? Why did The Master only speak to him? Dae Kim pondered these things and more as he grew bored on their stake-out.

A movement ahead caught Dae Kim's attention and he looked up. A man had exited carrying a cardboard box. Right behind him, another man jogged to keep up, toting a similar package. Dae Kim glanced at Pete's profile, now at attention, eyes trained on the strangers. Pete seemed to be making words inwardly and Dae Kim squinted to see more clearly.

The first man might have been mid-twenties, dressed in a white long-sleeved shirt unbuttoned at the top with no tie and dark grey slacks. Dae Kim couldn't make out his facial features, but he wore his wavy brown hair past his ears and he was tall and fit. The second man was a little older and completely bald. He also wore slacks and a white shirt, but with a too-wide plaid tie. His shoes carried an extra shine and clacked with each step.

"Is it one of these guys? Both?" he asked without looking away. Pete said nothing and Dae Kim sighed, watching the men place the boxes in the backseat of the car. The men chatted and were close enough that their words traveled to Dae Kim's bored ears.

"That's the last," the older man said. "Thanks for the help."

"No problem, Doc," the younger replied and the men shook hands.

"I was wondering," Wide-tie continued, "will you be bringing your father's work to our labs? I don't want to sound boastful, but our facility is more than capable of supporting his research. I will make sure you have the grants you need to fulfill Dr. Roberts's lifelong pursuits."

Fit-guy shrugged. "Naw, I mean, he had pretty much retired."

Wide-tie sighed and to Dae Kim, appeared irritated. "You should let me have a look at it. Let me into his lab. Will you?" Fit-guy hemmed. It looked like he respected Wide-tie, but still, he didn't automatically acquiesce.

"My father had military contracts, Federal government stuff, there are legal issues," Fit-guy said and mumbled a few more excuses that Dae Kim didn't catch. "How 'bout you let me look into it?" Wide-tie sighed, and they shook hands again.

Dae Kim watched the other man tromp back to the building, walking with long strides not necessary for a man of average height. Fit-guy slumped into his Charger and switched on the stereo. Trace Adkins' drawling voice flooded the parking lot.

Dae Kim nudged Pete's arm. "Well?" Pete made the same low noise in his throat and switched on the car. They'd come in Dae Kim's new Lexus sedan to increase their stealth. "Is that him? The pretty one?" Dae Kim asked again.

"Pretty. *Hmph.* That's debatable," Pete said watching the man check his appearance in the rearview mirror.

"What did The Master say? I don't hear nothin'."

"The Master doesn't trust you yet, DaeDae," Pete said and shot him a quick look. "He said we'd find a priority target here that we should destroy tonight. Let's see where he goes."

Dae Kim wondered who the young man was to The Master. Why did he matter? Pete didn't know either, but he was happy as hell to end him. Simply because The Master wanted him gone. Were they assassins now? Hit men? Dae Kim had millions of dollars in the bank; why did he listen to the edicts of an angry half-Rakum and a bunch of lunatic spirits?

"Want to hear from The Master, Dae Kim?" a raspy voice deep behind his ear uttered. *"The Master doesn't like you. The Master doesn't trust you. As soon as we get what we need from Pete, we're gonna have him eat you."*

Dae Kim jerked his gaze to Pete, but the man was driving, carefully and covertly keeping the Charger in view. *"I will serve you,"* Dae Kim answered back with as much humility he could muster.

The voice chuckled with derision. *"It's not enough. You're weak. Like a momma's boy on the teat. Soft and pink, plump for picking."*

Dae Kim frowned. He was none of those things. With an angry exhale, he answered back, *"I'll show you. I'm the one you want."*

The voice didn't speak, but made a few noises that could have been coughing, laughing, or breathing—the overall impression Dae Kim received back was that it would wait and see.

"Wook, he wikes wibwaries," Pete said in baby talk. "How tweet."

Dae Kim braced on the dash when Pete stopped suddenly to avoid the Charger's headlights. The man was making a circle before the library doors and he came to a stop at the curb in a No Parking Zone.

"Good way to lose your car," Dae Kim mumbled and Pete agreed with a grunt. He backed the Lexus into a shadowed spot across the empty lot. The library had been closed a couple of hours and Dae Kim figured it would be locked. On the contrary, their man heaved his boxes free of the passenger seat and toted them to the large glass doors. A security guard, complete with billy club and a gun holster opened the door and received the box.

"Hey, yeah, okay, I will," Dae Kim heard faintly the guard's responses, but he couldn't hear the stranger they watched. He shook his head, angry at losing his advanced hearing despite his work for The Master.

"Can you hear our guy?" Dae Kim asked Pete in a low voice.

"No, but the guard said he'd see him tomorrow." Pete frowned, probably just as sick of going deaf. "There he goes. He's on the move."

Dae Kim sighed, bored. He missed his independence, but The Master provided no complaint department. Pete fell in behind the stranger, again in stalk mode, and before they reached the interstate, Dae Kim had had enough.

"What are we doing? I'm hungry. And dammit, I want a hamburger!" He balled his fists and watched Pete's profile. Pete only grinned and then gave a small nod. "Well? Do we follow him home and end him there? Can I eat whatever's in his fridge?" Dae Kim said sarcastically. Pete gave him a quick glance.

"This is the mission, soldier," he said with a laugh. "Jump in or jump out, you can't ride my back about it. I just drive the car."

Dae Kim growled, feeling impotent and powerless. Not only had he been slowly losing his Rakum abilities, he'd been losing weight. What the hell was that about? Two weeks following The Master all over town and never did he get enough to eat. The main food the Unseen craved was blood and it did not nourish Dae Kim's body as it had before. He looked at Pete's midsection. He didn't look leaner; if anything, he looked stronger. What kind of unfair shit was going on? He was just about to remark on it when Pete decelerated and jerked the car onto the Denton off-ramp.

Within minutes they had followed the target to a large neighborhood with wide manicured lots and two-story homes. Dae Kim visually scoured the street and Pete crawled along, peeking to see which house he pulled into. When the brake lights came on, Pete stopped until they went off again. Dae Kim could just make out a man's shape exiting the car fifty yards ahead and walking up to a dark stoop.

"He's in," Pete said in an urgent whisper a moment later. "Follow me." His partner opened his door and slid out with more caution than necessary. Dae Kim snickered and followed him, hunched down with a quick step. At the man's front walk, Pete stood to his normal height and strolled toward the front door.

"Are we just going to knock—" Dae Kim began, but before he could finish, the stranger they sought stepped out of the shadowy stoop and faced them, arms crossed. He stood in silhouette so Dae Kim still could not make out his features.

"I only have one trick, fellas," he said in a lilting Texan accent, "but I'll pull it on ya if you don't tell me why you're following me." His left hand went to his belt and Dae Kim recognized the dark shape of a pistol butt poking upwards at his waist.

Dae Kim stopped his forward motion, thinking Pete would, too, but his partner ran forward as if to attack the stranger head-on. An explosion sounded all around them. With a flash of gunfire, Pete was thrown backwards into Dae Kim by a powerful hit.

"Pete!" Dae Kim hissed and caught him under the armpits. He dragged him backwards and made it to the curb before the stranger called for him to stop.

"The cops are comin', fella," he called to Dae Kim who jerked Pete's body back to the car. "Hey! Your friend needs an ambulance!"

"Shit, Pete!" Dae Kim barked and shoved him into the passenger seat. He jogged around to the driver's side and pressed the ignition. "Pete? Pete!" he yelled and hit the gas while spinning the wheel opposite the shooter's home.

"I'm good," Pete said, blood flying from his lips. "Didn't see that coming!" Bright red spittle bubbled from a punctured lung.

"Look at your blood, man," Dae Kim said too loudly. "Does The Master do anything he promised? We're not Rakum! We're human!"

"The hell we are," Pete said, pink saliva hitting the windshield. He choked and then coughed, catching a good-sized plug of moist tissue in his palm. He rubbed it with both hands, still laugh-choking. "Can a mortal cough out a bullet? N-O."

"Are you healing?" Dae Kim asked, unable to discern anything in his blind and dumb mortal state. Would The Master help *him* cough up a bullet? He seriously doubted it. "Do you need a doctor?"

Pete took a moment to look down at his chest and the red circle demarcating his entry wound. He was still breathing, less blood came from his lips and nostrils, and he'd grown pale.

"Do you need a doctor?!" Dae Kim repeated.

Pete popped open his shirt, the bullet wound the size of a quarter. He leaned up. "Did it go through?" he barked and hacked forcefully.

"You coughed it up, asshole!" Dae Kim barked. "You're delirious!" Dae Kim had gotten them on the interstate for the short hop to Corinth. His partner seized once and fell face-forward into the dash. "Pete?" Dae Kim grabbed his closest arm and yanked it. He was out cold.

Exhaling with rage, Dae Kim did what he would have done as a Rakum: he turned to his superiors, and these days his Elder was The Master. Aloud he said, "Master, what should I do with Pete?"

"Push him out of the car."

"No, let's use him a little longer, Master," Dae Kim said aloud. The Elders loved being flattered; perhaps his new master did, too. "You are powerful and mighty, it's nothing for you to heal his wound. When this is over, I'll show you I'm the better disciple. Until then—use him to perform your will. He's very capable..."

Dae Kim heard a small chuckle behind his ear and Pete sputtered. In another few seconds, the man sat upright, spat bile and frothy expectorate into his lap and took a deep breath. When he exhaled, he turned halfway to see Dae Kim's profile.

"What'd I tell ya? NOT HUMAN!" he shouted the last and fingered the closed bullet wound in his chest. He pound the dashboard and sang praises to The Master at the top of his voice.

"We can only maintain one of you at a time; your partner will rot," the collection of spirits laugh-talked in his mind.

Dae Kim gave Pete a half-smile. Things were going to be different now. *Much* different.

《回》

Kilmeade watched Chloe carefully descend the basement steps. It had been a week since Roman attempted and failed to talk her out of pursuing him and he'd tapped her blood in tiny doses three times in two weeks. As she reached the landing and looked around, he allowed his heart a little freedom. Previous to 11/13, a Rakum remained guarded against everything construed as weak or potentially *mortal*. Now there didn't seem to be a reason to follow such a tenet. The delicious pain the fragile female caused inside was as new as it was welcome.

"It's sorta dark down here," Chloe said as she reached the bottom step, "but it's clean. I'm surprised it's actually *very* clean."

"Canaan is a decent maid," Kilmeade said without joking.

Chloe laughed one short burst. "Canaan? No way." She reached his position and Kilmeade nodded when she indicated she'd like to sit by him on the couch.

"We can't hire anyone. Humans can't be trusted." Kilmeade studied Chloe's form as she shrugged off her light jacket and tossed it over the back of the couch. Tonight, she wore a pink long-sleeved collared shirt tucked into her normal dark blue jeans. The tiny ankle boots were a different touch and he realized they were the reason she'd descended the stairs so cautiously.

"You trust me," she said, by now accustomed to his roaming eyes. "I could clean it for you. I don't mind."

Kilmeade chuckled. "Oh, no. No woman of mine will ever clean up after filthy Rakum Elders with no hygiene whatsoever," he said and then coughed Canaan's name into his hand.

Chloe laughed high and giggly. "Where is he?"

Kilmeade considered her audacity to ask such a question—or any question. Yet was it audacious now that the Rakum were no more? Wasn't he simply a bloodthirsty oddity? Chloe widened her eyes, ready to repeat herself and Kilmeade offered a tight grin. "He returns tonight. Personal business."

"Oh," Chloe said thoughtfully and then turned her face suddenly. "Wait... you said *no woman of yours*." Chloe attempted to read his eyes, his thoughts, something, but Kilmeade remained quiet. "What's going on?" she asked and touched his arm.

"What?" Kilmeade asked milking the topic.

"You're acting kinda..." Chloe ran out of words.

"Speak your mind," Kilmeade said. "Have you not noticed my impatience?"

She grinned. "Everyone who meets you must notice that right away."

"Tick-tock," Kilmeade smirked enjoying the banter.

"Give me a minute," she said maintaining the same playful twinkle he'd seen at Javier's the day they returned. "We're not all as smart as you. I'm formulating my sentence now," she said slowing down on purpose.

Kilmeade tilted his head to the side. "I'm aging here..."

Chloe laughed a short burst. "You seem different tonight."

"Describe my different behavior. I'm new to this."

"New to what?"

"Opening up," he said plainly. "A Rakum's heart is a rock, solid and black. Not pink and hollow and filled with kittens."

"Like mine," Chloe replied. "Is it scary?" she asked and when his eyes flashed she added with a grin, "You said speak my mind."

Kilmeade nodded. "No, but it's painful."

"Which you also enjoy."

Kilmeade grinned. "Come close."

Chloe scooted closer to him on the sofa and allowed him to drape an arm behind her. He leaned into the couch and pulled her along, so her head ended up on his shoulder.

"You seem more romantic tonight," she said, her voice soft. "I think that's part of it. I think you might be in love with me and kinda freaked out about it." Chloe was looking at the basement ceiling illuminated only by the corner lamp. Kilmeade stared up as well, grinning at her openness. After all, he challenged her to speak plainly.

"Rakum don't fall in love like you think. You could fall in *my favor,* and that's the extent of it." Kilmeade sighed. "It is a limitation that prevents us from becoming weak."

Chloe blew a raspberry and nudged him with her elbow, still looking up. "Okay, Elder Kilmeade. We'll see how that goes now that the Brave New World is in play."

He huffed nodding, Chloe referring to their loss of the Rakum spirit. If that spirit prevented them from their most human behaviors, maybe Kilmeade's heart *would* drop the Rakum hardness. After all, Rafa and Roman held his favor. And didn't Canaan move into his heart a hundred years ago?

"What are you thinking about?" she whispered and turned her head to see if he'd meet her eyes. Kilmeade did and reflexively smiled as their gazes locked.

"You might be on to something there, little human." She grinned wider and Kilmeade definitely experienced an uncomfortable twinge deep in his core. "It's time to tell you that I've been thinking of you as my possession since the first time you consented."

"That's okay, isn't it?" she asked still locked in his eyes.

"Is it okay with *you?* You are my possession..."

"Like a nice table or chair?" she asked grinning. "I think of you as my own personal six-foot-two mosquito."

55

Kilmeade made a small chuckle. "Six-foot-three."

"Right," she giggled. "So, what? Is there a proper Rakum code of behavior with females?" Kilmeade nodded. "So, what do we do if you feel like you own me?"

Kilmeade gave a light chuckle. "You referenced Canaan and Marcy when Roman and I were trying to keep you away, remember?" Chloe nodded. "I have had innumerable lovers, but I have never taken a mate," he said and paused. Chloe smirked and he grinned and shook her with his arm. "I never liked anyone enough to pair up."

"You think you might like me enough, though?"

"Yes, but the mate-up is for the Rakum, not the human," Kilmeade said looking upon her upturned face. "It's about my comfort, not yours."

"*Pffft...*" With another raspberry, Chloe added, "It's been about you from the beginning."

Kilmeade chuckled. "Yes, it has." He rocked her slowly, preparing his next words. "A Rakum can mate up with a female for as long as he wants her around. We are extremely intelligent and we bore easily."

"No, you're just jerks," Chloe said shaking her head. She was grinning, though. "Big surprise. A Rakum wants a woman as long as she's young, pretty, and fun to be around." Chloe sat up out of his arm to face him. "It's not so different with humans. Look, my daddy raised me with self-esteem. If you and I were together and you treated me well, I'd stay. If you didn't, I'd leave. It's not complicated."

Kilmeade shook his head. "It doesn't work like that."

"Then it don't work," Chloe said using an exaggerated southern accent to soften the seriousness of her statement. Kilmeade fell silent and after a few seconds, Chloe leaned against him and sighed.

"If I asked you to be my mate, would you expect me to be like a mortal man—monogamous, home on time, be thoughtful, bring gifts?"

"Can you do all that?"

Kilmeade shrugged. "No."

"I love that you're so honest," she said smiling. "Can you at least be monogamous?" Chloe asked with a follow-up grimace. When he noticed, she clarified. "I couldn't be with a man who poked in strange places. *Ew.* No. I just won't." She faked a shiver but was serious about the sentiment.

Kilmeade had no problem answering. "I *am* monogamous." He chuckled quietly and lowered his voice. "All Elders slow down in that department after a couple of centuries. It doesn't mean we can't or we stop, but we become other-focused."

"Then that would be enough," she said with a single head tip. "But listen..." She met his eye again. "Last year, everything I wanted is completely different from what I want now. I think as I get older, I will expect more from you and from our relationship."

"That's a fair assumption," Kilmeade agreed. "Would you like to join me and see what happens? It's a brave new world, you said."

"Yeah," Chloe said and beamed another smile his way. "I'm in love with you. Human love. I can show you how to love. I'll be your teacher."

"Oh, that will be a new thing," he replied and squeezed her again. "I want to start now, then. Chloe Bushman, will you be my mate?"

"Yes, Elder Kilmeade, I will be your mate," Chloe said smiling.

"Okay, then, get naked. My hunger burns a different way tonight."

Chloe paled and sat up to see his expression.

Kilmeade grinned and laughed out loud. *"You should have seen your face!"* he sent silently and hugged her close. The new world might be more tolerable with such a funny little bird by his side. In the least, it couldn't be worse.

《回》

Chloe had been gone twenty minutes when Canaan finally returned from his trip. Kilmeade exhaled, an unfamiliar emotion squeezing his ribcage. Shaking it off, he started toward the hall.

"Honey, I'm home!" Canaan bellowed as he opened the front door. "My precious," he said with a goofy grin at the sight of Kilmeade at the foot of the stairs. "I know you missed me. Come on, fess up."

Canaan dropped his overnight bag, lumbered up to Kilmeade and yanked him close. He bumped their foreheads together and then went still with a jerk.

"That face," Canaan said and released him. "Have you seen your face?" With a soft laugh, he grabbed his bag and headed upstairs.

Kilmeade suppressed a grin, knowing he would tease about Miss Bushman's presence lingering so recently. "My face is fine."

When Canaan had dropped his bag on the bed, he turned and wagged his finger. "You finally took a mate."

"What does that have to do with my face? Your other senses have informed you of this—not my countenance," Kilmeade asserted.

Canaan pinched Kilmeade's cheek. "Sure," he teased. "You look happy. Really satisfied with yourself. That's on your face, not in the air."

"Huh," Kilmeade scoffed and then stated in a serious tone, "I sense it all worked out in Nashville."

Canaan sighed. "I didn't get a conjugal, if that's what you mean." Kilmeade smirked. "Oh, you were serious?" Canaan chuckled. "Yes, we're done. I'll have to take my rocks elsewhere." He lowered his gaze. "Got any ideas?"

"Don't look at me," Kilmeade said sardonically. "I'm in your brain— I know you prefer a lover who can't kick your ass."

Canaan burst out laughing. "Okay, okay—truce," he sighed and walked into the kitchen. "I'm in your brain, too. If you and your mate stay busy, I will be satisfied."

Kilmeade laughed at the thought of tangling with Chloe romantically and Canaan aware of everything. Canaan caught his eye and mimicked his chuckling.

"You are in my head more than ever," Kilmeade said in wonder.

Laughing still, Canaan said, "I know. This might really work out for old Canaan."

"It's because we're the last Rakum. Our minds are magnets desperately drawing together."

Canaan nodded. "Let it come. We'll need each other. I didn't like being apart."

"I felt stretched thin," Kilmeade reflected and the name of his earlier and unwelcome emotion came to mind. "I felt—"

"Anxious," Canaan said with authority.

Kilmeade nodded; his partner hit it exactly. "It wasn't natural. We need to remain together. No more trips out of state without Kilmeade."

"Agreed," Canaan said and gave up finding what he sought in the fridge.

"Drank it," Kilmeade offered. "We'll send Beryl for beer. He's in the den on the computer."

Canaan grinned. "Nerd."

Kilmeade winked. "He missed you, too."

"Awww," Canaan said and popped open a can of Sprite. "Maybe later, he'll show me how much."

Kilmeade smirked. "Be careful, he'll take you seriously."

"Ya think?" Canaan asked with a goofy smile. Kilmeade disappeared in his thoughts and after a few moments, Canaan tipped his chin. "What's on your mind? It's about your mate-up. Ask."

Kilmeade *tsked,* amazed again at their connection. "Chloe feels she understands our nature, but I'd like you to have Marcy call her, share her wisdom regarding how to please a Rakum Elder." When Canaan didn't respond immediately, Kilmeade added, "Marcy pleased you. I have read that correctly..."

"Oh, most definitely," Canaan replied with a nod. "Every second."

Kilmeade nodded, signaling the end of the topic, and Canaan made a noise of amazement. "Yes?"

"This other thing—you vowed to be monogamous," Canaan said watching his expression. "Did you want to ask me about that?"

Kilmeade rubbed his face. Now Canaan was seeing his unasked questions. "I suppose if we're going to seamlessly share our minds," he sighed, "we will both learn to only answer what is posed and not everything that streams past."

Canaan grinned and agreed. "Yeah, I don't need you asking me about what runs past my brain."

"At least make it interesting," Kilmeade joked. "I bore easily."

"I make no promises," Canaan retorted. He sighed and regarded Kilmeade with a long gaze. "So, tell me, is the great Elder Kilmeade finally going to limit his amazingness to one tiny mortal?"

"He is." Kilmeade looked to the ceiling. "I am woefully out of practice; it's been a long time since I initiated any sort of sexual activity."

"We got old," Canaan said with finality.

Kilmeade agreed with a small huff. Canaan's thoughts trickled over as his compatriot pondered why monogamy had no place before Last Assembly. Besides Cows who gave up anything a Rakum requested, Elders were never denied sexual stimulation, keeping nearby grunts especially gifted in those areas. These "fixers" had been dedicated to their trade and if ever they were unavailable, any grunt could take up the slack.

"Ish-mikhan,"[8] Canaan whispered with a wink.

With no argument and no reply, Kilmeade offered a sad grin.

After perusing the same memory hallways as Kilmeade a few more moments, Canaan sighed and clapped his shoulder. "You'll have fun. Marcy was young when we consummated our mate up and every day with her seemed like a new adventure. I saw things through her eyes—through human eyes—and it didn't make me soft as the Fathers feared. It made me a better Rakum."

"You're right. This *is* fun," Kilmeade said quietly. "Not knowing what to do or when to do it. Chloe called it a brave new world. We will learn new ways of dealing with daily life." Canaan agreed with a small noise.

---

[8] *Fix-it men*, used euphemistically.

"How do you feel about Miss Bushman?" Kilmeade asked.

"She's funny. She smells nice. I like her," Canaan said with a nod.

"Good. It only makes sense that you would like her, as much as you've crawled into my head."

"That goes both ways," Canaan said with a grin. He looked around the room comically. "I gotta find me a little birdie, too."

Kilmeade chuckled. "She told her parents we eloped. In a few weeks, I shall meet my mortal in-laws." Kilmeade grinned and Canaan scrunched his nose.

"This is so weird," he whispered.

"We will forge ahead," Kilmeade said with humor and placed his fists to his hips. "I missed you, Elder Canaan, and I have never experienced that sense of separation before."

"Aw, that's so sweet," Canaan said and batted his eyelashes. "This humanness is sneaking up on us." Kilmeade nodded. "Speaking of sweet..." Canaan inhaled deeply. "You've been at Miss Bushman's blood. Are you dumping me for a woman?" he asked smiling at his own joke.

"Not a chance," Kilmeade said with a tiny shake of the head. "I'm being polite. I'm quite ready to knock you over."

Canaan laughed and worked open the top button of his shirt. "No need. Whoa, horsey, *whoaaaa....*"

Kilmeade stepped closer and caught Canaan's eye. "How much further will our telepathic connection go?"

"We could turn into one person," Canaan said with a soft chuckle.

"I hope I get to keep my much better body," Kilmeade sent silently and then whispered, "I desperately missed your blood." He gently pulled the Elder's throat to his mouth.

"Sweet talker," Canaan said softly. As Kilmeade pressed in, Canaan switched to telepathy. *"Hope you consummate your mate-up soon. My room is right next door."*

"Shhh-hhh..."

"Shhh, yourself, I'm serious," Canaan sent grinning, and fell silent.

9, JAN 30

Seven days ago, Kilmeade asked Chloe to be his mate, which translated in her mind as "wife," so she had gone home and packed her bags. She wired her parents with the news and their response was to cut short their missions trip. Now they'd be home in a short three weeks instead of three months. They planned to meet Kilmeade at that time and her mom would most definitely make things tense. Chloe cleared her mind and retuned her attention to the wall color.

For now, she had permission to decorate the entire house any way she chose. Tonight, she'd been thinking about upholstery to match the pillow-top comforter when the hairs on the back of her neck stood on end; Kilmeade was coming up behind her. Within seconds, warm arms surrounded her from behind and a gentle kiss pressed into her hair.

"What? No startle?" he asked in her ear.

Chloe grinned with victory. "I developed Rakum radar."

"Oh, that is a talent," he cooed and encircled her more completely, snugging her body against his front. "I like rising and finding you here."

"I like you rising and finding me here," she said quietly and giggled at the sensation of his lips against her head.

"I don't hear Beryl or Canaan," he whispered.

"They went for some take-out," she replied, eyes closed and humming as he stroked her arm.

"What's that sweet noise you're making," he cooed and held her tighter against him. "You like this?"

Chloe's butterflies arrived and she shuddered. *"Yeah..."* she whispered her back melting into his front.

Kilmeade's hands remained around her body as he nuzzled her hair out of the way with his chin and gently kissed her throat. "You like this?" he asked softly.

"Yeah..." she replied, every nerve ending singing now that they were pressed together. The hand at her belly button slipped underneath the waistband of her jeans and inched to her lower abdomen. She inhaled sharply.

"And this?" he asked, this time in her mind.

"Yeah..." she sighed one more time and turned in his arms to kiss his mouth. He accepted her offer and pulled her into him. Fully folded into his embrace, Chloe sighed, her heart pounding. When their kiss deepened and her butterflies sought to tickle her lower and lower, he dropped back to arm's length, his hands on her shoulders. Chloe absorbed his gaze, certain hers must reflect the same desire. He didn't speak, yet she discerned questions in his eyes. As her breathing became more and more shallow and he hadn't yet moved or spoken, she opened the top button of his shirt.

Kilmeade looked at her hands going for the second button. *"Are you afraid?"* he sent silently. Chloe shook her head and the button came undone. *"Good, because I won't hurt you..."*

At his promise, Chloe's mother's words pinged around her mind. Mrs. Bushman had warned Chloe as a pre-teen that sex was painful and the best thing any kid of hers could do was avoid it completely. Kilmeade smiled, probably reading Chloe's rambling thoughts.

"Mother Bushman didn't know your lover would be an amazing and clever Rakum Elder. You will feel no pain," he sent and pulled the shirt over his head to drop it to the floor.

Chloe touched his chest gingerly, sought his liquid gaze, and knew he was telling the truth.

《回》

"It's midnight, Kilmeade," Canaan mumbled and dropped to the carpeted floor of the couple's upstairs bedroom. Chloe Bushman had shuffled off to the shower and Canaan wandered in to find the Elder drowsing and entirely too comfortable. "Are you listening to me?"

"I can tell time, brother," Kilmeade responded in a thick voice.

"Your brother is hungry," Canaan complained. Kilmeade did not reply. In the attached bathroom, Chloe sang pop songs as she bathed. Canaan sighed. "It's not easy finding good food out there."

"Come back in a half-hour. My ears work better in a half-hour," Kilmeade replied facing away on the king-size bed.

"We're reaching maximum frustration levels," Canaan added.

"Speak your mind." Kilmeade rolled over and met Canaan's eyes in the dim light. "You want permission to end somebody for their blood."

Canaan grunted. If he couldn't get it any other way, then yes, he would kill one of them. He always tried to leave them alive, but at the end of the battle, the blood donor needed to not tell the world he had been attacked by a vampire. Life was so much easier when they had Cows. Canaan closed his eyes, resisting the anger that welled inside when he became truly thirsty. Who was he angry with? His friends who put him in this situation.

Kilmeade shoved aside the covers to rise. He shrugged on boxers, jeans, and a wrinkled long-sleeve shirt, all three from the floor. "You ought to aim that fury a little higher," he said with a grin.

"No, the hell, no." Canaan remained as he was, on his back with his head resting on folded arms. "Not going there." Kilmeade might talk to the God of the mortals, but Canaan wasn't opening that box.

"If you don't drink blood, over time you will become human without even wanting to." Kilmeade stared down on him, standing now at the foot of the bed.

"Kilmeade, please."

"It is the opposite of the Lost Rabbit. Don't act like you didn't learn all this in Elder training."

Canaan held his breath a few ticks and shook his head. "I used to believe it—I marked Marcy before the shit went down in November thinking it might work on a woman—but I was being stupid—thinking like a *human*." Kilmeade only closed his eyes and Canaan huffed again. "It's a theory, that's all. *A theory*. No Rakum ever turned into a human from lack of blood consumption, just like no Rabbit ever became a Rakum from repeated ingestion of blood."

"Every myth is based in fact." Kilmeade shook his head. "What makes you non-human? The blood of the Fathers. Consumption of human blood is what increases our power and vitality. Scientifically, wouldn't the opposite also be true?"

Canaan slow-blinked. "Absolutely not. I am a Rakum and I will always be a Rakum. *Scientifically.*"

Kilmeade rolled his eyes. "You are being purposefully obtuse. As for the Lost Rabbit legend, if I mark a Rabbit and no one ever catches him, my blood will continue to replicate his cells. It is sound science."

"I don't agree," Canaan said growing impatient with Kilmeade's arrogance.

"How did High Father Abroghia create the Nine?" Kilmeade tilted his head awaiting an answer.

Canaan pressed his lips together. They had both read the book; Beth Rider nicely filled in what the Fathers withheld. "His blood..."

Kilmeade nodded with closed eyes, still in full professor mode. "The special demon-influenced blood of Ta'avah ingested by those mortal men—face it, brother, a demon's blood turned nine mortal men into the most powerful creatures on the earth. Why wouldn't an Elder's blood, if allowed, transform a mortal into something more?"

Canaan stood his ground. "A Rakum is not a human and a human is not a Rakum. The end."

Kilmeade walked out. "Okay, ostrich, keep your head in the sand, but when you pull it out and you're mortal, don't be mad at me."

"Just tell me to go out and get some blood, goddammit!" he growled, rolling over to rise and follow Kilmeade downstairs. "You're my superior—give me an order." Canaan and Kilmeade did not lord positions over each other, but tonight, more than anything, he wished he had a master to provide for him a gut-full of fresh hot blood.

"Ask one of your friends," Kilmeade said with a grin. They had reached the kitchen and he rummaged through the refrigerator. He paused and listened to the house. "Beryl's down the hall. Or David? You haven't tapped him, right? I wonder what that nitwit tastes like..."

Canaan toyed with the suggestions a nanosecond and eliminated them with a huff. "Go with me. Like the old days. Let's drive to the next town and find something new. Someone forgotten."

Kilmeade's gaze flashed. "A forgotten man I can finish off?" His eyes narrowed and he licked his lips.

Canaan nodded. His housemate pretended it didn't bother him, playing human, being careful, not taking risks. He was as hungry as Canaan for the adventure of the chase. When Kilmeade's stomach grumbled loudly, Canaan turned on his heel for the door. With the car keys in hand, he entered the garage happy to sense Kilmeade directly behind him.

Canaan and Kilmeade shared bloody hunting tales all the way to Birmingham. Both agreed that large cities made the best hunting grounds and once Canaan made a few turns off the interstate into the darker, unlit areas of downtown, they began to see their potential prey. Canaan and Kilmeade watched the pedestrians, men and women in shabby street clothes, going somewhere and nowhere. In a moment of inspiration, Canaan turned down a dark alley and hugged up against the curb.

"Feel like a walk?" he asked as he climbed out of the car. He joined Kilmeade on the curb and caught his eye; it was going to be a fun night.

Canaan led the way down the unlit alley toward the street. They each wore jeans, dark jackets and ball caps. On the sidewalk, Canaan shoved his hands deep in his pockets and started walking, head down. Kilmeade strolled beside him, watching the world from his peripheral vision and missing nothing. They were approached by a prostitute, but Canaan sent her away. She wouldn't be a consenting female, at least not for blood-letting. They needed a male. Even though their race was over, females still needed to consent. A man only had to be breathing. *Easy peasy.*

A bar patron stumbled out of a pub they passed and Canaan dodged him with a chuckle. Kilmeade caught the man's arm before he hit the littered sidewalk. The inebriated man mumbled a few thank yous and once righted and released, wobbled away.

"He smelled pretty clean," Canaan observed.

"Don't grab the first piece of candy you see, little boy." Kilmeade walked on, initiating a saunter Canaan recognized. He sought to *attract* his prey, a bad seed looking for trouble, one the police would be happy to find dead.

"You are a devil," he sent to Kilmeade and dropped back.

"I am what I am, and I always have been," he replied silently, repeating the mantra Canaan had heard many times.

Now walking casually fifteen yards behind, Canaan watched the reactions of the men and women who noticed his housemate. A Rakum Elder blended in to a point, but all mortals would notice something "off" if either man was studied closely; thankfully, humans regularly disregarded their natural instincts as a matter of course. Three youths passed Kilmeade from the opposite direction and spun around to drop in behind him. Two of them furtively slipped their hands into coat pockets and the one in the middle walked up briskly behind Kilmeade empty-handed, but aggressive in demeanor.

"I see them," Kilmeade sent, never altering his step. *"It's not what I wanted, though. These babies are faking."* The youngster in the middle lunged and missed.

"He's gonna grab you," Canaan chuckled.

"If I can't find a baddie, I'd rather have that first guy..." Kilmeade slowed his pace and the three boys did, too, still trying to decide how to attack.

"Snoozed and loozed, brother," Canaan sent, watching the young men.

"Nah, this is too much candy." Kilmeade abruptly stopped, turned, and faced the youths head-on. "No," he said in a controlled tone, meeting the eye of the man in the middle. Canaan also stopped and grinned; Kilmeade had the guy mesmerized with a glance. In the space of three seconds, his spooked buddies yanked the dazed thug away and all three disappeared around the corner.

Canaan reached Kilmeade and shook his head. *"Wanna go back for my first choice?"*

Canaan was teasing, but Kilmeade looked back the way they had come. The Beemer was tucked out of sight at least five blocks. If they found their guy and ended him between the buildings, it wasn't likely anyone would connect the victim to the car.

"He did smell pretty good," Kilmeade whispered. With a comical spin on one heel, Canaan did an about-face. As they passed the same bar this time from the opposite direction, a man stepped out with a companion, laughing and looking away. Canaan stopped short, avoiding a collision and when he glanced at Kilmeade, an odd look had hit his face.

"Elder Kilmeade?" a young male voice said, and Canaan jerked his gaze to the voice. "Elder Canaan? Shit!"

Canaan sucked his teeth and crossed his arms at his chest, surely looking scary and brutish, but Kilmeade grinned wide and grabbed the man behind the neck and shook him back and forth.

"Kite, you look good, little brother!" Kilmeade said his voice joyful.

Canaan played along, but he was not happy to be called out in front of the mortal Kite dragged alongside. Did the kid have a brain? Before 11/13, Isaac the Horrible, as Canaan had come to recall him, held him and Kilmeade veritable prisoners to siphon off their blood at whim. The grunt before them served Isaac voluntarily. Not only that, but he had abducted Marcy under orders and drank her blood more than once. Canaan clenched his jaw at the memory. Why Kilmeade felt the need to love all over him now was beyond Canaan's understanding.

"What a grouch," Kilmeade shot at him, still engaging their transformed little brother.

"This is Rodney," Kite said after a few more surprised expletives. "What are you doing here?"

Kite looked into their faces and Canaan thought, *are you daft?* But Kite was human now and wouldn't hear him.

Then Kite did a double-take, grinned as if embarrassed and whispered to his inebriated friend, "Wait for me inside."

Kilmeade released his neck and stepped out of foot traffic to the wall. Kite and Canaan followed. Kite whispered, "Having any luck?"

Canaan didn't reply and silently suggested to Kilmeade they move on, but he was smiling as if he'd just found his oldest friend.

"I know I shouldn't apologize, but—" Kite began and Kilmeade playfully covered his mouth with his hand. Canaan didn't mind hearing an apology for the kid's transgressions against them, but he was right; a Rakum would never regret obeying his master's orders.

"How goes it, this?" Kilmeade began and gestured to Kite's body.

ellen c. maze

Kite straightened his silk dress shirt and looked down at his fitted black slacks. "It's good. Took me three weeks, though. That was tough." Kite flicked his gaze to Canaan a split-second and resumed speaking to Kilmeade. "There are perks, Master," he said with a mini-eye raise.

"Do tell," Kilmeade replied which surprised Canaan. His cohort hated conversation, but something about this former brother had him stepping out of character.

"Sunshine," Kite said and again glanced to Canaan who remained expressionless. "My first day in full sun was worth every miserable moment of the transformation process."

"Worth every moment, yanh, yanh, yanh..." Canaan thought and pursed his lips, mocking Kite's happy statement. He rolled his eyes when Kilmeade shot him an irritated glance. The sun was a *killer,* a hated thing, threatening to murder him every dozen or so hours...

"Any of your brethren about?" Kilmeade asked.

Kite shook his head. "None. Zero. And I've been looking."

"They are connecting on a website," Kilmeade replied.

"Oh, good, what's it called?" Kite leaned in close enough to Canaan now to touch. He wrapped his fingers around Kite's neck as Kilmeade had earlier, but Canaan was beginning to have the thoughts. Kite's eye flicked his way and he swallowed.

"We'll find our first candy," Kilmeade asserted in his mind. *"I'm not ending Kite."*

"Why not? He's human," Canaan returned, enjoying his joke and grinning now on the youngster who was from his own pack and nearly two hundred years old in truth. *"Jack Dawn let me play with this one as much as I wanted. He's really fun and took a beatdown like a dream..."*

Kilmeade ignored Canaan's mental lobs. "Search the term Rakum and it will come up. Hundreds have connected there," Kilmeade told him and then added, "Canaan's not going to tap you, Kite. Calm down. Your heart is beating too fast."

"I'm cool. It's okay," Kite said, still speaking softly and hiding his sudden fear like a Rakum. "I didn't know any of us remained intact."

"Only Canaan and myself," Kilmeade said. "When you connect with the others, you can tell them you saw us, but they should stay away. We will initiate any contact that we desire. Understand?"

"Oh, sure," Kite nodded rapidly. "Shit, I don't blame you." He was still captive by Canaan's hand and he respectfully didn't try to break free.

Kilmeade caressed Kite's cheek with his fingers and then ran his hand

67

along his shapely scalp and across his tight afro.

"In that alley," Kite whispered, barely audible. "I'll bring him out the side door. No one will see me." He looked dead into Kilmeade's face and Canaan would have sworn they were communicating telepathically. Yet it was something else. A kinship, a brotherhood that went beyond human and Rakum. Canaan waited until Kilmeade sent the kid a very small nod.

"That was some voodoo shit there, brother," Canaan sent to Kilmeade and dropped the contact with Kite's neck. The youngster turned for the bar and clambered inside. *"Did you do that?"*

"I sent him a test thought and he didn't hear me, but..." Kilmeade replied and then took a step past Canaan toward the alley. *"...something transmitted. Something is still there deep down."* Kilmeade's eyebrows fluttered for Canaan's benefit and he slipped in between the buildings.

"Or maybe you're just really good," Canaan sent with a telepathic chuckle.

"Of course, there's that..."

They reached the alley exit of the bar and stood against the wall out of sight. Within five minutes, the door opened and Canaan recognized Kite's new scent plus the one he earlier called Rodney.

"This way," Kite mumbled to his friend and yanked him further into the dark. When all four of them were invisible to any passersby, he pressed the man against the chipped brick wall and waited to hand over custody. Canaan did nothing and Kite whispered, "Picked him up last night in South Carolina hitch-hiking. No I.D. Thought maybe I'd knock him around a little." Kite grinned. "I'm bored."

Bowing to Kilmeade's seniority, Canaan watched his expression. When he initiated a nod, Canaan shoved Kite's acquaintance hard against the wall. In the space of a moment, his left hand covered the man's mouth and his right jabbed a small knifepoint deep into his throat. Kite backed away and was gone. Canaan was semi-aware of Kilmeade standing guard, but no one happened by. Canaan pulled and pulled and did not stop draining the man until Kilmeade tapped his shoulder.

When Kilmeade took over, Canaan braced himself on both palms against the cold wall, breathing heavily, licking his lips, and sucking his palate. The transient's blood sent its vital medicine to his every cell and he closed his eyes to the sensation of fulfillment it delivered. It took less than two minutes for Kilmeade to finish the man off, and when he withdrew from Rodney's throat and looked Canaan's way, he grinned.

"Oh, Elder Kilmeade, how lovely you look," Canaan joked.

The Elder's eyes flashed robin-egg blue with lips now drawn away from his elongated fangs. The effects were temporary, but Canaan was tickled at the sight. Kilmeade giggled and covered his mouth. Canaan grabbed his bicep and tugged him through the alley to exit on the opposite street. Doing his best to keep his partner's monster visage in the shadows, he pulled Kilmeade through the intermittent foot traffic to the car. When they reached the BMW, Kilmeade was still laughing, and once in the car, Canaan laughed with him all the way home.

10, MAR 1

"Y ou can't drain folks in town like that, you know. Eventually, you'll get caught."

"You growing your hair out?" Canaan asked ignoring Javier's warning. "If you are—don't. You look stupid."

Javier put his fingers through his black hair. "Number one, I'm not, I've been busy. And two, screw you."

Canaan tossed back his head and laughed. A month ago in Birmingham when he and Kilmeade ended Kite's wayward acquaintance, they wondered how long they could go without repeating the adventure. Finding consenting blood did not get any easier and within three weeks, they headed out once more, this time to the state capitol of Montgomery. The two-hour drive gave them generous cushion, so when they found a transient to end on a dark downtown street, they returned before dawn as happy as they'd ever been. Telling worry-wort Javier about it might not have been the best idea.

"Don't give me any grief, pup. I can still zap you," he smirked.

"Okay, *Master,*" Javier grinned and fluttered a paperback book he had been shuffling through. He pointed to a page inside. "Check this out. When you kill one person, you've actually killed an unknown multitude, because you prevented that person from procreating. Get it? You've killed a generation in a single act of bloodlust."

Canaan regarded Javier with a bored look. "How many mortals did you kill before you grew all pink and fluffy, baby doll?"

Javier lowered his gaze and grinned to the side. "More than a few multitudes by that reasoning," he chuckled quietly. He raised his eyes and said, "I just thought it was a curious perspective. Might make you think twice from here on out."

Canaan processed his assertion. Before 11/13, when they still carried the demon Ta'avah in their spirits, he probably wouldn't ponder Javier's idea more than a moment. Now? Canaan peeked inside and asked the question—did he care if a million people died when he felt like ending someone? His brain said, *no, of course not.* But a tiny voice deep down raised

70

its hand and said, *Me! I care! I don't want to be held accountable for that!*

Canaan stomped the voice and lifted his boot to shove Javier's chair. "Get me something to drink. What kind of host are you, anyway?"

Javier stood. "Geez, I didn't realize you need a slave." Javier rose and headed for the next room. He, David, and Roman were staying in the same house for the time being. Tonight, however, he found Javier alone. Roman and David had gone to church.

Canaan chuckled softly and joined Javier in the large kitchen. "Gone to church," he laughed. "That's rich."

"What so funny?"

"Funny is my perfect memory recalling a myriad of crimes against humanity perpetrated by a certain Rakum Elder," Canaan said smiling. "I'm glad you can kill, maim, rape and pillage and still go to church."

Javier regarded Canaan with surprise. "It's called redemption. Shall I explain?"

"Nope." Canaan shook his head, sorry he had let his private thoughts slip. Javier had become an expert on the God stuff and Canaan didn't have the inclination to defend his position. "Forget I brought it up. I am not talking about *that* with *you*..."

"Whatever," Javier said and poured Canaan a glass of iced tea. "You never told me how you guys enjoyed your time in Biloxi. Did you gamble? Party? Sit in the hotel and pummel each other every night?"

"Yes, yes, and yes," Canaan replied, bouncing his pointer finger with each word. He laughed at a sudden memory and Javier asked what it was. "It's Kilmeade. You don't know him the way I do—he was a different man down there."

"What did he do?" Javier asked suddenly curious.

Canaan looked left and right, still grinning. "First, here's the picture. Two Elders striding through this huge casino—we're already rich and why play? We can win any game that requires intelligence or telekinesis. Having said that, what do you think a wealthy Rakum like Kilmeade would enjoy doing at a casino?"

"Well," Javier said thoughtfully, recognizing Canaan was not being rhetorical. "If I was a Rakum Elder with plenty of dough..." Javier grinned with a rare spark of mischief. "...I'd have the most fun finding high rollers and using my abilities to make him lose."

"Exactly!" Canaan said loudly pointing at Javier's face. "Now THAT shit is fun. Find the richest jerk in the place and ruin his night." Canaan shook his head grinning. "We didn't do that," he said, still shaking his head.

"Kilmeade says, let's find a loser and make him win." Canaan looked at Javier with a false expression of horror on his face.

Javier laughed. "What? That's nice!"

"That's nice," Canaan mimicked in a falsetto. "ANYWAY, he's the boss so we canvassed the casino for a sadsack. Kilmeade picked one out and we shadowed him. The guy started winning and after his third win, Kilmeade introduced himself."

"What could he possibly have said?" Javier asked eyes wide.

"He was having a ball, really played it up." Canaan grinned. *"I'm your lucky charm. Let's try roulette,"* he said in an imitation of Kilmeade's aristocratic tenor. "At the end of the evening, that little man cashed in a million dollars. Too bad we had to kill him in our room later."

Javier inhaled, horrified.

"Got you," he chuckled. "This idiotic New World—neither of us would have been entertained by helping some backward *Homo sapien* in the old days. Kilmeade hated mortals. Despised them. The world has become a very strange place."

"For a Rakum," Javier added.

"Asshole," Canaan said with a wry grin.

"How about you? Are you seeing things differently?" Canaan shot him a blank look. "You should speak to Michael Stone..."

Canaan interrupted him. "Stone and I don't get along. Didn't then, don't now." Canaan rubbed his face with both hands at the memory of how he and Stone traveled together to Jackson the night they destroyed Rufus. Stone had been uptight and unfriendly, a total downer.

"Well, if you start looking inside and asking yourself tough philosophical questions, talk to Mike. You two have similar personalities, you know..." Javier puffed his chest. "Tough guys."

Canaan humphed and rolled his eyes. "You're joking. I pummeled him senseless dozens of times before Last Assembly."

Javier lowered his chin. "You know what I mean. A non-Elder could never best you; you pummeled him because you enjoyed it."

Canaan licked his lips and grinned. "Damn, I miss those days."

"He doesn't miss being your punching bag," Javier said with a small grin. "Anyway, you guys might find you have more in common now. He will have some good advice."

"Screw him and his advice," Canaan said. "Plus, I don't have any problems. I'm awesome, handsome, and full of amazingness."

"Now you sound like Isaac," Javier said without apology.

Canaan was not offended. He leaned in with a tight grin and whispered, "He *was* damn adorable."

"Foooorrrrrrrrr a demon," Javier said comically and checked the time on his phone. "How about this—Kite contacted me last night."

Canaan looked up with his most innocent expression. "Oh?"

"I connected him with a few others who weren't seeking God. Also, a Rakum named Jersey asked for advice. He was really lost."

"Jersey, heheh," Canaan said and grew quiet. The appealing grunt had been a pleasant diversion in stressful times, yet another element of their old lives sadly long gone.

"Roman encouraged him to look for work in the medical field. Lots of the healers are doing that." Javier paused, catching something in Canaan's expression. "An old friend?"

Canaan grinned. "That one was an Elder's *best* friend, *shit!*" he said in a chuckle. "Ask Kilmeade or Roman about Jersey. He had this thing he did with his..."

Javier lifted one hand. "I know who he is." Then he raised his eyes to Canaan's. "And you're gonna want to let that go."

"You're mighty ballsy these days," Canaan returned and took a deep breath as if to begin a long tale. "I remember one cold, October night, Brandon and Roman swapped their *ish-mikhan...*"

"Moving on..." Javier exhaled, ignoring the bait.

Canaan settled on a barstool and jabbed Javier's near shoulder. "Are you blushing?"

"Roman feels he's living it up with no direction," Javier continued as if Canaan hadn't spoken. "It's not good."

"Okay, don't play. Shit," Canaan said with a soft chuckle. "What's not good? Living it up?"

"Right. As a Rakum, you do what you want, eat, drink, be merry. But as a mortal, there are consequences."

"Getting fat?" Canaan joked, but Javier didn't smile.

"Think about it—the first issue is venereal disease."

Canaan scoffed, but Javier went on.

"As Rakum, we never even caught a cold. Now, we catch everything the humans do and they have a head-start—they've internalized the consequences of risky behavior. Rakum need to be educated on basic avoidance of contractible diseases."

"We know what causes mortal disease, moron," Canaan teased. "Most of us are healers, experts in human anatomy. I think your brethren can figure out sleeping with prostitutes might give you crabs." Canaan was tickled at Javier's sudden seriousness, but he did not lighten up.

"Even so, hard living also includes hard drugs. They could easily become alcoholics or drug addicts. And consider how much Rakum enjoy pain and violence; I'm afraid some of our brethren might become murderers and rapists. *Geez,* if they don't find God, a Rakum would make a truly dangerous mortal."

Canaan raised his brow with a slow nod. "I see your point."

"They need to be counseled and I'm not reaching enough with the website. I want to find more of them. I want to go looking."

"Really?" Canaan sat up. "Interesting..."

"How would you like to go with me? The two of us." Canaan made a noise of surprise. "What else are you doing? You're sitting around, kicking Kilmeade's chair and waiting for the next buzz..."

Canaan smirked. "You think you're so smart. I'm kicking his *bed,* not his chair. His new squeeze keeps him in that bedroom—"

"Nuh-uh-uh!" Javier barked. "You made my point for me."

"I *am* getting pretty bored..." Canaan realized he had decided to go. Javier intuited the same, his entire countenance as bright as the moon.

"Fantastic," Javier said nodding. "Give me a couple of days and I'll get an itinerary. We will drive west using prayer, technology, and your nose to rat out the stragglers."

"And I'll have blood to drink. I'm sick as shit of going without. My little brothers won't mind," he said wagging his eyebrows. "Oh, wait." Canaan put his feet to the floor. "Kilmeade. We're a unit. It will be up to him if I go."

Javier conceded with a nod. "Both of you come. Two Rakum Elders are always better than one."

"*And* one Miss Bushman," Canaan added grinning.

Javier chuckled. "Is she melting your black Rakum heart?"

"Stop that," Canaan said and punched Javier's arm, holding back his strength. "Stop reading me, and yes, she is. She's ferocious."

Javier laughed. "Trust me, I know."

"Her parents will meet their son-in-law tonight." Canaan shook his head and then grew suddenly serious. "How did the grunts see Kilmeade back in the day?"

Javier shrugged. "He was a mystery. That night you and I met, I never saw him. I don't remember seeing him at all until Last Assembly."

"He had a close circle. I met him when I came over from England."

Canaan released a long exhale. "I completed my training at his side. I must know him better than anyone." Javier nodded awaiting more and Canaan grinned wistfully. "I don't think you realize what a giant he is among our people. Kilmeade would have been a Father."

"Geez," Javier whispered, and Canaan offered an exaggerated nod.

"Early on, I thought it was arrogance, but I quickly realized that he is much more advanced up here—" Canaan's finger went to his head. "—than the other Elders." Canaan paused.

Ever tuned-in, Javier inclined his head. "But?"

Canaan sighed. "He believes in the legend of the Lost Rabbit. That an Elder's blood could morph a mortal into a Rakum." Javier made a noise and he met his eye.

"I heard it happened during World War II. It was a story we told each other at Assembly to pass the time."

Canaan scoffed. "How did the story go?"

Javier scratched his head, recalling details. "It sorta made sense, I mean, an Elder marks a Rabbit at the same time the bombs start dropping. The Rakum always vacate war zones, so the Rabbit is marked and there are no Brethren chasing him..." Javier shrugged. "Would he eventually lust for blood? Could he figure it out on his own? We enjoyed embellishing the story, but that's the main plot."

"I don't see how it's possible," Canaan said thoughtfully. "A Rakum is not a human and a human can't become a Rakum."

"Sure, you're right," Javier said and shooed Canaan with a flick of his hand when he got to his feet. "Go see what Kilmeade thinks about our Rakum Hunt. I'm going to pray. I'll ask God to help us decide what to do. I'm certain it was His idea in the first place."

"I don't want a sermon, but how do you know? IN A NUTSHELL," Canaan stressed loudly.

Javier chuckled. "Because it's selfless. Good enough?"

Canaan's eyes widened. "Wow. Pithy, for once. Thanks." He turned away and headed for the door. Finally, an answer he comprehended. Maybe he was getting smarter. Or just more God-like. Canaan shooed the thought away and jogged out the front door.

《回》

"I have three months left in this class," Chloe said not sure if she was angry. In ten minutes, they expected her parents for the first meeting of husband and in-laws and Kilmeade announced he was leaving on an extended trip. "We've been together a little over a month," Chloe huffed. "You would go without me?"

Kilmeade directed his gaze away and Chloe regretted her last statement. She was still learning his eccentricities, but she'd been around the Elder long enough to know he didn't argue and he didn't bargain.

"Okay, forget I said that," Chloe said and stepped into his space. "It's safe—look down. You can look now." She stood under his nose and after a few seconds, he grinned and met her eyes. He might look human, but he was still an otherworldly being. "I'll join you when my class is over. How about that?"

"Perfect," he said and finally touched her. Cool palms cupped her cheeks and then one hand made itself busy in her hair against her scalp. Chloe closed her eyes to the sensation and the clock chimed downstairs. At the same moment, the doorbell rang and Chloe smirked.

"I told you she was punctual. And remember," Chloe began, but Kilmeade cut her off.

"Be myself, tell the truth as much as possible. Yes, Master," he said with a cheeky grin. Chloe nodded. Telling the truth would make it easier on them both and leaving out the Rakum stuff should be a breeze.

Galloping to the foyer, Chloe yanked open the door before her father rang the bell a second time. "Hey, Dad! Mom, come in!"

"Hi, Mina," her mother cooed blowing a kiss in the air, using Chloe's first name no matter how many times she'd been asked not to.

"Hey, shoog," her father said as he entered and kissed her head. He met Kilmeade standing a dozen feet away. "And you are Mr. Kilmeade?"

"Just Kilmeade," he said with a closed-mouthed grin. "Nice to finally meet you, Dr. Bushman."

"Just Jim, please, and this is Helen." Chloe's father turned at the waist and waited for the women to step up. Kilmeade offered a slight bow to Chloe's mother.

Chloe grinned. "So debonair," she chided and grabbed Kilmeade's arm. "Come into the living room, ya'll."

Chloe pulled Kilmeade along and maneuvered him to the sofa, forcing her parents to sit in either the love seat or recliners. In the end, her mother and father sat side-by-side on the two-seater. Chloe smirked inwardly, because at home they never sat together.

"Kilmeade, this is so unexpected," her father said, sitting forward over his knees, completely relaxed. "I always thought I'd throw Chloe a gigantic wedding at the country club."

"What possessed you to *elope* of all things?" Mrs. Bushman added with a clearly unhappy glare.

Chloe held her tongue and turned her shoulders to see Kilmeade reply. To her surprise, he slowly leaned into the couch, crossing one leg over the other at the knee and didn't speak. Chloe almost jabbed him but thankfully, he spoke before she did.

"Where I come from, you say a few words and there you have it." Kilmeade put his arms up and rest his head on his hands.

"I really didn't want a big wedding." Chloe gave Kilmeade a glare that maybe he should sit up. He sent her a wink and she looked back at her parents. "We both knew it was the right thing."

"I didn't want a big wedding either," her father offered with a tight chuckle.

"Isn't she too young for you, Mr. Kilmeade?" Mrs. Bushman asked, clearly being rhetorical. "How can you expect a barely twenty-year-old girl to know what she wants for the rest of her life?"

"Mom!" Chloe barked. Kilmeade's chin lowered a fraction and he regarded Chloe's mother with a weary gaze. He wouldn't answer rhetorical questions and Chloe knew it. Her father hopped to the rescue.

"Chloe didn't say where you were from."

"Yes, are you from Alabama?" Chloe's mother asked, peacocking from her seat: lower back concave, chest out. Chloe huffed with an amused headshake, hoping Kilmeade didn't say anything.

"Your mother's sort of sexy..."

Too late.

"I was born in Naples." Kilmeade looked Chloe's mother dead in the eye and sat forward. "But I came here very young."

Chloe's mother averted her gaze and scooted backward.

"Well, you have a beautiful place," her dad piped up. "You've found the one neighborhood not chock full of college students."

Kilmeade raised his eyebrows and made a sound of agreement. To Chloe, he sent silently, *"Your father's sort of sexy, too..."*

Chloe flashed her eyes with a tiny shake of her head. If Kilmeade got silly, she didn't think her mother could take it. Her dad could laugh it off, but her mother was *all* business *all* the time.

"Looks like you can more than provide for our youngest child and take her off our hands," Chloe's dad replied grinning and squeezed her mom's upper thigh. "I'm not prying, but Chloe said you're retired?" Kilmeade sighed audibly.

Chloe piped up, "Not exactly. Kilmeade—"

"I make wealth, Jim." Kilmeade wrapped his hand around the top of Chloe's thigh, mimicking her father's gesture. "Once I discovered how to manipulate the New York Stock Exchange, I stopped all manner of labor. Now, I make wealth and am worth well over seven figures."

Both of Chloe's parents puffed tiny courtesy laughs, but when Kilmeade's expression remained static, her father sat forward.

"You're serious."

Kilmeade stood and her parents followed suit. "Walk with me outside, Jim, and I'll tell you some man stuff."

Chloe's dad chuckled as if unsure, but Kilmeade had already left the room. Chloe started after him, but Kilmeade said with his back to them all, "Not you, little bird. Jim Bushman, you come. Ladies, stay indoors..."

"Well!—" her mother began, but her father grinned, waved comically, and trailed out the way Kilmeade disappeared. When the back door closed and they were alone, Chloe's mother shook her head. "You have married a weirdo. Loaded, handsome, and a nutjob. Good work."

"Two outta three ain't bad," Chloe joked and her mother didn't laugh. But then again, she rarely did.

《▣》

"Did you say when you moved in? I wished I'd built here—this neighborhood is quieter than ours. How big is this lot?"

Jim Bushman might have truly been interested or he may have been making nervous chatter; Kilmeade didn't know him well enough yet to guess. When Kilmeade didn't reply quickly, Jim turned to see his face, eyebrows raised. Kilmeade smiled.

"Oh, you are truly asking," he said. "My apologies. I don't do small talk. If we knew each other better, I wouldn't seem so rude. The lot is three acres."

He sent a genuine grin and Chloe's father matched the expression. He was a good guy without guile. Kilmeade didn't much care for humans up to now, but he had dealt with non-Cow mortal men for nearly four hundred years. He began to develop a feeling for this one's needs, desires, and disappointments. Jim Bushman wanted to be liked and respected by friends and colleagues. That gave Kilmeade an idea.

"Do you know any geneticists?" he asked, resisting for the moment to touch him. If anything, he might place a palm on the man's outer shoulder, but for now, he kept his hands in his pockets.

"Oh, sure, why? Need me to introduce you?"

"I would like that," Kilmeade replied and took a step away. Jim followed suit and the two of them walked across the immaculate lawn in the moonlight. "I'm a hobby scientist and have some projects in the lab."

Jim grinned. "Chloe has always been interested in science. I'm not surprised you hit it off. How did you meet?"

"Through mutual friends." Kilmeade had chosen his time and stopped walking, turned and placed a hand on the man's shoulder. "Jim, I am not keen on impromptu visits. I cherish my privacy and am accustomed to getting my way. Do you get my meaning?"

Jim flicked his gaze to the hand on his shoulder. Kilmeade monitored his thoughts so nothing unpleasant would translate through his face and watched for understanding to dawn in his mate's father. It wasn't a long wait. Jim forced a thin smile and nodded.

"I'll keep Mrs. Bushman from popping in day and night," he said whispering and looking about for spies.

"Ah, allow me to add, because of a medical condition, I avoid the sun. I sleep during the day and am awake all night taking care of business across the globe."

"I understand." Jim clapped his hands together, took a long look around the spacious property. "I feel like my baby is in good hands."

"She owns my heart and that seems to be the way these females want it," he said with a laugh, purposefully adding the unusual verbiage.

"Oh, sure, sure," Jim replied nodding and the two of them headed toward the back door. "I'm serious about getting some tips on the Stock Market. Got any help there for your new dad?"

Kilmeade laughed, unexpectedly amused. "This time tomorrow, you will have in your possession a portfolio valued at $210K."

Jim's eyes grew round and he began his head shake.

"Jim Bushman," Kilmeade said in a serious tone, "I don't waste words and I am not looking for anything in return. Your driveway is full of gravel and a person would like a rock for their drive. You hand them a rock. You never miss it. This stock is one of my rocks. Enjoy."

Jim still didn't understand, but at least he stopped trying to talk about it. "Thank you. I accept."

"*Shew*, you've exhausted me. Let's go in," Kilmeade said with a gentle smile. When they faced the back porch, Chloe exited and met them in the yard, clutching her thick coat about her neck.

"I made Mom some coffee. Do ya'll want any," Chloe asked, clearly trying to avoid her mother.

Kilmeade looked at Jim and they both said no. He prepared to walk them all indoors when he overheard Canaan having a bit of fun with Mrs. Bushman. Kilmeade altered course and turned the trio to the side. He asked Chloe to explain to Jim her interior design project.

"You're not seriously asking me to make small talk?" she sent telepathically while looking at her dad.

Kilmeade didn't respond and waited for her to comply. When she began, he listened to Canaan at the same time; his other half, as entertaining as always.

11

"Hello, there, pretty lady," Canaan said jovially when he spied Chloe Bushman's mother sipping from a coffee cup in the living room. He had promised to make himself scarce, but he was bored and curious, a bad combination. "Did they leave you all alone? A gorgeous thing like you?"

Mrs. Bushman rose to her feet and wasn't startled. On the contrary, she blushed and stepped toward him. "Canaan, is it?" she said and reached out her hand.

Canaan gave her a smile and took her fingers in his. "Since the day I was born," he said and kissed the back of her hand. "Chloe told us you taught dance in college…" Canaan allowed his eyes to scan her form and she blushed again without shrinking away. Chloe's mother must have been mid-forties, but she hit the gym and he liked her confident air.

"I haven't danced in ages," she said and looked aside.

"Aw, come on," he said with a wink. "I'll show you my magic if you show me yours." He eyed the sound system in the wall unit and switched it on from where he stood; when he looked back, she grinned, likely assuming some sleight of hand.

"You are strange," she said with a small smile.

"Strange and wonderful," he joked holding out his hand. Someone left the radio on a ridiculous oldies station, but Chloe's mother didn't object. "Strangers in the Night" trickled from the speakers and Canaan assumed a slow-dance pose.

"I do like this song…" she cooed, still considering his offer.

"My theme song," he said in a whisper. When she placed her right hand in his left, he positioned his right at her waist and snugged her close.

"You are *brazen,"* she responded in a breathy voice.

"Too much?" he asked with a dazzling grin.

She shook her head and cut her eyes the back door. "It will do my husband good to see me dancing with a younger man."

"You forgot to mention handsome," Canaan replied and glided the two of them in the space between the wall unit and the back of the couch. The woman reminded him very much of Marcy, and even as the comparisons made the circuit in his mind, his mate's favorite song came on next. *"I'm in a whirl over my beautiful girl,"* he mumbled during the first chorus. "I sang this song to my wife..."

The woman leaned away enough to see his face as they moved together. "And where is she? Chloe said you live here."

"Nosy, much?" Canaan teased and she gave him a sideways grin. Canaan laughed, a pleasant harmony filling his mind.

"I have some advice for your wife," Chloe's mother said, now back to the dance. "She needs to keep an eye on you. You're dangerous."

"Oh, she knows," Canaan responded and found a moment in the song to perform a dramatic dip. When Mrs. Bushman lifted upright, Canaan tucked her into his body more than before, enjoying the sensation of pressing against the soft and sweet-smelling mortal. Within a minute, his body reacted to their proximity deep inside and then more urgently in his lower regions. He'd been asleep in those places a long time and only when Marcy requested his attention in that way did he awaken. Something was changing and it wasn't this particular female causing it. Canaan grew warmer and he smiled to himself, humming.

"One more song," the woman mumbled.

"I aim to please," Canaan said in a lover's voice and stepped her gently to "Twilight Time" by the Platters, another one of Marcy's favorites. Mrs. Bushman's eyes were at half-mast, truly flowing with the dance and slightly hypnotized. This gave him an idea and he shot Kilmeade a message. *"Keep them outside five more minutes..."*

"You have two..."

"Spoil sport." Canaan stopped his movement and maneuvered to see into Mrs. Bushman's face. *"Would you like to dream about me tonight?"*

He had asked his question telepathically, but moved his lips. This test had worked for him in the past—if the woman heard his sentiment, she was open to telepathy. If not, she would ask him to repeat himself.

Chloe's mother whispered a reply. "What a crazy thing to ask..."

Canaan chuckled, moved to her ear, allowing his breath to fall on her neck as he laughed. The woman wasn't a philanderer, which Canaan discerned right away, but her thought-life ran wild with fantasies she would never entertain in real life.

"Would you like to dream about me tonight?" he asked again, this time, half-way through his question, he pulled back so she might notice he had spoken to her in her mind and not in her ear.

She inhaled sharply, but didn't pull away. Mentally, she decided she'd *not* seen what she'd seen. "If I did," she whispered, "what would we do in my dream? And don't be improper..."

Canaan grinned. *"Tonight, you will dream that I am a handsome vampire prince and I need a tiny amount of your blood to be satisfied. Wanna?"* Canaan raised his eyebrows a few times.

She made a *pish* sound, but her wry expression went to the side. "I'll do no such thing," she said in a whisper and Canaan touched her temple.

"Now, think to me what you really want to do," he sent telepathically. "Think hard," he said in a whisper.

"I. will. dream. about. you."

Canaan heard the words distinctly and purposefully formed, carefully separating each syllable so none would be missed. *Bingo.*

Embarrassed, the woman laughed. "You're quite the magician, Mr. Canaan. Let me go," she said, regaining her composure. She straightened her blouse and touched her pulled-up hair. "I never." But she was smiling.

Kilmeade, Chloe, and Mr. Bushman entered the back door and walked into the room as Canaan turned for the hallway. He stuck his phone to his ear and disappeared to the back of the house, switching off the music the traditional way as he passed.

《回》

"Hey..." Chloe mumbled as Canaan disappeared down the hall. Her mother looked odd and Chloe walked to her side and touched her arm.

Her mom startled and huffed with the usual disdain, "Mina, that Canaan *is weird.* You sure can pick 'em."

"Are you okay?" Chloe asked. Her mother's forehead beaded with sweat, so much so that the roots of her perfectly highlighted hair were damp. Mrs. Bushman dabbed her upper lip and swished Chloe aside.

"Please, really," she said and reached for her husband's arm.

"Mom..." Chloe tailed them to the door. Kilmeade remained in the living room, but his eyes watched everything. Chloe looked between Kilmeade and her mom and back. "Mom, wait."

"Let it be, Chloe." Kilmeade's voice in her head. Chloe's face pinched and she clenched her jaw. Once she saw her parents out the door, she spun on her heel to face Kilmeade.

"What happened to my mother?!" She had spoken too sternly, for Kilmeade regarded her as if she'd spoken goldfish instead of English. "I'm serious!" Chloe turned for the hallway and called into the dark, "Canaan! What did you do to my mother?!"

She heard no reply and Kilmeade turned away to enter the kitchen. Within a moment, she heard the two of them chuckling.

"CANAAN!" she shouted.

"You would yell at your master?" Kilmeade, in her head again.

Chloe ground her teeth hard enough to ache as she fumed internally. *"My master!"* she snarled to herself. *"CANAAN IS NOT MY MASTER!"*

But... hadn't Marcy Haddle explained it? Canaan's ex spoke to her for an hour on the phone, explaining how to be an Elder's mate. How to submit. How to follow his lead. But... *my master?!*

"Do this, Chloe," Marcy had told her, "always consent no matter what it is he wants—sex, blood, affection—always consent. And if you have to say no, understand that he will know the truth of why you're refusing. If it's your time of the month, or you are sick, or angry, or depressed—he will know, so be honest. And..." Marcy had paused a marked length of time only to finish with, "if possible, consent anyway."

And there was more; listing archaic edicts to follow, as if the Twenty-First Century never arrived. Marcy had said, "An Elder is never wrong. He will never want your opinion on anything concerning him or his business. He knows what's best for himself and his people, and entertaining your opinion is a waste of his time. Given enough years together, he could soften, but until then, don't be hurt when he doesn't care what you think."

"This is ridiculous!" Chloe had replied and Marcy laughed.

"You didn't fall in love with a man," Marcy had said with snark. "You fell in love with a god. He has no humility and no remorse. If you can't take it, get out now. He will release you."

Chloe took two steps toward the entrance to the kitchen and watched the Elders. Canaan rummaged in the refrigerator and Kilmeade leaned back against the center island. Taking a deep breath, but recalling her mother's wide eyes, she entered the room.

"What did you do to my mom?" she asked, controlling her tone. The Elder didn't turn, but flipped items around in the fridge.

"Do to her?" he asked and closed the icebox. "She showed me a dance step or two. She's a knockout." Canaan looked at Kilmeade tugging the crotch of his jeans. "She did things to *me*, though. *Shew.*"

"I'm serious. What did you do?" Chloe watched his eyes, but there was nothing there to read. The Elder's face was as blank as a wall.

"We danced. Now, will you make me a sandwich?" Canaan asked.

"Make you a SANDWICH?" Chloe hadn't meant to shout, but controlling her anger proved more difficult than she predicted. "How about stay away from my mother!"

Cool hands grasped her shoulders from behind and the gentle contact encircled her throat. Kilmeade leaned close and put his face against the back of her head. "Insolence is not permitted," he said softly.

"It's okay," Canaan said and wagged his finger in her face. "She's just feisty." Canaan stepped close and pet her head like a kitten. "I did *not* hurt your mother, little bird. Will you please make me a sandwich?"

Chloe's face drained and a fit of crying welled in her chest. *Insolence is not permitted? What did I consent to?* Marcy told her she could get out if she asked. *I could go back to school, find a job and a normal husband...*

Canaan stroked her head a third time; all the while, Kilmeade stood behind her, his fingers tenderly caressing the skin of her throat.

"Lotsa mayo, please," Canaan whispered, lowering his chin.

"I'll have one, too," Kilmeade said in her head.

This is a freakin' test, Chloe suddenly thought. *Can I suffer an injustice as wild as watching my mother manipulated by a Rakum Elder and then smile and make him a sandwich?*

Chloe didn't move for several seconds and Canaan stopped petting her head. The Rakum were waiting to see what she would do. How would she handle the disregard they had shown her? With her heart pounding in her ears from pushing down her anger, she finally nodded.

"Of course, Elder Canaan." Chloe stepped around him to the fridge and pulled out the condiments. "I'm sorry, Kilmeade." Chloe didn't look at him, but she regretted her emotionalism. She knew better; the Rakum weren't human, they would always behave according to their nature. *"Forgive me,"* she sent and turned to see Kilmeade's face. *"Master."*

Kilmeade offered a tight grin and lowered his chin. *"Fffffft.* Let's not be silly," he said and returned to lean against the island once more.

Chloe slathered ciabatta bread with mayonnaise, shaking her head. "I'm still new at this. I don't think Canaan's going to hurt my mom. It's just..." Chloe searched the right words.

Submitting to Kilmeade was no easier than submitting to anyone. She had never been obedient, not to her parents or instructors in school. Even submitting to God in order to be saved she found nearly impossible. Only when Elder Rufus had scared her half to death did she even consider turning to God for help.

Submit to God and the devil will flee from you...

That's what David Walker and then Father Theophilus taught her that night—the night she was rescued from death and her soul from hell.

Kilmeade abruptly left the room and Canaan lifted his gaze to meet hers. Innocent, as far as she knew, Chloe shook her head.

"Uh, Kilmeade?" She passed the finished sandwich to Canaan and had turned for the door when the Elder stopped her.

"He's fine." Canaan took a huge bite of his sandwich and spoke while chewing. "He doesn't want to hear about the God of the mortals. Go ahead and get his sandwich ready. He'll be back."

Chloe grew still, momentarily stunned. *I didn't think. Kilmeade? I'm sorry—I didn't know you were listening to all that..."*

"It's not your fault," Canaan said, guessing at her puzzlement. "When you're mated, your thoughts cascade," he said, flowing the fingers of one hand like water. "Over time you will learn to better control your thoughts when you're in the same room. The further apart you are, the less accidental reading you'll get."

"Oh." Chloe turned back to the fixings. "That's helpful. Thank you," she said meekly, sorry for being so mean to him earlier.

"Sure. You gotta realize, there are only two of us left. We're evolving to fill the void of thousands of our brethren." Canaan shrugged and returned to noshing his snack, looking out the large back window.

"You're losing power?" Chloe asked.

He laughed. "Not hardly." Gorilla-like, Canaan pounded his chest with his free hand. "Not sure how to explain it, but being the last ones, Kilmeade and I are *isolated.*"

"Having us around isn't enough?" she asked.

Canaan shook his head. "There's a thread inside that tied all of the Rakum together. We leaned upon it, depended on it. As Elders, we could tug a line any time we wanted to, just 'tug,' *hey, Jack...*" Canaan pretended to pull an invisible string at chest level. "Or 'tug,' *hey there, Tork.* But 11/13, the line was cut." Canaan took another big bite to chew-talk once again. "Imagine holding hands with a hundred thousand people and in a flash, they all disappear. That's how it is for us. Kilmeade and I have been telepathically connected to thousands of the brethren for centuries. Now? Zip."

He finished speaking, swallowed, and went back to his sandwich. His expression showed no unhappiness, no sadness, or lack of enthusiasm for life—facts were stated, life goes on. Chloe shook her head in wonder at his stoicism.

Kilmeade walked into the room with Beryl trailing behind.

"Hey," she said and his greeting was always a quick blush and tight grin. He'd been staying in the guest room and she rarely saw him. Canaan approached Beryl with mayonnaise on his chin and clapped him hard on the back. Beryl winced.

"Careful," he said with a glance at Chloe, his voice subdued.

"I have some homework to do," she said, taking the hint. Kilmeade kissed her head when she passed and she left the men to their discussions. Being a proud and independent woman around beings from an altogether different species would be the biggest challenge of her life. A little Psychology 101 homework should be a breeze.

((▣))

"Javier says you're hitting the road to find our brethren." Beryl made his statement to Canaan, including Kilmeade in a sideways fashion.

"You and Javie best friends now, B?" Canaan asked and feigned a jab to the man's shoulder. He flinched, which only made Canaan laugh again. "Such a Nancy now, shit."

"It *hurts* now, Elder Canaan," Beryl said, calling Canaan by his title.

"It's *Elder* Canaan tonight..." Canaan looked over to Kilmeade. "Hmm. It wants something."

Kilmeade grinned, as usual, watching their interaction with interest.

"What does it want? You want to come with us? Don't you have a job waiting for you in *New York City*?" Canaan pronounced the name loudly and with the southern accent from the silly salsa commercials.

"I would like to help, yes," Beryl said, rubbing his shoulder strike zone. "Javier liked the idea and the job with Polly will always be there."

Beryl looked a trifle pouty, as if he expected rejection, but Canaan had no reservations. He liked Beryl, enjoyed him, which surprised him a lot. Canaan reached for the guy slowly, exaggerating so he wouldn't flinch, and turned him to face Kilmeade.

"Ask Daddy, son. As usual, always ask Daddy." Canaan gave Kilmeade a wink. Canaan enjoyed deferring—it relieved a lot of pressure to not be the senior man.

"You may accompany us as long as you are a help and not a hindrance," Kilmeade said, end of chat. His superior spoke less and less since they came out of the storm drain and he grabbed Beryl's attention when he'd stared at the other Elder too long.

"Be prepared to let blood," Canaan said with a mischievous grin and Beryl shrugged. "Kilmeade's mate will join us in a few months," Canaan added. "Can you tolerate her?"

"I honestly have no problem with her, with Javier, with any of them." Beryl gestured to the fridge and Canaan pulled it open. He removed a bottle of water and unscrewed the cap.

"Even Simon Miller?" Canaan asked, testing the waters. A shadow crossed over Beryl's face and was gone. He had been morbidly infatuated with the man as a Rakum and it would be good to know how he handled the realization now. He lived his life as the perfect Rakum, so he had abused many of the mortals surrounding Javier and Roman.

Beryl lowered his voice. "His hang-up, not mine."

Canaan nodded, reading the man's sincerity. He prodded a little more for kicks. "Beth Rider? Wanna go see her? Selene Cherrie? Hmm?" Before Last Assembly, Beryl had violently accosted the Rider woman and raped the other who, in all fairness, had been rejected by her Elder-mate and thus, made available to all.

Beryl regarded him with a bored gaze. "Obeying orders, *Master,*" he said with emphasis on the last word. "The pride of my pack."

Canaan clapped his back with a nod of the head. "Just testing. Okay, so Beryl is in," Canaan responded and fluffed Beryl's hair. "Did Javie have any idea when he wanted to head out?"

"I saw the itinerary. It starts on Friday, whatever that's worth."

Still leaning against the granite-topped island, Kilmeade reached for Beryl's sleeve and reeled him in. Once they faced each other, Kilmeade ruffled his hair in the same manner Canaan had, looking into his face. Then his right hand went to Beryl's cheek and his thumb across his lips.

"Do not talk about the God of the mortals on this journey. Not to me, not to Elder Canaan. That is Javier's domain."

Beryl's lips parted as if to protest the unspecified accusation, but Canaan stepped behind him and took a firm hold of his shoulder.

"Because He saved you from the sun and healed your face. Because you're mortal now and will suffer human weakness—Elder Kilmeade is warning you to only talk about that stuff with Javier. Not us. Clear?"

"Clear," Beryl said nodding to both Elders and he did not attempt to extricate himself from the tight proximity. "So what are you doing tonight?"

Canaan glanced at the clock in the oven panel. "I have a date about one. You're welcome to watch some TV with me. Kilmeade?"

"I will go play with Chloe, thank you."

His expression did not reveal any euphemistic meaning, which made it even more humorous. Canaan waved a few fingers and squeezed Beryl's shoulder with his other hand.

"For your date tonight—don't make me sorry I approved it."

Kilmeade's telepathic message made Canaan grin wider and he dragged Beryl into the movie room. *"I won't, Daddy. I won't,"* he returned, anticipation of the hunt being nearly as fun as the execution of it.

The grandfather clock struck two as Canaan waltzed into the house and collapsed on the living room sofa, leaving the room dark. His "date" with Mrs. Bushman had been a gigantic success and her blood warmed him still a half-hour later. The plan had unfolded precisely as he expected; the woman would awaken with the memory of a nice dream and no wound on her neck.

He sensed his housemate entering silently and he grinned like a fool for him to see.

"You smell delightful," Kilmeade sent and joined him on the couch. *"Daddy is proud of you."*

"You should be. I was magnificent."

"You always are," Kilmeade said aloud. "I want you to tell Chloe about it tomorrow night. Spare no detail." His eyes twinkled with devilish humor and Canaan scrunched his nose.

"Training her up right, I see," he joked. With his eyes closed and his grin in place, he rolled up his sleeve and handed Kilmeade his beefy tattooed arm. It had been a good night and he had plenty to share.

12, MAR 2, DENTON, TX

"*F*ind them, drain them, make sure they're dead."

The Master informed Dae Kim that there were six thousand transformed Rakum remaining and he wanted Dae Kim and Pete to find and kill as many as possible. *"Before Elohim gets a hold of them,"*[9] he iterated deep in Dae Kim's mind.

"They belong to us, but the Maker will steal those He can." When Dae Kim asked if straight murder was enough, The Master expressed clearly, *"The life of the Rakum is in the blood. You must drain them or the ritual is a failure. If you can't perform this, we will find someone who can."*

Dae Kim could do it, and he would. But why was The Master so inaccurate with his missions? The past four days, Pete and Dae Kim went where directed only to find no targets. With Pete behind the wheel, tonight they headed to a long-abandoned Waffle House in Denton.

"I'm sure you heard just now," Dae Kim said, "The Master says there are three of them and we're supposed to do the deal to all three." It had been a week since The Master closed up Pete's gunshot wound and now spoke exclusively to Dae Kim. Being insane, Pete hadn't noticed.

"But we can't drink three guys..."

Dae Kim shrugged. "That's the mission. Jump in, jump out, but don't ride my back about it. Isn't that what you taught me?"

Pete chuckled. "The Master will empower us to drink all three."

Dae Kim nodded. *Sure. We'll vomit and go back. Vomit and go back. Yay.*

"This is great," Pete said and took the ramp to Denton.

Dae Kim stared out the windshield and thought of days past. He had lived in Manhattan most of his life, memorized that town forwards and backwards. He'd been in Texas by accident, brought Lonnie to celebrate a special award at Cowboys stadium. They were staying a month, tops. Then 11/13 screwed everything up forever. *Damn that stupid Cow!*

"There it is!" Pete chirped, soon studying the rutted parking lot for a place to park. "The Master says they're afraid and hungry," Pete said as he punched the ignition switch with his knuckle.

---

[9] Hebrew, "Elohim" is a biblical name of the God of Israel.

"Yeah, right, I'm sure he told you that," Dae Kim thought to himself, but to Pete he nodded. "The Master just told me to remind you what he told you last night—he wants me to lead this one to prove myself. Sound good?" Dae Kim waited to see if his suggestion would take root.

"Yeah, I told him, whatever he wants," Pete agreed. "He's The Master. I'll follow you. It'll be fun. You show him!"

"I'll try to do it the way you taught me," Dae Kim said and exited the car. He walked quietly to the rear of the abandoned eatery and in the shadows of the building, stood near the emergency exit.

"Testvér?" he called to anyone inside and then looked at Pete who gave him a salute. *"Testvér, itt vagy?"*[10]

"I'm here," a man's voice filtered out to them and Pete clapped his hands.

"Brother, it's Dae Kim, from Elder Dawn's pack." Using hand gestures, he encouraged Pete to calm the hell down. "We have news of the brethren."

Chains clattered and the door pushed open. Inside, a man no taller than Dae Kim leaned on a crutch, looking at them with bloodshot eyes.

"Dae Kim?" he asked.

Dae Kim nodded and pointed behind him. "That's Pete."

"Petrov, I know you," the man said with a sad smile. He touched his chest. "Newel. Elder Fawn's pack. He died."

"They all died, idiot," Pete said harshly.

Dae Kim spoke up. "Are you alone?" He craned his head to see into the dark building.

"No, I joined up with Turk and Mitch in December. We're trying to figure out what happened. They'll be right back." Newel peered around the dark lot. "Ya'll come inside. The police patrol this street every hour."

Newel disappeared into the blackness. Dae Kim took a deep breath and strolled in behind him, trying not to think of the dangers of trusting the guy simply because he looked pitiful on crutches. Once inside, his eyes adjusted and he stepped around debris on the dirty tiled floor, following Newel to a walk-in freezer the size of a small bedroom.

"Took us a while to change, got burned day after day trying to get to the dark. Then we found this place." Newel waited for Pete to be in the room and he sighed. "Now it doesn't matter. Nothing matters."

Newel must have been attractive in his Rakum life, but a couple

---

[10] Rakum Hungarian, "Brother, are you here?"

months of burning and healing had transformed his visage into a scarred mess. Also, he had wasted away, looking as frail as a stalk of grass.

Newel chuckled with a raspy cough. "I know; I look horrible. I don't go out. Turk and Mitch look a little better."

"How long till they get back?" Pete asked with a crazy urgency that caused Dae Kim to close his eyes and think calm thoughts.

"Any minute. You are still beautiful," he said wistfully to Dae Kim, with a human tear in his eye. "Did you learn a way to stop the change?"

"Yeah," Dae Kim answered, preparing himself for the attack. They could end Newel and lie in wait for Turk and Mitch.

"Thank you for coming. You give me hope. Thank you," Newel said, new water flowing from what used to be shining Rakum eyes.

Dae Kim furrowed his brow; if the man thanked him one more time, he was going to run out crying, himself. Without giving Pete heads-up, Dae Kim lunged into Newel and pinned him against the steel wall of the freezer. With one hand, he closed off his larynx, and with the other, he shoved his knife deep into Newel's middle. Pete leapt in to do his part. Dae Kim moved the throat hand to Newel's mouth and Pete jabbed his own knife into the brother's neck. Pressing into Dae Kim's space, Pete wrapped his mouth around the wound and sucked greedily. Newel struggled, but didn't last long. When his heart stopped, Dae Kim removed his hand from Newel's lips and released him. Pete did as well and they watched their former brother slide down the wall.

"Damn, you did good, DaeDae!" Pete said and clapped his back. "Let's move him outta sight." Pete grasped Newel's wrists and dragged him out of the freezer.

Dae Kim followed and stood at the door until he returned. In the next room, Pete retched with a splatter. Dae Kim rolled his eyes. The other two were heard laughing outside, headed in. Pete needlessly shushed Dae Kim and hunched over to sneak into the freezer on tip-toe. Dae Kim entered after him and they both stood in the shadows.

When Turk and Mitch came in, they'd meet their maker. Dae Kim knew exactly who that was, but he didn't tell Pete. The fool read the same book. If he didn't see the truth of it, whose fault was that? Not Dae Kim's. No, let Pete figure it out. It was every man for himself, so Dae Kim tensed his muscles to pounce.

《回》

Chloe giggled as Kilmeade expertly located every ticklish spot on her sides and ribcage. Wearing a strappy negligee, she straddled him as he lay bare-chested on their bed. He wore jeans and lay on top of the covers. Nothing too heavy had happened so far, but the tickling matches usually ended in a round of delightful petting.

"No!" she shouted when he squeezed the top of her thigh, the tickle going deeper on the larger muscles.

He squeezed again and she nearly bucked out of her straddle. Kilmeade caught her about the waist and brought her back.

"Okay, wait, wait, wait," she said breathless. When she looked down on his face, his grin could not have been wider. His gray eyes sparkled and his shoulder-length auburn hair fanned out around his head. Could he really be nearly four centuries alive? "You look like a teenager when you smile like that," she said in wonder.

Kilmeade touched her cheek and when she closed her eyes to move into his fingers, with his other hand, he tickled her thigh again continuously, and didn't let go when she cried uncle. Several seconds passed and she pushed away to her side of the bed, laughing so hard she couldn't fill her lungs. No longer atop him, she crossed her arms and hugged herself tightly and mechanically slowed her breathing.

"How do you do that?" Kilmeade asked and rolled up to prop on one elbow. "Humans can't control their autonomic systems."

"Some can!" Chloe's eyes flashed as she met his gaze in the light streaming from the attached bathroom. "I thought you knew everything about everything, smarty-pants."

"I know everything important," he said and winked.

"I've been able to slow my heart, my breathing, even lower my blood-pressure since I was a kid." Chloe shrugged. "It's my stress relief."

"Suburban princess, what could you possibly have to stress over?" Kilmeade asked with a laugh.

"Mortals and our tiny little problems? Is that what Canaan said?" Kilmeade thumped her nose. Just then, a knock sounded loud three times on the other side of their bedroom wall. Canaan's room lay next door. Chloe sat up. "What's he doing?"

"Ya'll get on with it!" Canaan shouted through the wall.

Chloe looked upon Kilmeade still lying on his side, propped on his hand. "What's he doing?" she asked again.

Kilmeade grinned and fell back, his arms behind his head. "Ignore him. He's lonely."

"He listens to us?" Chloe watched Kilmeade's expression, which remained jovial. Rakum had telepathy… Was Canaan in Kilmeade's head when they made love? "Well?" she pressed, her thoughts going wild. Canaan's detailed account of how he swooned her mother for her blood still pricked deep down. Mom wasn't hurt, but it had to be wrong. Something about it was terribly *wrong*.

On his side of the wall, Canaan made a loud panting noise and grew quiet. Chloe poked Kilmeade's side. "Why is he doing that?"

When she had stared at him several seconds, he exaggerated a few blinks her way and chuckled. Chloe pinched the skin over his pectoral muscle. He had very little chest hair and was too muscular for her to truly grab a goodly amount. Still she held the flesh between her thumb and forefinger and threatened to twist.

"What does he mean? Is he listening, or something else?"

"Do it. Do it," he said and bit his bottom lip. "We live for pain!" he said, his gaze filled with mock arousal.

Chloe released him and moved away, still on the bed. "Gross!"

Kilmeade leaned toward her and grabbed her into his embrace. She grinned, but as he pulled her down to snug her back to his front, she thought of Canaan on the other side of the wall virtually participating. She dropped her smile and began to wriggle free.

"Ew, ew, ew!" Chloe shimmied free and got to her feet. She tossed her silk robe across her shoulders and pointed at the wall. "EW!" Kilmeade *tsk'd* and reclined back. "Tell him to stop!"

Kilmeade met her eye considering her histrionics. Teasing, he opened his mouth as if about to speak, looked around and closed it again.

"Kilmeade," she said, openly begging. She crawled toward him on the bed. "Block him out. That's gross. I can't stop thinking about it. Ew."

Kilmeade took a deep breath and put one hand on her leg folded beneath her. "Do you hide from spirits?"

"What?"

"Spirits. They are always watching, right?"

Chloe shook her head. "It's not the same. I don't have to look them in the face."

"It's sort of the same," Kilmeade said and gently caressed her thigh. "Elders as old as we are have seen it all. You're not going to surprise either of us in the bedroom."

Chloe shook her head in rapid succession. "You're not getting it. I *know* Canaan. To think that he..." She couldn't stop herself and she said it again. "EWWW!" Her thoughts raced and she worked to slow them, select the ones she wanted to keep and toss the ones she didn't.

Kilmeade grinned. "You can control your brain, too?"

"I'll know he's there," she whined. "Can't you do anything about it?"

He moved his hand from her thigh to her arm she leaned upon near his head. "Canaan and I have melded into one brain. It's a fact. Part of our anomalous new existence. You waste your time and mine shaking your fist at reality." He brought his hand to himself and put both behind his head.

Chloe recognized the move, withdrawing, distancing; a rejection of sorts and instantly, she felt guilty. *But do I feel guilty enough to make love knowing Canaan's there with us?*

Canaan banged on the wall again. "You're killing me, GET GOING!" He laughed the last word and Chloe caught Kilmeade's eye.

"He's a big goof. He's just making trouble," she said hoping Kilmeade would agree. Instead, holding her gaze with enough ferocity to create a vacuum in the air, he sucked his teeth, his eyes smoldering.

Chloe dipped her head a fraction. "The blood, too?"

Kilmeade nodded in slow-motion, his right hand coming down to grasp her forearm. The tender contact reeled her downward and toward him millimeter by millimeter and Chloe didn't resist. When she'd made the circuit where her throat would meet her lover's mouth, she grinned finally and closed her eyes.

"Stupid old Canaan," she sent telepathically to Kilmeade. *"I hope he chokes over there with his imaginary blood meal."*

"He won't tease you anymore," Kilmeade replied in her mind. *"From this moment forward, he will be still."*

Chloe nodded, recognizing the mental command he simultaneously delivered his Rakum counterpart. "Thank you," she murmured giggling softly as Kilmeade nipped playfully at her neck. "I consent," she whispered and Kilmeade dug in.

The act no longer bothered her and had morphed into an extension of their intimacy. Deep down, her subconscious told her it was wrong, but she quashed the noise in her spirit and concentrated on Kilmeade's warm hands exploring her body. She did *not* think about the other Elder a few feet away vicariously experiencing everything they did. Well, she thought about it as little as possible.

A short time later, Chloe stared at the ceiling tingling from head-to-

toe from her lover's attentions. How could she possibly let him leave?

"I'm not gonna make it three months," Chloe whispered lying in the crook of Kilmeade's arm. He snugged her against him and made no response. Chloe sighed; he wouldn't experience a sense of loss or emptiness, nor would he suffer from fits of jealousy and paranoia. In the near-pitch darkness of their bedroom, she furrowed her brow and attempted to put herself in his place. *All I have to do is imagine everything in the world exists strictly for my pleasure.* Chloe paused her train of thought and then shook her head a fraction. *How sad is that...*

"Sad for who, angel? For me?"

"Yeah," she replied softly, aware that he was capable of answering her internal rambling if he so chose. "I'm trying to understand you and when I imagine it like you taught me, it makes me sad."

"Is a lion sad it is a lion and not an antelope?"

Chloe huffed, but smiled nonetheless. In his Rakum mind, they were the lions and her species was on the hoof.

Kilmeade lifted her to him with his arm and pressed his face into her wavy curls. He inhaled deeply and sighed, "I will miss you, Chloe."

She pushed against him until she could see the shape of his face in the dark. "You'll miss Chloe or what Chloe can do for you?"

Kilmeade smiled, his white teeth glinting. He chose his words and then chuckled deep within. "There's a difference?"

Chloe poked out her bottom lip, but she wasn't angry. His answer was one-hundred-percent Rakum. He never promised anything he hadn't delivered—everything she thought he lacked, she projected onto him. The most dangerous thing she could do was try to change him. *No, strike that. The most dangerous thing for my emotional health is to think he might change over time. Rakum are Rakum, they don't change.*

"I will miss your smile," Kilmeade said, his voice low.

Chloe turned again to see his silhouette. He was trying to name things besides blood and sex that he might miss. She propped up onto one elbow and waited for more.

"I will miss your sense of humor," he added.

"Yeah?" she whispered. Her hand landed across his chest and she stroked him slowly.

Kilmeade grinned. "I will miss..." he said and hummed a moment before finishing with, "...you arguing with Canaan."

"Uh!" she said and slapped his pectoral muscle. "Be serious!"

Kilmeade chuckled. "Harder! Harder! Get a hammer!" Chloe laughed, too, recognizing the truth. He enjoyed her banter with Canaan.

"Does Canaan like me all right?" she asked when they had both fallen quiet.

"He likes you as much as I do," Kilmeade said without missing a beat. Chloe propped up again.

"What?"

"What's not to like?" Kilmeade replied, but his question to answer a question gave him an out. Chloe leaned away from him to switch on her lamp. When she turned back, he had lain back flat and folded both arms behind his head.

"Is it safe, what you and Canaan are starting out on tomorrow? Do you have any reason to be cautious?" Chloe watched his eyes, happy now she could see them.

"The only thing we need to beware in the new era is sunlight, and we have centuries of experience avoiding exposure."

Chloe exhaled. "True," she said to convince herself. "The Rakum spirit is gone..." She mumbled the obvious and then sat up again. "Think about it, what spirit is keeping you and Canaan like you are?"

Kilmeade reached for her mouth and covered it securely with his palm. Tenderly, he pulled her to the pillow again, hand over her mouth, and switched off the lamp his way.

"When you're gone, I'm going to pray for you to be safe. All of you," she sent telepathically.

"Good," he replied and leaned in close. Playfully, he lifted his fingers only as much as would allow his lips to touch hers and then covered her mouth again.

"Are we finished chatting?" she sent with a grin and Kilmeade nodded and shifted his weight to drape across her. *"Two hours until sunrise, you know,"* she offered, closing her eyes.

"I know everything," he sent back. *"Haven't you figured that out?"*

Chloe giggled and he told her goodbye one more time.

13, MAR 3, DALLAS

"**O**ur mission has been altered regarding the one called Adam Roberts. We want him alive," The Master said, warbling when the voices fell out of sync at the last. *"He must be important, for Elohim is multiplying His messengers around him. So far, no flesh has been assigned to help. We have you; we can get to him first. You are clever and appealing. He will be drawn to you. Pete, no longer possesses the finesse required for this mission."*

Dae Kim agreed; he'd keep Crazy Pete in the dark. If anybody was eating the other, Dae Kim wanted to be the one holding the fork.

"The Master will empower you to sway him, open your mind to us and we will speak for you. You will seem like a Rakum to him; he will be fooled..."

Sure, why not? he thought and wove his wave through rush-hour traffic. He'd find the man in the research labs underground and show The Master he could do what Pete could not.

By 8 a.m. the rain arrived and fell in thick sheets. Dae Kim parked in the covered garage and headed for the labs in sub-level. In the elevator, he used the reflective wall to check his hair and attire. He looked sharp and had always turned heads, his ethnic mix of Caucasian and Chinese melding into perfect features. Plus, since The Master favored him, his physique had returned as strong and as lean as before. He snuck a little wink to himself as the elevator reached the bottom.

The hallway was quiet as Dae Kim walked smoothly past the lab doors. At one marked RESEARCH GRANTS/DALLAS, a nudge from The Master told him he'd found the place. Dae Kim peeked into the rectangular door window and viewed lab tables, various equipment, and three men in white knee-length coats.

As he pondered the next move, a man exited an office next door and stopped to consider him. One glance and Dae Kim recognized him as Wide-tie from the night Pete was shot. Up close and in the fluorescent light, Dae Kim noted his general pallor and hand-stenciled eyebrows. Dae Kim bobbed his head, mimicking the idiot mortals, but the guy didn't lose interest. Dae Kim averted his gaze and peered again into the lab; in his peripheral vision, Wide-tie continued to stare.

ellen c. maze

Maybe he's gay; I am quite beautiful... Dae Kim snickered inwardly. Just then, one of the men in the lab turned and made eye contact. Without direction from himself, Dae Kim's hand called the man over. The same height and weight as Fit-guy from the other night, only now Dae Kim saw his face plainly and thought he looked familiar. He busily searched for the correct file folder as the man pulled open the door.

"Help you?" he drawled, his eyebrows arching as he awaited a reply.

"Adam?" Dae Kim asked and the guy paused, looked back to his coworkers, and moved into Dae Kim to exit the room. A quick side-glance found that Wide-tie had disappeared.

"Who are you?" he asked and crossed his arms at chest level. The man stood a little taller than Dae Kim, and had bright gray eyes, wavy hair, and he drawled like a local. Dae Kim waited for The Master to take his tongue, but before he did, Adam spoke again. "You're one of the guys that tried to kill me."

Dae Kim ignored the accusation as The Master's words bubbled up from within. "That was a mistake. My name is Dae Kim. My companion that night was insane and I didn't know his intentions."

Adam tilted his head, his mouth a grim line. Was he buying it? Inside, The Master urged Dae Kim to wait, so he held his poker face.

"You're one of Bel's brothers?"

The Master shouted with glee. *"Elder Bel was somehow involved with this man's childhood. We want to know how!"*

Dae Kim nodded. He recalled Bel well enough from Assembly. "That's right, I'm one of Elder Bel's brothers," Dae Kim said. "My master sent me and I have answers to your questions."

Adam's eyes widened. "You know about the letter?"

"Of course," Dae Kim said faking it, finding it easier to meld his own voice with the suggestions of The Master. "Can we go somewhere private and talk?"

"Yessssss! That's it! Get us that letter!" The Master urged.

Adam looked back into the lab he had exited and then at his watch. The man was mulling over Dae Kim's story, his intelligence battling his curiosity. With a careful exhale, he allowed himself a half-grin.

"Yeah," he said, "You're not here to kill me."

Dae Kim flashed a wide grin. "Smart man."

"Follow me." Adam turned and walked briskly to the end of the hall. When they had made another turn, he pushed open a stairwell door. A voice called Adam's name and he turned.

99

"Does that guy need a visitor's tag?" Wide-tie called out.

"I'll take him to HR, Dr. Nankin," Adam said and waved. Baldy stared at them both a minute longer and disappeared into a room.

"My boss," Adam mumbled and entered the stairwell. When the door closed behind Dae Kim, he stopped on the landing. "There's an office down here we can borrow. Maintenance guy is on at nine so we have a little time."

"Great," Dae Kim said and shadowed him down the steps. The boilers rumbled and vibrated the walls and the chilly air was moist. The Master tossed Dae Kim more words. "Adam, you are very handsome; you know that, right?" Adam's head whipped around, a huge grin on his face. Dae Kim nodded. "What? I'm serious."

After meeting his gaze a few more seconds Adam said, "Well, thank ya. I don't swing that way, but you're mighty good-looking, too," and continued toward a set-in metal office door.

So he likes compliments. Vanity was something Dae Kim understood.

Once inside the small space, Adam closed the door and faced Dae Kim. He removed his lab coat and The Master inside Dae Kim caused him to look the man over. As a Rakum, Dae Kim appreciated the human form, but since his transformation, nothing held any interest except filling his stomach with cheeseburgers. Adam absorbed the ogling, accustomed to being noticed. He leaned against the cluttered metal desk grinning and showcasing his physique.

"Tell me about Bel," Adam said his head to the side, "if you really know him."

Dae Kim sent him another wink. "Our people are a hundred-thousand strong so I don't know them all. I know Elder Bel, though. He's this tall," Dae Kim said with his hand over his head, "with very dark skin and light brown eyes. He spent a lot of time with my Elder when we gathered in Nevada." Dae Kim stopped speaking.

"What was your Elder's name?"

"Show me your letter," Dae Kim said, tossing out a little test. If he could get his hands on it he might get to go back to bed.

"My questions?" Adam said and waggled his finger. "Anyway, I don't have it on me. I keep it locked up."

Dae Kim sensed The Master's agitation, as if in the spirit realm, his thousands of members sought the letter on their own.

"Who else did Bel hang out with?"

Dae Kim thought back, deciding to name some more while The

Master came up with a new strategy. "Elder Dawn, Elder Canaan..." Dae Kim pictured the Elders Dawn enjoyed the most. "Elder Tomás, definitely."

"Name one you don't like," Adam said. When Dae Kim didn't reply, he rolled his shoulders and flashed his grin. "I'm giving you a verbal lie detector. I invented it when working on my second Masters. First, I asked you to name folks who hung out with Bel. Then when I asked you who you don't like, you stop. Maybe you're trying to deceive me and just get your hands on my letter." Adam leaned upon his hands on the desktop and crossed one foot over the other.

Dae Kim shook his head with a smile. "My answer is simple; I didn't like Elder Kilmeade." Dae Kim paused as the correct file folder popped open. "SHIT!" he exclaimed and Adam's eyes grew wide.

"Kilmeade?" Adam repeated as a question.

Dae Kim snarled for him to be silent as The Master dug painfully into his mind seeking answers faster than he could pull them up. Aloud Dae Kim hissed, "Wait!" and he arranged his thoughts, his eyes squeezed shut, head bowed from the pain of The Master's search.

"Sounded like you said Kilmeade," Adam leaned forward. "You okay?"

Dae Kim held up a finger and gradually stood. Inside, he said, *"Master, this man is physically identical to Elder Kilmeade."*

A cacophony arose in his mind as The Master in a thousand voices cheered and hooted, hissed and moaned. He had already discovered in his research that spirits did not see into their dimension clearly unless they were fleshed. This explained why the imps were so excited with the news of Kilmeade's doppelganger. Dae Kim squint his eyes and peeked at Adam. What did it mean? Had they cloned an Elder? Was it a coincidence? Dae Kim raced to say what The Master commanded.

"The Master wants to see you. Will you come with me? Right now?" Dae Kim asked working to ignore the migraine The Master caused. As a Rakum, he handled pain as a way of life, but his human body could not compartmentalize it the same way; he hadn't become a Rakum again even though the Master said he would for this meeting.

"Tell me about Kilmeade," Adam said, his head tilted to the side.

Dae Kim disregarded his request, not interested in why the name sparked his interest. "Come with me. The Master can tell you all about Kilmeade, Bel–anyone you desire. Just come."

"No, it doesn't feel right..." Adam said and trailed off.

Inside Dae Kim's mind, The Master fell still and stroked his pain away. *"Now, do it now,"* The Master prompted and Dae Kim relaxed his will for his master to push his own.

"My master said you are being held back from discovering who you really are. He said you're not a simple research scientist."

Adam put his hands on his hips, his expression unreadable.

"With very little energy, my master can show you how to fulfill your potential. What do you say?"

Suddenly, a fondly missed urgency returned to Dae Kim's inward parts and he stepped into Adam's personal space. The man's eyes widened, but he didn't back away. Like the old Dae Kim, he brought his hand to the man's whiskered face, stroked his cheek, and Adam did not recoil from his touch. Instead, his breath hitched and he closed his eyes to the sensation. The Master was doing this, hypnotizing the young man, and oh, how Dae Kim wished he could keep such power forever.

"What a cruel trick of fate, locking you to these mortals," Dae Kim whispered, now running his hand into Adam's wavy hair. With incredible tenderness, he pulled the man close to his face and inhaled deeply. "Your destiny is with us. With Bel's people."

"I don't think so," Adam whispered, still pushing into Dae Kim's touch. "Something's off." Adam was barely audible now.

The Master inside Dae Kim caused him to scoff. "You look *exactly* like one of our greatest leaders—let us show you how to be as great as he is. Come with me. We will show you amazing things."

"No," Adam whispered.

Dae Kim lifted his other hand and ran them both deep into Adam's hair, massaging in slow circles. The Master was sending calming energy through the contact and Adam's heartrate slowed. Adam made a small noise in his throat as Dae Kim ceased rubbing his head and slid his hands to rest on Adam's inner shoulders.

"I want you to go now," he said without looking up.

Behind Dae Kim, the door to the office opened and a frowning man entered, his clipboard at half-mast. Adam languidly looked up to meet his eye and Dae Kim brought his hands to himself.

"Roberts, you and your boyfriend take it upstairs," the man said to Adam. "Ain't 'nuff room in here for all tree of us."

Dae Kim waited a second for The Master, but as had happened before, he didn't seem to be aware that they'd be one, interrupted, and two, unsuccessful in wooing Adam.

When no one moved, the maintenance man fell into his desk chair and met Dae Kim's eye. "You could stay, though," he said holding Dae Kim's gaze. "I'm not as purty as Roberts, but it *is* my office."

"We're leaving," Dae Kim said under his breath wishing with his heart and soul that The Master had made him a Rakum again. He'd kill the man in a heartbeat if he had the power.

"Suit yourself," he chuckled and turned to his clipboard.

Adam left first and Dae Kim followed without speaking. When they had both reached his lab door, Adam entered and closed it without acknowledging Dae Kim.

"Master?" Dae Kim thought and stood like a dolt in the empty hall. He was still seeking a word from his invisible helpers when Roberts's nosy boss popped out in front of him.

"I'm leaving. I'm leaving," Dae Kim muttered angrily, forced to walk past the man to reach the elevators. The boss made a soft *"Hhhh-mmm"* sound as he crossed and Dae Kim wrinkled his nose at the man's aftershave: oranges and formaldehyde. *Nice.* Dae Kim reached the elevator and the boss called him out.

"Son, did you see HR?" Wide-tie took a step closer.

Still hearing nothing from The Master, Dae Kim dumbly shook his head. The elevator doors opened and he stepped in backward promptly followed by Roberts's stinky boss.

"This is a private facility," Wide-tie said, standing shoulder-to-shoulder with Dae Kim as the elevator rose to the garage level.

"I'm leaving," Dae Kim replied, adlibbing since The Master remained mum. Wide-tie pressed the stop button on the elevator car. With a shudder the contraption slowed and came to a halt between floors. Dae Kim turned at the waist and waited for an explanation.

"Come to my office," he said and pressed a sublevel button. "There is a form for you to sign. Roberts should have given it to you."

Dae Kim read another emotion for a millisecond in the man's gaze, but naming it didn't come easy. Suspicious, sure. Irritated, yeah. Curious? Maybe... There was something else. The elevator headed back down.

"Master? What now?" he asked inwardly. When he heard no reply for several seconds, he sighed and gave up. The elevator stopped one level below the Lab Floor and once the door swooshed open, Dae Kim followed Roberts's boss to his office.

Inside, he asked The Master for some of his Rakum powers to work the guy over. Not kill him, just hurt him. Make him forget he saw Dae Kim in the first place. The Master didn't answer.

Maybe The Master wants me to play along, this is part of his plan... Or maybe the guy has the hots for me and exerting his puny mortal power is the only way he can get me to stay. Dae Kim smiled, after all, the man *did* eye him nonstop.

An expensive desk faced the door and a hand-carved plaque read, Cary K Nankin, PhD. From a three-quarter angle, Dae Kim studied a photograph of what was presumably his family: an attractive Oriental woman holding Chinese twin girls on her lap. Dae Kim rolled his eyes; a wife and kids didn't make a man straight. If only The Master would lend him the slightest power, not only would Dae Kim discern the truth, but woo Nankin to his will. *It wouldn't take much...* his heart called out, but again, The Master said nothing. The boss rummaged through a filing cabinet and flipped a sheet of paper on the shiny desk surface.

"If you'll fill this out, you can come and go as you please." Nankin handed over a pricey executive ink pen.

Dae Kim drew the item from the man's hand making sure their fingers touched. For the two seconds of contact, he looked up to catch the man's eye and Nankin might have broken a small grin. Up close, the boss's face seemed oddly slick, oily even, as if his alopecia required a prescription skin cream. *Maybe that's what smells so weird,* Dae Kim figured and lowered his eyes when he felt Nankin had received his flirtatious glance. He filled out the form, still standing and Dr. Nankin leaned on his palms across the wide desktop.

Name. "DAE KIM DAWN," he whispered as he wrote, using Elder Jack Dawn's name as his own. Why not? Chin down, he raised his eyes to the bald boss man. Nankin's hazel gaze watched his every move, but his impatient expression did not budge.

Address. He jotted Lonnie's old apartment downtown. *Phone.* He made up a fake Dallas area code landline. *Email.* He shared Lonnie's Cowboys email, long-since deactivated. *Car license tag and make*—Dae Kim told the truth, in case The Master sent him back. A few questions remained about health insurance and lastly, the form asked his relationship to the Baylor-Dallas employee. Dae Kim's pen hovered while he created an answer. Finally, he wrote, "FAMILY FRIEND," and handed the pen and sheet to Roberts's boss.

"Family friend?" Nankin asked eyeing Dae Kim sideways. "I've worked with Adam seven years. Why haven't I seen you before?"

Nosy asshole. Dae Kim didn't say it, but the words tickled his tongue. As a Rakum, he did not tolerate patronizing or condescending mortals.

This man's arrogance irked him, but with no power surge from The Master, he played along.

"He's a distant cousin. I'm new to town and my uncle told me to look him up," Dae Kim shoved his hands in his pockets. "I answered your questions. We done?"

"Write your uncle's name here and we're done."

Laughing inside at his joke, Dae Kim wrote in block letters, "BILLY BOB KILMEADE." Boss man gave him a bored stare and waved his hand in Dae Kim's face.

"Have a nice day." Nankin dropped into his chair and turned his attention to his computer monitor.

Still smirking at the idiot and his self-importance, Dae Kim exited. He trotted to the elevator and pressed the garage level. When the doors opened on his floor, a thick Hispanic security officer, complete with Taser and handgun, stopped him with an upraised hand.

"This is private property, sir," he grumbled with a thick accent. "Come with me." A large paw grasped Dae Kim's arm and he protested vocally as he was dragged to the door marked BDRH POLICE.

"I just left Dr. Nankin's office! Call him! Dae Kim Dawn. I filled out the form two minutes ago!" Dae Kim complained loudly and launched into profanity when the man muscled him into a small security office and forced him onto a metal bench, ordering him to wait. Dae Kim growled cursing under his breath. *'Master! Why aren't you helping me? Shit! This is impossible! You said I'd be a Rakum!'*

Five long minutes later, the giant re-entered and motioned for Dae Kim to leave. "Sorry 'bout that. From now on, wear this when you visit."

Dae Kim scowled and yanked a lanyard from the guard as he held it out. "Tell Dr. Nankin he can kiss my ass!" Dae Kim barked and walked double-time toward the cars a dozen yards away. Almost to his Lexus, Roberts's nosy boss appeared, standing up at Dae Kim's bumper.

"Just checking," he said with a snooty smile and waved as he walked away. Dae Kim cursed under his breath, hoping The Master never sent him back. He had no power and the mortals didn't respect him one iota.

In the car to Pete's house, he heard nothing from The Master. Dae Kim trudged back to the basement to keep up the façade; another morning wasted when he could have been asleep.

14, APR 2

"It's a fantastic idea," Roman acknowledged when informed of the plan to seek out brethren in need and tell them about the website. "But, brother," he said with a grin, "you realize that's no way to keep your shirts and slacks pressed."

Kilmeade flicked up his gaze and tossed another shirt into the duffle bag. *"Pssssh,* what need have I to worry about laundry?" He rolled up a pair of jeans and threw it on top. "I have a Canaan, a top-notch valet if there ever was one." He winked with humor and zipped up the bag.

"You are *truly* happy," Roman said smiling at his brother's joy. "Seems this one-of-two existence is going to work out after all."

Kilmeade regarded Roman with a smirk and lowered his chin. "Say what's on your mind."

Roman grinned. "I spoke with Rafael before he left town. He believes you and Canaan are in one brain. Is he correct?"

"Ah, my pet. I miss him," Kilmeade said wistfully and dropped into an armchair. "And, yes, Rafa discerned correctly. Canaan and I have melded into one." Kilmeade lowered his chin and winked at Roman with upraised eyes. "He's having sex with my mate sideways."

Roman laughed into his hand. "If you're in one brain, he's not at fault."

"Your brother Kilmeade is not bothered about it in the least. After all, I can't poke out my own eye," he remarked with a coy smile. "What else is on your mind? I see your wheels turning."

"Yes," Roman said and paused as he worked up his opener.

"Tick tock," Kilmeade teased.

Roman sighed. "I am concerned because Rafael said while you were with Isaac, you asserted you would die to protect me."

"What?" Kilmeade caught Roman's eye and shook his head. "Rafa spoke out of turn. Pitiful."

"Then it's true," Roman asserted his tone stern. "You need to—"

Kilmeade met his eyes with a snap of his head. "You would command Elder Kilmeade?"

Stiffly, Roman worked to rephrase. "I meant...

"Thank you," Kilmeade interrupted. "You have raced your little human heart for nothing. Yes, Isaac threatened your safety. When I grew weary of it, I told him to never mention you again."

"And you said, quote, I won't stand by and let you hurt him," Roman added.

Kilmeade narrowed his eyes and rose to his feet. "What do you want from me? A confession? I am a Rakum. My words are few."

Roman stood and touched Kilmeade's shoulder. "A Rakum, yes, and Rakum don't risk their lives for one another." Roman watched his eyes. "When you leave with Canaan, don't be careless."

"You insult me," Kilmeade replied. "I risked nothing. Isaac would not have killed me. Do you not know me at all?" Kilmeade asked growing indignant. "I know what I am doing at all times." Kilmeade turned away, discussion closed.

Roman frowned, not convinced. "Just for me, don't take risks. Now that we've reunited, I want to know you a long time."

Kilmeade looked back and waggled his eyebrows. "You're the one growing old."

"You got me there..." Roman forced a grin. Worry had become a close companion and that emotion did not come from God.

"Time to shuffle off," Kilmeade said and Roman asked him about Miss Bushman. "Oh, no. I'm not getting romance advice from an Elder who never took a mate," Kilmeade said grabbing the handle of his bag.

Roman grinned. "You're right, I can't help you there. I was going to ask you if she is joining you later."

"Three months." He shrugged. "She has me. Why go to college?" Kilmeade huffed. "Training her hasn't been easy."

"I'm sure you'll figure something out," Roman laughed.

"Seven years ago, you would have been a lot more help," Kilmeade said without malice. "I think now you're humoring me and expecting me to transform into a human before my problems grow out of control."

Roman widened his eyes. "Who me?"

Kilmeade put on an exaggerated shiver. "I should share what Father Damien told us the night Isaac ended him..." He paused when Roman huffed in disdain at his wording. "Contain your tears, old man." Kilmeade said with a lazy eye. "Father Damien informed me that there is a knocking on my heart and the One knocking is Yeshua, the Son of God." Kilmeade paused and swallowed. "Be encouraged to know that I am not offended."

Roman resisted a grin. "Thank you, that means a lot."

Kilmeade leaned in. "Did Rafa tell you about the voice?"

Roman's head tweaked to the side. "What? No. What voice? When?"

Kilmeade arched his eyebrows a few times and ran a hand over his face. "Just before Father Damien was killed, Isaac enabled me to see into the spirit dimension. He wanted me to see Damien as a traitor." Kilmeade rolled his eyes to the side. "Instead, I saw a Being of Light that eclipsed Damien's shape. A face like the sun turned to me and said, 'Kilmeade, you are My son and I love you.'" Kilmeade watched Roman's eyes and nodded when he was stunned too long to answer. "When my sight returned to normal, Damien said I had just seen your Yeshua."

"Oh, my God," Roman said and fell silent.

"And I *wanted* to be loved by Him." Kilmeade sighed and then squared his shoulders. "I *will* accept. It *will* happen. But not now…"

"Kilmeade," Roman said softly. How did his brother resist? Then again, hadn't he done the same thing? Roman had believed everything Beth Rider taught them about God, yet he resisted a long while. It had to do with being an Elder, with making sure Javier and his other pups were safe. It had to do with being responsible for everyone else *before* he could accept the promise of eternity and grace from his Creator. Was Kilmeade doing that? Waiting to be last?

"I will wait," Kilmeade said amazingly in sync. "I am glorious in this form and I will make the best use of it I can."

"Brother, you amaze me," Roman whispered. "Truly."

Kilmeade laughed and shook him by the shoulder. "Walk me to the car. Let's see what sort of conveyance the underlings procured."

Roman nodded, still marveling at what he had learned about his brother. In his heart he sent up a prayer for them all and followed him down the stairs.

《回》

The moon sat low in the sky as Javier stepped into the yard to meet Canaan at the new truck. In the glow of the Halogen headlights, Canaan flexed his muscles, even turning to the side for some Schwarzenegger flair. Javier shook his head.

"You are too full of yourself," he said laughing. "I guess Marcy encouraged this."

"You kidding? She couldn't keep her eyes off this," he said and struck another pose, arms curled with enough tension to bulge the veins over his bicep tattoos. He'd worn a tight-fitting T-shirt in the early Spring chill and made no notice of the wind.

Javier shielded his eyes with one hand as he passed. "Put it away, put it away," he teased and reached the driver's door.

Canaan laughed and held his phone up for Javier to see. "Marcy received the check." Canaan dropped the phone into his pocket and hefted his duffle bag over his shoulder. "She shit a brick, but she took it. I gave her half—ten million dollars." Chuckling to himself, Canaan grew quiet.

"I can attest the disbursement has been a huge blessing. I didn't expect to be included," Javier said as he tossed his single bag in the floorboard backseat of the Denali.

"Why not? Guap and Polly don't discriminate. Every Rakum alive will get their share of the Father's wealth. You, Roman, David, and the rest are no different."

Javier climbed in behind the wheel and waited for Canaan to settle on the passenger side. "I guess I'm saying, I didn't *assume* those of us who initially caused this huge change would still be considered brethren."

"You're happy about it, though," Canaan said with a grin. "Bought these nice wheels, I see. Very comfy. Elder Kilmeade will approve."

Javier laughed and headed away from the curb. Kilmeade enjoyed luxury more than any Rakum he'd ever met and the Yukon Javier bought the day before came with every possible creature comfort.

"I saw you checking out my Elder Emergency Box," Javier joked.

"*That* is damn genius. I love it."

"Good," Javier said. Earlier in the day, the dealership installed the largest lock-box they made, custom fit for the Yukon's cargo hold. Javier figured in an emergency, both Elders could use it to hide from the sun. Once he had the truck in his own garage, he drilled air holes in the away side and covered them with porous black cloth. Rakum were capable of slowing their breathing to a near stop when needed, so the box should certainly serve.

"I have us hopping from Jackson, Mississippi, to Dallas, to Los Angeles. I rented houses in each location so you won't have to stay in a hotel bathroom." Javier watched Canaan's face for approval and he winked. "Along the way, we'll follow our noses and pray for help."

"You pray. I'll sniff."

"Plan," Javier said and adjusted the mirrors.

Canaan checked his phone and chuckled. "Beryl is at the house along with Kilmeade and Roman. I guess you couldn't get the old goat to go with us, eh?"

"He has no calling for it. He'll stay with David and continue to work the website and the RA group in Tuscaloosa."

"Rakum Anonymous?" Canaan asked with a chuckle. "This is some freaky shit."

Javier agreed with a laugh. Their houses were only two blocks apart so when he turned onto Smithson, they were halfway there.

"I'm glad I went through that anomaly phase," Javier said thoughtfully. "It convinced me beyond all doubt that my faith is in the right Father."

"Don't make me clock you, Pastor Javie," Canaan joked. In a serious tone, he said looking away, "Kilmeade has become very touchy regarding this issue so don't press him."

Canaan's change of attitude piqued Javier's interest. The constantly jovial Elder rarely said a serious word, and just then he sounded quite concerned about his housemate.

"What's going on?"

Canaan looked his way. "Really, Javie? I tell no tales out of school, fool." Canaan forced a chuckle and fiddled with his phone.

"You can talk to me, Canaan," Javier said carefully to avoid inferring a weakness in the Elder. "You know I won't try to convert you." Javier watched him until he gave a combination shrug-nod. "Same goes for Kilmeade. He knows, right?"

"He knows."

"Okay, so everything is okay with you? Healthy, happy, all that?"

"Yes, love, I'm just dandy," he replied in a high octave.

Javier decided to take him at his word and pulled into Kilmeade's long driveway. The house had a wraparound porch and sitting on a hanging swing, he spied Chloe Bushman apparently awaiting their arrival. When he put the truck in park, she sprinted off the porch following the paved path illuminated by tiny solar lights until she reached the Yukon and crossed the headlights stream. She eyed Canaan with a miniscule snarl and met Javier at his door. He rolled down the window.

"Hey," he said to her, but she watched Canaan waltz up to the house. "What's wrong?"

"Canaan snuck into my parents' house and took blood off my mother!" Chloe hissed, both hands on the sill of the truck door. "And he's not even sorry. NOT EVEN A LITTLE. How am I supposed to deal with that? How would God want me to deal with it? I am SO MAD!" she fumed, whisper-yelling to avoid drawing the Elder's attention.

"Whoa. Is she okay?"

"Well, yeah," Chloe said, deflating. "But that's not the point."

Javier nodded and considered her base question. What did God think? He gave her the only thing he could come up with.

"You sleep in the bed you make, Chloe. Know what that means?"

"Come on, I'm serious." She waited for more.

"What do you want me to say? You're attracted to the Rakum and they are an abomination. You can't see the problem with that?"

"An abomination? Javier—"

"It's the same story from that night you slept in my bed," Javier said and she blushed deep red.

"Shhhhhh!" she hissed.

"Oh, he knows." Javier unlatched his seatbelt and Chloe backed from the door. "Why are you so red? Nothing happened."

"You're no help," she said and turned away.

"Chloe, come back." When she did, Javier apologized. "Look, you're not going to be able to control Canaan or Kilmeade. One day, God-willing, they will be mortal, then you might get through to them, but until then, they will do what they want, when they want to do it. It's the way of the Rakum, and especially, Elders."

Chloe sighed and crossed her arms. "I'm smart—I get it. I chose this life so I'll live with it even if they don't give a flip what I think."

Javier offered a sympathetic nod. "If it's any consolation, I trust them both a hundred percent. They know what they're doing."

Chloe's eyes childishly darted away, but she didn't disagree.

The front door came open and Beryl emerged carrying a knapsack and a brown paper bag. By the time he reached the truck, Canaan exited at a trot, laughing as usual, and Kilmeade followed with Roman, shaking his head. Chloe left Javier's door and jogged to Kilmeade before he got off the porch.

Javier watched them together, thankful she turned her attentions away—this second, and three months ago. As delightful as she had been for their forgettable tryst, Javier wasn't ready to commit any energy to romance. Being celibate had its merits.

15, Jackson, MS

Beryl steered the Yukon past the house Rufus and then Isaac called home before they died their own deaths. The place sat vacant, the lienholder obviously unwilling or unable to take possession. Beryl's mouth went to the side; oh, how he hated Elder Rufus.

Done with the unpleasant recollections, Beryl continued down the road, familiar with the area. His mind had just started to wander when the cell phone charging in the console chimed. Beryl waited to see if Elder Kilmeade would tend to it, but not too surprisingly, he did not. It was Canaan's cell, but he also ignored the alert. With an internal huff, Beryl glanced at the text. It was too long to read off the lock-screen so he unhooked the charging cable and held it up.

"Elder Kilmeade has a text on your phone," he said to Canaan, catching his eyes in the rearview mirror. Canaan looked back at him, his expression saying, *"And?"* Beryl sighed. "And I'm driving?" he said as a question. When he glanced at Canaan's reflection again, the big guy grinned. Beryl brought his hand down, but Javier took it before he dropped it back into the console.

"Ya'll stop picking on Beryl," Javier said and read the text aloud. "It says, 'Kilmeade, Dr. Claire Boone is the geneticist I told you about. Here's her number and email. She said she would enjoy some diversion. I told her you were a priority friend and my son-in-law. Ya'll be safe on your trip. Jim.'"

The geneticist contact was new news, but Beryl recalled Rafael mentioning *Kilmeade's babies* while in the storm drain the night Isaac was killed. He looked sideways at Kilmeade to gauge his reaction. The Elder sucked his teeth and nodded once in slow motion before returning to his quiet meditation.

Beryl worked to formulate a question and accidentally caught Canaan's eye, who winked. The wink said it all—the Elder knew Beryl was dying to hear more, but it was fun to watch him squirm. Beryl opened his mouth to ask, but thankfully, Javier jumped in.

"Elder Kilmeade, what do you think Rafael will do with them?"

"He'll leave it to Rafa," Canaan answered for his partner and Beryl took a chance in the next lull.

"I saw the key and the note. What's it about?"

Javier again took the lead. "In 1900, Kilmeade met a Cow who was a scientist, a pioneer in genetics and DNA, doing her research at a university in Dallas. Kilmeade and this doctor did experiments on his sperm to see why he couldn't procreate like the Fathers."

Javier paused and neither Elder interjected. They remained quiet, looking out the windows into the night. Beryl's brow furrowed at the amazing news—never in his long life had he ever pondered such a thing. The Fathers were fertile, the brethren were not. That was a fact. What had the Elder been thinking? It simply did not compute.

Javier commiserated with a nod to Beryl's reflection in the mirror. "Kilmeade and the doctor were able to fertilize some of the eggs. They prepared the samples for future technology and Kilmeade squirreled them away. That key represents the locker the samples are waiting in."

Beryl turned to see Kilmeade's profile. He was facing front, one arm on the window ledge and the other on the inside arm rest. A tiny smirk hit his mouth when he knew he was being watched. "You succeeded?" Beryl asked, glancing from the dark road ahead to the Elder beside him.

Behind him, Canaan popped his head with something papery. "Drive us toward the industrial center, B. I'm getting a feeling."

Beryl nodded and numbly took the exit for the bypass, still wondering what it meant that Elder Kilmeade might have offspring somewhere awaiting a bolt of lightning.

"Beryl, let's think about that later, okay?" Canaan said and looked out his window again. "Let's concentrate on finding our brethren who are here now."

"Okay," Beryl responded already compartmentalizing out of necessity. They had left Tuscaloosa at 8 p.m. and after grabbing a bite, they arrived in Jackson by eleven. Their first official night of the hunt and already, Canaan had a *feeling*. In ten minutes, Beryl reached the airport outskirts and slowed to await directions.

Canaan closed his eyes and turned his face to the window.

"Pull over right here," Kilmeade said and Beryl complied.

"Good boy! So obedient!" Canaan jibed in his usual teasing tone and climbed out of the truck. Beryl opened his door to exit and Canaan prepared to plant another painful noogie on his head. Beryl ducked.

"Shit! What a Nancy!" Canaan laughed and joined Kilmeade on the away-side. "I'm gonna put him in a skirt, I swear."

Beryl ignored his remarks, but Javier spoke up for him anyway.

"Geez, Canaan, leave him alone," Javier said stepping down. "I'm serious. *Com-a-rad-a-rie*. Say it with me. Damn." Javier didn't look at Beryl, but did come stand beside him.

"Mommy got mad," Canaan said, looking upward.

The black sky revealed few stars due to their proximity to the airport. Javier stood close enough to Beryl that their elbows made contact, but he didn't move away. Considering how much he hated the guy leading up to 11/13, Beryl marveled at the man's generous disposition toward him. Javier glanced over, gave him a *this-is-going-to-work* grin, and looked back to the Elders. Canaan and Kilmeade had been facing away, but they turned as a unit and looked wistfully over Beryl and Javier's heads.

"Two of our brethren are nearby. They're in a very bad state..."

Beryl thought it only fair that the Elders refer to them as *brethren;* after all, the 11/13 bunch did not voluntarily desert their birthright.

Canaan nodded in agreement. "Let's get closer." Canaan stepped quickly to the Yukon. "I'll drive. You two in back."

Beryl climbed in to the passenger's side rear and once Javier closed his door, Canaan hit the gas.

"Turn up here," Kilmeade said pointing ahead. They had been circling the airport and were turning into a residential area. Barely had they gone a mile and Canaan made a noise of surprise, checked his mirrors, and made a U-turn in the two-lane road. Aged street lamps revealed a rural expanse on the right and dilapidated houses on the left. The Elder pulled far onto the shoulder and shut off the truck. When he hopped out, Beryl followed suit and all four met in the shadow of the Yukon away from the road.

"In there," Canaan said and Kilmeade followed his line of sight.

"I'm picking up telepathy from one of them—he is much slower to transform," Kilmeade said softly and looked at Javier. "Are you armed?"

Javier patted his middle and Beryl hoped they didn't need a gun on this adventure. He'd been shot as a Rakum and it was bad enough then. Without meaning to, he glanced at Canaan. The Elder caught his eye with a mischievous grin.

"I know!" Beryl beat him to it. Canaan chuckled and turned back to Kilmeade. Any time a gun and Beryl were mentioned together, Canaan brought up the time the Elder shot him in retaliation for attacking his mate. *Whatever.* Beryl had moved on and he hoped one day, Canaan would, too.

"Follow our lead," Kilmeade said under his breath and had already headed into the brush.

Beryl clicked on his flashlight and jogged beside Javier. The overgrown path caused them both to move with caution. With the Elders twenty feet ahead, Beryl fell in behind Javier when the trail narrowed. Water ran close by and beyond his vision, tall deciduous trees surrounded their location.

Beryl's footfalls remained steady and rhythmic; being mostly mortal hadn't sapped his cardio endurance. He grinned at the thought and at that moment, Javier stumbled and caught himself a few feet ahead. He turned his face to speak, but both Elders stopped jogging and Javier collided with Canaan.

Canaan did not acknowledge the slip, he and Kilmeade staring ahead, holding the exact same posture. Beryl shined his flashlight to the grass at his feet to see the Rakum in the moonlight and it was as he thought—they were beginning to look very much alike. Not in facial features, but in an unquantifiable way, they looked like the same person. Beryl blinked, shook his head and lifted his light to illuminate the space before them.

"Okay, I got it," Canaan said in a low voice and turned. "Boys, see that chimney poking out of the trees? Don't shine your light on it, just look." When Beryl and Javier nodded, he continued in a low voice. "A shed and it's not light-tight. They've been holing up there, transforming, burned, but alive."

Kilmeade took a step away. "We need to hurry," he said and then walked with purpose toward the trees.

"These guys are likely insane. Stay behind me," Canaan instructed.

With matching nods, Beryl and Javier followed, using Canaan as a shield. They reached the tin shed enveloped by trees and Kilmeade approached the slanted door.

"Itt vagyunk, hogy segítsünk," he said at a conversational volume, telling them in Rakum Hungarian that they had come to help.

"Ki? Fő?" a man's voice returned asking if they were Elders. Out of the corner of his eye, Beryl noted Javier's hand under his jacket near the butt of his gun.

"Elder Kilmeade and Elder Canaan," Kilmeade said and put his hand to the door. "We are coming in." With a caution glance to Beryl, he pushed open the crooked door.

Beryl and Javier stood quietly and the two Elders entered, both ducking to fit the low clearance. The building could not have been more than fourteen feet deep and the roof sagged lower than seven. A shuffle sounded from the dark recesses and then a masculine "oomph." Beryl looked at Javier and neither of them breathed.

Beryl's lips parted to say something, but what could he say? The Elders knew more than he ever would about their business.

"You want to help them, too, eh?" Javier whispered with an excited grin. Beryl didn't return his grin, but he almost had. Suddenly, Canaan burst out of the door dragging a dark form behind him.

"Here you go, brother," he growled with effort and once he cleared the building, Beryl noted his captive trussed like a rodeo calf. "Whoa, dogey, whoa," Canaan said, now chuckling. Whatever stress he experienced in the shed had passed.

Kilmeade stepped out next, his hand on the shoulder of a young man with dark skin and bright hazel eyes. He approached Javier and Beryl, pulling the man with him while Canaan knelt beside the other, speaking in low tones.

"This is Kamron. One of Elder Tomás' pups." Kilmeade did not remove his hand from the man and Beryl nodded to the stranger. Javier inhaled and pointed at his face.

"I think I know you," he said and squint his eyes.

"You do," the man said, his voice raspy and carrying an evil edge. "Tomás brought us to Elder Roman's bunker a few times."

Beryl watched Javier's reaction. He would be speaking of Assembly, when all Rakum were called for mandatory meeting in Nevada. This Rakum seemed angry and unbalanced and Beryl wasn't sure how he discerned it, unless he hadn't yet fully transformed.

"I know you, too," Kamron said to Beryl, flicking a dark gaze his way. "Beryl and Meryl—ate shit for the Elders. *Judas Priest!* You two loved to suck—"

Kamron was silenced by a violent blow to the side of the head that sent him slamming into the damp earth. Kilmeade returned to his quiet stance and crossed his arms, looking off into the night.

Beryl wasn't offended by Kamron's insults, but had been taken aback by the Elder's savage reaction. The flattened Rakum worked himself into a kneeling position as bile dribbled from his lips. Beryl didn't meet his eye and when upright, the transforming Rakum looked up to those standing.

"That was fun," he remarked holding a maniacal grin. "Musta hit a nerve there with your handsome girlfriend..."

Beryl's eye flicked to Kilmeade, who stared calmly into the night, a slight smirk on his lips.

A glutton for negative attention, Kamron tried again. "What's this fairy clan of assholery doing out here, anyway?"

Barely had the last syllable left his mouth before Kilmeade squeezed Kamron's shoulder until an audible crack sounded in the small clearing.

"Ow, Master! SHIT!" Kamron hissed and sat on his rump, legs kicked out before him and stared up at those standing. "JUST BREAK IT!" he howled, his hand flying to the painful joint.

Javier knelt down and waited for the Rakum to lift his gaze. Kamron resisted and looked instead around the clearing, his gaze dancing off Beryl and finally landing on the dirt before him.

"Listen, we came to help you," Javier said, dipping his head, begging for an eye connection. "You guys are in bad shape. We can get you to shelter. Connect you with your brethren..."

"I HAVE ALL I NEED RIGHT HERE!" he bellowed and Beryl jerked his gaze to Kilmeade, but the Elder simply looked on.

"Kamron," Javier said and dropped out of his squat to rest fully on his knees, "You're burned up. Do you see that? You need medical care."

"These magnificent apes can heal me and move along. Apparently, the Elders are immune..." he mumbled, ducking a fraction as if expecting another belting. But again, Kilmeade was not disturbed by his words.

"They will. Look at Elder Canaan," Javier said and leaned over to see Canaan and the bound man. Kamron twisted at the waist, leaning on his palms to see behind him. Canaan did seem to be healing the man from something or other, hands on his torso, and looking into his face.

"Frankie's not a Rakum anymore," Kamron said. "I tried to finish him off, but ass-hat number one interrupted me."

Javier looked upwards, but Kilmeade was now looking far off. He looked to Beryl and seemed unsure how to proceed.

Beryl shrugged. "He doesn't want our help. Maybe we'll alter our mission to only help Rakum who want assistance." Beryl met Kamron's eye and the stranger winked and flipped his tongue lasciviously. Beryl grimaced.

"Elder Kilmeade," he said and stood. Kilmeade didn't look at him, but he continued nonetheless. "I think we should heal his injuries and move along. If I was Kamron, I wouldn't want to be coerced." He looked at Javier when the Elder continued to ignore him. "Kamron will figure it out. He's a survivor."

"Upsie-daisie," Canaan said with a comical noise of effort behind them. The man he'd been helping followed behind and Beryl only saw his leg and foot, shielded by the Elder's body.

"Frankie's coming with us." Canaan appeared beside Kilmeade and stood shoulder to shoulder with him. Once more, Beryl did a double-take. When posing side-by-side, the two Elders seemed identical somehow. Beryl wondered over it long enough that Canaan grinned at him and stepped close.

"Under the stars, you look so beautiful," Canaan sang and grabbed Beryl by the head. "I will dance with you by the light of the mooooon..." He ruffled Beryl's hair. "You look so worried! What's wrong?"

Beryl opened his mouth, but Kilmeade beat him to it.

"Beryl said leave Kamron to his devices. We should only help those who want it and not help anyone by force."

Beryl's eyes widened with surprise; the Elder had been listening and had considered his advice.

"Yeah, Beryl knows. He has insight we don't have." Canaan rubbed his head one more time and stepped back to Kilmeade's side. "Good call, B. Speak up. You're here for a purpose."

"Canaan is right," Kilmeade said and leaned down to lift Kamron off the ground by his neck. "Excuse us."

Kilmeade yanked the man away from the clearing and disappeared into the cabin. Beryl heard him yelp once and fall silent. The events of the past several minutes rolled past Beryl's memory as he watched the shed door. Javier spoke to Canaan in low tones and then to Frankie, who had been unshackled and was being led to the Yukon. Beryl overheard him thanking Canaan for healing him. And then for saving his life. Apparently, Kamron had truly been trying to end him just when they arrived.

Beryl sighed and rubbed his eyes. Just as he turned back to the truck, Kilmeade emerged from the darkness of the tin building. He strolled up, to, and then past Beryl without looking over, but he did not try to conceal his appearance—the robin-egg-blue shine to his eyes, swollen ruby-red lips, and fingers that had elongated into claws—Kilmeade had taken a Dying Buzz. No more Kamron.

《回》

Canaan watched Frankie the new human clamber into the Yukon and then stepped over to Javier.

"Frankie will receive all the advice and help you give him. His mind is intact."

Javier asked, "Want us to pick you up later?"

Canaan checked his cell screen. "Three a.m., right here."

Javier nodded and returned to the truck.

"You okay?" Canaan asked Beryl reading concern in his expression. "You're not upset about—" Canaan hooked a thumb toward Kilmeade and his Nosferatu impression.

Beryl half-smiled. "No, I was surprised at Kamron's rage."

"Ah," Canaan said softly. "Specifically rage directed at little Beryl."

"Yeah," he said with a faraway look. He shook it off and grinned, meeting Canaan's eye. "I think this is going to work."

Canaan agreed and clapped his shoulder, turning him for the Yukon. "Go keep an eye on Javier; you guys are a good team."

"Huh," Beryl said with a nod. "I guess so."

"We're proud of you guys. Get going and we'll catch up with you in a few hours." Canaan waited while he settled in the truck and with a small nod from them both, they pulled onto the dark road. Behind him, Kilmeade chuckled into his hand.

"What's so funny, Mr. Hyde? You're not making fun of old Canaan are you?" he asked as he reached his side.

Kilmeade dropped his hand and continued to laugh. His giggles rolled into guffaws and he leaned over, pressing his palms into his thighs to laugh harder.

"Let's get in the trees, idiot," Canaan said, chuckling. He'd seen Kilmeade much worse off than this and uncontrolled joviality had always been a side-effect of taking a Dying Buzz. "Help me find some blood."

"Bluh! Bluh!" his partner mumbled in a Bela Legosi accent, suddenly studying his own hand as if it were a new appendage.

"You are pitiful," Canaan chortled. "Methinks Kamron gave you flashbacks," he said and jabbed Kilmeade's near shoulder. Right after the mortal tragedy of 9/11, they'd run into the kid on an Elder outing. They weren't kind to him then, either.

"Flashback!" Kilmeade repeated with jazz-hands. Then he giggled and rolled his eyes. "He tastes a little off these days. Like a margarita made with rum instead of tequila," Kilmeade said around seriously elongated canines. "With a shot of vermouth..."

"Shit, you're wasted," Canaan joked finally pulling him into the trees. *"Giggle this way, Master,"* he sent telepathically and began a slow jog into the woods hauling Kilmeade along by the bicep. Kilmeade kept up with him, reaching for the odd branch now and then, lolling back his head as he loped along to open his mouth and stick out his tongue. When they had run nearly a mile, they hit another slow road between the airport and the outskirts of town. A trailer park sat just ahead and Canaan brought them both to a halt in the shadow of a forgotten barn.

"Okay, okay," Kilmeade sent silently. *"I'm coming around. I'm..."* and he giggled into his hand. Canaan shook his head smiling.

"That's okay, enjoy yourself," Canaan said as he scanned the mobile homes a few yards away. Dozens upon dozens of hearts beating, adults chatting, yelling, singing, romancing—his ears picked it all up and expertly, he sorted them. Somewhere in that pile of a hundred humans was one he could tap. By the time he found his mark, Kilmeade would likely be sober enough to come along.

"I'm sober now," Kilmeade said a little too loudly and Canaan whipped his face around to shush him. *"I'm sober now,"* he repeated in Canaan's mind.

Canaan faced front again and closed his eyes. He and Kilmeade stood against the barn's east wall in complete shadow, so he forgot about being seen by passersby and allowed his full attention to scout out the mortals in the park.

One male voice arced several times over the minutes and when he focused down on it, he heard individual words the man barked to whomever. *"She done that sheet for the last time! I'm gonna fine her an' give her two of dees!"*

Kilmeade held up his fists pugilist style, listening to the same banter.

"He's gonna give her two of dees," Canaan sent to Kilmeade without turning.

"After he fines her, of course," Kilmeade teased, still air-boxing. *"She's done way too much sheet."*

Canaan decided to find the guy and he turned to see Kilmeade had moved away. In that short moment, his brother was on the other side of the barn looking at the roadway. *"What is it?"*

"Heads up," Kilmeade sent from the shadows. At the same instant, Canaan discerned an approaching menace. From his location, Kilmeade saw them visually. Canaan heard and sensed them and Kilmeade filled in the direction. *"Twenty yards back the way we came, there's three of them. Oh, they are baddies..."*

Canaan took one last longing look toward the trailer park.

"My dear Elder Canaan, wouldn't you rather work for your dinner? These baddies are big..." Kilmeade sent with a snicker and quickly added, *"They have*

knives. Oh, dear."

Kilmeade's mental relay carried some humor, but his Dying Buzz had passed. Canaan jogged toward his partner who had reached the hooligans and prepared to make himself known.

"Don't be dramatic, brother," Canaan sent over. *"We have no cover..."* Canaan reached them and Kilmeade engaged all three.

The ne'er-do-wells were early twenties of varying builds, but all at least six feet. The man in the center carried a box cutter and he swiped it at Kilmeade when he refused to hand over his wallet.

"I only need one," Canaan sent and grabbed the largest of the three from behind. With a carefully measured jolt of energy, the man seized, twitched, and lost consciousness. Kilmeade followed his lead and repeated the move on the dark-skinned man holding the box cutter. That left Mr. Lucky.

The tussle had occurred in the open and being behind the bewildered bad guy, Canaan grabbed him around the middle and dragged him to the nearest tree line. It was dark and the area deserted, but just in case anyone happened to look over, they would not see him in the woods. Canaan covered the man's mouth.

"Shhh, shhh, little buddy," he whispered in his ear from behind. "You're safe. I'll take care of you." He dragged him backward further into the dark and didn't hurt him... much.

16, APR 3

Kilmeade was three hundred and eighty-one years old and didn't dream, so when a being shining too brightly to see its outline stepped down to join them in the basement, he assumed he was awake. Kilmeade sat up on the daybed and put his feet to the floor. Ten feet away, Canaan snoozed on the extra-long sofa lying on his front, his arm over the side, knuckles buried in the thick rug. Kilmeade thought to rouse him, but the light being shook its head.

"He will not awaken," the being said deep inside Kilmeade's mind. The voice was masculine, vibrating like a cello string just released. *"Kilmeade, the goodness of God endures forever."*

Kilmeade rubbed his eyes and held his breath. Was this real? And if he was awake, did that make this thing an angel?

"Your time in the flesh has come and gone," the being said, and although his words were harsh, they filled Kilmeade with peace. He wondered at his interpretation; why did he want to *cheer* when informed he was dead?

"...But the goodness of God endures forever, selah."

Kilmeade looked again at Canaan who rubbed his nose before his hand flopped back to the floor.

"For centuries, you eat up God's people as you eat bread, yet He stoops low to whisper His truths in your ear..."

Kilmeade narrowed his eyes. "I am helping my brethren find peace."

"True peace comes from the Lord and your peace is at hand."

Kilmeade narrowed his eyes. "At hand? Now?"

"Take and eat," the being said and held out a shining appendage.

Kilmeade looked into its hand with interest. It held a bright green apple. Kilmeade gingerly grasped it and the crisp and acidic flesh went down his throat smoothly. Kilmeade slipped to his knees, aware he had not been prostrate in centuries. Even the Fathers did not require an Elder to kneel, except under extreme chastisement.

"Your God will deliver your soul from death that you may walk with the saints in the land of the living."

"What am I not doing that the God of the mortals wants me to do?" Kilmeade asked wondering why he had been singled out.

"Remember, believe and come home," the being said. *"You were My son first and I love you. Remember. Believe. Come home."*

Kilmeade swirled his tongue as tiny flecks of the apple irritated his palate. He spat them into his palm, considered them blindly, his mind looping, *"Remember. Remember. Remember..."*

When Kilmeade looked up, the being had disappeared. He stood and turned a full circle. *"I remember, but what does it mean?"* he asked himself. Behind him, Canaan sat up.

"Brother, ignore it. It's a dream," Canaan mumbled. Kilmeade didn't respond and his partner turned away with a *humph.* "Go to sleep."

Kilmeade sat on the edge of the mattress and stared at his palms. The bit of apple on his tongue proved the visitation was real. Also, the light-being wasn't completely unfamiliar. It wasn't time to show Canaan, but it would be soon. Relaxing onto the mattress, Kilmeade pondered the nights to come, as well as when he should tell Canaan his secret.

《回》

"If this is Beryl, call me back. Simon 555-667-9090."

Beryl re-read the text message and looked around the quiet house. Javier hadn't left his room, probably sleeping in since the first hunt kept them out until 5 a.m. Beryl had risen, started a pot of coffee, and plopped onto the sectional sofa to play with his phone. And now this.

When he read "unknown number," he never would have dreamed it would be Simon Miller. The unrelenting visceral draw he held for Javier's Cow mercifully dissipated when Ta'avah's death excised the Rakum spirit from them all. Still, the memory of his obscene behavior toward the young man had not been forgotten. What could they possibly have to say to one another now?

Beryl's finger hovered over the number and his eyes glazed, recalling his last minutes with Simon. The man would have accompanied Beryl into the night had the evening gone differently. Maybe that's why he called. Maybe he needed the closure a simple chat might provide. *Maybe* Beryl would benefit as well. He didn't feel guilty, *per se,* but he didn't feel good about it, either. Decided, Beryl retrieved his calf-length duster from the foyer closet and stepped to the back porch. The deck furniture remained winter-proofed with covers on every chair, so he leaned against the wall out of sight of anyone in the house. Taking a deep breath, he pressed the number. The phone rang three times before a man said hello.

"It's Beryl," he said in as normal a voice as he could muster.

"Oh, hey," Simon said just as somber. "I texted every number that I had from that week." Simon offered a tight chuckle.

Beryl looked straight ahead an allowed a small noise.

"Yeah," Simon continued. "You heard I went back to the Sox."

"Mm-hm."

"And things are good at home," Simon added quietly. After a sigh, he continued. "How are you? You know, with the change and all."

Beryl sucked his teeth and narrowed his eyes. "Why did you call me?"

"I'm not sure," he said.

"Well, it's weird," Beryl snapped after a long exhale.

"I didn't call for any kind of apology," Simon muttered. "None of that was our fault. My behavior or yours..."

"Whatever," Beryl said under his breath and pulled the phone from his ear to consider the end-call button. Simon's next response relayed tinny through the earpiece.

"I called to tell you that I let it go. To see if you had, too." Simon sighed a frustrated sound. "I want to tell you something."

Beryl stared at the phone in his palm, the red hang-up icon prominent. "Hurry up, then," he said finally.

"Why after five months do I still wonder how you're doing? It doesn't make sense. I'm busy. I'm playing great. My wife loves me again. My daughter is an angel. I'm never bored." Simon's voice arced louder. "Why do I ask myself every single night before I go to sleep, 'I wonder how Beryl's doing?'"

Beryl shook his head and said aloud, "I can't say."

"It's because I miss you."

"What?" Beryl said with surprise and returned the phone to his ear.

Simon quickly clarified. "I meant that I miss you as a person. I told you then—if you weren't being a miserable jerk, you were okay."

Despite himself, Beryl huffed. "Right." He tried to think about Simon in the present tense, as if the man stood on the deck with him today. Would they get along? Beryl shrugged; his general feeling for the guy was positive.

"You still there?"

"Yeah, just trying to imagine what you want from me."

"I want to be friends," Simon said. "Of all the people I know, you keep coming to mind and that makes me think God has a hand in it."

"Huh. God," Beryl sighed and looked at his fingernails, imagining the two of them knocking back beers in a Boston pub in the off-season.

"Have you thought about me?"

"Maybe. Shit, I don't know." Beryl glanced to the sliding door absently. If he thought about Simon the past five months, he squashed the recollection immediately. "What about Stu Loudon? He still around?" Stuart had been a particularly obsessed Cow that latched onto Simon when his Cow-ness departed.

Simon forced a chuckle. "No, he's gone. Guap, Polly, and Rafael were all here for a while and they despised him."

Beryl smiled to the side. "Understandable. I didn't care for him in any capacity."

"I gave him half-a-million dollars to leave," Simon said with a nervous laugh. "I haven't heard from him since."

"Smart," Beryl agreed.

"Beryl," Simon said, his tone suddenly serious. "We went through a lot—together *and* apart. I think we'd enjoy commiserating with each other. If you don't agree, it's fine. You still have all your Rakum pals…"

Beryl inhaled, feeling he should interject, but Simon barreled on.

"But if you have any doubt at all, then why the hell not get together and see? We have nothing to lose."

Beryl chewed his lip. He *was* enjoying the conversation. Discussing his Rakum past with Javier, Roman, David, and the Elders felt natural because they were all Rakum. Would it be just as cathartic to have familiar recollection with a Cow? Beryl chuckled.

"What?" Simon asked. "You thinking it over?"

"I guess I am."

"Good," Simon said quietly.

"A lot of crazy stuff is going on even now," Beryl mumbled thinking of all the water under the bridge in just a few months and among his Rakum friends, he was the low man. Simon put him on an even level—that counted more than he realized the longer they spoke. "Maybe I feel the same way, shit, I'm enjoying our talk," Beryl said with a smile sneaking into his voice.

"We'll take it slow," Simon replied.

"When should I call you back?" Beryl peeked through the glass door. In the living room, Javier was moving toward him.

"Whenever you're free," Simon answered easily.

"Okay," Beryl returned as Javier pulled open the sliding door.

"Oh, sorry," he said when he saw Beryl on the phone.

"I'll text you," Beryl told Simon and hung up. He pocketed the phone and clapped Javier's arm. "I made some coffee."

Still waking up, Javier looked at the hand on his bicep and then turned back. "That's super. I think I'm going back to bed."

Beryl watched him shuffle to the stairs and then opened the message center to text, "Let's keep it between us."

Immediately, the dots informed him Simon was replying. Simon sent, "Agreed. Later."

Beryl grinned with a nod and deleted the message. Nothing wrong with making friends. Supposedly, it was one of the best things about being mortal.

17, May 4, Manhattan

A text from Roman informed Rafael that the Rakum Hunt had moved to Dallas, Texas, after a month in Mississippi. He grinned to himself and pocketed the phone. Knowing his brethren were getting help gave him great peace. Iago had seen the message as well and made a noise of surprise.

"And?" Rafa prodded. "The Elders are changing. One cannot maintain a Rakum heart without a Rakum spirit, sí?"

Iago shrugged. *"Sí, bueno,"* he said, wisely letting it go.

Rafael and Santiago had been in Manhattan two days before they reached Grand Central Terminal to retrieve Kilmeade's property. Rafael had been to the Big Apple dozens of times in his long life, but Iago hadn't visited at all. In addition, Rafael had never seen the city in the day, so upon arrival, they squeezed in as many tourist attractions as possible. They had reached day three and were ready to face the task of destroying whatever sat in locker 1191.

High noon and the terminal crawled with people. Blinding sunlight streamed through the windows as tourists and New Yorkers blended, going about their business. Rafael pulled Iago along more than once when he became distracted by the architecture.

"The ceiling!" he said, stopped, and gawked, his head back as far as it would go. Rafael let him look, unsure how much longer his cancer would allow him to travel. "Those are the constellations. *Stupendo,*" he whispered and turned to Rafael, his eyes watering. "Thank you for this wonderful life, Master. I wouldn't have had it any other way."

Rafael nodded, not offended that he referred to him as master when he was human now himself. He placed a hand on Iago's shoulder and looked at the ceiling with him. The travelers flowed around them and for five minutes they discussed the carvings and general craftsmanship that went into every inch.

As sometimes happened because of his approachable manner, a stranger stopped and spoke to Iago as he stared upwards. The woman agreed and complimented him on his handsome son. Iago's response was always the same, nod and smile. Rafael had looked thirty years old for the past century, so it charmed them both that up until Iago was thirty, people assumed he was Rafael's son. Then for a while, strangers saw them as brothers, which both of them enjoyed. Now he was Iago's son to anyone who looked on.

Rafael patted Iago's back. "How do you feel?"

"Good. Really good." Iago bumped Rafael's arm. "Come, son, let's find that locker," he said smiling.

"Yes, father," Rafael returned, matching his grin.

Rafael walked with purpose and as they covered the distance, they passed tunnels leading to the individual trains being loaded, unloaded, or awaited. Iago peeked into each one, which brought a smile to Rafael's lips. He had raised Iago from age five so the man dying of the most ravaging of diseases was his son in every way that mattered. Rafael refocused and reached the huge bays of lockers.

"This aisle," he said softly and Iago followed him, reading a pamphlet he had picked up from the floor. When they reached 1191, Rafael pulled the key free and unlocked it.

Iago peered inside. "That doesn't look right."

Rafael paused, numbly checking the locker number. He then reached inside and pulled out a handwritten note. The script curled and flowed, not in a feminine way, but with an Old World effect. And it had been written in the Rakum language. *"Az orvos elküldi a tisztelettel,"* Rafael said aloud. Iago touched his sleeve.

"What does that mean?"

Rafael said nothing and flipped the paper over.

"Rafa?"

Out of old habit, he pressed the paper to his nose, but of course, smelled only dust. "Hand me that envelope," he said to Iago who fished Roman's original manila envelope from his back pocket. Rafael unfolded it and and carefully inserted the odd message. "Elder Kilmeade may be able to discern who wrote this."

"What's going on?" Iago asked with respect. Rafael was still processing what the words might mean to the Elders. He mumbled, "Someone has taken Kilmeade's materials from this locker and I think it was a Rakum. We have to call Canaan. Follow me."

Rafael turned and headed for a quiet corner of the building where the cell phone reception would support his call. Five minutes later, Rafael found a corner designed for cell users and he leaned against the wall to dial

Canaan. It was nearing 1 p.m. and he would be in the dark, but probably not asleep; Elders slept little, as he learned from Kilmeade not too long ago.

"What's happening, handsome?" the congenial Rakum said when he answered the ring.

"Elder Canaan, is Elder Kilmeade with you?" he asked. "There's a problem with his babies."

A few moments passed and Kilmeade addressed him on the line. "Rafa," he said and waited.

"I opened the locker and found only a note inside. It says in Rakum, 'the doctor sends her regards.'"

Kilmeade did not respond for a moment. When he did, his voice barely carried. "Do you have the note?"

"Yes, Master," Rafael said and closed his eyes for the correction Kilmeade would send, but he didn't acknowledge the slip.

"Can you get here tonight?"

"Yes," Rafael said and motioned to Iago to arrange airfare on his cell. "Dallas-Fort Worth," he said to his friend and returned to the call. "I will text Canaan our arrival information."

"Kazak," Kilmeade said.

"*Kazak*," Rafael whispered and the Elder disconnected the call.

《回》

"Dear, you need to eat more. If you feel faint, get some protein. If you're nauseous, eat a cracker. It's not that hard." In full condescending-doctor-mode, Mrs. Bushman sighed for Chloe to hear. "How are you sleeping? All these things can result from stress. Are you stressed?"

Chloe stared at the phone and returned it to her ear. "No, Mom, I'm not stressed," she lied. In reality, she hadn't been resting or feeling well since Kilmeade left. "I'm just having second thoughts about this class. I should have gone with Kilmeade."

"That Canaan went with him, I hope?"

"Yes, Mom, they're business partners and this is a business trip, *duh*," Chloe replied realizing only her mother could cause her to regress into a pre-teen.

"Good. You don't need to be alone with that man. He's very forward. I wouldn't trust him for a minute."

"Methinks you doth protest too much, Mother," Chloe joked.

"What does that mean?"

129

"You seemed to enjoy his attention pretty well the night you were here. He said you showed him some new dance moves, some close and tight ones." Chloe decided to exaggerate a little; her mother brought out the worst in her. "He said you grabbed his butt."

"WHAT?" Chloe's mother shouted and instantly regained control of her tone. She spoke the rest in staccato syllables. "I certainly did *not* grab any part of that man's anatomy."

"Did you have a dream about him?" Chloe asked and then instantly regretted it, not wanting her mother to think too hard about that night.

"Wilhelmina Chloe Bushman!"

"Anyway, about the class," Chloe said to change the subject, "I'm probably dropping it. Don't worry, I'm paying for it."

"Kilmeade is paying for it," Chloe's mother retorted. "Speaking of, when will you two put that Canaan out and be a real married couple? Men don't have roommates at that age. It's time to focus on family and future. Time to make some grandchildren."

Chloe suppressed a snicker. Not only was Kilmeade infertile, but Chloe didn't think her mother would be a good granny, especially if the child ended up being a Chloe clone.

"Mom, *that Canaan* might never move out and Kilmeade's not able to father children." Chloe grinned with victory as her mother did not reply for a few seconds.

"I'll never understand why you're so mean to your mother," she finally responded.

Chloe deflated. "It's true, Mom, I'm sorry. Kilmeade's infertile. Facts are facts. As for Canaan, they're practically brothers." Chloe sighed. "If it helps, he lives on the other side of the house," she lied again. "It's a huge house..."

"It's a nice place, very ritzy, but you didn't think this through." Chloe's mother had returned to lecture mode. "Dear, wealth doesn't make a man a good husband. A good husband comes from upbringing, from breeding. Something is dreadfully off with both of those men. If you can't see it you might be a little off yourself."

"Gotta go, Mom. Bye." Chloe disconnected the call. Did her mother just say she was crazy? It wouldn't be the first time her mom passed judgment on her in non-motherly ways. Anyway, the joke was on her; all Rakum Elders were bred from human royal bloodlines. *So, nunh.*

Absently wondering about the identity of Kilmeade's "royal" mother, Chloe hit the favorites on her iPhone and *Km (C)* sat at the top. Kilmeade refused to carry a cell phone so any time she wanted to call or text, it had to be to Canaan. She checked her watch and hit send.

"Chloe," Canaan said on the second ring. "Do you have an emergency?"

Chloe frowned. "No." She kept her answer short to suit the Rakum Elder personality.

"Okay, good," he said and she thought he sounded relieved. "Kilmeade says, precious angel, don't call unless you have an emergency. You can text love notes and know I received them." Canaan paused. "That's the end of the message."

Chloe took a deep breath. *Tick-tock,* she could almost hear them saying. "Okay. I'm sorry. Ya'll be safe," she said and disconnected before Canaan did. *Showed you,* she thought with a head shake. *Happy to know the rules, Master.*

Chloe dropped the phone on the comforter. She wasn't mad, just lonely. She hadn't expected Kilmeade to speak on the phone with her; it never entered her mind that he might. He kept himself very far away, distinct, separated. Even more so than Canaan. *He doesn't want to appear human.* Chloe considered that notion. In Beth Rider's novel, *The Rabbit,* the Rakum protagonist explained it in detail—they were born and raised believing that they themselves were gods. *What a head trip.*

Chloe sighed. She wanted to be sad for them, but a demon spawned their race. God was merciful to allow them to live after Ta'avah was erased. Javier told her the remaining Rakum were allowed to live because they were born to a woman. They each had an eternal soul. *Kilmeade and Canaan each have a soul.* Chloe lay back on top of the covers.

"God, I don't want Kilmeade to spend eternity without you," she prayed internally, staring at the vaulted ceiling and picturing Kilmeade's paralyzing gaze. *"I'm full of myself and so selfish, but use me to save his soul."*

Chloe examined again what she had just prayed; God was going to fulfill it, she had no doubt. What would she have to go through? God allowed her to be abducted, terrified, and violently attacked by a monster, all because otherwise, she never would have seen His love and truth. *What will He want me to do to save Kilmeade's soul?* Chloe turned off the lamp and filled her mind with memories of Kilmeade and his kisses and not with what might come next.

18, May 4, Dallas

Kilmeade and Canaan refused the boys' invitation to find a restaurant for dinner. Instead, they jerked a heavy desk away from the wall in the rented house's office and challenged each other to several arm wrestling matches.

Javier had spared no expense on the short-time Texas rental, nabbing them a fully-furnished luxury four-bedroom monstrosity in the suburbs of Dallas, two floors, with a finished basement. In the month they'd been hunting, they had discovered and assisted twenty-two of their brethren. Only Kamron from the first hunt went sour; the rest experienced varying degrees of success and all of them enjoyed seeing the Elders in full glory.

"Yes, let your mind wander," Canaan whispered. The fifth match was at hand and he clasped his palm in Kilmeade's. Each round, the loser took a double shot of whiskey. Whoever lost the most at the end of the sessions would be pummeled by the winner.

"You can't win, pup," Kilmeade said with exertion. "I will always outrank you, and one doesn't best his master!"

"I'll show you a *pup*, Master," Canaan grunted and put more body weight behind his effort.

"Rafa's coming," Kilmeade whispered, resisting a new burst of power from his companion. "Isn't that wonderful," he said his voice tight with the game, "I've memorized his new human aroma."

"And he is DELICIOUS!" Canaan shouted and at the same time slammed Kilmeade's fist into the desktop. "VICTORY!" he yelled and hopped to his feet. He did a quick touchdown shuffle, spun around, and leaned on the desk, grinning.

Kilmeade lowered his head to his losing arm and laughed. "I let you win... I was thirsty," he said into the desk, his voice muffled.

Canaan chuckled and placed the whiskey by his hand. Kilmeade grabbed it, shot it down, and leaned into the thick cushioned chair.

"Judas Priest, I needed that," he said with a grin. "Rafa's going to be so serious." Kilmeade closed his eyes, mouth still in a half-smile. He hadn't been able to work up any excitement about the possibility of his genetic materials being stolen from the locker. What did it matter?

Canaan stepped to the front door, peeked at Rafa's progress, and pulled it ajar. When he returned to the office, Kilmeade watched his eyes—he was about to comment on the empty locker. Once he plopped back into his chair and leaned back, he did.

"Someone wants to bring your babies to life," he stated.

Kilmeade's internal reaction again was, *so what?*, so he remained silent and regarded Canaan with a glare.

His partner shrugged. "I don't care."

"Good. Neither of us care. Let them have it," Kilmeade said relieved. "You and I know the spirit of Ta'avah isn't there and all our brethren turned mortal. That seed is mortal, too. That is the end of it."

Canaan shrugged, eyes closed. "Don't care."

"My man," Kilmeade laughed as Rafael entered from the hall.

"Are you arm wrestling?" Rafael eyed the cleared desk and re-positioned seating. "Who's winning?" he asked as he headed for Kilmeade. It looked as if he was going to put out his right hand, but thought better of it moments before he initiated the move.

Kilmeade grinned. "Good. And forget it; I'm not hugging you," he said and leaned back further, arms crossed.

"Come close, I'll hug ya," Canaan said and stepped over to grab Rafael into his arms. "Tell me when to stop," he said, squeezing the man enough to prevent his lungs from expanding.

Instead of crying uncle, Rafael held his breath. When his face reddened and Kilmeade wearied of Rafael's stoic gaze, he stood and mentally insisted Canaan release him. Immediately, Canaan dropped his arms. When Rafael took in a few deep breaths, not yet smiling about the joke, Kilmeade clapped him on the back.

"He won't do that again."

"Aw, come on," Canaan whined, but Kilmeade meant it.

"No, it's cool. I'm fine," Rafael said, coughed and stood up straight. "It's fine. I like it," he said with a crooked grin. "Maybe you could wait until I pass out next time, or crack a rib."

Canaan cocked his head to the side. "You sassin' me, boy?"

"Let's see the note," Kilmeade said, disregarding Canaan's fun. Rafael pulled it from his pocket and handed it to him folded. Immediately, Kilmeade recognized the paper. He unfolded it and sure enough, it was his handwriting. He grinned and Canaan stepped closer.

"You wrote it? When? Why?" the Elder asked, always reading his stream of consciousness in their new anomalous condition.

"Call Javier back. I don't want to explain this twice."

Canaan turned to make the call and Kilmeade led Rafael to the living room. A sectional sofa circled the space and he sat on the end. Rafael sat beside him, inches away and leaned over his knees.

"Santiago's back at the hotel," he said with a sad smile. "He's not going to make it much longer. I'm filling his remaining days best I can."

Kilmeade paused, absorbing the pain in his former pet's voice. He tried to identify, but kept missing. Kilmeade sighed and played it as he always had—with truth.

"I can't know what it is like to lose a friend this way." Kilmeade put his left hand to Rafa's near shoulder. "The closest I can come to empathizing is the pain of losing you when you became mortal."

Rafael tipped his chin. "I know. I appreciate you caring."

"Yes, that's right. I *do* care. That's something, right? It matters to me if you are unhappy."

"Let's not talk about it," Rafael said softly. "Self-awareness leads to self-examination, which could cause you to open that door."

Kilmeade stared at Rafa's profile, stunned at his assertion. Where did that come from? Perhaps it was how Rafael came to believe in the God of the mortals—by being sad enough to examine these things. Kilmeade draped his arm across Rafael's shoulders.

"They're headed in," Canaan said entering the room. He didn't sit, but leaned against the bar that separated the space from the kitchen. "Also, that lady doctor texted and left her cell number."

"Google her," Kilmeade said still sitting beside Rafael. A little research on the doctor made sense, especially since Jim Bushman had no idea how odd Kilmeade's experiments had been or how long ago.

Canaan lowered his chin and stared at Kilmeade, eyes up. "I do not *Google*," he scoffed and looked to Rafael. "Have you ever known an Elder to *Google*?"

Rafael grinned and slipped his phone into his hand. "Her name?"

"Claire Boone, geneticist," Kilmeade said close to his ear.

"Got it," Rafa whispered half-smile in place.

So close. Oh-so-close... Kilmeade blinked. *He is so close to the way he had been.* Kilmeade's heart ached anew at the state of his former pet. While Rafael searched the internet, Kilmeade watched his profile. The man knew he was being studied and held his easy grin.

"Hey, brother, it's all good. Let's keep it together."

Canaan's voice. Kilmeade didn't look at him, but nodded his head.

"Seeing Rafa like this..." he sent back and paused. After another few moments, he withdrew his arm from Rafa's shoulders and got to his feet. He positioned himself shoulder to shoulder with Canaan facing the room. *"Looking at Rafa makes me angry at their God."*

"Don't think about it."

In agreement, Kilmeade reordered his thoughts and listened out for the boys. Javier entered first at a brisk walk with Beryl right behind him. The two men had been conversing on the way in about the upcoming topic and when they reached the center of the room, they fell quiet.

"Kilmeade," Rafael said softly and stood to hand over his phone. He hadn't called him by a title, which was a first. Again Kilmeade sighed, but he didn't allow his mind to wander backward.

Dr. Claire Boone's LinkedIn photo revealed an attractive black woman, mid-thirties, with bright brown almond-shaped eyes, shoulder-length black hair coifed in loose waves, and a pouty mouth that reminded him of Chloe. Kilmeade reflexively smiled at the thought of his new mate and always playing, Canaan poked at him in his mind.

"Whipped. Whipped. Whipped," he chanted silently.

Kilmeade ignored him and continued to read the woman's page. All those present waited and he did not rush. When he'd absorbed as much as he desired, he handed the cell back to Rafael and met Javier's eye.

"I wrote this note in 1901," he began and handed the paper to Javier. Beryl also examined it as Kilmeade continued. "Dr. Penny was the only woman in the lab, often complained about her coworkers' harassment. Also, she was half-Chinese which caused additional discrimination." Kilmeade looked to Canaan and prepared to hand off the telling. "I left this note for a gruesome toad of a mortal named Robert Roberts, a despicable character I nearly ended, but missed my chance when I made my attempt."

"Shi-i-i-t..." Canaan shook his head at what he saw in Kilmeade's memory stream. Forever weary of long dissertation, he prompted Canaan to finish in his stead. Canaan picked up without missing a beat.

"This man raped Penny when Kilmeade was out of town. The woman was only a Cow, but she was *Kilmeade's* Cow—his *property*. When he returned and found her in such a state, he set out to end Roberts."

No one spoke and Canaan allowed a pause to watch the rest of Kilmeade's recollection. When he reached the finale, he made a tiny grin and continued.

"When Kilmeade went to the guy's house, he wasn't home, so he left that note on the asshole's pillow..." Canaan wrinkled his nose at Kilmeade and bumped his arm. "He left the note along with the dead bodies of both of his dogs, his Siamese cat, and even the fish from the aquarium."

"The doctor sends her regards," Javier whispered, his eyes round and focused on Kilmeade.

Sporting the same facial expression, Beryl muttered, *"Judas Priest."*

"Kilmeade put Penny on an ocean liner the following night, sending her to her parents. He set her up with Elder Yu in Beijing. End of story." Canaan crossed his arms at his chest and shook his head with chagrin. "Yu, eh? Didn't know him, but I heard he was nasty."

"He was a friend," Kilmeade said with a thank you glance to Canaan. He returned his attention to Rafael, Javier, and Beryl. "I never laid eyes on Roberts and I moved on." Kilmeade shrugged. "I moved my babies periodically. Most recently the Manhattan locker, July 4, 1950."

Javier fell onto the couch nodding his head. "So Robert Roberts could have still been alive in 1950, depending on how old he was then. I'll do some research and see if we can't determine what happened with Dr. Penny and this creep."

"Don't," Kilmeade said and left it at that.

"Leave it alone, Javie," Canaan said. "Let's leave it alone and get about our Rakum hunting."

Javier, Beryl, and Rafael all stared at the Elders as if they'd gone insane. Canaan looked at Kilmeade who shrugged.

"We just don't care. Why should we?" he said and Javier stood.

"Because if someone fertilized your seed and successfully grew a baby, then you have little Kilmeades walking the planet!" Javier's voice grew higher and louder to the last word. Canaan left Kilmeade's side to approach him and put his hand to the back of Javier's neck.

"Whoa, little buddy," Canaan said and gently shook him back and forth. "Your blood pressure's spiking. I can feel it from across the room."

"This is serious, Canaan," Javier retorted and wriggled away. "Come on, Beryl, let's do some digging and see what we can discover about these scientists." Beryl sent a nod to both Elders, waved at Rafa, and was gone.

"Let them go," Kilmeade sent Canaan, who put his hands on his hips and watched them leave the room.

"Do you need anything from me? I'll go see how Iago's doing," Rafael said and crossed to say goodbye.

"He really does smell delicious," Canaan sent to Kilmeade. *"Hint, hint."*

"No, go check on him," Kilmeade said and Rafael bid them both farewell.

"How come he never asks me if I need anything?" Canaan asked with a put-on pout.

"Because he loves *me,* not you," Kilmeade said and spun around to square off with Canaan. "It's time to be pummeled, loser." Kilmeade reached him in a blur of movement and wrapped Canaan into a headlock from behind before he fully realized the game had begun.

Canaan laughed, his knees buckled under Kilmeade's weight and with a yank, he went down. "Okay, okay!" he said chuckling. "Make it count!"

"Oh, I will," Kilmeade sent silently and delivered several blows to Canaan's midsection and he deflected none of them. Two jabs to his kidneys had him on his side on the carpet, still laughing, but out of breath. Kilmeade rolled him onto his front and pinned one beefy arm behind his back. Finally, Canaan tapped the floor. Kilmeade released him and stood to watch Canaan recover. His partner rolled onto his back, blue eyes shining with exhilaration and grinning with white teeth. Only a small trickle of blackish blood unique to the Rakum came from his nose and he wiped it with the heel of his hand. Canaan remained on the floor a minute, catching his breath and then staring up at Kilmeade. A car horn sounded down the street and they listened to the world outside their rented house.

"Let's go find some trouble," Canaan said. Kilmeade put out his hand and yanked him to his feet.

"Oh, yes." Kilmeade straightened his shirt, tucked it into his jeans, and ran his fingers through his shoulder-length hair. Canaan was busy doing the same, but his hair was woefully short, loose blond curls all over his head.

"You're just jealous," Canaan said and gestured for the front door.

"After you, pup," Kilmeade said with a smile. Canaan grinned and they headed out.

《回》

Chloe needed to use the restroom. The urgent reminder slammed her just as she entered the restaurant. With a quick nod to the hostess, she zoomed past and found the bathrooms in the back. The hallway elongated as she walked toward the Ladies' sign, and then it darkened until she could barely see in front of her. Chloe put her hand to the wall; it was slick. *I must be dreaming...*

Chloe stopped walking and rubbed her thumb and forefinger together, the odorless substance slimy, viscous, and snot-like. Chloe wiped her fingers on her jeans and stared into the dark. Up ahead, a line of light shone beneath a door. Chloe stepped forward and slipped, the floor now coated with the same slime. Bracing her feet shoulder-width apart and holding out her arms, she balanced on the slippery mess.

Now what?

As if in response to her thought, the door ahead opened slowly, inch by inch, like in the movies, until a man-shaped shadow filled the frame. Chloe didn't speak to it, her dream-intuition telling her she was in danger. It moved toward her, but not walking and not floating. The man-thing wavered back and forth, moving forward snake-like with a faint hissing echo. Chloe shifted her feet and was thrown into thrashing frantically to stay upright. One, two, three seconds she fought her own legs as they placed and replaced her feet in the slime. Then she was down, her rear and both palms in the goo.

The man-snake-thing reached her position and lifted her off the floor with strong arms. "Sweetnessssss..." it hissed, pulling her close to its body as it swiveled to return through the door. "Come with me... my sssssweet, sssssssweet deliciousssssss angel...."

Chloe clutched her sticky hands at her chest, the to and fro method of locomotion turning her stomach. The thing breached the threshold of a cavernous room where a fire roared in a gigantic stone fireplace. The snake-man-thing carried her to the table and set her down.

"Sssssseeeeeeeee...." it hissed and pointed over her shoulder. Chloe startled with a gasp. Sitting at the previously empty table, a man in full clergy garb moaned low in his throat. As thin as a skeleton, his gaunt face hung from a back hunched several degrees.

"It's like this, ya see," the priest said in a W.C. Fields voice, its toothless mouth a black cave. "You're screwing everything up, ya see. I'm no sucker and you're no lollipop, so stop pickin' flowers in my bed."

Chloe scanned the room and found herself alone now with the horrible priest. The fire tossed orange and yellow light on his face causing shadows under his eyes and chin. His white hair hung in oily strands brushing a yellowed and frayed clerical collar.

I need to wake up...

The priest's hand snaked out and grabbed her wrist. "We don't need you, ya see? Steer clear or we will erase you. But we'll yank out your insides first and show you what they look like."

Unable to scream, Chloe pulled away as the hand on her wrist turned to claws.

"And you'll be alive several minutes. You can examine your innards while you wait to die," the priest said and his hideously forked tongue slithered out to wet his lips. "Let's have a look," the priest said and abruptly appeared on her side of the table. His opposite hand jerked to her shirt and pushed into her flesh. Her voice didn't work but she thrashed with all her might. Unaffected, he swirled his fingers and massaged her internal organs. A repulsive sensation of movement in her core brought fresh bile to her throat and the priest creature suddenly retracted his hand.

"Oh!" he barked. Pinched between his thumb and first two fingers was a reddish blob of tissue. He popped it in his mouth, swallowed, and licked his lips, again with that forked tongue. "You are such a treat!"

Finally finding her voice, Chloe screamed and sat up.

"Oh, God!" she breathed and wrapped her arms tightly to her breast. The moon flooded the bedroom with gorgeous blue light and she purposed to calm her heartbeat as she'd done since childhood.

Only a dream. Only a dream.

With practiced ease, she ordered the snake-man and horror priest to be buried deep.

I need to be with Kilmeade. I'm going to Dallas. Chloe leaned back onto the pillow, still holding herself tight. Picturing Kilmeade's adoring gaze, she fell back to sleep. And thankfully, she didn't dream.

19, MAY 10

A week after failing to convince Adam Roberts to join them, The Master compelled Dae Kim to try again.

"Bring Roberts to us. You won't have to coerce him, he will want to come. The moment you agree, you will feel a surge of Rakum power filling you to the core. Elohim has assigned flesh to protect Roberts, but you are more capable than anyone He would send of wooing the man to our will."

Dae Kim had agreed with no hesitation and as The Master promised, the fullness of his Rakum identity cascaded back like a long lost friend. Before Last Assembly, Dae Kim had been the best assassin of his pack— highly trained in torture and the special brutality a Rakum might need to extract information from a mortal. Tonight, for the first time in months, his body surged with the power he was born with and he found containing his joy difficult.

By 1:30 a.m. with his BDRH lanyard about his neck, he strolled down the kid's hall. As he pretty much expected, Adam's boss popped out at the sound of the elevator, nosy to the Nth degree. Dae Kim didn't break stride. Completely full of his own glory, he strolled right up to the oily jerk. Grabbing his reptilian gaze, Dae Kim stepped close enough to press one palm into the center of the man's chest.

"Go away," Dae Kim said in an undertone, pushing his will on the human like the old days. The boss's stenciled eyebrows arched, his lips parted, and he turned on his heel to disappear into the nearest office. Dae Kim smirked, happy finally with The Master, and took the last few steps to Roberts's lab.

Peeking in, Adam saw him, rolled his eyes, and came to the door. Dae Kim sent him a smile to die for, turned slowly, and walked away, his plan to lead Adam to the same office as before. The kid followed and with a teasing pause at the stairwell, Dae Kim again turned before speaking and disappeared from Adam's view. When he reached the bottom, Adam was at the top.

"You shouldn't be here. I don't want anything to do with you," the kid said descending.

Dae Kim entered the familiar office and flipped on the light. He then positioned himself to lean casually back atop the paper-cluttered desk as Adam poked his face in the door.

"If you don't leave, I will report you to security," he asserted with a hard edge and eyeing Dae Kim without fear.

"My master's offer stands," Dae Kim said, his voice like the old days, full of silk and power. "Yet he grows impatient for you. We both grow *very* impatient." He caught Adam's bright gray gaze and the man's protests dissolved, becoming putty in his hands. Stepping closer with his fingers unbuttoning Adam's shirt, Dae Kim maneuvered the young man so he now leaned back upon the desk.

"Stop..." Adam said in a whisper, his eyes unfocused and his breathing growing short. Instantly, a most rapturous sensation filled Dae Kim's body as his Rakum bloodlust returned in force. More than that, in his gums, The Master caused his canines to elongate into fangs.

"Oh, please, please, please," he begged The Master inside of him, *"please!"* he begged to keep them forever.

Adam's brow creased. "Wait..." he breathed, alarm in his gaze.

Following The Master's puppeteering, Dae Kim placed his palm to Adam's neck and pulled him close. Adam pushed into his chest with both hands as Dae Kim clamped onto the man's throat. The hot red tide had never tasted so good and Dae Kim allowed gravity to do the work without pulling with any fervency. Adam gasped in alarm and fell still, palms unmoving against Dae Kim's chest. When The Master's next edict translated to his consciousness, Dae Kim covered the punctures with his hand, trusting The Master to heal Adam's wounds. The punctures knitted together and Dae Kim bit hard on his own wrist to offer to the young man. Dae Kim did a double-take—his blood was black—like a Rakum's.

"Take my blood into you, Adam," Dae Kim cooed as the blood dribbled from his arm. "You will be one of us, as glorious as you look!"

His lips sealed, Adam flung his head to the side.

"You will learn to submit," Dae Kim whispered and forced Adam's lips to his wound. "...you will feel the power of The Master who loves you."

The counterfeit Rakum blood bubbled up and smeared Adam's lips and stubbled beard. He continued to resist, but Dae Kim forced him to swallow by covering his nose and mouth with one strong hand.

"Submit to The Master and the entire world will know your power."

With a wet gasp, Adam attempted to push away, his face turned aside.

Then he curled over clutching his middle. With a groan, he spat bile and blood onto the dingy linoleum. Out of habit and not entirely planned, Dae Kim yanked a handkerchief from his back pocket and put it to Adam's lips.

"Let it change you, Adam," he whispered now in a lilting voice. "The Master will make you as powerful as you are beautiful..." Dae Kim tenderly wiped his chin and cheek until Adam lifted his hand and took over the job.

"I... can't..." Adam choked out, still bent over but no longer heaving. "It... burns..." Adam stood up straighter and Dae Kim pressed him to lean back on the desktop. The man took a few deep breaths and on the second exhale, his eyes opened and he met Dae Kim's gaze. The Master had done it—in a small way, the kid's eyes smoldered with bloodlust.

"Yes!" Dae Kim said aloud and grabbed Adam by both shoulders. "Do you feel it, Adam? You have a taste of our *new* spirit! His name is The Master and he loves you! If you will only remain with me, I will show you how to become one with him forever! You will never die, you will never age, you will never see the first wrinkle or gray hair!"

With his newly awakened senses, Dae Kim heard a heartbeat approaching, then footfalls, heavy and businesslike. *"Adam can take this man for his blood, Master..."*

His hands still gripping Adam's shoulders, Dae Kim whispered, his gaze deep into Adam's, "This man is full of blood, Adam. The spirit inside you wants it. Do you feel it?"

Adam looked at the closed door, his eyes round and his lips parted. Dae Kim waited to see if The Master had been successful.

The door opened and an unfamiliar maintenance worker entered and looked at them both with a confused gaze. Dae Kim held his breath, willing with all his might for Adam to follow The Master's leading and attack. By the time the man's lips parted to speak, Adam did just that.

In a blur that surprised Dae Kim, Adam swiped a ballpoint pen from the desk and plunged it into the man's throat. Grabbing his new wound with both hands, the worker spun for the door and Dae Kim slammed it closed with his foot. With a one-millisecond glance to Dae Kim, Adam leapt into the man's space, grabbed him around the chest, and latched his mouth to the spurting puncture.

Dae Kim grinned and hugged himself, every nerve alive with the power of the Unseen mimicking his lost Rakum abilities. Yes, it was false. Yes, it could be removed at any whim of The Master. But it was *glorious just the same.* After a few short seconds, however, Adam pushed away from the man, yelped, and sprinted for the door. He brushed past Dae Kim and the maintenance man went to his knees with one hand pressed against his throat wound.

"Shit!" Dae Kim muttered and dropped to the ground to grasp the worker's shoulders. *"Master! You failed! Now I have to finish this guy and escape!"* Dae Kim sent to the Unseen, angry that once again his new master was not all he promised he'd be. Dae Kim pulled blood from the man, knowing if he didn't, the guy would survive. Adam had barely wounded him before abandoning the task. Seconds ticked by and Dae Kim became aware of a filtering away of his gifts.

"No! How can I take care of this mess without my Rakum abilities?" he shouted to The Master in his mind. When the man's blood threatened to cause him to vomit, Dae Kim grasped him about the throat and squeezed with all his might. Within seconds, his neck cracked and the maintenance man was gone. Angry and cursing, Dae Kim hastily hid the corpse and headed back to Pete's; another day's work for The Master gone to shit.

20, MAY 12, DALLAS

Javier dialed Dr. Claire Boone and leaned back in his chair. Finally warming up to being partners, Beryl sat nearby with notepad in hand, busily jotting ideas and questions for their interview with Mr. Bushman's professional friend. Three days exchanging emails and texts finally led to a phone call and Javier peeked at the woman's LinkedIn photo as he awaited their connection.

"Well, hey!" a bubbly southern voice answered. "Javier?"

"Hi, Dr. Boone. Beryl's here, too. You're on speaker," Javier said and sat up straight.

"*Fffft*, call me Claire," she said. "I found some *very* interesting things on our guy. You ready?"

"Shoot," Javier said and Beryl looked up, his bright eyes twinkling. Already, they had found the trail of the man that raped Kilmeade's Dr. Penny. Claire did not know anything beyond their need to discern her co-workers' identities and learn of her research, so when Dr. Boone related the rapist's name, Javier sat back as the dominoes fell into place.

"Dr. Penny Chao was an MD before she began to study DNA with a researcher named Robert Roberts. According to records, they worked together from March 1897 to December 1902, when she left the country. Her departure was abrupt and without explanation. I'm thinking since she was Chinese, she joined her family over there."

Javier nodded, absently thumping the desktop. Kilmeade sent Penny to China of his own accord. *Why did he go to such bother?* After working himself into Kilmeade's mindset of a hundred years ago, Beryl suggested he did it because he owed Elder Yu; Dr. Penny had been a payment. Whatever the reason, Yu's reputation was one of strict discipline and brutality with mortals; Dr. Penny would have had it rough.

Dr. Boone continued and Javier refocused.

"Later, Dr. Chao pops up in Beijing working again as an MD. Records after that are scarce. The more I dug, the more evident it became that China suffered upheaval after the turn of the century."

"I see," Javier said. "I guess you checked out Roberts's next moves?"

"Oh, sure, from 1897 to 1930, Roberts ran the lab at Dallas Regional

Research Hospital. He married and had a son, also named Robert Roberts. His son went into a non-medical field and drops off the radar." Claire hummed a moment and then came back on the line, her voice smiling. "In 1950, Roberts is working with his grandson, Robert Roberts the Third."

Beryl pushed a note to Javier, eyes raised. "KM'S BABIES MISSING AFTER 1950." Javier nodded.

"Claire, did you check on the research? Specifically, in 1950, what was Roberts working on?"

"I sure did…" Claire said. "Up until 1952, he published work on gene-splicing. In 1957, he changed up, publishing exclusively on geriatrics and the science of aging. My field, by the way."

"Interesting jump," Javier said and awaited more.

"I thought so, too. Bob the Third carried on his grandfather's research and in 1970, filed a patent for a few cosmetic treatments. Hmm," she mumbled and then laughed. "Youth Serum, I think we'd call it today. But the cosmetics industry took notice. In 1980, he lands a couple of big contracts and enters the private sector."

"Uh-huh. How about the photo I sent last night?"

"You wanted to know the identity of the people in the picture," she reiterated. "That was Bob the Third and his son Adam. The part that will make me the detective of the year is—are you ready for it?"

Javier made a short chortle. "Shoot."

"His son, Adam Roberts, works here, at Baylor-Dallas."

"You're kidding," Javier whispered and Beryl sat up, eyes wide.

Claire laughed. "Exactly. The irony! I haven't met him, but I asked him to come by tomorrow when you're here. He works nights in the grants labs, hired by my boss about seven years ago."

His mind racing, Javier mumbled agreement noises into the phone to buy time. *"Is that him?"* he mouthed to Beryl.

His partner shrugged and they both stared again at the photograph. It showed a pale and flabby man in horn-rimmed glasses with his arm on the opposite shoulder of a kid of about seven holding a fluted flask. The black and white newspaper clipping transformed facial details into useless dots. Was it ridiculous to think the boy in the image might be a science experiment raised up from Kilmeade's seed?

Javier made another noise into the phone.

Claire laughed kindly. "This was fun, playing detective. Are you still coming by tomorrow morning? I'll have more pictures and some of them are pretty vivid."

"Great." Javier found his voice. "We plan to be there at nine. Is that good?" Javier asked and watched Beryl's face. Claire said it was and both men nodded. On the doctor's end, a man's voice trickled over and she covered the mouthpiece.

"I'll see you tomorrow and we'll continue!" she said afterward and they made polite goodbyes.

Javier grinned goofily, Beryl's expression perfectly mirroring his: utter shock mixed with nervous excitement. Nine a.m. could not come soon enough.

The next morning, the temperature had reached 58° by 9, but the rain and clouds made it seem much colder. Javier jogged behind Beryl toward the door of the Medical Center holding the folder of collected research over his hair. Beryl did not shield himself, but strolled at a brisk walk, absorbing the water that landed on his skin and clothing. When they reached the overhang at the front steps, Javier touched his sleeve.

"You are allowed to stay dry, Beryl," he said with a grin. "There's no reward in catching a cold." Javier didn't sleight him; it would take time to drop the idiotic Rakum stoicism drilled into them from birth.

At first Beryl looked confused and then he offered a small grin and stepped aside for Javier to enter.

"Dr. Boone said she'd meet us at Information," Javier began as an attractive and petite dark-skinned woman in a lab coat waved at them excitedly and headed over.

"Javier? Beryl?" she said as she reached them, her fingers extended. Both men shook her hand and she smiled ear-to-ear. "You're soaked! Come to my office—you can towel off. Adam Roberts is on his way."

Javier and Beryl exchanged an excited glance as Dr. Boone whirled about and led them through the winding hallways peopled with medical professionals. She made small talk, mostly regarding elements of their emails or phone conversations, and when they reached a door with her name in gold letters, she turned.

"Adam Roberts must have been a child prodigy; he has three Masters degrees, the first earned at fifteen," she said and blew a strand of hair from her forehead. "My boss said he began work on a doctorate!"

"Does your boss care if we distract you with this stuff?" Javier asked probing the involvement of a stranger.

Claire shook her head. "No, and I have autonomy regardless." She handed them each a hand-towel from a shelf in her office lavatory and they swabbed their faces and necks.

"Good. We sure appreciate your help," Javier assured her.

"Dr. Boone, do you have a moment?"

All three of them turned at the request. A bald man in a suit and old-fashioned tie had poked in his head, his hand and arm wrapped around the threshold. He noted her guests and apologized.

"Come in, Dr. Nankin," Claire said in a sing-song voice. "What can I do for you?" The man seemed to consider her question and stepped in just enough to leave the hall.

"It'll keep," he said in a low voice. "Are these friends of yours?" He leaned in a bit more. Javier snickered to himself when he thought the man had checked Beryl out a little too long.

"These are friends of a colleague in Alabama. Remember when I asked you about Adam Roberts? These are the men I'm helping research Adam's father's work. Beryl and Javier, meet Dr. Cary Nankin."

"Pleasure," the man said making no move to shake their hands. "Good luck getting anywhere with Roberts. Baylor wants to see Dr. Roberts's work, too." Nankin removed his thick-rimmed eyeglasses to swab the lenses with his handkerchief. When he inclined his head, Javier noted his eyebrows were penciled on. "Dr. Boone, make sure they fill out the new HR261. Jackson is adamant we institute it."

"Ah..." Claire touched her forehead and walked behind her desk to pull out a sheet of paper.

"One for each visitor, please," the boss said and waited until she handed a form to Beryl as well. "Nice to meet you, gentlemen. I'll leave you to it." The man backed away, his eye falling again to Beryl before he sought Dr. Boone's smiling face. All three of them watched the man leave and then Dr. Boone shook her head.

"My boss." She shrugged one shoulder. "He's eccentric, but a brilliant mind. He comes from a long line of Texan Doctoral researchers. His father and grandfather directed the most prestigious labs in the Dallas-Fort Worth area since 1955."

Quietly, Beryl asked, "Why does Baylor care about this research?"

Claire shrugged. "I imagine the Board wants more government grants and this looks like *sure-thing* research."

"Oh," Javier said with a smile.

The doctor grinned. "After you go, I might look more into getting my hands on it. It's in my field, anyway."

Claire waited while they filled out the form. Both Javier and Beryl gave a false address, but the Yukon was recorded accurately so they could visit without attracting security. When they had finished, she collected the sheets and dropped them atop a small set of shelves near the door.

"I'll run those to HR," Nankin said appearing suddenly from the hall. He'd been walking quickly by and barely glanced at the room's occupants. When he was gone again, Claire laughed and shook her head.

"That man never slows down." She glanced at her watch. "He works third shift so he's likely late going home. Okay..." Claire composed her thoughts. "Let's see..."

"I assume you saw that last link we sent? It blew my mind," Javier said watching her face.

The article he spoke of regarded the latest Bob Roberts's death by suicide. In the man's most recent photo, he did not look eighty-seven years old. Beryl and Javier suspected a supernatural reason; what would a scientist with no knowledge of the Rakum think?

Claire crossed to sit at her desk and opened her laptop. "You're referring to his youthful appearance?" She glanced up and Javier nodded. "I did as you suggested and pulled all I could on the research grants we discovered already."

Beryl and Javier stepped to opposite sides of the desk to look over her shoulder. When she settled on the screen she sought, she pointed and leaned back for them to lean in.

"Robert Roberts who worked with Kilmeade's Dr. Penny was born in Manhattan in 1870." Dr. Boone stood up and Javier sat in her chair with Beryl leaning his palms on the smooth desk surface. "The Dr. Roberts we see in this newest article you sent, Bob the Third, started working with his grandfather in 1950 at twenty years old. Hit that cursor."

Javier tapped the mouse and the next screen revealed a photo gallery the doctor had assembled. The single picture of Bob I standing with Bob III had damage to the edges, but Javier made out their faces. The Bobs were stout, bald, round-faced gentlemen with glasses and small noses. The second and third photos revealed Bob III in 1970 receiving an award for his work in DNA research. He was forty and working at the premiere Dallas Research Hospital.

"Now, look at this one from 1981," Dr. Boone said, her voice giddy. "Bob III is fifty and receives a grant for YZ666." She waited until both men at her desk turned to see her face. "Youth Serum, yeah, uh-huh, just like I thought," she said with a sly grin. "The cosmetic industry paid him millions. And he was using it himself—look at 2005. He accepted another

148

award and brought fifteen-year-old Adam to the stage, told the world his work was so secret that the boy was his only lab partner." She reached past Javier and clicked the mouse.

"Oh...my...God," Javier said softly as the photo popped open. Javier and Beryl stared, mouths agape. The youth *was* Kilmeade, down to the strong build and movie-star smile. And seventy-five-year-old Bob III didn't look a day over fifty.

"Can you print that," Javier said, his voice cracking. Beryl put his hand to his mouth.

"Sure thing," Dr. Boone chirped and turned away to the machine nearby. Speechless, Javier and Beryl stared at the screen until she returned. When her desk phone rang, they both startled and Javier got to his feet. Dr. Boone picked up the receiver and chatted away. Javier took Beryl's bicep in his arm and pulled him aside.

"My God, Beryl, that's him," Javier said in a whisper. *"It worked."*

"Are you parked in Garage Level B? It's Dr. Nankin; security's checking your car right now to give you total access," Claire said to Javier, eyes wide awaiting an answer.

His mind racing with their revelations, he puzzled a moment and then shook his head. "No, it's outside, in the lot, in F."

Claire nodded and told security.

Beryl touched Javier's sleeve. "He did it. He really did it."

"The guy's mortal though, right? It's day so he lives in the light, right?" Javier rambled and Beryl agreed with a numb bob of his head.

"Text Canaan," Beryl whispered. "Now."

"Hey, ya'll sit tight. I'll be right back," Dr. Boone sang and disappeared out the door. As she exited, they heard her call out, "Adam? Yeah, nice to meet you! Right there, go on in. Be right back."

Texting the Elders would have to wait. Javier and Beryl regarded each other, took a deep breath, and watched the doorway.

Kilmeade's double walked in moments later.

"Hey, I'm Adam Roberts," the young man said in a soft local drawl.

Scrutinizing everything in order to report back to Canaan, Javier watched the guy consider both of them head-to-toe before breaking into an easy grin as he entered.

"What's up?" With a moment of amused hesitation, he closed the distance between the three of them and shook hands with Javier first and then Beryl, two strong pumps each. "Ya'll sure are lookin' at me funny," he said dropping his hands into his slacks pockets. He rocked his weight back onto one foot. "Have we met?"

Beryl answered first and managed a grin. "No. I'm Beryl, that's Javier."

Javier still marveled at everything about the man, his bright gray eyes, wavy light brown hair – not as long as Kilmeade's, but longer than Javier's. Like Kilmeade, he sported a scruffy five-o'clock shadow and was muscular and athletic in what appeared to be tailor cut shirt and pants under an open white lab coat. He met Javier's eye.

"Did you work with my father?" he asked.

"Dr. Roberts? No." Javier chuckled and shook his head.

Adam seemed to relax moment by moment. He squint his eyes and grinned, his pointer finger coming up. "You're not being truthful, sir," he said with a friendly laugh. His congeniality was infectious and Javier matched his expression shaking his head.

"No, truly," he chuckled. "We never met Dr. Roberts."

"He's wondering why two strangers and a geneticist hunted him down," Beryl said on Javier's left, studying Adam as hard as Javier was and marveling at the uncanny resemblance.

Adam chuckled softly. "Are you kidding? I'm in high demand; someone is *always* looking for me." He swiped imaginary dust from his shoulder. Then he winked at Beryl and pointed towards his face. "Ask him—he knows what it's like. Am I right?"

Beryl shook his head grinning. "This is some crazy shit."

"Okay, you win. I'm curious." Adam passed them both and leaned back on the edge of Dr. Boone's desk. "What's up?"

Javier inhaled and, with a quick glance to Beryl, decided to begin. He hadn't expected the man to actually *be* Kilmeade's offspring. Before he got the first word out, Beryl jumped in.

"We know your *other* father—your biological father. We want to take you to meet him."

Javier sent Beryl a glare, but to his surprise, Adam responded, "I had a feeling you guys were here about that."

Javier's ears perked. "Is it common knowledge that Dr. Roberts isn't your father?"

"No, but I see things others don't..."

Javier tried again. "You *had a feeling* strangers would come with news of your biological father?"

Adam grinned. "Spooky, eh?" He crossed his arms, still nodding. "I've had other visitors," he said, his grin dropping.

"What do you mean? Strangers... like us?" Beryl asked walking the line of revealing too much.

Adam nodded slowly, chin down. *"Exactly* like you," he said softly. "Only, I can see that you're not here to hurt me as they had come to do."

Javier licked his lips trying to read the guy's subtext. Had other Rakum come to see him or other scientists? What did he *see* and who or what did he think they were? Javier shot a look to Beryl who had nothing.

Hopefully obliquely, Javier asked, "What did they look like? Did you get their names?"

Adam shrugged. "There were two the first time, came at me at home. I'm a crack shot with my .45. I got one of them in the chest, but his buddy dragged him off before the cops arrived." Adam looked to the door, craned to the right, and returned his focus to Javier and Beryl. *"The Chinese one came here alone to my office later,"* Adam said in a whisper.

"Did you get his name?" Beryl asked at the same volume. Javier watched Adam work on his answer. He had clearly been shaken by the experience, yet appeared entirely too blasé about being visited by two strangers and attacked by two others.

"He said his name was Dae Kim and he spoke a lot about his master wanting me to come with him..." Adam shrugged and wrinkled his nose. "I'd like to know what, if anything, that means to you guys."

Beryl's gaze told Javier he knew the name. Adam shifted his weight and seemed about to say more and didn't.

Javier chose his next words carefully. "We might know that guy, but I promise you, we're not with him. We came to meet you. That's all."

"I know," Adam said softly then pointed to his right eye. "I can *see* the difference in you and those other guys."

"What does that mean?" Beryl asked and leaned closer to the young man. *"You see something beyond your eyes?"* he whispered.

"Since I was little." Adam nodded. "I can see you two are men of the light, men who mean no harm. Those two, live in the dark and have dark thoughts."

"Are you talking auras or—" Beryl began, but Dr. Boone entered at a trot and all three men assumed blank expressions. Thinking fast, Javier broke the silence.

"Adam was telling us about his work here and how he wished he'd met you sooner..." At his assertion, Adam reached for her hand and brought it to his lips.

"Are you spoken for, angel doctor? I hope not, because I'm recently uncoupled..."

The tension in the air dissipated. Beryl snickered and tried to catch Javier's eye. Javier didn't look, but he'd noticed the man's similarity in personality to a Rakum Elder he had never met.

The doctor laughed into her hand and shooed him playfully. "Stop, silly. Well, Javier?" she asked him then, fanning her face. "Do you think Mr. Kilmeade will be satisfied with the results of our detective work? Is this the guy?"

Javier grinned. "This is the guy."

"Dr. Boone," Adam cooed, still facing her and away from Javier and Beryl, "I'm serious. Marry me. I love you."

"You silly boy!" she said, her eyes shining. "I'm headed to another appointment, but Javier, Beryl, use my office, and ya'll call me any time. Adam, you behave." She pointed at him with a mock-stern expression and closed her laptop. When she had it under her arm, she waved at the three of them and left the room.

Adam sighed and looked at his cell phone. "I'm off the clock. Let's get some brunch. You in?"

"Will you come with us to meet Kilmeade?" Beryl asked.

"That's his first name or last?" Adam inquired, eyebrows raised.

Javier noisily cleared his throat. "Adam, we don't know that's what Kilmeade wants," he said apologetically. "We, um..." Javier stalled, seeking the right words. *Keep it human, keep it human.* "Beryl's excited that we found you. Heck, I am, too, but Kilmeade didn't ask us to find you."

"He doesn't know you exist," Beryl said eyes wide.

Adam stepped between them and draped an arm over each man. "You are both much too wound up. Let's eat—my treat—and then call him. No biggie. He'll want to meet me. I mean, who wouldn't?"

"It's amazing how much they favor," Beryl said to Javier. Then he shook his head and said to the kid, "You're going to freak when you see him. You even *act* like him. It's eerie." Beryl looked at Javier who agreed with a wry smile.

"I am very, very intrigued," Adam said with a grin. All three walked for the exit still under Adam's arm the first few steps and then he dropped the arm around Javier to fluff Beryl's hair.

"You said I look exactly like your friend..." Adam tossed them a teasing grin. "I guess that means he's *really handsome*," he added without apology.

Beryl chuckled and Javier sent the man an incredulous look. "Are you this familiar with all strangers?"

"Are you strangers?" he asked in a spooky voice, shaking Beryl with his draped arm.

Javier chuckled and resumed the trek for the truck. The rain had ceased, but thick cloud cover draped the cold morning in mist and fog. Behind him, Adam said to Beryl, "Even the bad guys think I'm adorable—your friend Dae Kim said I was the most handsome man he'd ever met."

"He lied," Beryl said smiling "because he's met me."

Adam grinned. "I knew you recognized the name."

They reached the truck and Beryl rode up front with Javier behind the wheel. Climbing into the back seat, Adam asked Beryl where he wanted to eat.

"We'll head to the Chop House," Javier answered for him. "If Kilmeade will see you, it's near our place."

"Good! Let's do it," Adam said cheerily.

Javier resisted the urge to call or text Canaan before they reached the restaurant. Once settled inside, Adam and Beryl launched into trying to get the server to choose her favorite between them. When she was thoroughly infatuated with them both, they released her to attend the other patrons.

Javier shook his head with chagrin and got Adam's attention. "I'd like to snap a photo of you for Kilmeade. Do you mind?"

Adam grinned wide and leaned into Beryl pressing their cheeks together. Javier snapped the pic and thanked him with a grin.

"No need to Photoshop the guy on the right, he always looks perfect," Adam said.

"You have a lot to learn," Beryl mumbled and Javier agreed with a grin as he excused himself from the table. "You'll *never* win that game with me."

It was more than eight hours until sunset, but Canaan would want to know what they found. Once Javier put distance between himself and the folks walking past, he pressed Canaan's icon. The Elder answered on the first ring.

"Bored! Bored! Canaan's bored!" he sang into the phone. "Javie, come play. I only need three hours sleep and Kilmeade's hibernating."

"Canaan, listen, we found something," Javier said knowing his tone would alert the Elder to his state of mind. "They did it—Kilmeade's seed is now a man and the similarities are unreal."

"You're shittin' me... Are you sure?"

Javier shook his head staring at his shoes. "A million percent sure.

We're around the corner, but I won't bring him over tonight without your permission."

"Let me kick the bear..." Canaan's end went quiet as he woke his comrade.

"He appears to be human," Javier offered while he waited, "but he might be precognitive or a seer. He recognized something was up, but doesn't understand what..."

"The boss says bring him at sundown."

Javier nodded and said, "Tell Kilmeade that two of our brethren tried to kill him over the past weeks, and one of them was named Dae Kim. He'll want to figure out why and what they know, etcetera."

"Damn... Okay. So...what's he like?"

Javier laughed despite himself. "He's funny, he's very likable."

"Just like his sweet poppa!" Canaan joked.

Javier agreed with a new chuckle. "Oh! And he's vain. He thinks he's better looking than Beryl." Canaan laughed boisterously. "Also, tell Kilmeade he's a genius; he'll get a kick out of that."

"He will," Canaan chuckled. "Did you get a picture? If you say no, I'm going to hurt you a little."

"You know I did," Javier returned. Javier fiddled with the phone until it sent Canaan the photo.

"Judas Priest!" he heard through the phone and the line when dead.

Javier took a deep breath and headed back to the table to tell the young man the news.

21, MAY 13

"Javier is beside himself," Canaan chuckled and settled back onto the basement couch. There were no windows to cover and the space already had one sofa, a daybed, and a pool table. Kilmeade lounged on the daybed, illuminated by a tiny night light, arms up behind his head, his gaze far off. More and more, his partner turned inward; Canaan recognized this was expected without the Rakum spirit in residence. Still, if he could cheer him...

"Catch," Canaan said and tossed the phone to his companion. Kilmeade glanced at the screen and tossed it back. "Yeah, right, like that reaction is genuine."

Kilmeade looked off again, guarding his thoughts.

"You wanna talk about it?" Canaan asked attempting to read his cohort's countenance since his mind was blocked.

Kilmeade made a small chuckle. "Do I ever?"

Canaan sighed. "You've been withdrawing," he said in a low voice. "You're unhappy."

"Unhappy?" Kilmeade shrugged. "Can a Rakum *be* happy in this new world? Are you, Canaan? Happy?"

Canaan thought a minute, poked out his chin and nodded. "Yeah. Things are different and we can't fix it, but I have you—I'm not alone. Face it, if it was little old Canaan against the world, I'd jump off a cliff."

Kilmeade chuckled. "That would hurt."

"Like a bitch," Canaan replied with a soft chortle.

"Wouldn't kill an Elder," Kilmeade replied and looked over. "Go into the sun. That's the way."

"Suicide is for cowards," Canaan spat, knowing his partner felt the same way. Kilmeade's mind opened up and Canaan sensed a great relief.

"Don't block your buddy, okay? My brain needs you," he said trying to sound tough while feeling the opposite. The sensation that grew in his middle when Kilmeade's mind closed off was akin to suffocating; even as he thought of it, his counterpart commiserated with a slow nod.

"In the storm drain, when Rafael and Boris began to transform right

155

under my nose..."

"You were alone in here," Canaan said pointing to his forehead. Kilmeade nodded.

"Utterly." Kilmeade took a deep breath and send his next words telepathically. *"We suffered stinted telepathy for seven years, but that night, someone pulled the plug."*

Canaan agreed with a small noise.

"Brother," Kilmeade added, "for those few minutes before you called to me, I was the only Rakum on the planet and..." he stopped speaking and he didn't need to finish.

"Same here. I was ridiculous, cuddling Beryl like a momma bear."

Kilmeade nodded. "Our shared telepathy must be on par with the Fathers. Together, we're going to be able to hear any of the brethren that call us." Kilmeade stared at the ceiling as he pondered. "The ones who are struggling, the ones who are in danger, those are the ones we hear."

"I guess we can figure out why that is."

"Don't say it," Kilmeade whispered.

Of course it was Javier's God doing whatever He wanted to with them. But at least the mission ran congruent with both Elders' desires.

"Yes," Kilmeade said, answering what hadn't been mentioned.

His partner shook his head and Canaan discerned topics floating past his mind that he wouldn't discuss, conversations he wouldn't begin or entertain, they all had to do with agreeing with and speaking with the God of the mortals.

"This kid is gonna make things interesting again, eh? He looks like you, only better," Canaan said attempting to lighten the mood.

"That is not possible," Kilmeade parlayed.

"Show me how it happened. You said Dr. Penny used human magic on the samples. What do you mean?" Kilmeade nodded and closed his eyes. As soon as Canaan closed his, he zoomed into Kilmeade's memory of that time.

1901, Dallas, Texas.

The laboratory had been thrown into darkness and candles burned around them, reflecting the flames on Bunsen burners, flasks, scales, microscopes, test tubes, and in the center of the room, looking through Kilmeade's eyes, Dr. Penny sat on the floor of the lab in a circle of various symbols drawn onto the linoleum. Petite, with soft round cheeks and expressive brown eyes, Kilmeade's doctor Cow held her arms out with a serious expression.

"If your Fathers cast a spell on your seed, we'll counter that spell with another. Watch," the woman in the light blue lab coat said. Words mumbled in Latin and then a few sentences in what translated as gibberish to Canaan flowed from the woman's lips as she stared at nothing above her.

Canaan huffed when in the memory in Kilmeade's body, he lowered himself to the floor alongside Penny and removed his clothing. She did the same until they were both nude. Without a word they went through the motions, methodically, scientifically; then they were finished. A short time later, they redressed and Penny continued her incantations.

Canaan wondered over it, having been alive a few centuries, and never seen witchcraft performed. The Rakum avoided all things spiritual and as far as they were concerned, black magic equaled Catholicism in its idiocy and uselessness. From the entire episode, he learned that the sexual act empowered the witch and her spell; the fertilizing of the doctor's eggs took place in a dish hours later.

Canaan pulled his inner eye back and pondered what he saw. Kilmeade had asserted that Father Abroghia used *his* type of magic on the Rakum's seed so it would not procreate. Penny successfully using magic *against* him proved it had been a curse after all. Where did Javier's God fit in?

"I asked Roman that question," Kilmeade said softly. "He insists none of that which you just saw has anything to do with the Jesus stuff."

"Huh," Canaan said and shook his head.

"Huh," Kilmeade repeated with a sad smile. "This man that grew out of my seed didn't grow because of any magic of Javier's God." He shrugged. *"I am concerned he'll be like Isaac."*

Canaan didn't respond; Kilmeade hadn't sent that thought to him, he was simply thinking it. Yet, Canaan had the same concern. What spirit entered that union when they brought it to life with 21st-Century technology?

Neither Elder spoke again and Canaan daydreamed about Marcy, Beryl, Javier, even Dae Kim. But he didn't think about Adam Roberts or Javier's God.

《回》

"So why sundown?" Adam asked from the passenger side of the Yukon for the ride to the rental house. Beryl rode in the back, but listened, scooted forward. "Is it because it's sundown or it just happens to be at sundown when he is available?"

Javier glanced at him. "What's the difference?" So far, they had learned much about the kid's past and present, but only the last hour did they begin to touch on anything paranormal about him.

"Well, the more time we spend together, the more I see." Adam turned to see Beryl. "You two avoided the sun for a long time. I'm not sure yet what it means..."

Beryl whispered with a grin. "I bet you're a hoot at parties."

"With the ladies, mostly." Adam tossed him a genuine smile. Then he continued in a serious tone. "I've never shared my special sight with anyone. Not even Dr. Roberts—who, by the way, I knew wasn't my father. In mutual agreement, he and I presented to the world as father and son, but I was always a lab assistant and test subject."

"No way," Beryl hissed and caught Javier's eye in the rearview.

"No, it was like a job," Adam asserted. "He wasn't a mad scientist."

"You're serious..." Javier had reached the house. He stalled and pretended to be thinking of what to say and got the young man to the porch where the Elders could overhear him. He put his hand to the knob and said, "So you knew all along you were a test subject?"

Adam nodded and stepped into the house, looked around and then followed Beryl into the living room.

Javier repeated one more thing for the Elders. "What did you mean when you said you think Beryl and I avoided the sun a long time? That's a weird thing to say to someone you just met..."

Adam shrugged and seemed to daydream as he watched Beryl find a seat. When he sat, he chose one cushion away from Beryl. Thoughtfully, he leaned over his knees. "I see a spectrum of light around everyone, and the longer I see it, it develops edges."

"Edges," Beryl repeated with a nod. "Edges with facts attached."

Adam looked up, his eyes wider. "Yes, exactly. How did you know?"

"Maybe I've seen that, too," Beryl said quietly.

"These edges said Beryl and I were like Dae Kim in the past?" Javier asked. Adam didn't answer, still looking at Beryl. They couldn't be communicating telepathically, but their posture resembled the behavior.

"I was kidding you earlier, but..." Adam began, looking at Beryl a few feet away on the couch, "do you hypnotize people with your—" He used one hand to showcase his own face in lieu of finishing his question.

Beryl's eyebrows went up. "What?"

Adam grinned. And did he blush?

"Ya'll are asking me about my special sight. *Quid pro quo.* Your face...

Is it supernatural?"

Beryl looked at Javier, not sure how he should respond.

"It's just a face," Javier said, but felt sorry for the guy. Before 11/13, Beryl *did* use his unique appearance to manipulate others. Now this anomaly from Kilmeade's seed was seeing that power still.

Adam rubbed his eyes with the heels of his palms. "I'm not an imbecile. None of this is normal. Give it to me straight." Adam looked hard at Javier. "My biological father made his *deposit*..." he said with finger quotes on the word, "...more than one hundred years ago and you're introducing me to him at sunset?"

Javier considered his words; the kid knew something more than they realized and either wouldn't or couldn't say.

"Kilmeade will fill you in if he deems it necessary." Javier lowered his chin. "Trust me, when you meet him, you'll understand."

Adam started to object, but Beryl touched his arm. "When Dae Kim came to see you the second time, did he tell you who he was? What his intentions were? Why did you trust him if you knew he had tried to hurt you before?"

Javier turned to Adam at Beryl's excellent queries. "Yeah, why did you trust him?"

Adam looked between them a few times. "I plead the fifth until I meet your guy."

Javier didn't like his reply, but what could he do?

"Fair enough," Beryl said with a grin. "Continue then, before my beautiful face mesmerized you, you were explaining light and dark people."

"Yes!" Adam nodded and in a flash, his happy-go-lucky demeanor returned. He leaned back. "Both of you *used to be* people of the dark." He touched the corner of his eye.

Javier didn't respond and worked to keep a blank expression. Was the man seeing backward and forward? Would he see that the Elders weren't human? If he did, what then?

"You shouldn't stress over it," Adam continued ignoring their stunned silence. "I have seen my own aura—I am both, light and dark."

Javier narrowed his eyes. "What does that mean?"

"It means he's in the middle, am I right?" Beryl asked not nearly as disturbed by the guy as he should be.

Adam grinned revealing white teeth, and then he scrunched his nose playfully. "You get it, B. You get it."

"You called me B," Beryl said. "Why do you think you did that?"

Adam looked around the room. "Felt right. Someone important to you calls you that, right?" Beryl's eyebrows lifted and Javier cleared his throat.

"It's time to meet Kilmeade."

Adam rose to his feet. "I'm ready."

With a strengthening nod to Beryl, Javier led them to the hall and pointed to the basement door. Canaan's text said to send him in alone so Javier had a parting word. "Kilmeade is a good man, you read me?"

"More than you know," Adam said with a wink and knocked on the door. Javier smirked as he disappeared into the basement and Beryl got his drift.

"He's about to be knocked down a few notches," Beryl whispered.

"Maybe more than that," Javier replied. "He can't possibly be *that* calm. He should be freaking out." Beryl agreed.

Too bad they hadn't been invited down; it was going to be a good show.

《◉》

As prepared as he was going to be, Kilmeade indicated to Canaan he was ready. He switched on a floor lamp for the kid and stood toward the back of the room. Canaan saw him first and instantly, Kilmeade read his cohort's shocked surprise.

"Adam, you will call me Elder Canaan," he said and stepped aside for the youngster to descend. Canaan's eyes were huge and his smile to the side as Kilmeade focused his gaze upon the one they rose up from his seed.

No doubt the young man resembled him, but Roberts's behavior remained the oddest thing about him. The man didn't try to shake hands or move into Kilmeade's space. Rather, he stopped in the center of the room and stood with his hands clasped behind his back. Then he nodded like a Rakum.

Kilmeade narrowed his eyes. "Explain yourself."

Adam exhaled as if he had been holding his breath. "You look really young," he marveled in a Texan accent. He looked back once at Canaan and returned front. "My name is Adam Roberts. I was born in 1990, here in Dallas. I learned recently that Dr. Roberts had been using *your* preserved cells for decades. I also learned that I am the product of whatever you left behind."

Kilmeade watched him for deceit as he spoke and saw none so far.

"That accent is great," Canaan sent playfully. *"Maybe he'll say 'darlin' for us next."*

Kilmeade ignored him and asked, "Explain how you learned this."

Adam nodded rapidly. "Dr. Roberts had records of experiments carried out in his grandfather's lab. I think he stole your genetic materials and studied the notes by the original 1901 researcher."

"She made notes," Kilmeade said under his breath. He hadn't realized the woman recorded their experiments on paper. But why wouldn't she? Scientists must document everything.

"Dr. Roberts committed suicide on November 14th last year. He left me this..." Adam slipped a fold of papers from his pocket and opened them up. "They mention you. This was how I pieced it together." He held the paper out and did not move.

Canaan stepped from behind him and took the papers to carry to Kilmeade. After handing them over, Canaan engaged Adam in banter.

"You look like my man Kilmeade." Canaan reached for Adam's chin and he flinched backward. "Aw, now, don't be like that," Canaan teased and grabbed Adam's throat with one big hand. "Never resist an Elder," he said close to the guy's face. "We don't like it." Adam mumbled an apology and stood unblinking as Canaan released him. "We also despise apologies. Just don't screw up in the first place."

"Yessir," Adam whispered.

Canaan inclined his head still grinning. "Do you really think you're better looking than my little Beryl?"

Kilmeade shook his head at Canaan's chitchat and scanned the first page of notes. Reading quickly, he finished all three sheets of hand-written scrawl in the space of a minute.

"I hate to be the one to tell ya," Canaan was saying to the kid, "but no one will ever win a beauty contest that man enters." Kilmeade touched his partner's shoulder and Canaan moved away, whispering to Adam as he passed, *"I'm watching you."*

Kilmeade grinned and quickly resumed a serious expression for Roberts. "This last page is written in our language. Can you read it?"

Adam shifted his weight. "No, sir, and when I tried to have it translated, they told me that dialect was abandoned long ago. Nobody could read it anymore."

"Mortals can't read it," Kilmeade said derisively and handed the pages to Canaan. "Page three is written by one of *my* people, a brother your Dr. Roberts served. What of that makes sense to you?" Kilmeade again watched his eyes.

Unnerved, Adam averted his gaze. "The one who wrote that—his

161

name was Bel. I saw him often up until about seven or eight years ago."

"Last Assembly," Kilmeade reflected.

Canaan grunted in agreement and muttered, "Bel, what the shit..."

Elder Bel ran in the same circles as Jack Dawn and Tomás in the Rakum heyday, a tall, thick, black Elder with extreme abilities in many areas. He had written the note on the last page to Kilmeade, purposefully using an unreadable language, saying the Fathers sent him to collect the samples and he was too curious to destroy them. This meant Robert Roberts the First had been the Elder's Cow.

"And Roberts the Third, too, according to this," Canaan sent just finishing with the letter.

Kilmeade looked aside. *"I was too distracted, I should have noticed him sneaking about when I was playing scientist."*

"We just got back from two years' quarantine. You were still waking up," Canaan sent in an effort to help.

"Adam," Kilmeade said and the guy jumped. "Do you know the extent of their relationship?"

"Sir," Adam began with respect and lowered his shoulders. "Dr. Roberts hid me out of sight when he visited, but I could see them..."Adam glanced behind him at Canaan.

"And?" Kilmeade prodded.

"Bel used to drink Dr. Roberts's blood," Adam whispered and touched the crook of his arm. "That paper says I am the result of the fertilized egg spoken of in those notes. That means you're over a hundred years old, so you must be like Bel."

"Excellent deduction," Kilmeade jibed. "And what exactly is Bel?" Kilmeade asked watching his eyes. The kid gulped, afraid or unable to explain his trepidation.

"I-I have to guess. I don't know, exactly. That paper is all I have to go on."

Canaan stepped to Adam's side and handed the paper back. "You watched Bel sucking your adopted father's arm and you don't know what to call it?"

Adam put his hand to his throat and Kilmeade watched his expression flicker. *"He's been attacked and he hid it from Javier,"* Kilmeade sent Canaan. *"Try to read him. I want to see that attack."*

Canaan was already within arm's length behind the boy and so he placed both hands on his shoulders. Recalling the earlier lesson, he startled, but did not pull away. After a moment, Canaan slid both hands towards his throat and forced his fingers under the material of his shirt to touch skin-to-skin. Adam's pulse spiked, but he remained in place.

"Kid," Canaan said behind him in an urgent whisper, "Who attacked you?"

Canaan raised his eyes to Kilmeade's the instant the images trickled in. It was Dae Kim, as Javier had informed them earlier, wooing, swooning, and then viciously attacking the boy in a dark office.

Underneath his hands, Adam suddenly tried to wriggle free and Canaan tightened his grip. "Be still," he commanded and the kid's movement ceased.

"Oh, look," Kilmeade sent silently as Dae Kim forced Adam to drink his blood. *"But he's no longer a Rakum..."*

Canaan agreed. *"He's delusional..."*

"Yet his blood is black..."

Canaan shook his head. *"Javier would know. This is his area..."*

"Tell the boys to join us up top," Kilmeade said in a low voice.

Canaan dropped the contact with Adam and clapped his back. "Let's do it." Canaan waited for Kilmeade to move toward the stairs, but he first put his fingers to Adam's sleeve.

"We overheard everything you have said here at the house," Kilmeade told him. "Explain what you think Javier and Beryl used to be. And answer forthrightly; I despise dodgy, oblique responses."

"Yes, sir," he said, his voice shaking. "When I first saw Javier and Beryl, they emanated light. Javier more than Beryl. Also, I knew right away they had come about the experiments that led to my making."

Kilmeade nodded. "And?"

"And the more time I spent with them, the more I saw. By the time we got here, I could see that both of those men *are* or *were* like Bel."

Kilmeade nodded. "By contrast or comparison, when you first saw Dae Kim, what did you see?"

Adam paused, keeping something back. When he answered, he spoke carefully. "He is surrounded by a dark cloud. I have never seen a thicker darkness around one person."

"What if anything do you see around Elder Canaan and myself?"

Adam dropped his gaze. "Your aura looks like mine—vacillating nonstop between both extremes."

Kilmeade nodded, pondered his words, and said no more.

《▣》

Javier and Beryl chose to kill time upstairs and landed in Beryl's room. Javier situated himself at a dainty corner desk and opened his laptop. Beryl dropped noisily long-ways onto the bed and Javier grinned at him. "Yes?"

"Kilmeade did it," Beryl reflected while staring at the smooth ceiling. "Three thousand years and never did a Rakum procreate; that's hard to wrap my mind around."

Javier answered with a nod, his mind wandering the same paths. How many millions, maybe billions of seed refused to take root because of the spirit inside their High Father?

"Are there more fertilized cells to make more Adams?" Beryl asked, still looking up so Javier figured the question was rhetorical. "He's spoiled rotten," Beryl said with a grin and rolled his gaze to Javier's. "He's been riding life on that face, brain, and physique given to him by our most powerful Elder. He's completely conceited."

Beryl was chortling by the end of his observations. Javier agreed with a grin.

"But I'm better looking, right?" Beryl asked and Javier met his eye.

"You're serious?" Javier huffed gently. What a sad-sack Beryl was going to be as he aged. "According to the entire population of Rakum," Javier said leveling his gaze, "and every mortal who met you and Meryl, you have no competition." Javier watched his face and he nodded. "Now, what did you think of Dr. Boone's boss?"

Beryl hemmed a moment. "He stunk, had some weird stuff on his skin. He didn't look healthy, I'll tell you that much."

"I mean, was he staring at you more than normal?" Javier asked with a shake of the head.

"Everybody stares at me. I don't notice."

"I did," Javier said. "He stared at you. *Hard.*"

"Of course. Look at me." Beryl fluttered his eyebrows.

"You and Canaan. Thank God I was never so full of myself."

"When you got it, you got it," Beryl said in a chuckle and rubbed his eyes. "I'd love to have seen Kilmeade's face when he saw this kid."

Javier nodded and turned to open Explorer on the laptop. "Kilmeade is so reserved; he'll reveal nothing. He'll look Adam in the eye and ask him what he knows." Javier scanned the email and continued, "And Canaan will do his best to keep it light."

Beryl chuckled. "That's for damn sure. Canaan can't let anything alone. He'll make fun of Adam's face, his walk, his accent."

Javier nodded. "Cute little cowboy accent," he said and then straightened. "Chloe's flying in. I'm supposed to pick her up in the morning. She sent me her itinerary."

Beryl sat up. "Looks like six weeks is her limit."

Javier laughed. "She got lonely. Don't girls get lonely?"

"Not that. What am I missing?" When Javier only returned a blank look, Beryl huffed. "She's a chatty, opinionated twenty-year-old teenager..." He jerked his eyes to the floor as if speaking to the Elders. "And I mean that in the nicest way."

Javier only chuckled.

"You feel me," Beryl said forcing down his grin. "What is it about her that grabbed the attention of our most powerful Elder?"

In his mind Javier immediately put the onus on God, but for Beryl's sake, tried a more worldly answer. "We don't choose who we fall in love with."

Beryl gave him a dead-eye. "Come on."

Javier laughed. "What? She's cute, she worships him, and you know God must have some big plan in the works about it."

Beryl pointed at Javier's face. "THAT is what I wanted to hear."

Javier furrowed his brow pondering Beryl's meaning. Out of the corner of his eye, his email populated and he read a familiar name. "Look at this—Roman forwarded me an email from two Rakum in Dallas." Javier read on and Beryl rose to stand over his shoulder.

"Imagine that—Dae Kim and Pete," Beryl said quietly. "By the way, I know Dae Kim very well. Same Elder. He was born in 1946."

Javier nodded. All Rakum had perfect memory and total recall, but the longer they lived as mortals, the more the old life and its memories melted away. Javier used to know the birthdates of every Rakum he'd ever met. Today, he remembered Canaan's and Roman's. He couldn't remember Beryl's anymore and he didn't ask.

"Do you know Pete?" Javier asked and Beryl said no. "Me either. *Pete.* Peter, maybe? What Rakum would name his ward Pete?" Beryl shrugged. Javier turned back to the screen. "This was sent before they went after Adam... They were asking about the Elders."

"Yeah, right. Like we'd let them near this place."

"They are trying to get to Adam before us," Javier said thinking. "First to kill him, and then to woo him over. Who or what do they think he is and what use is he to them?"

Beryl returned to the bed and leaned back, arms folded behind his head. "In other news, I got a text from Rafael. He joined the God team."

165

Javier couldn't read Beryl's take on the information, so he simply said, "Yeah. He told me. I wonder if the Elders can cure Iago. They're growing stronger every night."

Beryl dismissed his idea with, "They won't bother."

"Why not?"

"Healing consumes too much energy. Imagine what it would take to heal cancer, and he's old already. What's the use?"

Javier stared at Beryl unblinking. Iago was only fifty-one and soon enough, Beryl would realize fifty wasn't so old after all.

"I'll still mention it," Javier said quietly and looked back at the computer. If he had the power to do it, he'd hop on it in an instant.

Just as he pulled up the next email, Canaan called.

Showtime.

22

"It's the dynamic duo," Canaan said as soon as Javier peeked around the living room threshold where the party had been moved. Kilmeade stood at the far end of the room, leaning against the ledge of the built-ins, arms folded, his face unreadable. Canaan took a position beside Kilmeade and mimicked his posture. Adam stood awkwardly in the center of the room sideways to the Elders and now Javier and Beryl.

"So, what did we learn?" Javier asked parking beside the armchair. Beryl stood next to him, apparently just as unsure as to where they should land.

"Adam," Canaan prompted and the guy startled. He stepped to Javier and handed him three sheets of old paper. His eyes were huge and his movements jittery; he'd been spooked just as they expected. The top two were hastily jotted pages of formulas, symbols, and doctor's notations. The third was handwritten by a Rakum.

"You two read that," Canaan said and Javier had already begun after settling into a chair. Beryl sat on the edge of the couch and waited for the first sheet to be passed across.

Javier was no scientist, but the surface meaning of the papers was obvious. Someone from the turn of the century jotted down the details of samples collected from Subject A, various extractions made, and methods of storage. Javier handed the two top sheets to Beryl. The last one was from Elder Bel.

"Elder Kilmeade," Javier said, looking at the letter, "it says he stole the materials and gave them to his Cow." Javier lifted his eyes and looked at Adam. "Dr. Roberts?" Adam made a tiny nod. Javier handed the note to Beryl and worked up a new question. "You knew... what? About the Rakum? What did you think was going on?"

"We asked him the same thing." Canaan uncrossed his arms and pulled out the desk chair. "We called you in here to continue. Go on, Adam. Have you ever heard that term? Rakum?"

"No," Adam said, his energy completely different than before.

"Out there, you said you were a lab assistant," Beryl said, his tone accusatory. "Elder Bel suggests you were more like a lab rat." Before Adam could answer, Beryl turned to Kilmeade. "Bel must have recognized the boy looked like you. How did he keep it a secret?"

Kilmeade's eyebrows went up as if he'd been daydreaming. As easily as he got bored, Javier thought he probably had been.

"Think. Has no one ever kept a secret from the Fathers?" he replied with familiar arrogance. Holding Beryl's eye, he slowly sucked his uncommonly sharp teeth.

"As far back as I remember, all our tests were voluntary," Adam said quietly, drawing everyone's attention. "Dr. Roberts took blood and tissue samples on a schedule. He has books and books of notes in his study about me. Now that he's dead, they're all mine. I inherit everything. I have started looking for things related to this research." He indicated the old papers. "We can go there, I have the keys."

"Let's not get ahead of ourselves," Canaan said in Kilmeade's tone and Javier suppressed a grin. The two Elders were melding into one man. Did they notice, and what did it mean?

"What now?" Beryl asked. Everyone turned to Kilmeade, who paused a long moment before replying.

Finally, he said without inflection, "Adam is mortal. He should go his merry way and forget this night ever happened." Beside him, Canaan agreed with a grunt. Adam parted his lips to counter and Kilmeade silenced him with a raised palm. "You have *my* excellent genes, Dr. Roberts's wealth, and Javier tells us you're already a success."

"You lack nothing," Canaan added with finality. "The end."

"Canaan, be realistic," Javier dissented with as much respect as possible. "He's not going to forget this."

"Oh, we'll help him forget," Canaan said firmly, holding Javier's eye.

"Sir," Adam whispered, "those men who tried to kill me will be back."

"Pete and Dae Kim," Javier offered. Neither Elder reacted to the names which meant they had attended their daytime conversations.

"Did wittle Adam get fwightened?" Canaan asked in baby talk. He crossed to Adam and looked at Kilmeade, eyebrows raised.

"Go ahead," Kilmeade said and Canaan gingerly grasped the kid by the forearm, pushing up his sleeve.

Canaan sent him a wink. "I'm gonna read you again."

"Wait, wait," Adam protested.

Canaan laughed. "That's funny," he said and moved his hold to Adam's throat using more force than necessary. "As if it could tell me what to do."

"But..." Adam whispered, his brow creased in worry.

Canaan looked at Adam's face, three seconds passed, and he grinned. "This is..." He turned to Kilmeade. "Judas Priest."

"What? What is it?" Adam asked, his eyes roving. "I can explain..."

Canaan laughed low in his throat. "Wait," Canaan said, laugh-talking. "Wait, seriously. Kid—try to read me. Try. I'm sending you a present."

"What? Wait..." Adam said, his eyes growing larger. Then he flinched and jerked back, but Canaan's grip held him in place.

"Nuh-uh. Keep watching. You need to see this..." Canaan looked back at Kilmeade still chuckling. Then he released Adam, smiling on the young man as if he were an exhibit in a zoo. He returned to Kilmeade, an eyebrow indicating they were discussing the man telepathically.

"What?" Adam said with a mixture of frustration and fear, rubbing his neck where Canaan's fingers had been. "What's going on?"

Kilmeade rolled his eyes and walked past the group toward the door. Canaan followed, turning to Javier as he tailed them to the foyer.

"Tell him the history of the Rakum."

"What just happened?" Javier whispered to both Elders. Kilmeade wouldn't meet his eye and Canaan was still laughing to himself. He then leveled his gaze.

"Javier, do what I told you to do." Canaan glanced at Kilmeade who frowned.

"You know I will," Javier replied softly.

Canaan huffed and shook his head. "That cocky air?" he said jerking his chin back the way they had come. "A put-on. He's scared to death. He's no Kilmeade."

"He's been raised by a man with hand-me-down Rakum knowledge." Javier didn't know what else to say. The guy *couldn't* measure up if the Elders' expectations were that high.

"Follow my orders. Do it now." Canaan pat Javier's shoulder. "And don't let him fool you; he's scared shitless. He thinks we're all *vampires.* Hollywood vampires. You and Beryl, Dae Kim and Pete." Canaan shook his head. "And wittle Adam wants to be a vampire, too."

Kilmeade growled and exited the front door.

"We are a proud people and there are only two of us left," Canaan said stepping out. "Please tell the human with my man's face that his seed donor is a Rakum, *not* a vampire."

"Okay, you know I will, but what else could he think?" Javier glanced at the open door. "Maybe Kilmeade is overreacting."

Canaan scrunched his nose in fun. "I'll pretend I didn't just hear that. Do as I said and send the kid home. We will decide tomorrow what we will do about him." Canaan held out his hand for the key fob and left.

Javier trudged inside deep in thought. Beryl and Adam were speaking, on the sofa, turned toward the center. When Javier entered, both stood. He dragged a heavy dining room chair closer and faced them as they re-settled on the couch.

"Why the theatrics?" Beryl asked, tipping his head toward the door.

"Adam," Javier said and waited for the young man to meet his gaze. He looked lost. "You added everything up and want to know if we're vampires. Does that sum it up?"

"Vampires?" Beryl mumbled.

Adam's lips tightened into a line and he shrugged. "I told them I had to guess. He saw into my mind? Elder Canaan touched me and could see what I have in my mind?"

Javier nodded. "Yes, but he's not a vampire. Vampires are make-believe." Javier looked at Beryl, wondering if he should tell the story of the Rakum as he knew it before, or as he knows it now. He decided to tell it the way Kilmeade or Canaan would.

Javier cleared his throat. "Thousands of years ago, a spirit expelled from God's presence took the form of a man and created a race of men that he called Rakum. He empowered the Rakum and gave them supernatural abilities. For more than two thousand years, exactly one hundred thousand Rakum lived under the radar of mortal mankind. Rakum are born—not made—and a Rakum is always male. Rakum eat, drink, have sex, party, work, whatever humans do, a Rakum can do better. You saw Elder Bel taking blood from Dr. Roberts because the Rakum drink human blood."

"And can't go out during the day?" Adam asked.

Beryl and Javier both nodded.

"So, you can see that the Rakum aren't make-believe."

Adam said nothing, but he had questions and sought the right ones to ask in what order. Finally, he said, "Why are there only two left?"

Beryl nodded to Javier, leaving it to him to explain. Javier thought a minute and said, "We don't know precisely why the Elders didn't transform into humans, but seven years ago, the Rakum became aware of the Creator of the Universe and His salvation, so many transformed to human at that time by faith in Him. I was one of those. On November 13th last year, the spirit that I told you about was erased from existence. When that happened, his power disappeared in every remaining Rakum. They all began to morph into humans. That happened to Beryl."

"November 13th?" Adam said and looked between both men. "Dr. Roberts hung himself the 14th."

"The Cows reverted, too," Beryl said.

"And all Cows were notoriously unstable," Javier mumbled. "My condolences."

"Appreciated, but..." Adam shrugged one shoulder. "What about the other part." Adam looked at them both and put his palms to either side of his head. "The *Creator?* Is that a religion? The Creator and His Salvation—are you talking about Jesus Christ? The religious figurehead?"

Javier slowly shook his head. "The real Jesus, or Yeshua, is not fiction. The Jesus Christ of the churches is mostly created by emotionalism, and here in America, by wealth and greed."

Adam looked at Beryl. "You have an opinion on this?"

Beryl leaned back into the sofa. "He's real. He showed me more than once that He is the strongest of all and the Creator."

Adam stared at Beryl, blinked once, and then looked back to Javier. "The Elders, what do they believe?"

Javier chuckled. "They both know that God is real. For their own reasons, they are choosing to not receive His salvation. They will, probably, I hope..." Javier said and trailed off. He truly wanted them both to be saved, but would they give up their deity to serve the true Deity?

"So it *is* Jesus Christ—you have to believe Jesus is the Son of God to be saved." Adam watched Javier's eyes.

"No, you have to believe Jesus died on the cross for your sins, and then you will confess it with your mouth. At that time, His Spirit comes to dwell in your heart. You will spend eternity with Him and not in hell."

"Deep, isn't it?" Beryl mumbled.

Adam got to his feet. "Where did the Elders go?"

"They don't tell us their movements," Beryl said. "One thing you don't know yet is that the Elders were our immediate leaders. They were bred differently, trained differently, and have unimaginable power that they keep tamped down."

"Tamped down?"

"They can kill a mortal with a thought," Beryl offered.

Adam shook his head. "I don't like them," he said in a low voice.

Javier rubbed his eyes. "Don't form an opinion about the Elders until you've known them longer. Imagine what it's like from their perspective. Can you do that?"

Adam shrugged and said okay. Then he met Javier's eye. "I don't like having my mind read like that. By force. It's... invasive. It makes me feel—"

"Helpless; we understand," Beryl said grabbing his attention. "If you give them a chance, you will find they are the wisest men on the planet and you can trust their decisions."

Javier nodded. "When Dae Kim visited you the second time, what did he want? If he didn't want to kill you, what did he say?"

Adam swallowed and didn't answer. Beryl discerned the meaning of his hesitation. "Did he coerce you to do something you didn't want to do?" Beryl asked softly.

Adam shrugged. "You could say that."

"What happened?" Beryl tried again.

"Just tell us. We've seen it all before." Javier's impatience grew as he recalled how indignant the Elders had been. Adam was hiding something and he'd like to suss it out before the night was done.

"He seduced me," Adam blurted and looked aside. "That's why I asked you about your face. This guy... once he had me, he had me."

"Don't be ashamed," Javier said. "Before the Rakum spirit was expelled, we could seduce any mortal we set our whims upon."

"But Dae Kim is mortal, right?" Beryl asked Javier.

"Yes, but a demonic spirit can mimic his Rakum powers." Javier caught Adam's eye. "You blushed when we asked you. How successful was he? What happened?" Adam dropped his eyes, still holding back. Javier exhaled. "Adam, we want to help you."

"Tell us what happened with Dae Kim." Beryl scooted a few inches closer to him on the couch. "Did Elder Canaan see? It's something you are hoping we won't find out?"

Adam shook his head and stared at his hands. "I'm sure he saw it. I'm sure that was when he laughed and started sending me the most god-awful images I've ever seen," Adam said quietly.

"He's a prankster, Adam," Javier said and forced a laugh. "Dae Kim seduced you and what happened?"

"He had fangs," Adam said and looked up when Beryl made a noise of disbelief. "Elder Canaan saw it—Dae Kim had fangs."

Javier absently scratched his neck. "Demonic spirits can do that, too. So he bit you? Took your blood?"

Adam nodded and his breath hitched before he recovered. He had feared for his life; Javier felt for the guy. But there was more. Canaan wouldn't storm out because the guy was attacked.

"And then what?"

"He forced me to swallow some of his blood," Adam said again looking to the side. "He went on and on about his master and how he wanted to make me like him..."

Javier's eyebrows arched and he nodded to Beryl, familiar with the verbiage.

"And then he tried to make me kill a man that walked in on us..." Adam said very small. Javier and Beryl both inhaled.

"Who? What happened? Is he okay?"

Adam shook his head. "Dae Kim killed him after, but Elder Canaan saw what I did. I'm so embarrassed."

Beryl tenderly touched Adam's knee. "You attacked the man?" Adam nodded. "Don't be embarrassed. Dae Kim knows exactly what to do to have his way with any mortal."

"Plus, the demonic influence you're subject to..." Javier offered. "I'll teach you about the spirit realm and it will be much more difficult for them to manipulate you, I promise."

Adam nodded, still obviously miserable.

Javier suddenly remembered Chloe was coming and jumped up. "I forgot something. Excuse me." He crossed to the far side and dialed Canaan who picked right up.

"Javie! Did baby Adam cry when you explained nobody's gonna make him a vampire?" Canaan laughed at his joke.

After a courtesy chuckle, Javier barreled on. "Chloe's coming tomorrow. I'm supposed to pick her up at the airport."

"Yeah, we heard you, dummy. We hear everything," Canaan said. "Tell Rafael if he wants me to heal Santiago, I'll give it a go."

So he heard that, too. Javier smirked. Before he could say any more, Canaan was gone. Beryl was patting Adam's back when Javier returned to the living room. The young man sat on the couch leaning over his knees.

"What's going on?" Javier asked and sat near them.

"It has to do with Canaan," Beryl said in a quiet voice.

"He's harmless. He likes to tease. It's his thing."

"I'm fine," Adam whispered, but didn't raise his head.

Javier read Beryl's face; his partner was just as curious. *What did Canaan show him that made him so afraid?* Javier took a stab. "Did he show

173

you a murder? Maybe, him killing someone?"

Adam nodded. He raised his face and his eyes were wet. "He wanted to scare me, and he did. I'm a genius, guys; I have a Masters in Psychology. I realize what he was doing." Adam took a deep breath. "He knew a man my age and kept him a long time. Kept him like a dog, fed him garbage, used him like a toy for his own debased jollies, and attacked him in every bloody manner imaginable..." Adam's voice fell inaudible and Javier looked to Beryl who shrugged.

"A Rabbit?" he mouthed and Javier didn't know.

After a long silence Javier exhaled and touched Adam's shoulder. "Could you see the era? By what they were wearing or the setting?"

Adam shrugged. "What does it matter? He's a monster. And you guys adore him."

After exchanging glances with Beryl, Javier shook Adam's opposite shoulder. "Look at me," he said and Adam met his eyes. "I'm a mortal now, but I lived that life more than a century. It wasn't evil for Canaan to do those things—it was normal, it was proper. Use your genius mind to step outside of your box and imagine being one of us." Javier awaited a nod from Adam. "If you live in a society apart from mankind with your own rules and social norms, obeying your leaders is not wrong."

Adam swallowed. "Elder Canaan was commanded to abuse that man?"

Beryl and Javier both nodded.

"We're assuming it was before he was an Elder because what you're describing is a Rakum Rabbit," Javier offered.

Beryl explained before the guy could ask. "A Rabbit is a mortal that has wronged us; usually he tried to murder one of our brethren. When he is caught, he is fed the blood of an Elder; from then on, he's a Rabbit. His body heals like a Rakum so the grunts can attack him over and over forever. It's punishment for those who turn against us."

Javier agreed with a noise. "And Canaan did his duty to punish whoever that guy was. After a Rakum becomes an Elder, they no longer chase Rabbits, so your story is really old."

"I wish I could unsee it." Adam shuddered. "I couldn't think fast enough of how to get away..."

"You can't resist," Javier said gently. "He's a Rakum Elder."

Adam leaned back into the couch. "Elder Canaan is going to tell you. Since I was born, I've been drinking human blood. It was part of Dr. Roberts's program. But not like Bel, I never drank from a living person,"

Adam clarified beginning to pale. Javier and Beryl both stood up and looked down on Adam as he reclined.

Finally Javier asked, "Why? For what purpose?"

"Various positive outcomes," Adam said like a research scientist.

"Such as?" Beryl added.

"We stopped experimenting after my fifteenth year, but the experiments showed increased physical strength, increased performance on intelligence testing, increased acuity in my five senses. Even increased sun-sensitivity."

"Wait—we were with you in the sun yesterday," Javier said.

Adam opened his eyes. "Were you?"

Beryl looked at Javier and shook his head. "It was overcast, but it was day."

"I can go out when the sun isn't too bright, but I stay in if it is. I work at night, sleep during the day. I blend in."

"Dr. Roberts was trying to see if you were a Rakum?" Javier asked.

Adam nodded. "I assume so, now that I know about you. At the time, he was only assuring me that I was *special,* and the results proved it."

"Geez," Javier whispered and ran his fingers roughly through his hair. "That's enough for tonight. The Elders have the truck. Beryl, will you call Adam an Uber?"

Beryl nodded and pulled out his cell.

"Do you sleep light-tight?" Javier asked as Beryl worked the app.

Adam shook his head. "No, just curtains."

"What happens if you get in the sun? Do you burn?"

"No, I get weak, sort of nauseous."

Javier nodded, the guy's sun sensitivity similar to his when he suffered under Isaac's blood. But what did that mean? He crossed his arms and Beryl got off the phone.

In another ten minutes he was gone and Javier and Beryl crashed in front of the television. By two a.m., Javier roused and checked the garage for the Yukon. The Elders hadn't returned and what they were up to was anybody's guess. Back in the living room, he nudged Beryl with his shoe.

"I'm heading to bed. Good night."

Beryl sat up and looked around. "Canaan back?"

Javier shook his head.

Beryl stood and stretched. "I had a dream just now of that guy Adam burning our Elders to death with sunlight. I didn't dream as a Rakum and I sure don't like it now." Beryl blinked rapidly. "This was much too vivid to not be some sort of warning." He shook his head.

"A warning?" Javier repeated, knowing Beryl was new to such things. "Like from God?"

"That's your department." Beryl shivered. "I'm turning in."

Javier clapped his back as he passed. When he disappeared up the stairs, Javier sat and lowered his face into his hands.

"I'm glad You kept us all safe today," Javier said in a whisper. *"My prayer is that we fulfill Your purposes on this mission. That's all. Amen."*

Javier remained bowed a few seconds longer. None of them prayed like Beth Rider, with practiced phrases, memorized scriptures, or Hebrew blessings, but it was enough to direct his heart to the Creator. Javier said amen one more time and headed to bed.

23, MAY 14

While waiting for Chloe's luggage at the carousel, Javier texted Rafael concerning the possibility of Canaan healing Iago. Instead of texting back, Rafael called.

"He thinks he can do it?" Rafael asked in a soft accent that likely drove the ladies wild. "Last November, Kilmeade assured me he didn't have the power to heal cancer."

"Since we last saw you, the Elders' abilities have increased a hundredfold. When Canaan overheard us discussing it, he offered to try." Rafael was quiet a few seconds and then came back on the line.

"*Grácias,* Javier. I'll speak to Iago. *Kazak.*"

On the drive to the house, Chloe said she had been having nightmares about their Rakum hunt, so when Javier filled her in on their adventures, he kept it light. When they were five minutes from the rental house, he asked her if she knew anything about Kilmeade's babies.

Chloe huffed. "Rakum Elders can't make babies..."

"I'm sure Kilmeade would want me to get you up to speed," Javier said and proceeded to tell her about his experiments from 1901 and how they found out days ago that the locker had been raided. "So with a little detective work and the help of a geneticist your father knows, we picked up the trail." Javier paused because his next news would be shocking.

"Where did they go? Can we make babies from them?" Chloe had turned in her seat watching Javier with round eyes.

Javier gave her a quick look and turned back to the road. "Brace yourself, but someone already did. Twenty-seven years ago to be exact."

"What?" she said loud enough to cause Javier to wince. "No way!"

"Shh," he said, "We met him and his name is Adam. Open the photos in my phone."

"No way!" Chloe said again and did as Javier suggested. When she saw his photograph she reverse-pinched it to zoom. "NO WAY!"

"Calm down." Javier turned into the neighborhood and slowed to give her time to accept the news.

"I'm calm," she said and flipped her long hair to one side. "Can I meet him? Is he normal?"

"Unless Kilmeade has some reason not to. He's human and he seems okay." Javier looked at Chloe. "As you can see, he's the spitting image of Kilmeade. Be prepared."

"Just...wow..." she said and leaned back in her seat as Javier pulled into the drive. "This is nice," she remarked looking at the house. "It was very cool of you to rent houses for the Elders," she said far away.

"I've slept in enough bathrooms to know this is much better."

She shot him a grin. "Hah, it's easy to forget you used to be one of them. You're so normal now."

"I'll take that as a compliment," he said with a chuckle and hopped out of the truck. He came around to open her door and she jumped down like a child.

"I want to see him. Do you think I can? You know they're not asleep." Chloe had stepped into the foyer and looked in every direction.

"No, Kilmeade specifically asked me to have you wait up here." Javier showed her to the living room. "Just get a feel for the place, look around. They'll be up soon." Chloe pouted and walked away.

Javier shook his head and left her to her explorations.

《▣》

When the basement door opened, Javier watched Canaan exit at a jog. Right behind him, Kilmeade grabbed Canaan's heel. It looked like they had been wrestling, remaining sane in a Rakum-free world.

"*Shiiiit!*" Canaan yelped, went down to his palms, and violently jerked his foot free. Kilmeade reached the landing and closed the basement door. The Elders noticed Javier at the same time; Canaan pointed Javier a finger gun while Kilmeade only smirked.

"Chloe's in the living room," he told them and they headed that way in unison.

"Kilmeade!" she screamed, hurting Javier's ears as she passed and leapt into the Elder's arms. Javier thought to find a place to sit, but immediately a dark look passed the Elder's face.

"What's wrong?" Javier asked out of impulse and Kilmeade did not respond. His expression recovered and he wrapped his arms around Chloe's small form. The identical cloud remained on Canaan's face a few feet away and Javier caught his eye, mouthing, *what is it?*

"Boys," Canaan said and turned for the kitchen. Javier and Beryl exchanged a glance and walked past the couple.

"Good to see you, Chloe," Canaan said pulling Javier by his sleeve. "Ya'll chat." To Javier and Beryl he said, "Kitchen."

"I am totally confused," Beryl said. "Is she sick?"

Canaan reached the island and leaned against the counter. Milking the moment, he crossed his arms and grinned.

"Canaan," Javier said and stepped closer. "Come on."

Canaan scrunched his nose. "Chloe's pregnant."

Javier looked at Beryl and no one said anything for a long while.

《回》

"But you said you couldn't, we couldn't, I wouldn't..." Chloe said, looking into Kilmeade's killer gray eyes. After a quick mental count, she calculated a minimum of four months along. Chloe put her hands to her tummy. Was it softer? Her breasts had been more sensitive, but not enough to ponder. She felt sluggish, but had attributed that to stress-eating, bad dreams, loneliness, and quitting school. Even when her menstrual period ceased, she blamed stress. *Never* did it enter her mind she might be pregnant.

Kilmeade's head went to the side and he gave her a tight smile. "There is no doubt," he said and stroked her hair. "I hear our child's heart beating, very strong and very healthy."

"Wow..." she said faraway. "That means you and Canaan..."

Kilmeade gave a miniscule nod. "Ta'avah held that curse on our seed. I assume since he's gone, the curse is gone." Kilmeade took her face in his hands and kissed her forehead. "It never occurred to me that such a thing might happen."

Chloe put her hands to his chest and worked to read his expression. Was he happy? Was she? She was only twenty. Wasn't she going to do a bunch of stuff before she started having babies?

"Yes, I am happy," Kilmeade said in her ear and kissed her cheek and then her lips tenderly, as if she'd been gone decades and not six weeks. Before too long, she was flush with romantic notions and Kilmeade scooped her up and carried her upstairs.

After a short but passionate love session, Kilmeade snugged her close and whispered embarrassing and delightful compliments in her ear. Chloe giggled and dug in further with Kilmeade wrapped around her from behind. When he removed one arm from around her to tickle her side, she shrieked and scooted away.

"They're waiting for you!" she squealed and shoved herself to the other side of the king-size bed. "We better go see what's happening." She clutched the blanket to her chin and watched his eyes prepared to jump off the bed if he tried to tickle her again.

Instead Kilmeade smiled and rolled onto his back, calling her back with his fingers. "Come close, little bird," he whispered. Chloe comically crawled toward him and he pulled her close to rest her head on his chest.

"Don't you want to see what they're doing down there?" she asked and stretched her arm across his body. "They sure are patient with you."

"Why not? They've waited on me their entire lives. I am Kilmeade," he said with a grin and kissed the top of her head.

"Don't you mean, you're the master?" Chloe asked with mischievous flair, maybe still stinging from the reprimand received when she lost her temper with Canaan.

Kilmeade chuckled. "I'm evolving. I'm only Canaan's master in this new world. You're off the hook."

Chloe pivoted to see his profile. "Is that good or bad?"

"It just *is.*"

Chloe made a noise of agreement and settled against his side. At one time, he was master to the entire population of Rakum grunts, and many Cows, too. The loneliness and helplessness of his loss struck her deep and she shuddered. "I'm sorry, Kilmeade."

"I forgive you," he said and when she looked to his face, he was grinning. Chloe's mind turned to blood and she wondered if she should mention it. Before she spoke, Kilmeade saw it coming. "Until the baby comes, keep your delicious blood to yourself."

Chloe nodded in agreement. She caressed his chest and remembered the biggest news in the world aside from her pregnancy. "What do you think of Adam?"

He didn't answer for a long moment and finally exhaled. "I don't think anything. We spoke to him a short time and we left. Maybe tonight he can make a better impression." Kilmeade nudged her with his arm. "You haven't explained why you're here. What compelled you to quit school and fly to Texas?"

"Can't you see it in my mind?" she asked and fluttered her eyelashes.

"I see you were having nightmares. Why did you take them seriously?"

Chloe sighed. "I don't dream much at all and these were so specific... They reminded me of Bible stories where God speaks to the prophets in their dreams. Roman said—"

"Ahh," Kilmeade interrupted. "So I have my brother to thank for this impromptu romantic rendezvous." Kilmeade rolled away and sat up to shrug on his clothing.

Chloe scooted after him. "Well, I asked Roman about the dreams."

"Tell me more later tonight," Kilmeade said and handed over her T-shirt. "We will go save Canaan from Beryl and Javier. They're turning him into a little girl."

"What?" Chloe laughed, but Kilmeade was already at the bedroom door and he turned to wait. "I'm coming, I'm coming." She pulled up her socks and trotted to his side.

"Let's not give Canaan any fodder for his games," Kilmeade said as he straightened her hair, lifting and fluffing it across her shoulders. Chloe closed her eyes to his clumsy grooming. "Be nice to Canaan. He will be the one taking care of you if anything happens to me."

Chloe's eyes flew open. "What?"

But Kilmeade had turned and opened the door. He walked when she did and led her to the living room. *What does that mean? Is Kilmeade in danger? What? What?* Chloe worried and tried to smile anyway.

《◙》

When Kilmeade and Chloe abandoned the living room, Canaan returned and collapsed dramatically on the long end of the sectional.

"I need to get me a little woman," Canaan said to no one, his arm over his eyes.

Javier chuckled and entered with Beryl. They sat at opposite ends and Javier jabbed Canaan's foot. "Don't spy on them."

Canaan peeked at Javier under his beefy arm. "You're such a pervert," he said grinning and covered his eyes after placing a decorative pillow over his lap. "Now hush, I'm concentrating."

Javier laughed and slapped his foot again as his phone chimed. "It's Adam. He wants to know if he can come over."

"Gotta ask Daddy," Canaan said with a grin, face still covered.

"Beryl, tell Canaan about your dream," Javier said.

"*Ffft*, he won't care." Beryl stared at his cell phone, but Canaan sat up and swung his feet to the floor.

"Tell me, B. You're a bigger part of this mission than you think."

Beryl set down his phone and rolled his eyes. "I don't know what it was, but I had a flash of him opening a door to a dark room and you and Kilmeade were killed by sunlight. End of dream."

"Damn, that's terrible," Canaan said making a face.

"I took it seriously," Javier said, not sure what the Elder thought. "We don't know Adam yet and Dae Kim was able to swoon him."

"I'd like to get my hands around his neck," Canaan said to himself. "Did he ask the kid for anything? Did he know about the letter?"

"I didn't think about that," Javier said and looked at Beryl. "Adam told us Dae Kim wanted to take him to his master. To me, it sounds like Dae Kim and Pete are following demonic spirits; maybe these spirits are giving them power. It sounds like something Ta'avah or Zahdone would have tried."

"I hate those invisible troublemakers," Canaan hissed. "Life was a lot more fun before I knew about them."

Javier gave a weak laugh.

"Let's save this for Loverboy." He grinned and looked in the general direction of the stairs. "When he disentangles himself, tell him what you just told me."

"Stop trying to make me picture what you can see, sir," Javier said, chin lowered. "Not our business."

"What?" Beryl said looking up from his phone. "What?"

"Nothing," Javier said and changed the subject. "Canaan, listen," Javier began and Canaan regarded him with a humorous eye roll. "I'm serious. Beryl and I noticed that you and Kilmeade are changing. It's hard to put a finger on it, but do you feel okay?"

Canaan dropped the silliness and took in a gaze from Beryl, too. He tilted his head and asked Javier, "Does it worry you?"

"No. Yeah." Javier shook his head. "Maybe. It looks like you are becoming one person in two bodies. Is that even possible?"

"Ask Beryl," Canaan grinned. "B? Didn't you and Meryl share a brain?"

"But they were identical twins," Javier answered for him. "I guess I just wondered if it was a good thing or a bad thing. For you. For your health. For the future."

Canaan arose and stepped to Javier's side.

"There you go, worrying for old Canaan again." He grabbed him by the neck and gently shook him back and forth. "Both of you, you're doing a great job with this Rakum hunt. We'll help a lot of our brothers before we're done. You care a lot, and you know Kilmeade and I care about all of them. We're unhappy that Boris flipped out. We're unhappy that Kamron rejected our assistance. How many others out there are in need of our guidance? How many others just need to hear someone say, hey, little buddy, you're not alone."

Clapping erupted from the hallway as Kilmeade entered the room smiling. "Bravo!" he said and paused for Chloe. She appeared beside him and he pointed to an armchair. "How about, hey, little buddy, you're not alone. Here's twenty million dollars to buy booze and women," Kilmeade said with a grin. "If they would only give us a chance, we have some really good news."

Javier watched Kilmeade take a seat against Chloe who scooted over in the wide chair. Javier smirked and glanced at Beryl. He noticed it too; Kilmeade's positivity had skyrocketed.

"Somebody's in a good mood," Canaan said and winked at Chloe, who blushed and looked away. "Now that Elder Romeo has rejoined the class, tell him about your dream, B."

Kilmeade stopped him with one hand. "I heard. Let's talk about those two wild cards that tried to kill Adam. Pete's real name is Petrov; he was Emil's pup. I am familiar with both he and Dae Kim."

"Why would anyone want to kill Kilmeade's son?" Chloe asked. Kilmeade turned and looked at her. Of course, he wouldn't consider the young man a son, but being human-born gave Chloe an entirely different perspective on everything.

"Adam shot Pete in the chest," Canaan said with his fist at his sternum. "If he recovered, he has spiritual help. Isn't that how it works?"

Javier nodded, flattered Canaan openly deferred to him.

"Get him over here," Canaan instructed, again sounding like Kilmeade. "Tell him to remain alert."

"What's going on? I thought this wasn't dangerous? Who's trying to kill Adam?" Chloe scooted forward to touch Kilmeade's arm. He looked at her hand and then covered it with his own. She looked at his face and grew quiet.

Javier texted Adam; in less than a minute, the man responded and Javier gave Canaan a nod.

"I know Dae Kim," Canaan offered. "I never met Petrov."

Javier shook his head. "I don't know either of them."

"Elder Dawn settled Dae Kim in Manhattan," Beryl offered. "Meryl and I partied with him a lot. Nothing remarkable to say except he loved the ladies. Dae matured very early and had more sex than any Rakum I knew; neither Meryl nor I could keep up with him."

Chloe giggled and then zipped her lips. "My bad."

Kilmeade kissed her fingers. "Dae Kim never impressed me," he said dismissively. "Petrov, though—he was a delight." Kilmeade set Chloe's hand back on his thigh. He grinned at Canaan. "You would have liked him. He was like Beryl—so pretty and cuddly."

"Hey," Beryl said with no true angst evident in his objection.

"Call my brother. Roman knows Petrov. He and Emil left on assignment together when the Fathers split the two of us up."

Javier dialed Roman and when he picked up, he put him on speaker. "Roman, everyone is listening. Do you remember a Rakum named Petrov with Elder Emil?"

"Hey, guys," Roman said and then hummed a moment. *"You must mean Pete."*

"Yes," Javier and Beryl said together.

"Pete was with us for several years, Emil favored him. Why?"

"I'll fill you in, but tell us what you remember about him," Javier added.

"First, he's a looker—ask Kilmeade. He teased him a lot."

Kilmeade rolled in his lips with a slow nod.

"He didn't much care for humans. We caught him torturing a man once, some Cow, and not one of his own."

"How awful," Chloe mumbled.

"And he was a leader. Emil thought he was simply bored, so he made him captain. The grunts idolized him."

"Thanks, Roman," Javier said and stood. He looked at Kilmeade, gesturing he was going to speak privately. The Elder nodded and turned back to Canaan. Javier went into the hallway. "How's it going?"

"I'm sure you saw my last email, but fifty-five Rakum have come to the site today and been authenticated by the Bankers," Roman said and then added, "Remember your suggestion?"

"For Guap and Polly?"

"Right. They are taking your advice. Only our group plus three or four others received the disbursement before the new process. Now, every Rakum must check in with us before his money is dispersed. He won't have to do anything but listen. That's fair, right?"

"I think so. It has saved lives already," Javier answered. "I need to know if Pete and Dae Kim received their money."

"I'm looking right at it. Yes, Pete in December and Dae Kim in January." Javier filled him in with a few basics and promised to call him the next day. Back in the living room, the Elders and Chloe had risen and headed for the foyer.

"Keep our mini-me occupied," Canaan said to Javier.

"We will return in two hours and continue this investigation," Kilmeade said, his eyes also on Javier.

Javier nodded and the Elders ushered Chloe out the front door. When they were gone, Beryl had come to stand beside Javier and he made a noise.

"What?" Javier asked him.

Beryl inclined his head to the front door. "It's like you said. I mean, in some way, when they stand together, they seem to be one person."

Javier nodded. No matter the Elders had vastly different hair styles, facial features, and Canaan was an inch taller with fifty pounds more muscle; when they were side-by-side, they optically blended into one.

"I want to show you something," Beryl said quietly and started flipping internet pages on his phone. "I came across this accidentally when this photo popped up in an ad..."

Javier stepped closer and watched his fingers as they selected pages. When he found what he wanted, it was an advertisement for a role playing game called Archangels III; its box cover showed two angels standing over a man whose head came to their shoulders. Both angels were shrouded in shadow, slightly stooped, angled in toward their ward, each with their wingtips touching their heels.

"Isn't this what the Elders look like?" Beryl shook his head. "It's eerie. And I've seen a lot of shit."

"Is it good or bad?" Javier sighed and then shook Beryl's shoulder. "At least you and I aren't starting to look alike."

"If only you could be so lucky," Beryl returned, but neither felt much like laughing.

24

Unconcerned with the guys' comfort, Kilmeade invited Chloe out to dinner. Canaan tailed behind them and once to the car, they both asked her where she wanted to eat.

"Italian?" Chloe said and Canaan nodded from the driver's seat. In the back seat with Kilmeade, Chloe asked for more information about Adam. "Javier told me he might have special abilities. Like what?"

"Javier should have filled you in," Kilmeade said with a sigh. "Adam is still a mystery. Tonight, he will consent to a closer examination."

"What does that mean?" Chloe's mind raced working to interpret Kilmeade's oblique answer. *I'm not a Rakum; is it too much to speak plainly?*

Kilmeade pulled her close and blew in her hair. "Dr. Kilmeade will lay hands on him. He can see inside the man's spirit."

"Dr. Kilmeade has amazing and unfathomable talents nearly as impressive as Dr. Canaan's!" Canaan offered from the driver's seat.

"Indeed," Kilmeade chuckled. "Dr. Canaan will now fill you in." Chloe looked to the rearview mirror, not surprised Kilmeade handed off the conversation.

"Yes, Dr. Kilmeade," Canaan joked. "Miss Bushman, the man smells human, but he's been consuming blood since childhood. Kilmeade's DNA combined with the ingested blood of humans did not make him a Rakum." Canaan nodded and looked back to the road. "He should *smell* different if he *was* different."

Kilmeade gave her a squeeze. "Canaan thinks it's in his head, that he's been deluded by what he thinks he knows."

"He's crazy?" Chloe asked, restating Canaan's assessment.

"Delusional," Canaan said, softening the diagnosis.

"You like him," Chloe said to Canaan in the reflection.

Canaan shrugged and caught Kilmeade's eye. "It's your mini-me. How could I not love it?"

Kilmeade chuckled and looked out the window. "I am not responsible for that person. I had no hand in bringing him here and I wish he hadn't been turned up."

Chloe gently squeezed Kilmeade's leg where her hand rested.

"He's not bad," Canaan said, pulling into the parking lot of a busy restaurant. "I saw right into him, all the way down to his inward parts. Kilmeade knows. I dug down deep with my mind shovel."

"Mind shovel," Chloe giggled into her hand. Kilmeade laughed too, still facing the dark world outside the window.

Canaan parked, unbuckled, and swiveled to meet Chloe's eye. "If Adam was dangerous, you would never meet him. I saw his core. He is soft-hearted and believes in happy endings. He is not a Rakum."

Kilmeade popped her thigh. "You ready?"

"I'm starving," she said and Canaan and Kilmeade opened their doors simultaneously. She giggled at their synchronicity and Kilmeade saw in her mind what made her laugh. Leap-frogging off Kilmeade, Canaan did, too, and he grinned.

Heading to the door, Kilmeade walked on her left, his arm draped across her shoulders with Canaan directly behind. A gaggle of twenty-something girls rushed past, shouldering Kilmeade in the process. The one who made contact apologized while moving forward to break in line. Two of the women sought eye contact with the Elders, who ignored them. Chloe waved her fingers and they smirked. When the hostess told the girls the wait was thirty minutes for a table, two different girls turned to eye Kilmeade and Canaan. Chloe leveled her gaze at them both and they moved to the other side of the lobby.

Kilmeade snickered and leaned down. "I shall return. Stay with Canaan, little bird," he said and wove his way around the hostess stand and toward the restrooms in the back. A chill ran up Chloe's spine as she recalled her skeletal-priest dream.

Canaan moved behind her placing warm palms on her shoulders underneath her hair, his fingers close together so the pointers stroked the front of her throat. "You good?" he asked in her ear. "You shivered."

"I'm great," she mumbled, now fixated on the contact between his skin and hers. "You're...you know..."

"This? Does this bother you?" he inquired softly, his impossibly tender hands still on her shoulders.

"Canaan," Chloe whispered. She had to mention it; there were no secrets with the Elders being in one brain.

"Yep?" he said, bending down to speak softly in her ear again. *Precisely the way Kilmeade does.*

"You're touching me *exactly* the way Kilmeade does. It's a little freaky," she whispered covering her mouth with one hand because of the nosy girls who watched from their side of the room.

"This?" he said and moved his hands in tiny massaging motions. "Or do you mean this?" Canaan's hands became still, palms open on her inner shoulders. Warmth increased beneath them and within moments, a tingle of pleasure grew like a bubble from the middle of her body.

"Don't do that!" she gasped, embarrassed. Yes, Kilmeade did that, but only in private. Canaan chuckled and reeled her back.

"Wait, wait," Canaan said quietly with a smile in his voice. "Does he do this?" he said and removed one hand to poke her in the ribs from behind. When she squealed and jumped forward, he caught her shoulders and brought her back snug against his front. "Huh? Does he?"

"Canaan!" she hiss-whispered through an involuntary grin caused by the tickling. *"You're freaking me out!"*

"I got one more," Canaan said near her ear. "Wanna see it?"

"No!" she said and accidentally caught the eye of one of the more brazen party girls. The woman nudged her friend to get her to look over.

"I have to show you one more..." Canaan moved one hand forward to entirely encompass the front of her throat and he brushed it with his palm, as if asking her to turn toward him via the contact.

"No," Chloe said frowning.

"One more," Canaan whispered in her ear. *"Kilmeade wants you to see it."*

Panic flooded Chloe's body; Canaan had to show her something that she wasn't going to like. The Elder was leaning down again, his mouth now at her cheek, and when he spoke, his breath fell on her skin like butterflies and smelling of peppermint—just like Kilmeade. He was teaching her something she sincerely did not want to learn.

"Turn around," he whispered, his voice nearly inaudible.

Chloe stared hard at the rude girls, swallowed, and turned in Canaan's tender grip. He was even taller than Kilmeade and she craned her neck to meet his eyes. "What?" she said.

One hand remained on her inner shoulder, but the other touched her cheek and his fingers stroked her ear. Chloe moaned deep in her throat; he was moving in to kiss her. She put her hand to his chest, but he continued until he pressed his lips to hers. *One, two, three* seconds, she did not respond, her mind battened down and waited for Kilmeade to come back and explain himself. If he put Canaan up to this, it was extremely thoughtless. *Four, five, six* and Chloe relaxed a fraction. Canaan's hand on her cheek moved into her hair, fingers spread out against her scalp, and he held her face to his. *Seven, eight, nine* seconds, and Chloe gave in and realized what was happening—Canaan's kiss was indistinguishable from Kilmeade's. Everything about their contact, the cadence, the pattern of his tongue against hers matched her love play with Kilmeade to the smallest iota. When he disengaged and licked his lips inches from her face, a hot tear fell from Chloe's eye.

"Don't cry, little bird," Canaan said and kissed her forehead. "This is important. You need to know."

"Know what?" Chloe said, her voice hitching as she resisted crying.

"You'll figure it out," Canaan said. "And Kilmeade's headed back."

Chloe wiped her cheeks and turned in Canaan's grip. Kilmeade walked over nonchalantly and when he reached Chloe's side, the Elders changed guard—Canaan backed away and Kilmeade stood behind her to place his hands where Canaan's had been.

You'll figure it out...

Chloe placed her hand atop Kilmeade's at her shoulder and kissed his fingers. She placed her other hand on her belly where little Kilmeade or little Chloe waited to enter the world.

"Be nice to Canaan," Kilmeade had said. *"He'll take care of you if something happens to me."*

"God, please don't take Kilmeade away. Please," Chloe prayed silently. Behind her, Kilmeade kissed her head.

《回》

"Have you had any trouble? Any sign of Dae Kim?" Javier asked Adam as they walked in the door. Over hamburgers, they talked about everything except immediate current events, instead, discussing women, movies, politics, and the way different types of cheese taste when melted. As soon as they pulled into the driveway of the rented house, the mood dipped and seriousness reigned.

"No, but I had nightmares about your buddy, Canaan."

Javier disregarded his statement, while Beryl felt the need to reiterate Canaan's trustworthiness. Adam shrugged and then sat purposefully close to Beryl on the huge sectional dominating a third of the room. Javier chose the adjacent recliner and leaned over his knees.

"Can ya'll teach me the telepathy thing?" Adam asked haltingly, giving Javier only a small glance.

"We're not Rakum anymore," Javier answered. "And you're human, why bother?" Javier wanted to watch his eyes, but he faced Beryl instead.

"I've heard voices in my head since I was very small. Some speak

English and some don't," he said directly to Beryl. "I ask because there's probably a method of controlling them, some sort of mind exercises." He looked at Javier and added, "I've studied up on it over the years, but human mentalists are full of crap. I think true telepathy can be learned and since I hear voices, maybe I'd be a candidate."

Javier prepared another dismissive objection, but Beryl said okay.

"All Rakum had telepathy with varying degrees of talent," he told him. "My brother and I were the best in our generation; I'm sure I could give you some pointers." He turned to Javier, "Do you think Kilmeade's DNA made him open to it?"

"Wait for the Elders," Javier said, although he nodded to the query.

Beryl winked and turned back to Adam. "I'll be careful. Javier is right—it's dangerous. But, he forgets... I'm an expert."

Javier huffed, but he also was curious. Whose voices were filling Adam's head? Demons? Or was he insane?

"First, take a d-e-e-p breath and release it as slowly as possible. Drag it out forever." Adam nodded and they both closed their eyes to perform the first exercise. They finished at the same time and Beryl tipped his head to the side looking into Adam's face.

"Relax, man. It's as natural as pissing. You piss, don't you?"

"Okay," Adam said with a small laugh.

"Now, keep looking right here..." Beryl pointed to his right eye. "Be careful; we don't want you falling in love with me."

"*Ffft*, works both ways," Adam weakly retorted.

"You go both ways?" Beryl asked maintaining eye contact.

Javier leaned forward. "Don't make me be the adult in the room."

"He's so bossy," Beryl whispered, the last word fading to inaudible. Then, with a surprising jerk, Beryl looked away and got to his feet. He said to Javier with flashing eyes, "He can do it."

"What?" Adam sat up. "Why did you stop?"

Standing over him now, Beryl sent him a gentle grin. "It's intimate, and I don't have the control over it as I did as a Rakum."

"But..." Adam protested. "I didn't see anything."

Beryl caught Javier's gaze. "We touched minds." Beryl stepped to Javier and leaned to his ear. *"His mind reached for mine,"* he whispered. *"He looks like a Rakum in there. Canaan would've seen that."* Pulling back a few inches, Beryl's eyes revealed to Javier the extent of his astonishment.

Javier nodded. The initial contact with any open participant always felt like jumping into a bottomless pool of warm water. You trust that when you enter it, your feet will find purchase, but a tiny warning deep within whispers you might disappear forever. Why Canaan chose to keep the revelation from Adam, he didn't know.

"Drop it," Javier said tersely. "Let the Elders take it from here."

Adam frowned and Javier's phone chimed before he addressed the guy's hurt expression. He read the screen and showed it to Beryl.

"The Elders are headed back; they want us to tell you about Chloe." Javier paused to consider how detailed his information should be. Canaan hadn't given any additional instructions, so he would wing it.

Adam's eyebrows went up. "A woman is with ya'll?"

"She's with Elder Kilmeade. Like a wife, in human terms."

"How is she not scared to death of that guy?" he asked mortified.

Javier chuckled at Adam's naiveté. "She's seen the worst of the Rakum, trust me, and these Elders are saints in comparison." With a quick glance at Beryl, he prepared to provide cliff notes of Chloe's short history. "All of us gathered last November in Jackson, Mississippi, and Chloe was abducted by an insane Elder named Rufus. She was rescued and we regrouped. When the dust settled, she was with Elder Kilmeade."

"*Shiiiit*, Javier," Beryl said with a laugh. "You summed that up very well! Bravo!" He turned to Adam. "He left out a lot of stuff that would make me look *very* bad." Beryl sent Javier a tiny bow. "Continue, sir."

Javier grinned. "Yes, Elders are extremely protective of their mates; don't speak to her too much or look at her too long, okay?"

"Great," he mumbled his eyes more worried than ever.

A car door slammed out front and Javier stood. "Chloe might act silly, but you just do as I said," Javier said to Adam. "I have no idea how much training she's had on how to be an Elder's mate." His words were lost on Adam, but Beryl agreed with a knowing stare.

"Where's my greeting party? Your master has arrived in all his glory!" Canaan bellowed from the foyer. The Elder entered the living room halfway and caught Javier's eye. "Pitiful. Just pitiful."

Javier grinned and shook his head, figuring Canaan would have enjoyed a little demonstrative groveling when he entered. "Next time, I promise," he said to the Elder in a smiling voice.

"I'll hold you to that," he replied and stepped aside as Kilmeade entered with Chloe. She appeared fragile and feminine in her soft pink V-neck blouse and belted low-rise jeans. She held Kilmeade's arm and her eyes sought Adam. When she saw him, her mouth fell open.

"*Ohmygod!* You weren't kidding!" she said and dropped contact with

Kilmeade to step toward their guest. "Hey, Adam. I'm Chloe!"

Adam held a cautious smile as he shook her hand. When she released, he clasped both behind his back. "Honored to meet ya, ma'am."

"How sweet!" Chloe turned to Kilmeade. "He's a Texan, through and through!"

"Precious," Kilmeade retorted, but Javier read adoration in the Elder's gaze as he watched Chloe's face.

"The menfolk will now accompany me to the basement," Canaan said with authority and stepped back for Beryl and Adam to pass. "This way, kiddos." Javier watched Adam follow direction, his expression pensive. "MARCH! MARCH!" Canaan barked, following after them.

Javier lingered as Kilmeade kissed Chloe's head and whispered in her ear. She smiled and covered her mouth with both hands. Javier marveled at the tender affection the Elder displayed. Tonight, he looked like a love-struck teenager.

He had been staring too long; Kilmeade finished with Chloe and met Javier's eyes. "If you're a man, get downstairs."

Javier trotted to the hall. Kilmeade was right behind him and comically popped him on the head on the way down.

"Nosy Nelly," he said and passed him once they reached the floor.

"Okay, let's get this show on the road," Canaan said in a high voice, making fun as he always did. It was good, for Adam appeared scared to death. "Kilmeade?"

All eyes went to the more reserved Elder who offered a small smile. "This is a teaching night, Adam," he began. "Circle up and let's begin." Everyone fell still and Kilmeade said, "Adam, Canaan looked inside you and found no avarice. This is the only reason I allowed you to return." Kilmeade was facing Adam and Canaan flanked him on his left. "Those men," he said gesturing to Beryl and Javier, "this Elder, and the woman upstairs are under my protection. I would end you with a thought—" Kilmeade held up one hand, palm out, and then closed it into a fist. Adam jerked his palm to his temple with a soft yelp. "If you ever made a move against any of them."

Adam gasped, "I swear—!"

"But I don't need to, because Canaan saw you deep."

"I-I..." Adam stuttered, his hand coming away from his head. He was petrified but Javier understood Kilmeade's reasoning; the jolt assured he had the man's full attention.

"When Canaan and I touch you now," Kilmeade said to Adam, "it will be painless. Understand?"

Adam nodded with round eyes.

Kilmeade rubbed his hands together, thoughtfully sizing the man up. He then tossed a head-tip to his partner. Canaan stepped close and grasped Adam's arm.

"You will submit to a blood sample," Kilmeade stated and Adam watched without breathing as Canaan gingerly punctured his arm with his knife tip. A few drops of blood bubbled forth and Canaan brought it to his mouth via his pointer finger. He closed the tiny wound with no effort and backed away. Adam exhaled and stared at his arm.

"Your blood is human," Canaan said without emotion.

"As we guessed it would be," Kilmeade said with a smirk. "Adam, Dr. Canaan does physical testing and I do the *metaphysical*. You ready?"

"Yes, sir," Adam whispered, clearly terrified but holding it together.

The Elder took a deep breath, his right hand hovering chest-level between them. Then, with a wink to Canaan, he put out his hand and cupped the back of Adam's neck.

"Uh!" Adam exclaimed and fell silent. Close together, their differences were more pronounced. Slightly taller with a man's more mature build, Kilmeade's long reddish-brown hair held a sheen that Adam's more curly brown hair did not. And now that an expression of fear had been revealed on the young man's face, in his mind, Javier no longer compared him to the Elder at all.

"Canaan," Kilmeade whispered and Canaan stepped close. "Look..."

"What? What?" Adam asked his eyes flicking to both Elders.

They ignored him as Canaan also put his hand to the back of Adam's neck. Flanked by Elders, their guest's eyes swiveled to Beryl who used his hand to instruct him to be still.

"Oh..." Canaan said far away and then both Elders raised their eyes.

Kilmeade turned to Javier, his smile in place. "If Adam had been raised with our people, he would have been a Rakum."

Stunned, Javier only stared back.

Kilmeade nodded, looking into Adam's eyes. "As soon as Bel recognized the child, he threw up a block and avoided that memory for the rest of his life."

"What? Why?" Adam whispered. "I don't understand,"

"The Elders' minds were monitored by the Fathers. If he thought of a little Kilmeade in the world, they would know," Canaan answered and then caught Javier's eye. "Bel tucked that memory away for decades. That is one powerful brain."

"Bel stopped contributing to the experiments," Kilmeade added and moved his hand to Adam's shoulder. "If Adam had been exposed to Ritual training, he'd be a full Rakum today."

Canaan stepped to Adam's side and shook his head. "Freaky shit."

"What does it mean now?" Adam asked. Both Elders looked at each other several seconds and then Canaan crossed to Javier.

"He was born a Rakum," Canaan said in a low voice, but not as a secret. "They didn't stress his flesh as our leaders did." Canaan pointed to the kid. "Without Ritual training, he remained weak and human."

"Now his problem is metaphysical," Kilmeade said looking into Adam's face. "I have only recently been made aware of the immensity of the spirit realm. When we fertilized my seed, Dr. Penny used what the humans call black magic. The curse that she placed on our union is what gives you your special sight. The auras. The precognition..."

Beryl bumped his arm and Javier cleared his throat.

"What?" Canaan asked, eyebrows raised.

"We realize you both must have seen this, but he hears voices in his head," Javier said and Beryl nodded along with his update. "He asked us to help him with it, but we told him we'd ask you about it."

"After you touched his mind," Canaan said admonishing Beryl.

"Do not go back in there," Kilmeade said catching his eye. Then he said to Javier with a lowered chin, "The boy is an open vessel."

Javier nodded with understanding: Adam was open to possession.

"What am I missing?" Beryl asked.

"Isaac was an open vessel after Zahdone left," Javier said.

"Ohhhh," Beryl sighed and looked back to Adam. "We have to warn him," Beryl said to everyone. "He told us what he understood about the spirit realm and he has it all wrong. He doesn't understand anything."

"Then that makes him a liability," Kilmeade said and turned to Adam with a hard gaze.

"What? Please, tell me what this all means?"

"Oh, we will," Kilmeade said. "Have a seat. This might take a while." Kilmeade waited for him to sit in a stiff chair nearby.

Javier never would have guessed what he would say next.

"Javier," the Elder said with a glint in his eye, "pray for us right now. Pray he will understand, because he is this close..." Kilmeade held up two fingers an inch apart. "...to accepting a deal from Ta'avah's kind."

Javier nodded and drew near.

《 ▣ 》

The boy sat stiffly, back rigid and jaw clenched as Kilmeade moved to stand behind him, purposefully keeping him alert and uncomfortable. Javier discerned correctly regarding the youth's natural propensity for telepathy; Canaan and Kilmeade recognized it from the first reading. His mind was a tiger trapped in a kitten's body, struggling to break free, yet only driving Adam Roberts toward the brink of psychosis. Kilmeade hoped tonight they would discover if Adam could overcome the limitations he adopted from his mortal guardian.

"Adam," Kilmeade said and the man startled. "You refused Dae Kim's offer to meet his master because of voices," Kilmeade said in a low voice and seeing into his thoughts. "What did they say?" Adam floundered with a few false starts and ceased speaking. Kilmeade took his shoulders from behind. "Spill your words; we will sort them out," he whispered into his ear and willed the man to loosen his tongue. "What did they say?"

Adam inhaled abruptly. "I don't always understand them," he gasped. "With Dae Kim, the one voice I fear the most told me to go."

"Why do you fear this one the most?" Kilmeade asked.

"It's the easiest to understand..." Adam visibly shivered, his eyes still tightly closed. He spoke the next in a rush. "And it has been telling me to kill myself since as far back as I can remember."

Kilmeade looked at Canaan who stepped up and placed his palm atop Adam's head. Instantly, a soothing energy flowed through the youth's body and he opened his eyes to look into Canaan's face.

"Hey," Canaan said and removed his hand. "So you didn't go because the voice you don't trust wanted you to. Do I have that right?" Adam nodded. "What about the other voices. What are they saying?"

"They don't always speak English and when they do, it's all scrambled up." Adam slow-blinked and exhaled. "The only one I can understand is the one that hates me."

Kilmeade looked at Javier, assuming he'd have a spiritual theory.

Javier nodded. "Ask him to actively recall these voices and see if you two can decipher them."

"Fun," Canaan mumbled and standing behind his chair, placed his palm to the back of Adam's neck. "Do it. Recall the voices."

Kilmeade acknowledged Javier's contribution and placed his hand under the collar of Adam's shirt. At first, Kilmeade neither saw nor heard anything, but after a few silent moments, a flash of color appeared in his mind's eye and he focused his attention. Canaan received the same spark and in a three-way share, Kilmeade grinned as the sounds evened out in his spiritual ears.

"*Shit,*" Canaan whispered so low that Kilmeade doubted the boys heard. His partner met his eyes and shook his head in wonder. Kilmeade grinned wide, an unexplained excitement building deep inside.

"Enough," Canaan said and jerked back his hand. He crossed his arms and stepped away from Adam's chair. Javier was the first to notice Canaan's demeanor.

"You okay?" he asked Canaan and walked to his side. When he touched Canaan's forearm he pulled away.

"I'm fine," Canaan said and watched Kilmeade.

"Please, tell me what's happening," Adam said quietly, alternating his gaze to all four men standing. "Can you hear what they're saying?"

Kilmeade sought Canaan's eye. *"It's to be expected,"* he sent silently. *"Why didn't we guess this was what it was? It makes perfect sense. It is amazing..."*

Canaan made an imperceptive shake of his head. *"It's too much to sort out. Adam Roberts has become a liability. You know he can't handle all this. We should destroy him. He's still only human..."*

Kilmeade held his gaze, pondering his suggestion. They were in one brain for a reason—to work things out in tandem. Now what do they do? Canaan wanted the boy ended and he wanted to investigate more fully. *"Javier?"* he sent and Canaan nodded. They'd ask the one in their group most capable of offering a useful outside opinion.

"Adam, Beryl, I am going to speak to Javier now. Do not speak until we ask you to." Kilmeade looked at Beryl who nodded. He caught Adam's eye and he gave an urgent tip of the head. Still in his gaze, Kilmeade added for Adam, "Beryl knows how to obey. You, control your tongue or I will make you incapable of speaking."

"I will," Adam said with a more convincing nod.

Kilmeade nodded to Canaan who communicated more easily with Javier. Canaan turned a grim face toward Javier and began.

"It's not gibberish. It's us. The Rakum. He's been hearing the Rakum, as if they played across a radio frequency. It must be what the Father's heard, all of us at once, but they could sort and choose."

"My God," Javier whispered.

Canaan nodded. "He heard more before Last Assembly, then less and less. Now he only hears Ta'avah's kind. The demons. They speak to him in English." Adam made a sharp noise of surprise and Canaan looked at Kilmeade. *"Shall I ask?"* Kilmeade nodded so Canaan turned back to Javier.

"I can see Adam has no avarice, but I also see his thought-life."

Adam's head swiveled to Canaan but he held his tongue.

"Since his youth, all of his fantasies are drawn from our daily lives as Rakum." Canaan looked then to Adam who didn't understand the depth of his assertion. "Adam, your fantasies of sex, violence, and bloodlust are actual experiences of our people. You experience guilt for having them, and you should—you're human. Sane mortals don't dream to do those things." Canaan returned his eyes to Javier. "The problem is that the degree of violence he's witnessed subconsciously for twenty years has unhinged his sanity."

Kilmeade made a small noise. *"Rephrase."*

Canaan huffed and licked his lips. "It is *my belief,*" he stressed for Kilmeade, "that Adam will never be able to straighten this out. *I think,*" he stressed again, "he is irreparable and borderline schizophrenic. He could snap and hurt you, our mortal friends."

Again, Adam made a sound, but didn't speak, warily watching all who encircled him.

Javier looked at Kilmeade. "You disagree on what to do."

Kilmeade sent him a grin. "I feel he has a super-intelligent mind that the proper instruction will enable him to sort it out."

"And for what? He still won't be a Rakum," Canaan said softly. "If he's not a Rakum," Canaan said aloud, but finished privately to Kilmeade, *"why do we give a shit? End him and let's get on with our mission."*

"Elder Canaan," Beryl said, daring Kilmeade to punish him for speaking. Kilmeade tightened his lips and warned him with his eyes and the man fell quiet.

"I'll hear what B has to say," Canaan sent, his eyes on Beryl. Kilmeade nodded for Beryl to finish.

"Sleep on it," Beryl said simply and looked at Javier for support. His cohort nodded.

"Twenty-four hours." Javier met Kilmeade's eyes and stayed there. "It gives me time to pray and see what God wants to do."

"Canaan?" Kilmeade said and Canaan nodded with a sigh. "Javier, go home with Adam." Kilmeade stood Adam up with a hand to his upper arm. "Adam, spend the day with Javier and see what you can figure out. Tomorrow at sunset, return here. Will you do this?" he asked, looking deep into the young man's eyes.

"I will," he said shakily.

"Good," Kilmeade said and sent the men upstairs.

Canaan had a right to be concerned. When they looked into Adam's mind specifically for the voices, they heard Ta'avah more than once. The spirit was long gone, erased by the Creator, but his voice and his suggestions to the boy remained deep in his subconscious. Because of that, Canaan was more right than he realized—if they hadn't happened upon Adam Roberts, eventually he would become the worst serial killer in the history of man.

"That is not an exaggeration," Canaan sent over.

"No," Kilmeade returned morosely. *"No, it's not."*

25. May 15

The following evening, Javier drove back to the rental in silence, pondering everything and nothing. Adam followed in his car, his headlights in view. There were no huge revelations during his time with the new Anomaly. The sun had set and Javier dreaded telling Canaan the results of his prayer time. The usually jovial Elder had texted him no less than three times during their separation to ask his opinion. Each time, he respectfully declined to answer. Now he would have to say what Canaan didn't want to hear. Javier pulled into the driveway and Beryl met him before he came in the house.

"Canaan's texting me, wondering if you've arrived."

"He's obsessed," Javier said with a shake of the head.

"There's something going on with him that isn't about Adam," Beryl said at the front door, whispering even though the Elders likely heard.

Javier agreed. "I'm thinking part of it will come out tonight."

Adam parked and slowed his stroll as he neared. "I sure hope Canaan is wrong about me."

Javier patted his back. "Kilmeade thinks you're smart enough to handle it, so let's think positive."

Javier led the way and assumed the Elders would be in the living room. From the sofa, Chloe informed them they'd meet in the basement.

"I put some snacks and drinks down there. Have fun," she said and turned back to her novel.

Javier sent Beryl a half-grin. "Clueless," he joked.

In a rare gesture, Beryl smiled, too. "Let's have hors d'oeuvres and tea while we discuss demons and ending this man's life!"

"Not funny," Adam grumbled and paused to wait for them.

At the door, Javier turned to Beryl with an apologetic expression. "I need five minutes alone with the Elders. I'll explain later." Beryl shrugged and leaned against the wall. Adam copied his movement, probably glad to prolong the suspense.

Javier headed down. What he needed to say to Canaan could be misconstrued as weakness, and since he and Javier shared the tighter bond, the Elder would not feel exposed. At least, that was the hope...

"Okay, enough mystery." Canaan looked hard at Javier. "Let's hear your decision. Cut the baby in two?" he asked and fluttered his eyebrows.

"King Solomon? Really?" Javier said with levity.

"An evil witch wants to slice a child in half and a pagan king is the richest man in the world? Bible folks don't own that one, sweetheart," Canaan countered, his impatience only increasing.

Javier grinned, and took a deep breath delaying the inevitable. Canaan's countenance darkened as he interpreted the move.

"Shit," he muttered and folded his arms at his chest.

Kilmeade sent Javier a go-ahead nod.

"I asked them to wait because—"

Kilmeade grunted. "Your Elders understand. Continue."

Javier nodded with a small eyebrow raise. "Okay, yes. Bottom line, you both think I have a direct line to God..." He paused and their lack of reaction proved his point. "And I can't say whether or not that's a fair assumption, but Beth Rider taught me to pray and then believe He responded. That said, here's what I heard from God."

"Thanks for the useless preamble, Javie," Canaan deadpanned and rolled his hand. "Proceed."

Javier nodded. "Canaan, your desire to kill Adam is a reflection of your trepidation," Javier carefully avoided using the word fear, but Canaan saw through him.

"What? You think I'm afraid of Adam?"

"No, you're afraid, period."

"The hell I am," Canaan said without venom. "Maybe I'm lazy, I don't want to bother with him, I'm heartless, or I'm evil. I'm not scared of the little shit."

Javier rephrased. "You're not afraid of Adam at all. I get the feeling that you're afraid he will somehow hurt our cause, hurt Chloe, or me or Beryl, that he can somehow hurt Kilmeade." With a sudden inspiration, Javier added, "you don't want anyone to be hurt simply because we're curious about Adam."

"You should have said that to start with," Canaan said, still not angry. "I admit it—it's not worth the risk. We have you guys, we have Chloe up there—I've seen enough shit happen to those I care about, shit I can't control. I have no power against these invisible forces your God manhandles with ease." Canaan turned to Kilmeade. "You're buying trouble, brother. I'm worried we will stick our hands in the snake pit and this time, you or I will die as a result."

"What does Solomon recommend?" Kilmeade asked softly. Before Javier responded he angled his head toward Canaan.

"Right there—" Javier interjected with respect when he noted they were communicating telepathically. "What is that about?"

Canaan exhaled, his mouth drawn down. "Kilmeade?" he asked and Kilmeade shrugged. Canaan looked to Javier, still frowning. "Elder Kilmeade is convinced he will die soon. I will not discuss it further."

Javier turned to Kilmeade. "Why do you feel this way?"

Instead of responding, the Elder stepped in front of Javier to wrap his arms around Canaan. He squeezed him tightly and Canaan rolled his eyes, his arms dangling at his sides.

"This makes it *allllllll* better. I'm so happy now," Canaan said without inflection.

Still wrapped around him, Kilmeade said in Canaan's ear, "We lost control of this train a long time ago, brother. We're passengers, now." Kilmeade released him and fell to the side, one arm still about Canaan's shoulders. "I will not speak of it with you, Javier, but I'm glad you know. Prepare your heart."

"Prepare your heart, sweetness," Canaan mimicked raising his voice like a woman. "Screw that." He shrugged out from under Kilmeade's wing. "Solomon says?" he asked now looking at Javier.

"God brought us to Adam in time to keep him from breaking apart. That means we got to him before the enemy did. We can help him."

"If he doesn't first give his body to a demon and kill my friends. Great." With a quick glance to Javier, Canaan dropped his posture a fraction and grabbed Kilmeade by the back of the neck.

Before 11/13, a Rakum Elder never exuded anything less than 100-percent confidence and Javier averted his eyes to preserve the Elder's dignity. *But...with only two left, isn't this evidence of Canaan's burgeoning human strengths? The transforming of his heart?* Javier swallowed and held his thoughts close.

Holding Kilmeade's neck, Canaan took a slow deliberate breath. "I'm behind you, brother. I'm all in. Let's save the little shit." With his free hand, he slapped the side of Javier's head to make him look over. "Happy, asshole? I'm in. Let's rescue Adam from those invisible jerks."

Javier braved to sock Canaan's arm. He grinned, joviality returning to his countenance, and then shook Kilmeade playfully by the hand on his neck.

"We're doing the jobs of angels." He released Kilmeade and took a firm hold of Javier's upper arm. "Beth Rider described an angel nine feet tall that killed Jack and scared the ever-loving shit out of our Fathers." Grinning wider than ever, he put his pointer finger to Javier's nose tip. "You have an angel like that, too, don't you?"

Javier parted his lips to answer and Canaan interrupted him.

"Beth Rider said that all believers have a guardian angel..." He looked to Kilmeade, who maintained a secret smile. "That means Javie has one of those nine-foot creatures with him all the time. This is good." Canaan put his hands together. "We are going to *KICK SOME SPIRIT ASS!*"

Javier laughed. "I think Canaan is right. Let's kick ass!"

Kilmeade clapped his hands and the basement door opened. "Good! Let's start by digging into that man's brain. Together—two Elders, a God-man, and the man with the heart of gold," he said pointing to Beryl as he neared, "will help Adam choose correctly."

The atmosphere lightened and Javier clapped once loudly, mimicking the way Kilmeade unlocked the door. Canaan clapped several times, and with a goofy grin, popped Beryl's shoulder to get him going. Beryl slapped his palms together, at first with a bored stare at the Elder, but then smiled at Canaan's joyfulness. Beryl booted Adam's behind and within moments, all five men were clapping and laughing. Kilmeade hooked Canaan's elbow and pulled him into a jig, clapping all the while.

Beryl's idiotic expression tickled Javier and he guffawed, unable to contain the sudden joy in his spirit. Javier closed his eyes to listen, their impromptu cacophony sounding like a gigantic waterfall. A flash of light appeared behind his lids and the sound amplified as a figure emerged in his mind's eye. He immediately thought of Emunah, Beth Rider's angel mentioned minutes ago.

The light-being opened detail-less arms as a hole in its featureless face called out, *"Behold, the glory of the God of Israel comes, His voice like the sound of many waters, the earth is bathed in His glory!"*

Javier's heart pounded in his chest. Was he seeing an angel? Afraid he'd never have another chance to find out, he turned his attention to the being and sent the question, *"Can I know your name?"*

The being directed its head to Javier and said, *"I am Baruk, who stands with you in the presence of the One Who is and Who was and Who is to come."*

Javier's heart grew too big for his chest and he opened his eyes. The men were still clapping, only now in a Jamaican beat as Beryl and Adam contorted into embarrassingly pitiful dance moves.

Javier's eye met Kilmeade's. "Baruk..." the senior Elder whispered with a wink. Javier turned away, his mind racing. Kilmeade saw him, too? A quick glance assured Javier no one else had. What did that mean? Did it have anything to do with Kilmeade's assertion he would die? Javier decided not to think on it; the angel was with them and that was enough for now.

《回》

It *was* a little like looking in a mirror. Kilmeade held Adam's face in his hands, a palm on each cheek and sank into his gaze. The man was perfect in appearance and his intelligence shined through his bright blue-gray eyes. Now that he had allowed himself to invest energy into the one they raised from his seed, he saw more than before and much more than his cohorts.

In Adam, Canaan saw his partner's death. Javier saw a lost lamb that his God lovingly called back to the fold. Beryl saw a man like himself, a little lost, a little worried, but capable of doing anything he set his mind to. And Kilmeade?

I see me, as a mortal, unbroken, unadulterated, unassaulted...

Adam Roberts wasn't pure in the sense of Javier's Bible, but compared to a Rakum? He was innocent and unblemished. Canaan turned, attending Kilmeade's inner monologue. Kilmeade paused in his reflections on Adam and began a few on Canaan. *Never have I had such a bond as the one I share with Canaan. From the day we met, our life-threads entwined, finding instant balance. The centuries we spent apart did nothing to spoil the perfect camaraderie of the Rakum's two finest Elders...*

"*Shi-i-i-t...*" Canaan looked away snickering. "*Go back to work, asshole.*"

Kilmeade grinned to the side and looked back at Adam whose eyes revealed his discomfort at being held by the head. "After 11/13, there were no more telepathic relays to overhear, and you have never heard an Elder; we guard our thoughts as a matter of course. Understand?"

"Yes, sir," Adam said holding Kilmeade's gaze.

"First, Canaan and I will help you bury the worst visions..." Kilmeade readjusted his fingers. "Try to bring up the worst, most disturbing memories you have and we will send them under."

Adam nodded and closed his eyes.

Kilmeade did the same and peeked over the wall. Adam's psyche was as dark as his outward appearance was bright. Roiling and swirling in an oily ocean of viscous fluid, the boy's thoughts, memories, and unfulfilled fantasies sloshed about, perverted and depraved, as black as Kilmeade's own heart before Last Assembly when the Rakum race began its slide to obliteration.

Then Kilmeade had an idea. Without moving, he opened his eyes and sought Javier's gaze. Javier stepped close and Kilmeade whispered to come even closer. Javier put his ear to Kilmeade side-turned lips.

"He needs your kind of help. Try to connect with us."

Javier exhaled and with a most serious expression, he placed his palms atop Kilmeade's. Energy from the Elders buzzed him, but he fell still, concentrating on allowing the sharing to happen. Much of telepathy had to do with being open to experience more than one could with his five senses. Javier spent a hundred and forty years in their world and the technique had not changed. Soon, on the far side of the rolling black ocean, Javier appeared as a wisp of white smoke.

"What can I do?" he asked in Kilmeade's mind.

"Canaan and I cannot make even the slightest dent here. Twenty-seven years it has piled up and once I saw it, I knew we needed the help your God brings. Pray and see what He will do."

Javier's essence hovered over the vacillating fluid that periodically splashed up as if reaching for him. In the space of a moment, he began to telepathically pray in Hebrew; Kilmeade spoke the words in English for Beryl and Adam to hear.

"What will you do to help this man, oh God? His mind is full of evil that he had no hand in putting here. Will You bring light into this mind? May I stand in the gap for this man until he comes to know You?" Kilmeade stopped talking when Javier paused.

"B'shem Yeshua, avinu malcheinu..."[11] Javier began again and his essence gave Kilmeade a directive. *"Have Adam ask God for help. 'Please help me,' would be sufficient."*

Kilmeade opened his eyes and looked at Adam. "Do you want the God of the mortals to help you?" Adam nodded, his eyes huge. "Then say, God, please help me."

Adam said the words and Kilmeade returned to see Javier's mist spread across horizontally, and as he did so, the movement in the viscous body below grew still. Kilmeade exhaled and Javier was gone. He opened his eyes and both Javier and Canaan looked back at him, completely disentangled from Adam's mind.

Kilmeade returned his gaze to Adam and slowly released his head, bringing his hands down to clasp at chest level. Adam blinked and rubbed his face.

---

[11] (Hebrew) "In the name of Jesus, our God and King."

"OKAY!" Canaan said loudly and Beryl jumped. "Hah!" he teased and popped his head.

Kilmeade grinned and said to Adam, "Try to bring up something disturbing. Something you could always bring up before…"

Adam looked at his hands and after a few seconds, he shook his head. "I can't remember anything like that."

Canaan huffed. "Can you hear the voices?"

Adam shook his head. "Only the ones I understand, not the gibberish ones."

Javier caught Kilmeade's gaze. "He hears the demons, but not the Rakum cacophony."

Kilmeade nodded and gestured to Canaan. "Enough. That is all his brain can take tonight. Javier, spend some time with Adam explaining those voices. Determine if he wants to be like you or Dae Kim."

"Sir—" Adam protested, but Kilmeade raised his hand.

"One thing you will learn—if you live long enough—an Elder is never wrong." He caught Canaan's eye and winked. "And if he ever seems to be, keep it to yourself." Adam huffed, but Javier and Beryl agreed with a grin. "Now, Javier will take Adam upstairs. Beryl, you stay."

Kilmeade didn't watch the men leave; instead he watched Beryl's eyes. When the basement door closed again, Beryl removed his shirt and Kilmeade raised his eyebrows.

Beryl shrugged. "You're not going to ask them and I don't care."

"Come here, sugar," Canaan said and crossed to meet Beryl where he stood. Kilmeade snickered into his hand at the scene he had witnessed many times at Assembly, when an Elder noticed Meryl or Beryl and approached them for a buzz. Now, as then, Beryl turned his face away and waited it out.

"That is a beautiful thing," Kilmeade said. "Generous to a fault."

"I do what I can…" Beryl closed his eyes as Canaan drew his blood from a new puncture in his neck.

Kilmeade collapsed heavily onto the short couch. When Canaan finished, he'd buzz off Canaan. And then, he'd see Chloe to sleep. Kilmeade grinned and leaned back. It was a good night and it took all he had in him to not thank Javier's God for it.

26, MAY 16

Galleria Dallas seemed to be made of windows. Chloe craned her neck repeatedly to see the black sky through the glass ceiling as the Elders escorted her through the gigantic indoor shopping mall. This evening when Kilmeade located her in the kitchen after sundown, he invited her to go into town. Something about his behavior made her think he wanted to buy her a gift. She didn't dare think on it or he'd know and she didn't dare want him to do so, or he'd know. Chloe instead purposed to simply be happy about the invitation.

The mall closed in an hour so the crowds weren't as bad as they could be. Kilmeade walked beside Chloe, his hand resting under her hair on the back of her neck. Canaan walked on her other side, talking over her head whenever he wanted to speak to Kilmeade. As they neared the food court, Kilmeade steered her to the wall out of traffic.

"Stay with Canaan. I'll find you shortly," Kilmeade said in her ear, pecked the crown of her head, and turned away. Chloe watched him go and when she looked at Canaan, he had leaned against the wall pretending to be asleep.

"Hey," she said and poked his chest. "Is Kilmeade getting me a gift?" she asked, thinking Kilmeade might be far enough away to avoid accidental mind-reading. "He has a look in his eye."

"I tell no tales outta school," Canaan laughed and turned his face to hers. "I mean, maybe."

"Yay," she said and beamed him a smile.

Canaan's grin grew and he shook his head. "Time for ice cream," he said and stepped away from the wall. He put his hand under her hair precisely as Kilmeade had earlier and she expected nothing less. In ten minutes, they each had a cone and Canaan sat them at a small table against the Plexiglas skating rink wall. He watched outward, always on guard, and Chloe watched the skaters and noshed her mint ice cream.

"Have you ever gone ice skating?" she asked him thoughtfully and he shook his head. "Ever gone hang gliding?" Canaan again shook his head, a half-grin on his face. Chloe smiled. "Water skiing?"

Canaan laughed and rubbed his face with one big hand. "Lean in, newbie," he said and she did. "Rakum don't float," he continued quietly and in her ear. "So, no, I don't do anything in the water."

Chloe sat upright, her mouth ajar. "Really? That's weird."

"Only if you're human," he returned with a wink.

"Did you like riding horses before they made cars?"

Canaan chuckled. "None of us ever rode a horse for fun."

"There weren't cowboy *Rakum?*" she said whispering the last word.

"Please," Canaan replied with false offense.

Chloe hummed at his sudden attitude. "It sounds like you don't like animals in general."

Canaan didn't respond until he could do so gently. "The animal did a job; it's a *thing*, a tool." He shrugged. "The end."

Chloe gazed off, pondering how lonely she'd be without pets in her life. Her last pet had been a Persian cat and since he passed away, she hadn't found time to replace him. Maybe the Rakum didn't get lonely. Chloe hit Canaan with a new question.

"You lived with Kilmeade in Canada when…" Chloe said lowering her voice even though she hadn't said anything odd to outsiders. *"His two-year quarantine,"* she whispered. When Canaan nodded his reply, she sighed. "Were ya'll lonely? I mean, isn't it kinda like that now?"

Canaan shook his head without reservation. "This is not even remotely similar, little bird." His tone softened as she had touched on what appeared to be a melancholic subject. "Remember the connection I told you about?" Chloe nodded and he continued. "To answer your first question, no, we weren't lonely back then." He chuckled with an eye raise. "Who could be lonely with the amazing Elder Kilmeade around?"

Chloe grinned. "He is amazing, isn't he?"

"Affirmative," Canaan answered.

Chloe finished her ice cream and blushed as her mind wandered to Kilmeade's last intimate visitation. Canaan appeared to be walking down memory lane, too, looking handsome and intelligent, staring off over her shoulder, his famous half-grin in place.

He dropped his eyes to hers. "Are you looking at me, ma'am?"

Chloe quickly asked, "Did everyone think Kilmeade was amazing." Canaan rolled in his lips with a thought he didn't automatically share and Chloe poked his forearm. "What? Who didn't like him?"

Canaan laughed once. "Little bird, when you're the great Elder Kilmeade, being liked isn't a priority." Canaan noted she awaited more and he smiled when she did. "He and I always enjoyed each other, but you'd have to ask him if anyone else liked him." Canaan sent her a wink. "He could easily kick the ever loving you-know-what out of anyone not a Father. Does that help you appreciate the issue?"

"Fighting? That doesn't sound like him..." Chloe shook her head, unable to imagine Kilmeade engaged in any sort of violent showdown.

Canaan tilted his head to the side. "How do you think Kilmeade controlled everyone around him?"

Chloe answered the only thing that fit. "With his will."

"Yes!" Canaan sat up and scrunched his nose in fun. "By the time he graduated to Elder, the collective consciousness of my brethren discerned he was not one to cross."

Chloe's eyes grew as she digested information Kilmeade hadn't yet shared. *Would he ever?* He didn't reveal much about himself. Then Chloe smiled when Canaan leaned in conspiratorially to add a little more.

"Your mate acquired his first pup by stealing him from the very man who promoted him—his *Master,* a Rakum Elder *twice his age.*"

Chloe blinked. "You're blowing my mind..."

Canaan shook his head with a new laugh. "As the story goes, Emil's favored pet became Kilmeade's overnight. And trust me, Elders don't share easily." Canaan grinned at his memories and Chloe smiled back with a funny thought.

"That would be like you stealing away Rafa," she said and Canaan scrunched his face with a nod. Chloe giggled, enjoying the lost look in his eyes whenever she laughed. Across from the Food Court, a woman walked out of a store carrying a puppy and Chloe stood up. "Oh! Let's go look in there!"

Canaan rose to follow her line of sight. He then cleared his throat and said in a flat voice, "You're kidding, right?"

"You act as if I asked you to look into a garbage can!" she laughed. "Everybody likes puppies."

Canaan licked his lips. After a quick inhale he said with his usual oblique opener, "My people do not like puppies."

"Ohhh..." Chloe walked around the table to stand closer. She lowered her voice. *"In nearly four centuries, you never had a pet?"*

Canaan straightened his shoulders with an expression of disgust. "I've been in the possession of many beasts, but I never desired a pet."

"Is it too *human?"* she asked mouthing the last word.

"No, it's *weak,*" Canaan imitated her, chin down. "There is no weakness among my people."

Chloe put both hands on his nearest forearm and said very low for his ears alone. "It's a new world. Come with me and I will show you what a puppy feels like with Uncle Ta'avah out of the picture."

"She wants me to pet a puppy," he said in a whisper, looking into her eyes. Chloe grinned and nodded like a child, figuring he was speaking to Kilmeade. He shook his head and one side of his mouth went up. "Lead the way," he said finally and allowed her to pull him to the store.

Inside, after two aisles of product, the store transformed into a petting zone. On either side of a wide path, four separate pens had been erected with solid walls four feet high and a swinging door. Each enclosure contained scampering puppies and various toys.

"Oh! I see," she said, still holding Canaan's arm with both of her own. "You can choose the kind you want to cuddle."

"Cuddle?" Canaan said, his eyes scanning the furry forms.

"Yeah, this one," she said and carefully opened the door, walked them in, and closed it back. "These are large breeds. What kind did you keep? Working dogs, I bet."

Canaan looked behind him at a gray Weimaraner tugging his jeans cuff. "You're learning," he said still looking down. He lifted his leg until the puppy released him and Canaan stood on one foot. Chloe dropped his arm and scooped the puppy.

"Look." She held it close to her face and it licked her nose, wiggling is entire body. After a few more spastic motions, it started trying to reach parts of her to gnaw on and she giggled. "You hold him like this," she said, assigning it a gender and handing it to Canaan.

Canaan received the puppy and mimicked the way she held it.

Chloe laughed at his expression, lips parted, his eyes wide with unease. "Look at his face. Look at how cute," she said watching Canaan and not the puppy.

"Adorable. We done?" he asked as the puppy wiggled in his hands.

"Not until you look at his face. Lift him up. He'll lick your nose."

Canaan regarded her with his chin lowered. "Be serious." He scoped the mostly empty store. *"I'm a freaking Rakum Elder. Puppies do not lick my nose,"* he whispered.

Chloe giggled. "New world, new Canaan," she said and waited for him to comply. He stared at her and she poked out her bottom lip. "Just once? For me?"

Canaan rolled his eyes and lifted the puppy close enough to lick his chin. Chloe erupted with glee.

"AWWW! That's the sweetest thing I've ever seen!" she squealed and received the dog as he handed it back scowling. She could see he wasn't truly perturbed. "Did he melt your heart?"

"You're the only one melting my heart," he said and turned away. "Let's go and look into some garbage cans."

Chloe laughed and set the puppy down to follow him out. They headed for the exit and she grabbed his shirttail.

"Do you think I could get Kilmeade to hold a puppy?" she asked as they began a slow walk down the mall concourse.

Canaan scoffed. "No way. Absolutely not." He put his hand to the back of her neck and squeezed her playfully. "No," he said again as if he'd been trying to picture such a thing.

"Yeah," she said softly. Chloe fell quiet and strolled past various stores wondering why the Elders were so different. The more she pondered her evening, she was convinced she'd never be able to ask Kilmeade any silly questions. Kilmeade remained set apart and Canaan made himself available. Had it to do with them being in one brain? One played the lover and the other the friend? Getting nowhere with her vague concerns, Chloe cleared her mind and elbowed Canaan.

"Thanks for that. The talking, the puppy, everything. That was fun."

"Happy to oblige," he said looking ahead. Suddenly, the Elder stopped moving and stared hard to his left. Chloe took his near arm in both hands and watched his profile. Something had happened that involved Kilmeade. She prayed and waited to see what it could be.

《回》

Kilmeade strolled out of Tiffany's, tiny blue bag in hand. The best jewelry designer in Texas created and customized his treasure after asking specific questions regarding Chloe's personality. The rose gold band featured an 8ct white diamond in the center of twelve rubies selected for their unique translucency. The engraving would probably make her cry and Kilmeade didn't mind the anticipation of seeing how she received it. The food court was half-a-mall away and he walked at a comfortable pace, absorbing the energy of those around him. Two steps past GameStop, his internal alert system pinged. Kilmeade stopped walking and simultaneously, Canaan touched his mind.

"Where is he?"

Kilmeade hummed and concentrated on the suffering brother. Canaan waited patiently and within ten seconds, Kilmeade turned to the shoe store on his immediate left. There were no customers evident and he stepped inside. Kilmeade was drawn to the back of the store. *"The stockroom,"* he sent to Canaan.

"I'm going to the car," Canaan responded, getting Chloe to safety.

Kilmeade reached the cash register and detected two heartbeats. One beat faster than the other, but since 11/13, his brethren's heartsounds matched those of the general population. Kilmeade circumvented the counter and stepped to a partition dividing the space.

"Testvér, jól vagy? It's Elder Kilmeade," he said in a calm voice.

After a short pause, a shaky male voice responded, "Elder Kilmeade? It can't be..."

"I'm coming back there," Kilmeade said and pushed the moveable divider to the side. Two steps in and he viewed a small stockroom lined with shelves. A young man in a store uniform lay on the floor barely alive and a transformed Rakum stood over him. This brother looked healthy, was tall and broad-shouldered, with a crewcut and a square jaw. His only obvious problem was his misery. "Brother," Kilmeade said when their eyes met.

The Rakum covered his mouth with his hands. "Master, I... I don't understand. What are you doing here? What happened? Where?" he stuttered through his fingers.

Kilmeade gave him a gentle smile while at the same time reading several medical problems with the youth on the ground.

"Come close," he said and held out both arms.

The Rakum stepped over the employee and folded into Kilmeade's embrace. Before 11/13, Kilmeade was the only Rakum he knew who fancied such contact. Now that the brethren were human, none refused his invitation to be tactilely comforted.

"You look well, brother," Kilmeade said over his shoulder and the man cried openly, fat tears staining Kilmeade's leather coat. Kilmeade sighed at the youth on the floor. He would be dead in minutes; it was time to get the brother safely away.

《回》

To no big surprise, The Master hadn't allowed Dae Kim to keep his Rakum powers. A week ago, when he failed to entice Adam Roberts to come away with him, the frustration nearly drove Dae Kim to suicide. But he chickened out. *Again.* Back to normal and fully mortal, Dae Kim physically restrained Crazy Pete and watched Elder Kilmeade enter the shoe store. Tonight, The Master led them to the mall promising to deliver another pining brother into their hands. Unfortunately because of his partner's insanity, Pete engaged a stranger in a brawl at the mall entrance. That brouhaha took thirty minutes to dissolve; if Dae Kim had come alone, he would have killed the sad transformed brother and been gonc before the Elder Goon Squad even arrived.

"Where's Elder Canaan?" Pete hissed, his yellowed eyes also trained to the quiet store across the aisle. The man smelled of death, which was no wonder considering The Master never intended him to live this long.

Dae Kim scanned the area and didn't see the blond Elder anywhere. He got a little thrill, though, when he laid eyes on Kilmeade. He had only glimpsed the rear three-quarters of his head, but his confidence, his arrogant carriage, his stride, every ounce of the man exuded his Rakum essence. The injustice of it boggled his mind.

"He's not so great," Pete whispered and Dae Kim glared at him. "He didn't sense us? Some Elder."

"Yeah..." Dae Kim said softly and returned his gaze to the door. What Pete still didn't get was that *they* were human. Kilmeade would have discerned if Rakum were stalking him, but Dae Kim and Pete's scent and sounds blended with humanity. The Elder would have to *see* them to know they stalked him. It was better to let Pete enjoy his delusion.

《回》

"Brando, correct?" The man nodded. Kilmeade hadn't met him formally, but being in Kilmeade's periphery at some point was enough. "What happened here?" Kilmeade asked looking at the dying employee.

"I lost my temper," the brother said softly no longer weeping. "This jerk fired me over the phone. I came in to reason with him..."

Kilmeade found it funny and he chuckled. Brando nodded his head, remembering the Rakum attitude about humans and their little problems.

"I will get you out of here. Show me to your back door."

"Thank you, Master," Brando whispered.

Once he identified the security cameras and exits, Kilmeade disabled surveillance inside and out, and very shortly, had them both in the rear mall parking lot, ducking behind a van as they awaited Canaan. Kilmeade sent Brando a wink and he smiled, relief flooding his bloodshot eyes.

"Have Chloe in the front with you. I'll ride in the back with Brando," he sent and Canaan was underway. *"Tell our sweet little human not to look at or chat with our new friend,"* Kilmeade sent with wry inflection. To Brando, he said, "do

you have a car?"

Brando shook his head. "I have to hitch. That's why that jerk fired me. I can't get to work some days..." Brando repositioned from a hunker to rest on both knees and he stared into Kilmeade's face. "Are there others, Master? Others who are intact?"

Kilmeade reached out and cupped Brando's cheek. "Every living Rakum has transformed. Only myself and Elder Canaan remain intact. Ride with us and I'll tell you what's going on," Kilmeade said and Brando nodded several times. "Listen close..." Kilmeade waited for the man to notice his serious tone. "My mate is in the front seat. Do you remember the protocol?" Brando nodded again. "Good. I want you to prosper, but I will protect her without prejudice."

Brando replied, his eyes wide. "It will be as you say, Master. I understand."

Kilmeade nodded. "We have excellent news for you. Here's our ride..." Kilmeade remained low to avoid eyes from the direction of the mall and directed Brando into the backseat of the Yukon.

《回》

When several minutes passed, Dae Kim jogged to the shoe store and tip-toed inside. It was a gamble, but to his memory, the likely *modus operandi* would mean the Elder ushered the Rakum out a back way. Dae Kim went as quietly as possible to the rear of the store and peeked past the partition. Crazy Pete followed hunkered low with a lunatic gleam in his hazel eyes. On the floor of the stockroom a man lay still. Dae Kim stepped past him and found a back door. When he'd gathered his nerve, he squeaked it open. This one ran straight to an exit out of the building.

"Quick!" he whispered to Pete and led the way to the door at a jog. The reinforced steel door had a two-by-two mesh-embedded window and he motioned for Pete to stay down. With care, he peeked over the bottom edge in time to see a beige SUV roll up, driven by Elder Canaan. His heart swelled and he made a noise of surprise. Pete stood fully and looked out the window, catching Canaan's attention. Dae Kim dropped his weight, pulling Pete down with him and hissing curses at his carelessness.

"He saw us, you idiot!" Dae Kim said and when he dared peek out again, the truck had vacated the lot.

《回》

Once Kilmeade and Brando were inside and the door closed, Canaan pulled calmly away. Only when they exited the mall property did Kilmeade and Brando sit upright in the back seat.

"You were watched," Canaan sent to Kilmeade, his tone noncommittal. Kilmeade responded with a tiny nod and Canaan addressed their passenger. "Brando!" he said in a loud voice. "Where's Bonny?"

Brando shook his head. "Dead, Master. He couldn't take it. He leapt off a building when I was out."

"Aw, shit," Canaan mumbled up front and fell silent.

"But if he had seen you guys," he burbled, being extra careful not to look in the direction of the front seat passenger.

Kilmeade scooted to sit against him and rest his hand on Brando's leg, knowing he would find the gesture soothing. "Do you have a place to stay?"

He shook his head. "I have been at the shelter." Brando looked back to Canaan's reflection. "I couldn't get a job for a long time. I lived off my Cows. I was lost." He turned to Kilmeade. "How could I have known? How could any of us have known this would happen?" Brando's gaze fell to Kilmeade's hand on his knee. "What happened?" he said in a forlorn voice and tentatively touched Kilmeade's fingers.

"Go ahead," Kilmeade said and Brando covered his hand with his own. "Canaan, take us to the Ritz-Carlton on McKinney. Chloe pull it up for him if he needs it."

"Master, I can't aff—" Brando began, but Kilmeade shushed him.

"Call the guys; have them meet us at the Ritz," Kilmeade said, eyes on Brando who did not look at Chloe.

"The guys?" he asked as he reverently stroked Kilmeade's hand.

"Your brothers have fantastic news for you." Kilmeade sat up to put his free hand to Brando's cheek. "You *will* be happy again."

Brando lifted Kilmeade's captive hand to his lips. "Thank you, Master. Thank you."

"Elders take care of little brothers," Kilmeade said and draped an arm around his shoulders to pull Brando close. He turned his mind to Chloe. *"My beautiful little bird, I haven't forgotten you."* Respecting his request to ignore their passenger, she did not look back, but she smiled. To Canaan, he sent, *"Pete and Dae Kim are unstable. I'd like to find them."*

Canaan caught his eye in the rearview mirror. *"I'll put the boys on it."*

Kilmeade nodded and squeezed Brando's shoulder, happy to help one more of their brethren find peace.

《回》

The clock chimed midnight and Chloe nodded off where she reclined waiting for Kilmeade to tell her goodnight. They had left the strange Brando character at the Ritz with Javier and Beryl and then brought her back to the house. After a quick shower, she waited in the huge bed she shared with Kilmeade whenever possible and watched the door. When he touched her arm, she startled.

"Oh! I must have dozed off."

Kilmeade sat on the edge of the mattress and stroked her hair, his face illuminated by the nightlight on the far side of the room. "I didn't mean to keep you up this late, little bird," he whispered and moved a strand of hair from her cheek.

Chloe maneuvered out from under the covers and sat up, leaning on her palms. Kilmeade still wore the jeans and shirt from their excursion, but the buttons were open all the way down and she reached out to touch his chest. "Will you stay with me?" she asked, fearful he'd say no and then angry with herself for hemming him in with her emotions.

Kilmeade smiled and shrugged off his shirt. "Make room," he said and when he was undressed, he snuggled her to him, her back to his front. "I have a gift for you," he said in her ear.

"You always do," she said teasing and wiggled in his embrace.

Kilmeade poked her once in the ribs. "A gift to treasure when I am long gone."

"Don't say that, please," Chloe said, keeping her tone light even though her mind longed to ponder the meaning of his frequent mentions of departing. She squeezed his arms and forced a new giggle. "So...what is it? I want a present!"

Kilmeade playfully nipped the skin of her neck with his lips. "I'll show you later," he whispered. "The timing must be perfect." He lowered one hand to her tummy to caress in a circular motion. Kissing her neck, he whispered, "You will give birth to a daughter."

"A girl..." Chloe repeated smiling and rolled onto her back. She pulled him close. The sun would chase him out before long, but for now, she had his undivided attention and she would cherish every minute.

27, MAY 17

"We can't reach Adam," Javier told Canaan as he exited the basement at sundown. "He's not answering his phone and he's not texting back."

"I've texted him fifteen times over the past twenty-four hours," Beryl added coming up behind Javier in the hallway. "I think something's happened to him."

Canaan regarded them both with a blank look that they interpreted to mean *tell me more.*

Javier added. "Three nights ago, Kilmeade gives him that elaborate testing and warns him not to accept deals from demons. Now he's missing?"

"And?" Canaan said. "So what? He's working late. He has a date. He ran off with the circus. Jumping to conclusions is not my thing."

"Why would he visit every day and then suddenly stop contacting us?" Beryl asked, waiting for concern to dawn in Canaan's eye.

Canaan called to Kilmeade inwardly to settle the matter. Staring at two anxious faces the minute he rose for the night was not his idea of fun. *"Your mini-me is missing. Our boys think Dae Kim and Pete grabbed him..."* To Javier and Beryl, Canaan said, "Kilmeade is coming up. Show him these miserable mugs." Canaan walked around them both for the kitchen.

"Canaan, this is serious," Javier called after him.

Now out of sight, Canaan listened as they shared their concerns with Kilmeade who immediately came to his defense.

"Do not hop on Canaan's back the moment he arises," Kilmeade said down the hall. "Adam will turn up, and if he doesn't, we did all we could. It has never been our job to watch over him day and night."

Canaan grinned and poured two cups of black coffee, holding one out for Kilmeade as he walked in. *"That was good,"* Canaan sent silently. *"I like the little shit, but I'm not a freakin' babysitter."*

Kilmeade nodded. *"We have no connection with him unless we touch him, so he's beyond our protection. He's been warned; he's on his own."*

"Oh, wait," Javier said, still in the hall with Beryl.

"Oh, me, too," Beryl added his voice growing as he approached the kitchen. "I just got a text. He lost his phone. He's okay." Both men entered the room looking at their cell screens.

Canaan set down his coffee with care and then spun around, grabbed Javier's shirt in both fists, and shoved him against the wide double refrigerator.

"Don't..." His first word he left alone, saying it right in Javier's ear with a measured tone. "...ever..." He pulled back slightly to catch the man's eye. He finished the threat standing nose-to-nose. "...throw that meaningless shit at me right when I get up."

Javier's face read shock, regret, concern, but not fear or anger. Canaan considered that and lowered him to the ground, still pressing him against the cool steel.

Behind him, Kilmeade rubbed the top of Canaan's head. *Kiss him, drink him, or release him."*

Canaan said he would, but his muscles hadn't unlocked.

Still close enough that their noses bumped, Javier's face relaxed. "It won't happen again," he whispered.

Canaan cut his eyes to Beryl who tossed up his hands in surrender. "Same here. Please don't shove me into the refrigerator."

"You're losing it, brother," Kilmeade sent and stepped closer.

Canaan opened his fists and pressed the cloth across Javier's chest until it was flat. His anger still burned, but entirely out of character, he had misdirected it. He backed away and Javier stepped forward, one hand to Canaan's arm.

"What's wrong?" he asked.

Canaan wouldn't meet his eye. Nothing was wrong. What could be wrong? Javier tugged as if to lead him to the other room, but Canaan pulled out of Javier's grip. He turned around and picked up his coffee. Kilmeade remained quiet, keenly observing everything.

"They need to leave the kitchen," he sent, his back to them all. Kilmeade shooed the two men out and Canaan worked to pinpoint the problem. His anger sat like a lump in his stomach and his head pounded with violent images. Kilmeade had joked about taking Javier's blood by force just then and he had imagined it. Standing behind him, Kilmeade attended his thought-stream and said nothing. *Maybe I just need a quiet moment... Everyone—back—off—*

Kilmeade exited the kitchen without a word. Still facing the sink wall with his back to the doors, Canaan stared into his coffee cup. What was it?

217

Kilmeade's dreams came to mind; Javier's God meddling in everything, threatening to take his other half off the planet. Could Kilmeade have misinterpreted that? Then, there was Chloe Bushman, breaking his heart every time she smiled. Kilmeade wasn't the only one experiencing the pain of re-making the Rakum heart; Canaan felt everything he did, only worse, because he had no physical release.

"Canaan! There you are! Look at what I got for you!"

Canaan turned to see Chloe enter the kitchen the back way. A quick check assured him that Kilmeade was aware of her arrival, leaving the moment between them.

"What's the matter?" Chloe said and walked to his side. She put a hand on his arm and her palm felt unusually clammy. Canaan's anger dissipated in a flash.

"You okay?" he asked and put his hand to her cheek. No abnormalities presented, no viruses, no imbalances. He took her hand in his and rubbed it between his palms. "Your hands are cold."

Chloe laughed and stared at his treatment. "Silly, we just got back from the mall." She watched his face and added, "It's the A/C in the car. Look..." She held up a white paper bag. "It's a present." Canaan abandoned the rubbing and Chloe lifted her hand. "Ooooo! My hand feels great now. Thanks, Doc!"

Canaan gave her a har-har and peeked into the sack. He sought the anger that flooded him minutes ago and it was gone. Canaan pulled a wad of wrapping tissue from the bag and carefully opened the fragile paper. Once revealed, the item sat in his palm and he stared dumbfounded. Chloe burst into fits of happiness.

"It's the puppy that licked your chin!" She plucked the gift from his hand to display it. "See? *This is your puppy.*" She watched his face. "Canaan?" she said, still smiling. "It's a keychain. There's a machine. You take a photo and it will make it into a keychain or a mug or a plate—whatever," she rambled, her eyes as excited as they had been the night before. "I found our puppy and took a photo with my phone. Voila!"

He still hadn't responded and she held out her hand.

"Give me your keyring."

Canaan reached in his pocket and passed over his keys. Chloe worked the new item with the circular acrylic-coated photo onto his keyring and gave it back to him.

"Now you will always remember the first time a puppy licked your face."

Canaan's mouth curled into a half-grin and he looked at the photo again. It showed Chloe's face scrunched tight and a gray puppy having a go at her nose with its pink tongue. His heart pressed against his ribcage and he put a fist to his sternum.

Chloe noted the movement and wrapped both small hands around his tattooed forearm. "Do you like my present?" she whispered.

Canaan nodded. "I will smile every time I look at it."

"Awesome," she said and stepped closer, raising up on her toes. Canaan lowered and she pecked his cheek. "I got Kilmeade something, too. Later." And she left the room.

Canaan leaned against the counter and scrutinized the personalized bobble. His smile had nothing to do with the ignorant animal squirming its way into her human heart.

《回》

"Dammit. He doesn't need this," Javier muttered, shaking his head.

Arms crossed and leaning against the living room threshold, Kilmeade watched Javier and Beryl lament their decision to ask Canaan's opinion so early upon rising. The more he studied the two men, the more displeased he became at Canaan's improper response. With only two Elders left, neither could afford to fall into undisciplined behavior.

"Why did we jump to conclusions like that?" Javier asked Beryl who returned a woeful expression. Kilmeade had had enough.

"Javier, Beryl," he said sternly. Both men immediately met his eye. "Stop this inane whining. Every uncomfortable thing that happens is not your fault. Do you understand?"

Not ready to agree, Javier and Beryl held his gaze.

Kilmeade added, "You asked for his help. An Elder's entire *purpose* is to help and guide the brethren. Do you understand?"

Beryl conceded first with a slow nod, but maintained his apologetic posture. Javier followed, and nodded as Kilmeade's logic sunk in.

"When he feels better, we have some good news," Javier said and rose from the couch.

Kilmeade rolled one hand to have him proceed. "He will hear you."

"We have a street address for Pete," Javier said. "He combined his name with his Elder's and goes by Emil Petrov in city records. I drove by today to have a look."

"Well done," Kilmeade said. He sent his mind to Canaan. As expected, although still in deep listen-mode with Chloe, the Elder also

219

attended Javier's current revelations. "What else?"

"They both have their disbursement. There is a new Lamborghini registered to the man and it sat in the driveway. We didn't find anything with Dae Kim's name, but I ran the plates of the Lexus at the house and it's registered to a Lonnie Richardson."

Beryl added, "He's a retired pro-football player. Five years ago when he dropped out, he was photographed by paparazzi at a night club." Beryl flipped through the photos on his phone and showed the screen to Kilmeade. "That's Dae Kim."

"*Very* well done," Kilmeade said and enjoyed the twinkle in Beryl's eye at being complimented, a shadow of his Rakum response, but enjoyable just the same.

Javier and Beryl engaged in chit-chat about their findings and Kilmeade again peeked in on Canaan. Chloe had given him a memento and the big guy was melting. Kilmeade shook his head with a grin.

"Hi!" Chloe entered the room making a beeline for Kilmeade. He received her embrace and she spoke rapidly about her day while holding him about the waist.

"This is for you," she said under his nose, holding up a slick pearlized ring box with no insignia. "It's not jewelry. Don't panic," she said probably noting his dubious expression.

Kilmeade opened it with a grin. Inside the box sat a smooth, oval-shaped polished pink quartz roughly the size of a quarter. One side had the word "Chloe" engraved into the rock. The flipside bore the date January 30. His grin remained, but he caught her eye, chin lowered.

"Our mate-up date is the 23rd..." he said softly.

Chloe's smile grew huge and she placed her hand on her softening tummy. "True, but more amazing is the date a Rakum Elder made this..."

Kilmeade nodded and allowed himself a little happiness. He pulled her close and when she looked up he kissed her.

"You put it in your pocket, carry it like keys or coins. Always have it with you so you will be reminded of your little bird and her *littler* bird."

"*I will, I promise,*" Kilmeade said low enough that only Chloe heard him. He kissed her head one more time and Canaan finally joined them.

"Javie, B, I owe you an apology," Canaan said, standing square. Both men objected, but he hushed them with one hand. "Listen, I'm a goddamn Rakum Elder and none of that was acceptable by any stretch."

"I've never heard an Elder apologize for anything," Javier said with respect in his gaze.

"And I never would before, but things are different now. This is it—Kilmeade and Canaan—are we even Rakum anymore? We're more akin to the Anomaly you called yourself before 11/13." Canaan looked to Kilmeade. "*We* are the Anomaly. Presuming we remain this way, eventually, we will stop referring to ourselves as Rakum at all."

"Brave New World," Chloe said sending Canaan a gentle smile. "You're still plenty awesome, though."

Canaan cracked a small grin. "Thank you."

"Very well! Come, my gorgeous Anomaly!" Kilmeade said with aplomb usually seen in Canaan alone. "I want to put a scare in those two sneaks in Corinth."

Javier and Beryl took a step toward him and he and Canaan shook their heads simultaneously and in sync. "This little trip is Elders only." He winked at Canaan who grinned at the promise of adventure and pulled out his cell.

"Text me the address," he instructed the men and watched as Kilmeade released Chloe and pocketed his gift. At the door, they overheard Javier ordering pizza and Canaan grinned. "Maybe I will taste one of these sneaks..."

"You never know," Kilmeade said and followed Canaan to the car.

《回》

Dae Kim climbed the basement stairs, groggy from sleep. The Master kept them up all night and most of the day interrogating their captive, and only Dae Kim's hunger for a PB&J dragged him upstairs now. They'd turned off Adam Roberts's phone before having the brilliant idea of using it to misdirect his friends. And when they needed a break, Pete stashed Adam in the same tiny room they'd stuck Lonnie in.

Crazy Pete was fast asleep and he *still* believed they were Rakum. Dae Kim frowned; The Master only loaned Rakum powers when he needed them to do a job. The latest? Grab Roberts by force.

It hadn't been difficult. The guy had no sense of caution and, because of Dae Kim's temporary strength, had barely struggled when he wrestled him to the ground next to his car at Baylor-Dallas. Pete gagged him and sat on top of him as they drove back to the house.

As senseless as it was infuriating, The Master refused to let them torture the man. Dae Kim repeatedly bragged that if they allowed him to use his talents, he would get the information they sought. But the ridiculous overseers never gave permission. Once, a faceless spirit replied,

"Elohim forbids it!"

Dae Kim shook his head; the spirit world was a chaotic place and once again, he regretted being introduced to it. As a result, hours of interrogation without significant physical duress had provided nothing. Tonight Dae Kim hoped The Master might see things his way. *I can get that guy to talk. It would be so easy. He loves his body. That's the way in...* But for now, Adam Roberts sat bound in the dark. When Pete came to, they'd go at him again, hopefully Dae Kim's way.

For now, Dae Kim yawned... *I'll have a sandwich.* In the kitchen, Dae Kim flipped on the overheads and nearly had a stroke.

"JUDAS PRIEST!" he yelped. The Elders sat casually at the dinette, leaning back, each with an elbow hooked in the chair, one leg kicked out in front, as if they'd simply been discussing the weather. Dae Kim's mind said, *"RUN!"* but he stood frozen to the spot, his eyes locked with Elder Kilmeade's bright gray gaze.

"Kazak, Dae Kim," the auburn-haired Elder said and came to his feet, followed directly by Elder Canaan on his left. "You're human. Why are you sleeping in the basement?"

Still in shock, Dae Kim didn't answer. Both Elders shone with the glory he remembered, as if they had stepped out of time. As if Last Assembly and 11/13 never happened. *Why? Why them?*

Canaan had walked into his space as his mind rambled and pinched a lock of his hair between two fingers, studying the texture. Dae Kim parted his lips to speak and the Elder gave him the shush signal.

"Let's call Pete up here," Elder Canaan said in a thoughtful tone, standing close, scrutinizing Dae Kim head to toe. "And do I smell a special guest? You're in deep shit, Kemosabi..."

When the Elder's eyebrows flicked a millimeter and he grinned with a secret, Dae Kim realized he and Kilmeade were communicating telepathically. *Oh! The injustice!*

Likely responding to Canaan's silent remarks, the senior Elder came close and touched Dae Kim's cheek with his palm. Dae Kim's contact with Canaan had always occurred during violent military instruction; Kilmeade, on the other hand, stood out in his memory as a handsy, relentless teaser. No matter; violent or romantic, in their day, Elders did what they wanted without exception.

"Come close, Dae Kim," Elder Kilmeade said quietly and pulled him slowly by the back of the neck. In his peripheral vision, Canaan nodded and left the room, presumably to fetch sleeping beauty from downstairs.

"Master..." Dae Kim managed, happy he'd finally found his tongue. Where was *The* Master? Why hadn't he warned Dae Kim that the Elders were waiting for him?

"You were always such an obedient pup, Dae Kim," Kilmeade said in the same low voice and leaned in to sniff dramatically near Dae Kim's jawline. He then sought Dae Kim's eyes. "Have you lost your senses?"

"Master..." Dae Kim mumbled again, unable to look away. The damn human body he was left with provided no defense.

"You have made some bad choices since your change," the Elder whispered, nearly nose-to-nose now, his palm growing warm to the back of Dae Kim's neck. He was being read. Digging inside his mind, Kilmeade pulled Dae Kim closer so his lips spoke against the skin of his cheek. "Black magic? How utterly human of you..."

"They tricked me," Dae Kim whispered, his mouth at Kilmeade's ear. "I-I didn't want to be mortal..."

"But you are, my brother." The Elder's breath tickled as he spoke. "You are fully mortal. I'm reading you *deep,* deep. Do you realize this?"

Dae Kim closed his eyes and swallowed hard. The Elders surely noted the identity of their guest, especially since Adam was the spitting image of Kilmeade. *Why? How?* Dae Kim had no answers, because Adam had not opened up. Now Kilmeade was probing his inner mind. He would see The Master, and Dae Kim was mortified to admit his magic included demon possession. *Why aren't the Unseen helping me resist?*

"*Ohhhhh...*" Kilmeade breathed the word and moved back to catch Dae Kim in his hypnotic gaze. "You thought *demons* could give you the power you had as a Rakum..."

"Yes," Dae Kim whispered, knowing a lie was a waste of breath.

Behind him, Pete shouted in pain as Elder Canaan manhandled him into the kitchen. Kilmeade turned his head to see them enter, but maintained firm contact with Dae Kim's neck.

Canaan held him by the front of the throat, Pete facing the Elder, mouth agape, and eyes bulging, with both of his hands wrapped around the beefy tattooed arm dragging him across the ground. The Elder's other hand supported Adam by the bicep. The guy looked ragged, but otherwise untouched, which meant the Elder healed his slight contusions. Dae Kim's heart sank; he truly was in deep shit if they cared that much for the spoiled clone.

"They abused your mini-me a touch, but he'll live." Canaan directed Adam to a chair and he fell in, his eyes semi-glazed. "Petrov looks rough,

Kilmeade," Canaan said standing him up by the contact with his throat. "You told me he'd be pretty and cuddly, but this? Entirely unappealing." Canaan spun Pete to face the rest of them. Dae Kim didn't meet his partner's eye, too miserable to feel or transmit the misery they both experienced.

"Master, whatever I have is yours," Pete said and dropped to his knees. "We found you by accident, we didn't want to disturb you; it says on the website that the Elders don't want contact... and the kid? He has a letter, Master. A letter you need. We will get it for you. Give us time..."

"It sure is talking a lot," Canaan said about Pete, referring to him as an object. Dae Kim remembered that about the Elder and grimaced as he continued. "It should know that even though it's human, I see right through those lies."

"No, Master, I'm not lying," Pete said and sought Dae Kim's support. "And I'm not mortal, Master. Look, look." Pete pulled a small folding knife from his pants pocket and jabbed the tip into his forearm. Bright red blood issued forth in a thin line, running down his arm and dripping to the floor. "See? See? I'm a Rakum."

Elder Canaan moistened his pointer finger and tasted Pete's obviously human blood. From the dinette, the Adam guy inhaled with surprise or fear, but Dae Kim's eyes were drawn to Canaan as he grabbed for Crazy Pete's hand.

"Human, and oh-so-tasty," he said and lifted the man to his feet. "Let me see that." The Elder snatched the knife from his hand and plunged it into Pete's throat. When he buried his face in Pete's neck, Dae Kim and the Adam guy both yelped, albeit for different reasons.

I'm next! They're going to kill me! Dae Kim's fists clenched and Kilmeade tightened his grasp.

Unable to break free, Pete cried, "I'm a Rakum! I'm a Rakum!"

Kilmeade chuckled and returned his attention to Dae Kim, his palm now massaging where he held his neck. "You enjoy Petrov's delusional state, don't you?" The Elder offered a small *tsk-tsk* and stroked Dae Kim's face twice with his free hand. "What to do with you..."

"Whatever I have is yours, Master," Dae Kim rasped.

"We're past that, pup. You're working against us." Kilmeade watched Dae Kim's face. "Your demons are killing our brethren. Canaan and I are rescuing them. How can we resolve this issue?"

"I'll stop, Master," Dae Kim whispered, wondering if he could. If he did not obey The Master, he would die. And Elder Kilmeade couldn't leave him alive if he didn't stop his mission.

Behind and to his right, Canaan ceased his blood meal with a loud smack and Dae Kim angled his eyes in time to see the Elder drop Pete to the tile. Their mystery clone moaned and covered his mouth. *Who was he to the Elders?*

Everyone fell silent as Elder Canaan closed his eyes and turned away, enjoying the buzz they all used to get from ingesting human blood. Then the Elder straightened, winked at Adam, and fixed his gaze on his partner. Dae Kim wished desperately that he knew what they were saying to each other silently, and after a moment, Canaan knelt to one knee, still looking at his comrade.

"His mind is gone," Canaan said to Kilmeade in a flat tone. Dae Kim swiveled to see Kilmeade nod and in his peripheral vision, Canaan laid his hand on Pete's body. Crazy Pete seized once without opening his eyes and fell still. Again, Adam Roberts cried out in alarm. Ignoring him, the blond Elder stood, stepped over Pete's body, and drew near.

"How's this one's brain?" Canaan asked and put a heavy hand on Dae Kim's inner shoulder adjacent to Kilmeade's palm still around the back of his neck.

"His mind is intact, but he invited an entire legion of demons into his body." When the Elder finished speaking, he glanced at Adam. "Don't mess with spirits," he said and turned back to his prisoner.

Dae Kim looked between the Elders; they were about to end him. He had to think of something and fast. "Masters, I beg you! Look deeper! You will see I'm worth saving!"

"It still looks pretty," Canaan said to Kilmeade on top of Dae Kim's pleas, roughly rubbing once across his pecs with his free hand.

"Please, I was stupid. I was afraid. Look again. I want to live!"

"It's making entirely too much noise from this region," Canaan said his pointer finger inches from Dae Kim's lips. Canaan looked to Dae Kim and gave him a sad smile. "It won't hurt."

Dae Kim looked back to Kilmeade, who at least seemed to be considering his words. The more reserved Elder stood an arm's length away, head to the side, eyes unfocused. Maybe they wouldn't kill him...

"I don't want these spirits," Dae Kim said weakly, afraid The Master *would* suddenly return. "Help me, Masters. I made a horrible mistake."

The Elders were speaking telepathically again and Dae Kim alternately watched their faces. Elder Canaan wanted to play it safe and stop his heart as he had Pete's. Kilmeade's brow furrowed much more; this Elder wanted to keep him alive.

"Please," Dae Kim whispered. "I'm so sorry..." Dae Kim opened his mouth to beg again, but Elder Canaan covered his lips with one hand. Before he could send his mournful gaze to the softer-eyed superior, the world went black.

《回》

"We did the right thing," Canaan said behind the wheel and pulling them away from Pete's spread. "Petrov died when Adam shot him. Those spirits kept him moving, but talk about your systemic shutdowns... He was barely alive." Canaan shook his head.

"A mercy killing, it was."

Canaan agreed and sighed. "So, about our pretty little DK—what do you think? A month? Three weeks?" he asked and Kilmeade shrugged.

Instead of kill the man, his partner put Dae Kim in a coma. The time the kid spent begging, Kilmeade and Canaan had been discussing how to keep him alive. They had no authority over the spirit realm and Chloe needed to be insulated from the liability Dae Kim presented. This way, by the time his human brain recovered from the jolt it received, Chloe would have returned home.

"If he truly wants help, we will find him when Chloe is safely away," Kilmeade said looking out the window.

"And then Javier can do his thing," Canaan added thinking aloud. They had both read Dae Kim deeper as he suggested and discerned dual agendas—Dae Kim suffered punishment when he didn't allow his spirit masters to work their will through him.

"This is what will happen to Adam if he doesn't choose wisely," Canaan said and Kilmeade made a noise of agreement.

In the rearview mirror, Adam looked back at him, his eyes wide and rimmed red with stress and terror. Canaan hadn't healed him entirely and gave him no rejuvenation; the man needed a reality check, and thanks to Dae Kim and Pete, he got one.

"Drop Adam at his place and send Beryl to stay with him," Kilmeade sent silently and Canaan pressed the Bluetooth.

"Hey, order a car to Adam's," he said when Beryl picked up. "He's been accosted by those two turds and you'll make him feel better." Canaan caught Adam's glassy stare again in the rearview. It looked like he might have nodded.

"Shit!" Beryl said over the speakers. "I'm on the way. I hope you ended those guys."

"Pete's gone. Dae Kim will come around in a few weeks."

"Time to teach Adam *kazak!*" Beryl barked and disconnected.

"Thanks," Adam said in a tiny voice.

"Kazak means be strong. You saw some heavy action from two indignant Elders tonight, Adam," Canaan said looking at him now and then as he piloted the truck. "We want you to prosper and live a long, happy life, but if you take demons into your body, we will zap you into eternity. *Comprende?*"

Adam's chin bobbed once, but his eyes said it all—he did not ever want to be on either Elder's bad side. Canaan grinned and in his peripheral vision, so did his cohort.

"Pissed his pants," Canaan sent and Kilmeade covered his mouth to chuckle, still looking out the window.

"He's only human, after all," Kilmeade returned silently.

In the backseat, Adam wiped his eyes and took a slow, deep, breath. "I didn't talk," he whispered. "I didn't talk..."

"But you screamed like a little girl when I attacked Pete," Canaan thought to himself. Again Kilmeade laughed facing away. "This is fun," Canaan said. "This was a good night." He laughed louder and didn't care that Adam looked more frightened than before. Time to man-up, the sooner the better.

28, JUNE 16

"I love this," Chloe said to Javier as she passed him for the kitchen, her arms hooked to the max with plastic grocery bags. It had been a month since she arrived and the revelations of her pregnancy and the existence of Kilmeade's offspring had normalized in her mind. Her body displayed only the slightest changes, but both Elders assured her that they read her health status at a glance. Kilmeade told her eventually Canaan would lay hands on her to chart the baby's growth and she wondered exactly what such examination entailed. *It'll be weird, I can guarantee,* Chloe giggled to herself and plopped her bags onto the counter.

What about Adam? They informed her he'd been abducted and rescued a month ago no worse for wear, but she couldn't get any details.

Behind her and similarly burdened with bags, Javier made an *oof* as he plopped his parcels on the granite countertop.

"You love what? Buying groceries for a house-full of bottomless pits?" Javier joked and helped her set down her collection.

Chloe laughed one *hah* and nodded. "Yeah. I feel so grown up!" Javier had no response and she shooed him away. "I got this. Thank you for taking me to the store."

The sun had been down ten minutes so after she put the cold items away, she peeked around for the Elders. She found Beryl in the office, his back to the door, tapping away on a laptop. Kilmeade lounged longways on a leather couch across the room with his feet propped up facing the door and speaking on a corded landline. He met her eyes with no expression and immediately her mind raced with human female concerns, none of which could realistically be applied to a Rakum. After another cold-shoulder moment with no recognition of any sort, she backed out and turned to the hall to seek Canaan.

She found Kilmeade on the phone every night and always with a serious expression. Often, she overheard snippets of conversations surrounding property and banking. Once, she heard him say Roman's name, so maybe he was simply getting help with his accounts. But why so serious? Kilmeade held secrets, and she expected him to, but something big was coming and she hated that she didn't know how to ask about it.

At the basement door, Chloe knocked and turned the knob. She suppressed her concerns and forced a smile. "Canaan? You down there?" she called into the dark without opening the door more than an inch.

"Nobody down here but sexy beasts, missy. Beware!" Canaan said mimicking her voice.

Chloe clomped down the steps, prepared to be cheered.

《回》

"I hope you're decent."

"Depends on your definition of that word," he said shrugging on his blue jeans at the far side of the space.

Chloe reached the floor and flipped the light switch. "Why do you leave the lights out? Can you really see that well in the dark?" She walked toward him looking around. "It so clean down here."

Still shirtless, Canaan chuckled and combed his curls in a small mirror hanging on a nail. "Why, I thank you."

"*Ffff,* yeah right," Chloe scoffed.

Canaan only grinned. He'd been cleaning up after Kilmeade since their reunion; and before he met Marcy, someone always did the same under him. Chloe stopped in the center of the room and he looked at her sideways. "Yes, ma'am?"

"I thought Kilmeade was joking when he told me you were a good maid," she said with her smile to the side. She tried to hide it, but she had noticed his nakedness. Canaan turned and reached the open shelf where he kept his T-shirts.

"Wait! Wait, what is that?" Chloe asked and closed the distance. She put her fingers to the tattoo that inked most of his back. "Is that a wolf?"

Canaan froze in place enjoying the 40-year-old memory of Marcy Haddle shooting him where Chloe's tiny fingers moved across his skin.

"*Whoa,*" Chloe whispered reverently and her hand traced the wolf to his shoulder. The tattoo covered his back and one side of his body from ear to fingertips. Everyone saw parts of it when he was clothed, but it was most impressive when viewed in total.

Canaan cleared his throat and turned slowly, trying to force Chloe's hand to draw across his chest. She yanked back with a grin.

"Marcy designed that. You like?" he asked and pulled on a white undershirt. "She drew it herself and the tattooist filled it in."

"It is *very* cool." Chloe stepped back and he moved toward her to grab his long-sleeved Henley off the edge of the couch. She scurried out of the way and he chuckled.

"Did you need something or were you hoping to catch old Canaan in the nude?"

"Canaan! Shhh! Geesh!" she barked embarrassed. "No, I noticed Kilmeade on the phone again. Is everything okay?"

Canaan regarded her with a half-grin. "Why are you worried about a few phone calls?" he asked and then answered for her. "It's because you're *nosy*, yeah. That's it. *Nosy...*"

Chloe shrugged. "No, it's just... he looks so serious." She came a little closer and Canaan gestured for the couch. She sat on one end and clenched her fists in her lap. "He didn't acknowledge me when I waved at him..."

Chloe did not meet Canaan's eye and he heard in her voice that she was unhappy with speaking her complaint aloud. He refrained from teasing her, and when he was quiet too long, she looked up.

"No snappy retort?" she asked with a small smile. "You're stepping out of character."

Canaan played it cool by chuckling and dropping heavily beside her. "Tell Dr. Canaan your troubles, little lady. I am a *killer* psychiatrist. I will diagnose your schizophrenia and multiple personality disorder forthwith."

Chloe laughed and leaned back to stare at the ceiling. "Tell me something about yourself." She turned her face his way. "Kilmeade's not much for talking."

"You're a real newbie," Canaan said with a *tsk*. "Imagine a hundred thousand of us not much for talking."

Chloe stared on, not understanding.

"It's the way of our people. Humans love to chatter away, so we do *not*. Anything a mortal enjoys, we enjoy the opposite. We are the anti-man." Canaan grinned at his explanation, but Chloe still frowned. "I don't talk much," he said and shrugged. "You only think I do because I answer your questions. I don't initiate, do I?"

Chloe furrowed her brow. "I don't know. I guess. Will you tell me a Kilmeade story?"

Canaan grinned to the side. "A Rakum doesn't have pretty pink tales to share." He ran his mind through a few good ones, none of which would appeal to the petite figure on the sofa.

"They're all bloody and murderous?" she asked in all seriousness.

"Bloody, yes," Canaan answered. "How about this; in more recent history, remember the day you ran up to me outside Javier's place and asked me about Kilmeade?"

"Sure," she said and folded her legs beneath her.

"I told you that he had mentioned you to me."

"Yeah," Chloe said softly. "You gave me a really hard time, by the way." Her eyes begged for an apology and Canaan didn't have one.

"In the words of our beloved Kilmeade, I yam what I yam."

"Well, you yam kind of scary," she said with the same eyes.

"Grrr," Canaan growled lifting his hands into claws. Chloe grinned at his antics, which made him smile wider. "Okay, here's your story. My man Kilmeade didn't only mention you once. He talked about you for two nights. What did I think, what should he do, should he do anything, what would I do, do I think she's pretty, and on and on and on." Canaan nodded for emphasis. "For an Elder of such power and might to notice a mortal in this way is incredibly rare. In fact, it's been more than a century since Kilmeade expended any energy on a female. The end."

Chloe's smile grew and she blushed. "That's really nice. Thank you for telling me."

Canaan nodded. "Happy to oblige."

Chloe hugged herself and rocked back and forth a few times. To Canaan she looked like a tiny angel, perfect and shining.

"That's all the fluffy memories I have of Kilmeade."

Chloe released a pent up breath. "He's going to send me home soon. Javier said the bad guys would be out of jail by now—"

Canaan laughed one short burst and covered his mouth. Javier had spun some wild tales for her feminine ears and an Elder's mate didn't require such protection. He gave her a kind smile.

"Javie means well, but this is what happened. The two transformed Rakum who hurt Adam were possessed by demons. When we went to rescue mini-me, we ended the crazy one. The other seemed to want help, but he's too dangerous to have around when little Chloe's here."

"Geesh, this story makes so much more sense," Chloe said with a small shake of her head. Canaan could see she wasn't angry at being lied to, simply glad to hear the truth.

"Your sexy other half incapacitated Dae Kim into a coma. He has since recovered. Javier and I will go see him in the hospital tonight. If he can be saved, Javier will know."

"Am I going to have to leave now?" she asked with round eyes.

Canaan touched her cheek without thinking, blinked, and dropped his hand. "Kilmeade doesn't set his life around an idiot's. He'll send you home when he determines it is time."

Chloe smiled and got to her feet. "This entire visit has been great. You don't realize how much I need you. I'm glad you like me okay."

"*Pffft,*" Canaan sputtered and stood. "Let's not go crazy," he teased and pointed to the ceiling. "Kilmeade's off the phone."

"Oh!" Chloe bolted for the stairs and trotted up. Canaan watched her go and shook his head. Javier needed to give it to her straight from here on out.

Stuffing his pockets with his wallet and keys, Canaan headed to the main floor. Soon, he'd look in on Dae Kim and if the guy was irredeemable, he would drain him. Plan set.

《回》

"Thought you and Kilmeade were attached at the hip," Javier said to Canaan as he led the way to the front door. The Elder chuckled so Javier jibed him again. "I mean, he's right up those stairs. I'm sure you could *extricate* him..." Javier gestured pulling apart two objects. "...if you put some muscle to it."

Canaan didn't laugh. "Let the man have some quiet time."

"So serious," Javier said and shook his head. "You really are turning into Kilmeade."

Canaan turned to catch Javier's eye. "And stop watering down information for Chloe. From now on, give her the details. *All of them,* no matter how unsavory your now-human mind thinks they might be. *Comprendé?*"

Javier nodded, truly surprised. "Geez. I understand." Canaan pulled open the door and Javier followed him to the Denali.

"Javie, listen," the Elder said, back to his more familiar tone. "You've been soft and fluffy a while so I sort of expect you'd forget a few things. I'll just have to remind you sometimes. Now, chauffeur your master to see the demon-possessed idiot."

"You will is my will," Javier said with snark.

"Oh, 'tis sweet, sweet music to my ears," Canaan cooed with drama. When he was forced to adjust his seat, he grumbled, "Buncha midgets."

"Chloe," Javier said with a smile.

"Ah," Canaan chuckled and his demeanor instantly softened. "I'm in Kilmeade's head," he said knowingly. "I can say with authority, she'll stay one more month. Let's go see if we can't buy some time."

"Should I pick up Adam?" Javier glanced at Canaan for his expression.

"You guys scared him to death that night and it was the best thing for him. Those demons call to him all the time, offering whatever his heart desires. We've got to make him understand they will eventually succeed if he doesn't turn to God."

"I'm glad I don't hear them," Canaan asserted.

Javier chuckled softly. "But all the Rakum did, daily, from birth until November 13th."

Canaan turned to see Javier's profile. "What? I didn't hear a voice promising me the world, *yada yada yada.*"

"No, but the voices told us how to behave as Rakum. It's the same thing."

"Javie, really," Canaan scoffed and looked out the window.

"It's better if you face it," Javier said with respect. "You end a guy, you want to, you agreed with a demon. You drink blood, you liked it, you agreed with a demon. Etcetera, etcetera."

"You can be a real downer, d'Millier. *Shit.*"

"Geez, you're right," Javier mumbled with a sigh. He hadn't meant to steer their adventure to miserable thought spaces. "Cripes, I need a vacation."

"Nope. We forge ahead," Canaan answered flatly, then tapped his thighs. "Yes, pick up Adam. Let me poke at him a little. I need a laugh."

Javier grinned and texted Adam with one eye on the road. When done, he dropped the phone between them.

"They put Dae Kim at Regional South. Had to do some digging because they listed him as a John Doe. Apparently, he did all of his business through his Cow. He doesn't even have a driver's license."

"Guess he didn't intend to stay. Maybe he got stuck here by 11/13."

Javier nodded. "I gave the receptionist my name and number, said I would ID him. Told her I was his brother." He grinned at Canaan.

"That you are," Canaan agreed. "That you are. Speaking of our brethren, I never heard from Rafael about our experiment."

"Oh," Javier said recalling the topic, "Iago's cancer. I got one text the following day. It said Iago wasn't interested. I didn't answer, figured they were still talking about it."

Canaan shrugged. "Suit himself. I am amazing. I bet Kilmeade and I together could even send that man's clock back. Hey..." Canaan chuckled. "Let's experiment on you! Let's try to make you young again."

"No way," Javier said laughing. "Keep your stethoscope over there, Doctor Canaan."

Javier's phone dinged and the screen read a *thumbs-up* emoji from Adam. In another twenty minutes, he pulled up to the man's home and honked the horn. Adam trotted out wearing jeans and a loose red Polo. When he slid into the backseat, Canaan turned to see his face.

"You losing weight?" Canaan asked.

"A little," he replied softly.

"Better reverse that or you'll lose your sex appeal—I know you want to be like me, gorgeous and mighty as shit."

Adam nodded and remained quiet behind Canaan, looking out his window. Javier headed for the indigent hospital and told Adam some of the things they had been up to since he last saw him. Beryl had been visiting the guy nearly every day, but Javier mostly stayed with Chloe during the daylight hours and worked online with Roman. In addition, he'd begun an email friendship with Claire Boone, the geneticist, but didn't want Canaan to know or tease him about it.

Adam listened, but offered no new information. When they reached the hospital, Canaan turned in his seat and caught Adam's eye.

"Just go in with us, it's going to be okay. Your eyes are too big and I'm going deaf with the pounding of your wittle heart."

Javier also looked at Adam and tried to comfort him with a kind grin. Canaan was right. He seemed to be expecting something horrible.

"Get out," Canaan said brusquely and exited to stand beside Adam's door. Adam stepped out of the truck and faced him, looking as petrified as the other night. What did he think Canaan was going to do?

Javier realized he didn't know, either. Was he losing touch? Every morning he awoke feeling less and less like part of their mission.

"We want you to succeed, remember?" Canaan asked in a kind voice. Squared off, he fairly towered over the guy, even though he was only an inch or so taller. It was the Elder's posture, width, and authority that made him appear much larger than he was.

"Yes, sir," Adam nodded and Canaan put one hand to his inner shoulder, maneuvering to touch the long side of his finger to the skin of the man's throat.

"Hmmm," Canaan hummed and scrutinized Adam's face. "You're not eating enough." Then Canaan's eyebrows went up and he turned to Javier. "He changed his diet."

"Oh," Javier said realizing what Canaan hinted; Adam had stopped ingesting blood. "That's good."

"Whatever," Canaan mumbled and returned his attention to Adam.

"Look, I can also do nice things. Feel this," he said and moved his fingers a trifle. Adam's lips parted and his eyes grew wide. Canaan dropped his hand and turned away with an evil smile.

Javier looked at Adam.

"Don't ask," Adam said in a raspy voice as he followed after Canaan, tugging his jeans.

Javier grinned with a roll of his eyes; just like Canaan to keep a guy on his toes.

《回》

Visiting hours ended at nine so they had a little time. Canaan sent Javier to fill out papers for the nurse and he took Adam in to see Dae Kim. The man appeared thin and his skin sallow and when he recognized Canaan, he inhaled sharply.

"We wave the white flag, DK," Canaan said and wiggled his finger. "White flag. See it?"

Dae Kim relaxed only a fraction and sought Adam's gaze. When Adam wouldn't look at him, Dae Kim went back to Canaan. "*Sajnálom,*[12] Master," he whispered in mortal Hungarian. *"Köszönöm, hogy nem engem megöl..."*[13]

"Hush that." Canaan glanced behind them at the door with a grin. "That scabby nurse out there might be from the Balkans," he said with a wink. He stepped closer, bringing Adam along by the forearm. "Nobody wanted to kill anybody. Now tell Adam something nice."

"I take it back, man. I've been screwing everything up since 11/13. I'll make it up to you." Dae Kim stared Adam's way and at the end, they made eye contact and Adam nodded.

"Awwwwww," Canaan said and patted Adam's back. "All friends." Canaan took Dae Kim's near hand in both of his. "Let Dr. Canaan read your chart..."

Just then, Javier walked into the room followed by a woman and Canaan assumed without turning that it was the nurse. He looked into Dae Kim's body and found him functioning well. His brain had re-set from the jolt and only a few metabolic imbalances from being bedridden remained. Javier cleared his throat and Canaan turned his head.

"Canaan, this is Dr. Claire Boone," Javier said and Canaan gave the woman a surprised nod. Kilmeade's geneticist was a knockout.

---

[12] (Hungarian) "I am sorry."
[13] (Hungarian) "Thank you for not killing me."

"Your LinkedIn photo needs some adjustment," Canaan jibed when she met his eye. Canaan released Dae Kim's hand and straightened, noting he'd grabbed the doc's attention. Her eyes widened and her breath rate increased. When he sent her a wink, she looked down.

Adam shook her hand, expressionless, the doctor no doubt interpreting the morose faces as concern for the patient. She pulled Dae Kim's clipboard chart from the wall and did not raise her eyes to Canaan. *Oh, I still got it,* he laughed to himself and waited to see what she'd say.

Across, and standing beside the doctor, Javier mouthed, *"Stop,"* and rolled his eyes her way. Javier had a thing for her. Canaan crossed his arms to bulge his muscles if the woman should look up.

"So, doc," Canaan said in a lover's voice, "will he survive?"

Dr. Boone took the tiniest glance at Canaan and averted her eyes. "He looks good, Mr. Canaan," she said and patted Dae Kim's shoulder. "You'll be discharged today."

"Great news," Javier said to her a starry-eyed.

"How have you been?" she asked, adding, "I spoke to Jim Bushman yesterday; he said your friend Kilmeade is also a scientist..."

Canaan grinned when the doctor put one hand to Javier's forearm; it was about time Javier had some action. He retook Dae Kim's fingers in his own and waited for the doctor to go. In no hurry to move along, she continued to engage Javier in conversation.

"I'm so surprised to run into you here. I have a consultation two rooms down. How amazing you'd be here at the same time. How long will you be in town?" She looked at Adam. "And are you doing well?"

Canaan sighed for Javier to notice and he steered the doctor into the hallway. Once the door closed, Canaan used gentle pressure on Adam's forearm to lure him back to his side. During the last several minutes, he had decided on a treatment his patient wasn't going to like.

"We need another month, little brother," he told Dae Kim. "Javier gave the nurse your information and they will move you to the city hospital. You'll have a private room and the best treatment available for coma patients."

"Master—" Dae Kim protested and closed his hand around Canaan's fingers.

Javier walked in shutting the door behind him. "Okay, what are we doing?" He stepped to the opposite side of the bed. "Want me to pray?"

Canaan rolled his eyes. *"Meh,* I'll put him under. It's a sure bet. That praying thing takes too long and is so noisy." Canaan nodded to Adam's confused gaze. "You should hear the racket the demons make."

Adam gulped and said nothing.

Javier wanted to object, but he didn't. "You're the Elder," he said and leaned over Dae Kim. "When we come back, we'll help you get rid of those demons, okay? Trust Elder Canaan. They want you to survive. It's their mission. Got it?"

Dae Kim nodded and before he could blink, Canaan sent him out. Adam jumped when he realized Dae Kim had been jolted so invisibly. Canaan couldn't help himself. With an evil grin, he dropped Dae Kim's hand and grabbed Adam's neck with the other palm. In the space of a moment, he sent a jolt of pleasure to the guy that had him collapsed and twitching in the fetal position on the cold linoleum. Canaan laughed boisterously and left the room.

Damn, those guys are so much fun...

He watched the nurses run into Dae Kim's room, alerted by his leads that he'd had a relapse. Still chuckling, Canaan headed for the truck.

"KILMEADE," he shouted telepathically.

"Bravo," Kilmeade sent when their minds touched. *"Come back. We have a brother to hunt down in Plano."*

Canaan honked the horn as Javier crossed the front bumper, causing him to leap to the side and grab his chest. Canaan burst into a new fit of laughter. He would keep them jumping all night if he could. He needed some laughs and he'd take all he could get.

29, JUNE 30

The days passed too quickly and two weeks after Chloe's basement chat with Canaan, Kilmeade was still making calls nearly every night that lasted forever. She asked Kilmeade about them earlier tonight, but as before, he kissed her nose and changed the subject to lovemaking. Chloe sighed. *I won't complain about that.*

Still tingling from his romantic visit, Chloe exited the bedroom fresh from the shower and trotted down the stairs. Their daughter had reached eighteen weeks and her tummy finally showed the smallest round protrusion. Her breasts had only grown slightly and she had no morning sickness or negative side effects of any kind.

Except those dreams... When Chloe's nightmares attempted to surface, she grunted and cleared her mind. *Everything is perfectly fine. The end,* she told herself, using Canaan's distinct way of closing a thought.

She called Kilmeade's name at the landing and Canaan summoned her from the living room.

"Chlo-*eeeeeeee,*" he said again, turning the "e" into an incredibly long syllable. She rounded the pillar and found him reclining in one section of the sofa. He righted the chair and patted his knees. "Come close. Dr. Canaan needs to check the baby." Chloe huffed as if he were joking, but he pat his lap again.

"Where's Kilmeade?" she asked.

Canaan put one finger to his temple, squeezed his eyes closed and hummed. Then he peeked at her with one eye and the finger at his temple pointed to her left.

Chloe laughed out loud—Kilmeade was in the same room on a landline beside a small table against the wall. She took a step toward him and he pointed to Canaan. When she didn't move, he swished his hand.

"See, I told you," Canaan said. "Come close."

Her grin to the side, she stepped over. "What are you going to do?"

"Standard prenatal examination, ma'am. Turn around and sit here." Canaan tapped his thighs

"This is not how you check a baby," she said grinning. A quick glance to Kilmeade and he sent her a wink, still speaking on the phone. "Is he talking to Roman?"

"If it is for you to know, you will know," Canaan quipped and leaned forward to touch her arm. She rotated and he pulled her onto his lap. "Okay, I'll open this up..." he said and kicked open the footrest.

Chloe yelped and remained upright as he reclined. She peered back at him, balancing on his middle, laughing. The mirth in Canaan's eyes only made her laugh more. "This is not how you check the baby!"

"Are you a magnificent Rakum Elder, missy?" he asked. Chloe grinned shaking her head. "Lean back. Don't make me tranquilize you."

"You wouldn't..." she said, still looking backward.

"Only if you're naughty," he said trying to look serious. "Be good."

"I'll be good." With a tight grin, Chloe gave him a last warning. "If you tickle me, Dr. Canaan, I will never trust you again. Got it?"

Canaan crossed his heart. "I promise, ma'am."

"Okay," she said and relaxed backward onto his front after arranging her waist-length hair over her outside shoulder. "What do I do?"

"Lift your arms a little..." Canaan put his arms under hers. "Now, arms down, relax, think of nice things," he said in his doctor voice.

Chloe took a deep breath and exhaled slowly. Ignoring the fact that she lay on top of a man with whom she normally maintained a platonic distance, she forced her mind to remember they were Rakum and not men at all. They were *weird* and they would always be *weird*.

Canaan's hands on either side lifted the hem of her shirt enough to place his warm palms against her skin. She didn't react and the tips of his fingers carefully pushed an inch beneath the waistband of her low-rise jeans so his hands surrounded her entire belly.

"Um, Dr. Canaan," she said suppressing a grin, "your hands are in my pants and my husband is right over there."

Canaan chuckled and she giggled at the bounce it caused. "Keep your mind out of the gutter, ma'am," he said and grew quiet.

Chloe closed her eyes and wondered if she'd feel anything. Canaan's hands were still and nothing seemed to be happening. He breathed slow and steady beneath her and she resisted new giggles as his lungs expanded and she rose up with every respiration. She had been busily counting them when he said okay.

"You are 100-percent healthy, ma'am," he said, but did not remove his hands. "Now, Dr. Canaan is giving you a rejuvenation treatment. This should feel very excellent."

"What's the treatment for if I'm healthy?" she asked while trying to remain still. Her abdomen grew warmer under his hands before a delicious heaviness drew her attention. She felt as if she weighed a thousand pounds and that she must be crushing Canaan, but the sensation felt more than wonderful. "What are you doing?" she gasped.

"Your cells replenish all day long. A Rakum's replenish faster," he said in a breathy voice right at her ear. "That's why we heal so quickly." He took one last big breath and exhaled peppermint. "I sent healing energy through your body which will speed up your cell-replenishment to match the rate of mine. The effects will last a few hours and you'll feel fantastic, so don't do anything crazy."

Chloe smiled. Both of them were quiet a few long seconds and she rolled her eyes to Kilmeade. It looked like he might be finishing up. "He won't carry a cell phone. Why not?"

His gentle hands still in place, Canaan followed her eyeline. "Doesn't need one," he said in a soft voice.

"Heh," she mumbled and closed her eyes again. The heaviness dissipated and a feeling of positivity pierced to her core. "You should do me every day," she said and Canaan laughed.

"Say what?"

"You know what I mean," she giggled and he hadn't removed his hands. "Is that it? Are we all done?"

Canaan chuckled. "I've been done a while. I'm just copping a feel."

"Canaan!" Chloe sat up and shimmied off his lap. "Gross!" she said laughing and jogged to Kilmeade. He was saying goodbye and he replaced the handset in the cradle and took her under his arm.

"Dr. Canaan fixed you up?" he asked, his expression saying he enjoyed the entire spectacle.

Chloe shook her head. "You're *weird.*"

"And you love it," he said with humor and pecked her cheek. "If you would like to stay, I will permit one more month. Then you will return to your mother and finish your pregnancy."

Chloe agreed, expecting such a commandment sooner or later.

Kilmeade kissed the crown of her head. "You must never go out after sundown and never let anyone in the house. In the day, trust Javier to protect you."

"I promise," she said.

"Okay, pretty little human," he said with a wink and backed away. "The Elders are headed out."

"Beryl! Javier!" Canaan barked and clambered out of the recliner. "Who's coming with us?"

Chloe watched the men plan their evening. Kilmeade caught her eye and sent her a wink. Chloe waved and placed her hands around her softening tummy. When Javier agreed to stay behind, she giggled as both Canaan and Kilmeade turned in synchronicity to the front door. The union of minds—as *weird* as it was utterly amazing.

30, July 14

"W*ait... I've seen this before...*"

Chloe forced herself to awaken from what was about to be a repeat of the worst nightmare so far concerning Kilmeade and Canaan. Releasing a deep purposeful breath, she turned to sit up from bed.

Wait. The floor flowed with black ooze.

"*Oh, God... I'm not awake.*"

The sudden realization caused the scene to reset and she opened her eyes again in her own bed, in her parent's house, the morning sun streaming in warming her with its glow.

No, that wasn't right, either.

"*Wake up, Chloe! You're in Dallas!*"

This time without sitting up, Chloe slapped her cheek hard. Squeaking her eyes open, finally the scenery fit. She carefully studied the details of the ceiling, the bedspread, the thickly-curtained window of the bedroom of the rented house in Texas. Sighing with relief, but her heart thrumming with adrenaline, she put her feet to the floor.

Normal brocade rug, a little scratchy on my feet...

"Thank God," she whispered and woke up her phone with the touch of her finger. Midnight.

Wait. Hadn't she gone to bed after two? Realizing she was in a dream, Chloe braved the dark hallway. She was downstairs, not up, and her "bedroom" sat where the living room should be.

"Please don't let this be another nightmare..." she begged and stepped toward the door ahead. It was the basement, or at least, in the real world, it sat where the basement door was located. Chloe took another halting step and behind her, every window on the first floor opened simultaneously, filling the hallway with sunlight. It wasn't midnight, but high noon.

A person shoved past her then, walking hurriedly for the door ahead. It was a man, not especially tall or thick, but moving with a purposeful step. Before Chloe could react, the silhouette flung open the basement door. Silent screams filled Chloe's throat as the faceless man turned, hands on his hips, and said, "That ought to do it."

"No! No!" she shouted, her heart bursting at the sound of the Elders struggling to avoid the sunlight flooding their sanctuary. She couldn't reach the basement as every step moved her nowhere. "Why? Why?" she whispered, her voice exhausted.

"Why not?" The man with no face shrugged. "They're not human."

Chloe awoke, her cheeks wet with tears. The nightmare had repeated after all. Two weeks ago, she had seen the shadow-man kill her beloved in a dream and she had no qualms about sharing it with Kilmeade at the time. Was it a warning? Chloe checked the time. Roman would arrive soon for a short visit before he took her home. Without meaning to, her heart searched for Kilmeade and immediately their minds touched.

"Little bird, it's only a dream, we are safe," he sent, soothing Chloe's panic.

Embarrassed to have disturbed him, Chloe apologized. *"I'll see you tonight,"* she returned silently and the connection slipped away.

Feeling more like herself, Chloe stretched and yawned and hopped into the shower. By the time she exited and initiated the ritual of grooming her long hair, the evil image of the shadow-man had faded. An hour later, with her suitcase packed and her souvenirs bagged, she took a deep breath and exhaled. One more night. Her final month with Kilmeade had flown by and although she cried herself to sleep a few times, prenatal vitamins and periodic visits to Dr. Canaan were not enough. It was time to see a human doctor and begin the countdown in earnest.

Chloe's cell phone chimed and she lifted the screen to read a group text from Javier, addressed to all in the rental. *"Getting Roman, will return in ~ hour."* As she watched, Beryl sent back a thumbs-up emoji. Canaan was next. He texted, "Roman" with a thumbs-up. Then, "Javier," followed by a hand flipping a bird. Chuckling, Chloe caressed her growing bump and smiled.

《回》

Javier shook his head at Canaan's humor and looked up in time to catch a glimpse of Roman heading his way.

"The more things change, the more they stay the same," Javier said as Roman came within earshot. Love-Field rumbled with foot traffic and Roman didn't reply until they walked to the edge of the concourse.

"I was just thinking about that as I disembarked," Roman said near his ear to be heard over the crowd. "Nine months ago, you picked me up at the airport to figure out what to do about Elder Rufus." Roman remained in Javier's gaze an extra moment and Javier shook his hand.

"No one to fight this time," he told him, hoping to draw some cheerfulness into his eye and Roman forced a tight grin. "Can I assume your brother filled you in on our adventures so far?" Javier asked as he took custody of Roman's overnight bag and turned them toward the exits. "He'll want me to fill in any blanks before you arrive."

"Kilmeade and his royal patience," Roman replied with chagrin. "I'm caught up. He has a daughter on the way, his mini-me—as he said Canaan is calling him, and what has happened with Dae Kim and Petrov. Does that about cover it?"

"Sounds like it." Javier led the way and toyed with the idea of asking Roman if Kilmeade shared anything else—like about the angel visitations or the idea that he would die soon. Could he ask Roman about his own angel vision? How would he open such a conversation in the short visit they had lined up?

"Javie, what's wrong?" Roman asked suddenly serious. "Kilmeade— is he okay?"

Javier glanced his way to judge any deeper meaning. He decided to play it safe out of respect for the Elder. "He's fine, but he'll be glad to see you. He's not the same Kilmeade that went into the storm drain last November."

Roman made a sad chortle. "And how alarming it must be to be one of two remaining. Whatever the Lord is doing with them, I hope He's done fast. How long can they go on like this?"

Javier glanced over to see if Roman was truly asking. "Canaan's still Canaan, if that's any comfort."

Roman shook his head with a grin.

"How's David?" Javier shoved open the glass exit door and Roman went through. "He didn't want to come?"

"He is holding down the fort. We have eleven brothers staying in the house this week for a *Bible camp*, of all things." Roman paused at the sidewalk and stretched his back. "David wants to plant a church for Rakum. He'll probably start construction next summer. You'd be amazed at how well he works with the brethren seeking God."

Javier smiled. "No, I can see it. He has a huge heart."

"Indeed. I will share a program we developed together. It's been helping the brethren understand God, and it should help you on the road just the same."

"Fantastic," Javier said nodding. "God has enabled the Elders to sniff out the suffering Rakum. Kilmeade estimates only two or three left in this area. When you leave tomorrow, we're going to Los Angeles."

Roman clapped his shoulder and resumed their trek to the car. "You haven't mentioned Beryl," Roman said as they reached the Yukon. "Can you believe Simon Miller called me to ask how he was doing?"

Javier stifled a curse and Roman agreed with a wry nod. *Why?* Javier wondered, truly mystified. Why would Simon be concerned for a former Rakum who repeatedly attacked him and then wickedly tried to seduce him every waking moment?

"I'm supposed to tell Beryl," Roman said shaking his head.

"Please, don't," Javier replied sincerely. "Ever since we left Tuscaloosa, Beryl has become progressively more affable."

"I understand," Roman nodded. "I will speak to Beryl privately, encourage him, see where he is spiritually."

"Good," Javier said. They headed away from the airport and would be at the house in thirty minutes. Javier reached for the radio, but Roman asked another question.

"Kilmeade speaks of Chloe often. She has cheered him, I gather."

Javier nodded. "His devotion to her is off the charts and I can tell, she pleases him a lot." Javier then clarified, "With very little training in how to be an Elder's wife."

Roman huffed. "The Old Way is out the window. I doubt he has trained her at all."

Javier grinned. "I guess you're right. But she hasn't complained or been a problem." Javier couldn't help but chuckle when he thought of Canaan's problematic one-brain situation.

Roman noticed. "Tell me."

Javier shook his head. "Canaan..." Javier laughed and wiped his eyes. "He has a crush on her. He's proper. He's very proper."

Roman offered a knowing nod. "They're in one brain, so you know what that means..."

Javier laughed again, his heart light. "Kilmeade stubs his toe and Canaan feels it?"

Roman's eyes sparkled with humor. "Yes."

Javier laughed again and sighed. "I've missed you, you make my heart glad."

Roman reached across and shook his shoulder.

"By the way," Javier said. "Adam isn't welcome any longer. After all of our efforts, he still hasn't chosen sides. He's too unpredictable in this headspace, so Beryl visits him some away from the house. The rest of us are waiting for the guy to make his choice."

"Does he understand that if he doesn't keep his guard up, the demons will succeed in drawing him away?" Roman asked.

"Yes, and Canaan gave him front-row seats to an Elder's fury," Javier said with a head shake. "Twice."

Roman made a noise of agreement. "Ironic that Roberts is a scientist," Roman said, looking out the window. "Kilmeade loves science, too. Always loved using his brain."

"And what a big brain it is," Javier said in a silly voice to get Roman to laugh. When he did, it was almost like the old days, when Roman was an Elder bigger than life and Javier his little proselyte following him in awe and wonder. Javier didn't mind rehashing those days, and deep down, he hoped God didn't mind either.

《◎》

"Can you talk? 555-667-9090."

Beryl rose off the couch and walked to the back deck. It was noon and the house sat quiet. Chloe was upstairs and Javier had not yet returned with Roman. Since their first phone chat in February, Beryl had found talking with Simon enjoyable. As it turned out, he was funny and now that he'd lost the desire to latch onto a Rakum, he had commendable confidence and self-esteem, two qualities Beryl never saw in him before 11/13. Beryl hit the number and Simon picked up at the second ring.

"I'm free the next two weeks. Lisa-Marie's taking Jessica to her mom's for a wedding and I'm batching it in Oklahoma City. Didn't you say you guys are in Dallas?"

Beryl leaned over to look in the house; the coast was clear. He stared at the landscaped lawn, his mind racing. No one in their party, including Javier, would understand why Beryl wanted to visit Simon.

"I'll be discreet," Simon said and Beryl's eyes grew wide.

"How'd you know what I was thinking?"

Simon chuckled. "Because of the lecture Roman gave me when I spoke to him earlier."

Beryl considered Roman's perspective, always trying to protect everyone in his circle. He didn't like Simon and didn't try to hide it.

"We'll be here another day or so." Beryl grinned, suddenly looking forward to seeing Simon in the flesh after all their phone calls. "Come on down and text me when you get a room. I have some interesting news."

"Sounds good," Simon said. "I have an appointment at noon so I'll be there about six. See ya then."

Beryl disconnected the call and turned. Roman had arrived. Good timing. Beryl smiled and prepared to lie to a man who discerned lies as an Elder for two centuries. Worth a try.

《回》

At the house, Roman tailed Javier into the living room and Chloe greeted him across the open floorplan.

"Congratulations," he said noting how small she remained even at six months along.

Chloe came close and grabbed him in a hug. "Your brother is awesome. I love him so much." She squeezed him tighter. "I'm sorry I was rude to you when you tried to help me before."

"Don't even think about it," Roman said with a wave of his hand. "In all of our phone conversations, my brother talks more about his little bird than anything else."

Chloe's smile erupted and her dimples deepened. "Thank you for saying that," she replied and turned away. Roman watched her head up the stairs as Javier returned to the living room.

"I found him," Javier said and gestured for the sliding glass doors.

On the large back deck, Beryl peeked around to see him through the glass. Wearing a fitted maroon T-shirt and faded jeans, the guy still looked like a true college freshman. Roman pulled open the door and Beryl shook his offered hand.

"You're looking well."

Beryl met his eye and looked away smiling. "I almost called you Elder," he said and chuckled.

Roman grinned and led him to the side where they both leaned on the railing. "Javier said you've made a huge difference in the mission."

Beryl shrugged with a half-nod. "Javier's doing all the work. I feel like a cheerleader; I'm not really contributing."

"Trust me, you are." Roman looked out across the yard, putting his thoughts in order. As an Elder, he had viciously punished the youth for following the orders of his Master, Jack Dawn. As mortals, no animosity existed between them. While he chose his moment, Beryl spoke up.

"Do I need to apologize for what I did before? Seems it was my business to hurt everyone I came in contact with," he finished without

247

humor. "You, Javier, Canaan, Beth Rider, Simon Miller..."

Roman shook his head. "You might apologize to mortals if it comes up, but not to your Rakum brethren. We all followed orders and the crueler we were, the more Rakum we became. When the time is right, you will apologize to God, but your brethren don't need it."

"Apologize to God?" Beryl asked. "I was the best Rakum I could be," he said and grinned. "And I enjoyed it."

Roman chuckled softly. "We all enjoyed it. Ta'avah inside us made sure we were only satisfied when we suffered and caused others to suffer more." He looked to the cloudy sky and sighed wistfully. "One day, you'll say inside, *what I used to be was abominable.* That's when you'll repent."

"Okay. I think I get it," Beryl agreed in an undertone.

Roman put a hand to Beryl's shoulder. "I feel strongly that I need to tell you not to worry and stress over joining 'the God team,'" he said with finger quotes. "I can say with confidence that at some future point, you will begin to feel a need to repent and you'll do so. No stress. You are covered in prayer and you know He loves you." Roman referred to Beryl's miraculously-healed cheek—the one Isaac's curse reduced to an oozing mess during his short reign. Beryl nodded and his bright eyes sparkled. Javier was right—the man was very close.

"I wish you had been my Elder. My life would be a lot easier now, for sure. I made a much better Rakum than I make a human." He then chuckled into his hand. "The way you protected him in the Cave..." Beryl shook his head smiling. "So many bones were fractured when I slammed into that wall, *shhhhi-i-i-t.*" He held Roman's gaze, his head to the side. "I was so jealous of Javier after that night."

Roman clapped his back and stood off the railing. "Don't sell yourself short. You were brave to stand up to me," he replied. "And don't regret being raised by Jack Dawn. Everything that happened then led to where we are today. Your personality was formed by your upbringing, which caused you to do your part in the salvation of our people. Do you understand?"

Beryl didn't react or respond, so Roman added more.

"At Last Assembly, you and Meryl brought Simon to the Cave where he gave his life to God. Javier and I had left him at Mike's house—I *insisted*—I didn't know he was supposed to come with us. Think of it— God used you to save Simon's soul."

Beryl hemmed and Roman continued.

"Years later, you attacked Marcy Haddle, which caused Canaan to join

248

up with us to defeat Rufus." Roman watched the truth dawn in Beryl's eyes. "When Isaac needed to be eliminated, you gave Canaan focus and companionship—which you still give him to this day. He's crazy about you," Roman said shaking his head with a wry grin. "The only Elder I knew whose favorite of life's little pleasures was pummeling the snot out of his brethren. Now he hugs them. Figure that out."

"Yeah," Beryl huffed also shaking his head and pondering the changes in them all since November.

"Carry on, Beryl," Roman said and headed for the glass door. "I'm proud of you. We all are." Roman meant the Elders and he saw in the youth's eyes that he read it that way.

Beryl nodded. "Thanks."

Roman headed inside. The kid would be fine. Now, to catch up with Javier before the world's last two Rakum arose and set the plan for the evening.

31

Roman had only the briefest conversation with Kilmeade before the two Elders left to take Chloe out for a meal. They returned by nine, and when she had been made comfortable to Kilmeade's satisfaction, he joined Roman in the kitchen.

"Change-up tonight, D'Millier," Kilmeade said to Javier also at the dinette. "Roman will accompany us in your stead."

Javier nodded and Roman noted he appreciated the break.

"Beryl may visit Adam, but not here. Understand?"

"I'll tell him. I'll stay with Chloe," Javier said and stood to stretch his legs and crack his back. Canaan entered the kitchen, patted Roman's shoulder, and widened his eyes at Javier's motions.

"Are you getting old and rickety, little brother?" Canaan asked Javier and crossed the room. "See Dr. Canaan..."

Javier laughed and said to Roman, "His head is so big since he became Kilmeade's preferred physician." Javier stopped speaking as Canaan gently clasped his throat.

Roman smiled and watched Javier's eyebrows go up in surprise.

"Damn," he whispered as Canaan withdrew the contact with a sly grin. "Threw something extra in at the end, didn't you?"

Canaan laughed and clapped his back hard. "I'm sick of you dragging around. Clean this place up while we're gone. You're a sorry-ass housekeeper." Canaan shot his gaze to Roman. "How did you put up with such service?"

Roman's grin widened. "You'll never hear me complain; he was the perfect valet."

Javier shot Canaan a sideways bird while straining to reach the strike zone.

"Wimps," Canaan said to Kilmeade and left the kitchen. "I bet you a million dollars Roman doesn't bitch when I slap his back," he yelled from the front door.

"Be careful and good luck," Javier said to Roman as he followed Kilmeade out.

Roman calmed his spirit, excited that he was to participate on the hunt. It never occurred to him that he'd be invited, so now as they climbed into the truck, he prayed for God's will and their safety.

In the driver's seat, Canaan pulled them away from the house and Kilmeade turned to Roman. "I hear you have a novel approach for our sad little brethren. Do tell."

Roman nodded. "It involves Scripture," he said and watched Kilmeade's eyes. His brother had said before he left Tuscaloosa that he was close to accepting the Lord. Because of this, Kilmeade resisted hearing the Word. To his surprise, Kilmeade asked for more, so Roman continued. "The Lord led me to a specific Rakum scripture and so far, it has been 100% effective."

Kilmeade nodded and turned slowly to the front deep in thought.

"It seems our brethren group in twos—have you noticed?" Canaan asked him in the rearview mirror.

"I have," Roman agreed. "Who wants to be alone?"

"Not me," Canaan said sternly with a look to Kilmeade.

Soon, they exited at Plano and Roman watched with interest as Canaan pulled the car to the shoulder, both Elders looking to their right. Roman stayed put as they exited the car and stood shoulder-to-shoulder facing town. Roman scanned the electric horizon. Across an expanse of grass and cement culvert, an Econo Lodge loomed over a few restaurants. Behind that, signage for a wooded preserve.

The Elders conferred in low tones and then returned to the car. Once underway, Canaan offered an update. "Two Rakum in this motel," he said and Kilmeade nodded. "It's bad."

"Hurry," Kilmeade said and Canaan spurred quickly into the parking lot. As soon as he was in park, they jumped out and Roman followed.

The two-story rectangular building had the room doors on the inside. Kilmeade reached the side entrance and opened it with no obvious effort. Once through, both Elders stopped and listened. Roman stood still, as a former Elder himself, recognizing every move the two made. Canaan then spun away and hit the door to the stairs followed by Kilmeade, and Roman brought up the rear.

On the second floor, they reached their target and Kilmeade spoke through the door in their language. A clatter, a yelp, and a thunk emanated from inside and Canaan opened the door.

"Brothers, it's Elder Canaan," he said and entered. Kilmeade gestured for Roman to wait and disappeared inside. After a muffled cry of alarm,

Kilmeade called him in.

"Master! Please!" the ailing brother begged, crying openly and hanging onto the leg of a dead dog in Canaan's arms. "Pleaasseee..." he cried and collapsed on his face to bawl.

Roman looked left and Kilmeade's hand rested on one of Roman's pups from days long past. This brother, Thelo, sat under Kilmeade's palm composed and sorrowful. Both little brothers were thin and pale and neither had bathed in a very long time.

"Master!" the man with Kilmeade barked when he recognized Roman. Kilmeade crossed his arms and winked to Roman; this one was to be *his* project. On his left, Canaan set the animal's corpse out of sight and knelt beside the anguished Rakum with dog blood on his chin.

Adrenaline pumping, Roman nodded to Thelo. "Come close."

"What happened? How did you find us?" Thelo's eyes went to Kilmeade and back to Roman. "Why are they intact and you're not?"

Roman sat in the rickety chair beside the desk. Thelo remained on the carpet and scooted to Roman's feet.

"I will explain," he said with a kind grin. Then with his next words, he caught Kilmeade's eye. "I have some words to share that will make everything right again." He held Kilmeade's gaze until he was certain his brother understood; the next few sentences could change Kilmeade, too.

"Proceed, brother," Kilmeade said with a wink, his eye shining with an odd gleam. When Roman leaned down and placed his hand to Thelo's cheek, Kilmeade turned away and leaned against the closed door. Listening, but facing the wall.

"Thelo, at Last Assembly, you were there?" Roman asked. The man nodded. "Do you recall the story the Rabbit told us about the Creator?" He nodded again. "That night, you chose to remain as you are. Many of our brothers did, too. Elder Canaan and Elder Kilmeade were two of them. I chose to follow Him, the One who made me."

"He's real, Master," Thelo said in a whisper. "He's real. I missed my chance. I want to die..."

"Shhh," Roman said and moved his hand to Thelo's oily hair. "You haven't missed out. The true Father that loves you is here, the One that has watched over you every day to bring you to this motel room tonight is here right now."

"H-He brought me here?" Thelo asked.

Roman nodded. "You eat to feed your body, correct?" Thelo nodded at rapt attention. "You also have a spirit that it eats only spiritual food. Do you understand?"

"I-I think so, yes," Thelo stuttered, "my soul. I have a soul."

"Will you eat this spiritual food I am about to give you?" Roman asked him and he nodded without hesitation. Roman glanced at Kilmeade's back. His brother's head rested against the door, his shoulder pressed against the wood. Slightly louder, Roman sent him one more oblique warning. "These words will change everything."

Kilmeade did not react and Roman returned his focus to Thelo. He slipped from the chair and joined the pup on his knees. Dropping his hand to the man's shoulder, Roman said, "Repeat these words after me. Have mercy on me, God, blot out my transgressions. Wash me clean of my iniquity and cleanse me from my sin..."

Thelo repeated precisely, eyes closed, brow furrowed. Roman did not look at Kilmeade again, but it was an effort not to.

"I acknowledge my transgressions, my sin is always before me..."

Again Thelo copied his words carefully.

"Behold, I was brought forth in iniquity, and in sin, my mother conceived me..."

Thelo paused, exhaled and then repeated Roman, meeting his eye when he mentioned the mother.

"Wash me, and I will be whiter than snow and the bones You have broken may rejoice."

Out of the corner of his eye, Kilmeade's head turned to Canaan. Roman did not allow it to distract him. The former Rakum before him grew bigger in spirit every second, the furrow gone from his brow and his frown fading.

"Deliver me from the guilt of bloodshed, O God, the God of my Salvation, and create in me a clean heart..."

Thelo said the last few words with his eyes open and ablaze, looking at the water-stained ceiling tiles.

"Thelo, do you believe what the Rabbit told you about the Son of God?" Roman waited for the man's answer, but watched Kilmeade out of the corner of his eye. If his brother admitted the Truth of the Gospel, he might be human by the time they reached the car. Roman wanted him saved, but he had also promised not to convert him by subterfuge.

"I do, I believe. I see Him on the cross in my dreams," Thelo whispered with reverence. Kilmeade quietly left the room and Canaan got to his feet, the miserable brother with him following with his eyes.

"Then accept Him. Right now, tell Him you want to serve Him..."

Thelo rose to his knees and looked upwards. A grin played with the sides of his mouth and Roman could almost see the glory of God around his head.

"Father! I see You! I have served an earthly Father my whole life, but now I see only You. I have shed blood my whole life, erase my past! You have broken me, and I asked to be lifted up again in You! Take me to Your side! Show me Your salvation!" Thelo raised his hands high.

Canaan watched with round eyes and the man at his feet put his hands to his mouth. What had been only in Roman's mind was now an actual manifestation of God's glory in the dank hotel room. Electricity buzzed around them and Canaan looked away, going to his knees beside the transformed brother.

Thelo fell silent and the room slowly returned to normal, the shining aura dissipating altogether in the space of five seconds. Thelo regarded Roman a split second and leaned forward to pull him into a hug. Roman patted his back in wonder; that hadn't happened back home. He turned his eye to Canaan.

The Elder shook his head. "That was some freaky shit."

Roman grinned despite himself. Thelo said in his ear, "He loves me. He loves me so much that He died so I can live."

"I know, I know," Roman said and after another moment, Thelo pulled away and rose to his feet. Roman and Canaan followed suit and all three looked at the man on the floor.

"This is Brill," Canaan said in a quiet voice.

Roman waited for Brill to meet his eye. "Would you like some food like that?"

The miserable lump of humanity nodded, his eyes wet and his nose running fluid. Roman approached and joined him on the carpet. Above him, he sent Canaan a wink.

"I'll be in the hall," he whispered and left the room.

Roman placed a hand on Brill's shoulders and told him about the Father who loves him more than life.

《回》

"Brother," Canaan said softly as he joined Kilmeade in the stairwell adjacent to the room. "Come close." Canaan put his hand to Kilmeade's neck and reeled him in. He pressed him to his chest and they stood together quietly. When five minutes had passed, they overheard Roman's parting words with the two brothers. Kilmeade stepped out of their lengthy embrace and leaned against the cinderblock wall.

"Don't say it," Canaan whispered. "There's no need."

Canaan watched his eyes and requested again telepathically that Kilmeade not discuss what he was thinking. His companion was leaving, and neither of them fully understood the extent of that knowledge. A sense of panic touched Canaan's heart and it was so foreign that he put his fist to his chest.

"Not yet," he hissed, glaring at Kilmeade in the quiet stairwell. Canaan lifted that hand to Kilmeade's face and cupped his cheek. "Not yet," he said again, tipping his chin down, his eyes locked fast with his brother.

"Soon," Kilmeade whispered and placed his hand over Canaan's. "Watch over our Chloe."

"GODDAMMIT, KILMEADE!" Canaan shouted loud enough to reverberate the cement wall. Roman pushed open the door beside them, covering his ears. Canaan backed away. "I'm not doing this alone!" he barked and trotted briskly down the stairs.

"Canaan?" Roman called after him. "Canaan!"

"He'll be fine," Kilmeade said, his voice subdued. "You did well in there. Two more of our brethren have found peace."

"Amen," Roman replied with typical seriousness.

Kilmeade sent him a tiny grin. "I'm leaving the flesh when I receive Him, brother."

"No, you're not," Roman huffed. "Why would you say that?"

Kilmeade pulled him close and touched foreheads. "Let's go comfort the child pouting downstairs," he said, his humor returning.

Downstairs, Canaan leaned against the car fuming. Kilmeade stood before him and crossed his arms. He regarded Canaan with his head tilted, a half-smile on his face. Canaan exhaled and met his eye.

"I have a passie you can suck on, you big baby," Kilmeade jibed using one of Canaan's favorite sarcastic retorts.

With a sad grin, Canaan shook his head and then looked at Roman. "Your God is messing with my shit!"

Roman grinned. "I know. He does that to get your attention."

Canaan looked up to the sky and waved dramatically. "Howdy!"

"And it means He loves you and knows what's best for you," Roman finished and Canaan shot a bird to the night sky.

Kilmeade chuckled and jabbed Canaan's shoulder. "Let's take Roman clubbing. Preachers are so uptight."

"In my defense," Roman said deadpan, "I have always been uptight."

"Will there be blood-letting at this club?" Canaan asked without joking.

"If you're as good as you think you are, sure," Kilmeade replied and headed to the passenger side.

"Oh, I'm excellent. Better than you, old man," Canaan bantered and slipped behind the wheel.

"I'll go, but don't let me see any of that Rakum business, Canaan," Roman said as he fell into his seat.

"I make no promises, Elder Roman, Master, Sir," he returned and laughed at his own joke. "Might even be you. I can take you easy, now that you're a cute little human man."

Roman sent an exaggerated laugh and turned to look out the window, probably wondering if he was kidding.

《回》

Dae Kim ordered another shot and scoped out the room. The club hopped with young people and the music vibrated to his core. When he first returned to consciousness after the second Elder coma, The Master told him he should hunt down and kill the Elders, promising he'd have the power to do it when the time came. This was not even *remotely* possible. He hadn't heard from The Master since and Dae Kim grinned, cautiously optimistic for the first time in months.

Today, after a little banking and shopping for immediate needs, he was ready to relax tonight at the club, perhaps hook up with one of the local beauties, and head to Manhattan in the morning to start over. Hopefully, leaving town meant The Master and all his various parts would find a new patsy for their ridiculous missions.

A gorgeous woman leaned on the bar beside him and her perfume reminded Dae Kim of better days. When he met her eye, she smiled shyly and looked away. Was she alone? He met her gaze in the mirror behind the bar. His lips parted to speak when three faces crowded the reflection and he nearly released his bladder.

"It's DK! So handsome! Looking so fly!" Elder Canaan said and wrapped his beefy paws around Dae Kim's outer shoulders. The woman received her drink and dashed away, but Dae Kim hardly noticed. Elder Kilmeade hopped onto the stool next to him and impossibly, a *human* Elder Roman sat on his opposite side. Canaan remained behind, grinning at him in the mirror.

"She wasn't right for you, little brother," Elder Kilmeade said close to his ear. "Whatever he's having," Kilmeade said when the barkeep offered his services. "When did you wake up?" Kilmeade did not touch him, which gave Dae Kim a little solace. Elder Roman, did, though. Roman had aged since he'd last seen him and was obviously mortal. The tipsy Elder put his arm across Dae Kim's mid-back and gave him a sincere smile.

"They told me you're possessed by demons," Elder Roman said too loudly in his ear. Elder Canaan laughed and Kilmeade shook his head, but none of them were concerned about Dae Kim's fear. "Come out, come out, Satan!" Roman shout-whispered and Canaan shook Dae Kim back and forth by his shoulders still chuckling.

"Masters!" Dae Kim hissed, his eyes asking for mercy. "Please don't zap me again!" He repeated the request louder in Rakum Hungarian and Roman hugged him with the one arm.

"*Gyere velünk,*[14] Dae Kim," Roman said in his ear, in *mortal* Hungarian and again louder than necessary. *"Beszélni akarunk veled..."*[15]

"Helló polgártárs!"[16] a man beside Roman shouted loudly and reached his opposite arm over to shake hands. Dae Kim watched as Elder Roman dropped the arm around him and grasped forearms with the stranger. He turned away and they began loudly and animatedly discussing Hungarian politics. Canaan playfully squeezed Dae Kim's shoulders.

"Elder Roman can no longer hold his whiskey," Canaan said in his ear. "We don't want you to come with us tonight. But we could do it tomorrow night..."

Elder Kilmeade leaned in and snakclike, grasped his wrist where Dae Kim's skin was exposed at the cuff. Skin-to-skin, the Elder had no trouble seeing his plans to flee the city.

"Oh, little brother, stay one more night," he cooed, holding Dae Kim captive with his gaze. "You wanted our help, remember?"

"I can leave town, I think the demons are gone," Dae Kim began, but Kilmeade shook his head, his eyes full of mock sorrow.

"No, they remain, little brother," he said in a sad voice. Dae Kim held his breath as Kilmeade looked at Canaan behind him and started up with the telepathy. Expecting to be zapped any moment, he tensed for the jolt. But Elder Canaan nodded in the reflection and took Dae Kim by the arm.

---

[14] (Hungarian) "Come with us."
[15] (Hungarian) "We only want to speak with you."
[16] (Hungarian) A greeting to a fellow countryman.

"Come along, DK," he said and steered him away from the bar, moving his guiding hand to wrap around Dae Kim's neck. Dae Kim did not resist, but kept up with his stride and only when they reached the exit did he ask what was going to happen to him. The Elder maneuvered him past the exterior bouncer and reached the curb before he spoke. "Ride with me," he said and flagged the valet.

"What then, Master?" Dae Kim asked in a whisper. Inside him, The Master awoke and told Dae Kim to attack Canaan. The demons were shouting, *choke him! choke him!* Canaan turned then and looked at him as if he were insane.

"Did I just hear your demons?" Canaan asked with a new expression Dae Kim couldn't name. He nodded and Canaan rolled his eyes. "Choke me?" Canaan gestured to the man pulling the truck near and mumbled under his breath, *"Idiots."*

Their now familiar pearl-colored Yukon parked and Canaan helped him into the front seat. When the Elder crossed to the other side, the demons shouted, *run away! run away!* But Dae Kim resisted. The Elder could gain on him in a blur of movement. What use would it be to run?

"You'll like this," Elder Canaan said and pulled off the curb. In a couple of minutes, he had located a quiet side street and he entered the alley. "Come on," he ordered and exited the truck.

Dae Kim paused only a moment, still shutting out the demons' bad advice. He slid out of the seat and Canaan met him by his door. Without a word, he took Dae Kim's upper arm and gently ushered him to the tailgate and opened the back. A dark grey box nearly the size of the cargo area filled the space. With one finger, the Elder opened the box and he pointed inside.

"Get in."

Dae Kim didn't move.

Canaan sighed. "It's our Elder emergency box, but humans who don't want to be put in another coma can use it, too."

Dae Kim looked inside the dark space and saw only an abyss. The alley had almost no light and the Elder wouldn't care if he couldn't see in the dark. Dae Kim took a hesitant step toward the bumper and when the Elder reached out to help him in, he flinched.

"Trust me," Elder Canaan said and took his elbow tenderly. "Kilmeade and I want to help you. You've been incapacitated because we are protecting others. Do you understand?" The Elder waited a few seconds and then drove his point. "If you are not psychopathic, do you understand?"

Dae Kim crawled into the blackness and replied, "I understand. You can't trust these demons and I'm afraid of them and might do what they say..."

"Good," the Elder said with what looked like sincere satisfaction. "You're not insane yet. This box is ventilated sufficiently for a human. Shortly, we will bring you some water and snacks. You will be in here twenty-four hours. You can do this, or go back into your la-la land. I don't recommend it, though. Your brain needs to heal and rebuild." Canaan put out his hand. "Your phone."

Dae Kim handed over his cell and sat cross-legged leaning over his lap. There was room for at least two men his size and he nodded his head. "Thank you, Master. I will stay here until you get me out."

Elder Canaan grinned and pinched his cheek before closing the box flap and slamming the tailgate. In the black space, Dae Kim scooted to the side and then onto his back with his knees bent. His plans had been altered again, but these masters wanted him to live. If they could help him correct his earlier bad decision, he would welcome it.

"We will kill you in here, Dae Kim," The Master said in an unknown number of voices. Dae Kim hoped the threat was an empty one.

After a short and bumpy ride, the vehicle stopped and Dae Kim heard the voices of the other two Elders. Once underway, the three spoke on mundane topics all the way to their destination. When the truck stopped and the engine switched off, the voices trailed away and a new one spoke into the air vents on the inner edge.

"Dae Kim, my name is Javier. I'm the one who came with Adam and Canaan at the hospital. Are you okay?"

Dae Kim nodded and said aloud, "I'm okay."

"Good."

Dae Kim heard the lid open and in the space of a second, Javier shoved a cardboard box in with him and re-locked the flap. "That should hold you until tomorrow night. As soon as they get up, we'll get you out. It's the only way to keep everyone else safe, you understand?"

"Yes," Dae Kim said softly.

"Okay, listen. When those demons say scary things to you, ask Jesus to protect you. They will torment you over the next twenty-four hours. I know because I've heard them. When it gets bad, ask Jesus to help you and He will. Got it?"

Dae Kim didn't reply, but Javier was gone anyway. He felt around in the box and his knuckle slapped a flashlight. Once on, he saw chips, cookies and three bottles of water. A fourth bottle had a wide mouth and was empty already—a urinal. How nice.

Still, I'm alive and I'm not unconscious...

"We're gonna suffocate you in here," The Master said.

Dae Kim didn't respond and he didn't call out to Javier's God. At least not yet.

32

The Lyft driver carried Beryl from Dallas to Fort Worth in record time with absolutely zero chit-chat. Now crossing the lobby of Simon's hotel, an odd excitement tickled his spirit. As the elevator stopped at the correct floor, Beryl's phone chimed with a new text.

"I'm off work. Where are you?" It was Adam, looking for adventure.

Beryl had been spending his free time with the guy and a month had passed since the Elders scared him to death at Pete's house. All three of his friends were hard on him, but *damn it*—the guy was fun.

Without a care, Beryl texted back: *"Worthington Renaissance, Frt W, Room 2233."* Adam sent a thumbs-up and Beryl knocked on the door. Simon yanked it open, his blue eyes smiling.

"Come in here! I mean, shit! Look at you!" They shook hands and Simon led him into the enormous room gesturing at two sitting chairs. He sat when Beryl did and whistled. "You look exactly the same."

"Control yourself," Beryl cautiously bantered back, unsure how much teasing either of them could stomach so soon in their reunion.

Simon held up both hands. "I'll do my best," he said with a chuckle. "But if memory serves, you're the one with the roaming hands."

"*Shit,* good one," Beryl said and shook his head. Simon looked great, strong and lean, dressed casually in jeans and a tailored pale-blue dress shirt. Since November, his hair had grown out, more like the way he wore it seven years ago. Of course, back then, Beryl was a Rakum and had designs on the kid he wouldn't deign to contemplate as a mortal.

"This is so cool," Simon said. "First things first." Simon hopped up, jogged to the wall and yanked four tiny liquor bottles from the minibar. He handed two to Beryl and held his two up for a toast.

"My first alcohol since 11/13," Beryl said surprising himself with the news. "Cheers."

"*La-chaim!* Let's get drunk!" Simon said grinning. "You couldn't get drunk before, right?"

Beryl made a second *cheers* gesture. "Let's see what has all you mortals in a spin..." Beryl downed both minis with a comical grumble at the end.

"Wow."

"You like?" Simon laughed. "Now, time to spill." He caught Beryl's eye. "What's your big news?"

In all of their renewed conversation, Beryl had not divulged their mission. Tonight, since they were heading to Los Angeles soon, he thought it okay to share.

"I told you I was traveling with Javier, right?" Beryl asked and Simon nodded. "We're helping our brethren with the transformation. The bigger surprise is that Elder Canaan and Elder Kilmeade are with us."

"You're kidding..."

Beryl nodded, a fuzzy numbness growing in his head.

"You okay?" Simon teased.

"Get this," Beryl said, ignoring Simon's question, "they're still Rakum and they're stronger than ever. Maybe as strong as the Fathers."

"*Shit!*" Simon said incredulous. "Why didn't they change?"

"No one knows. And there's more..." With Simon at rapt attention, Beryl shared the miracle of Chloe's pregnancy, and then Kilmeade's science experiment. Simon asked a few questions about Adam and then histrionically crawled onto the stiff Berber carpet to lay spread-eagle.

"My head is exploding," he said pretending to go into a seizure. Flaunching his arms and legs as the performance came to a climax, Simon mimicked brains spewing out of his head and closed his eyes.

Beryl laughed in guffaws, wondering when he had ever been so joyful. He caught his breath and told him, "I didn't know you were so funny."

"I'm much funnier now that there isn't a beautiful and bloodthirsty Rakum shaking my tree," he said with a grin and sat up on the floor.

"Ouch, shit!" Beryl returned and fished his phone from his pocket. "At least you thought I was beautiful..."

"Yeah, *past tense*. And don't let it go to your head." Simon rubbed his face and crawled with a final fake spasm to the chair.

"It's a fact, that's all; Beryl is beautiful," he said and pulled up the photo of himself and Adam at the restaurant. "Here he is. Adam Roberts. From Kilmeade's seed."

Simon furrowed his brow and retrieved the cell phone. When he looked at the picture, he blinked and then zoomed it in. "This isn't real."

Beryl grinned as Simon examined the photo again.

"My brain is gone. I need another drink."

"Hit me again," Beryl said and Simon tossed him two mini-bottles of Svedka. "Too bad I killed your brain. I have one more surprise." Simon regarded him with a lowered chin and shook his head. Beryl laughed. "Adam is headed over here now to meet you."

"Pshewwwwwwww!" Simon demonstrated a huge explosion using his hands opening outward from his head. He tumbled to the floor and again lay on his back and twitched mostly his face. "I'm dead now," he said.

Beryl chuckled and tossed back another mini. "I'm getting drunk," he mumbled and Simon opened one eye.

"Hurrah!" he said and put out his hand. Beryl yanked him to his feet and didn't release right away. Now they stood inches apart, face-to-face, both out of breath from laughter, and Beryl squeezed his hand.

"How now, former Cow, say it. Am I still beautiful?" he asked watching Simon's eyes, his mouth, his eyes again.

After a miniscule pause, Simon tipped his chin. "No comment." He looked away grinning to the side.

"Hah!" Beryl shoved him back. "Let's drink to an oddball friendship my friends don't approve of!" Beryl saluted his next vodka to the air, completely buzzing now on the alcohol, wistfully wishing Javier had been there to see it.

Simon held up his bottle. "Here's to Beryl!" he said and swigged the entire contents. When it was empty, he added announcing, "WHO'S STILL BEAUTIFUL AND VAIN AS HELL!"

"Hear, hear!" Beryl said and considered his empty bottles. "Have more of those?" he asked and Simon returned to the box for four more.

"Okay, how's Javier?" Simon said and dropped into the chair.

"Javier's great. The lot fell to him to guard Mrs. Kilmeade tonight." Beryl snickered. "He takes her shopping. It's funny," Beryl said and chuckled, then made a serious face. "He's my bud. We're friends now." Beryl slurred his words, the alcohol numbing his tongue and he enjoyed having to think about each word. "He's kind to me, takes up for me before the Elders. I have no idea why I ever hated him."

Simon clinked his fifth mini to Beryl's fifth. "Because of me, *duh.*" Beryl chuckled and leaned back in his chair. "How are you enjoying those horrible Elders?" Simon asked raising his eyebrows.

"Hell, you need to shut up about my Elders," Beryl said and closed his eyes. "Mine, all mine. You only wish you had one..."

"Hah!" Simon scoffed and made a grab for Beryl's unopened mini.

Beryl shook his head. "Mine," he said moving his hand out of reach and settling back into the cushion. Just then, his phone alerted with a new text. "Adam's coming up," Beryl said in a renewed effort to speak clearly.

He tweaked open his eyes. "And listen, he's kinda shell-shocked. He got abducted last month by two angry brethren. The Elders rescued him, but he was spooked good. Don't bring it up."

Simon narrowed his eyes. "Great timing, bro," he finished and rubbed his face. "You almost sobered me up."

Beryl laughed. "Then you're a candy ass."

Simon shot him a bird and rose to his feet as a knock landed on the door. He jerked his eyes to Beryl. "Kilmeade's spooked man-child!" he whispered.

"Shhhh, don't! Be cool," Beryl said and shakily stood. "I like this a lot," he mumbled, but Simon was turning the door latch. After he greeted Adam and introduced himself, Simon ushered him through the door. Adam had worn dark jeans and a black pullover, his long hair tied into a ponytail at the nape of his neck. Beryl sent him a nod and watched him make his way over. Simon invited him to sit and Adam relaxed moment by moment.

"How do you know that creature?" Adam asked then in his Southern drawl, hooking a thumb casually Beryl's way.

"Try to guess," Simon said, lighting on the edge of the bed to leave the last chair for his second guest.

"Okay..." Adam flicked his gaze between the two and said with a sideways grin, "You're his... boyfriend?"

"Very funny." Simon flashed his wedding band. "Try again."

"And be nice," Beryl slurred to Adam.

"Okay," Adam said with a quiet chuckle. He peeked shyly back to Simon. "You look sort of spoiled. Maybe a rich kid—that Chloe-girl's brother?" he asked, eyebrows arched.

"No, and *excuse me,* but I've worked hard to get where I am." Simon rose to hit the bar again. He pulled six minis and handed them out. "You give up?"

"Um..." Adam unscrewed one tiny bottle and tossed it back. Beryl watched him grimace at the end and he scrunched his nose when their eyes met. Adam grinned back and looked to Simon. "You an actor? You look sort of familiar. Like I've seen you on TV."

"BERRRRP!" Beryl buzzed loudly. "Adam is dumbfounded!"

Adam sighed and drank his second shot more carefully. One hand tugged at his neck and his hair fell free, falling to touch each shoulder.

"Don't pout, little fella," Beryl told him, kicking him with the toe of his shoe. Adam had ceased drinking blood and no longer saw the auras. All in all, Beryl thought the guy was doing well, despite the fact that he spent twenty years trying to be supernatural and in the end, failed miserably.

Adam reached out suddenly and yanked Beryl's two minis from his loose fist. "You've had enough." He tossed them back in short order and rubbed his face hard. When he had focused upon Simon, he narrowed his eyes in thought. "I'm guessing you let blood to the Rakum?" Simon held his eye and nodded his head. "Ahhh," Adam said and pointed to Beryl's face. "And this one was your favorite?"

"Wrong again." Simon shook his head and laughed. "Not *even close.*"

"Simon," Beryl said suddenly in an undertone and the man raised his eyes. Beryl regarded him with a forced serious expression and scooted his chair closer to Adam. "This copy-cat-Kilmeade-shit thinks he's better looking. Tell him the hard facts." Simon's face broke into a grin.

"Beryl the Beautiful wins every time!" Simon shouted and fell to the carpet, bowing low before Beryl in a comical display. "Handsome and wonderful! None can compare!" Then he laughed into the floor and mumbled, "I am so drunk..."

Adam rose to his feet standing over Simon. "You are so *queer*," he drawled and crossed his arms.

"Sticks and stones, Cowboy," Beryl retorted and leaned over to put one hand to Simon's hair, still folded over before them on the stiff carpet. "Adam, sit down. This is serious." Beryl made his tone as even as possible. "Be quiet and learn something."

Simon straightened his spine and crossed his legs Indian-style without dislodging Beryl's hand. "Please, don't ask me to get up, buddy," he said under his breath, grinning and sipping his last mini.

"No, you stay," Beryl said as if speaking to a small dog. Simon panted a few times and then relaxed his face. Beryl stroked his hair, his eyes on Adam. "Simon used to be a *Cow*. He used to *worship* us."

"That's so very sweet," Adam said, the liquor loosening his tongue and personality. *"Queer,"* he coughed into his hand, his eyes smiling.

Beryl hissed for him to be quiet. "Shush and learn. I was trying to teach you more about how Dr. Roberts served Elder Bel."

Adam tilted his head still in Beryl's gaze. "Served?" he said with innuendo. Beryl grumbled without emotion—he was too tipsy to care if Adam comprehended any of it. Some Rakum were sexual with their Cows, but Javier hadn't been with Simon—he knew that much for a fact. Plus, Adam didn't need to go to that corner every time something about the Old Way arose. Finally weary of trying, Beryl gave up. Dropped his hand and leaned back into his chair.

Simon clambered back to the side of the bed and leaned onto his palms. "I *schmerved,*" he said with comical mispronunciation, watching Adam who's eyes were still on Beryl. "I schmerved Javier, not Beryl."

"Ohhh," Adam said with apparent revelation and renewed interest. "What was he like back then? He's *so serious...*"

Simon regarded Adam with a tiny one-shoulder shrug. "He was awesome. Didn't you read *The Rabbit?* We're both in there. We're like the *stars* of that whole novel."

Beryl's eye flicked to Adam, recalling with effort what Beth Rider wrote about him and Meryl.

"Da-n-n-n-g," he whispered and met Beryl's eye. "And you're one of the twins..."

Beryl wagged his head. "Next topic."

Adam regarded him a moment before asking, "Does Simon know the Elders?" Beryl nodded and he faced Simon again. "You like them?"

Simon fake-guarded his lips from Beryl mouthed the word "no."

"They're frickin' monsters," Adam added with a knowing head bob, his voice finally garbling more than before. "They do this..." He set his pointer finger on one knee. "And you're dead."

Simon looked at Beryl. "Who'd they kill?"

"Adam needs to hush," Beryl said and popped the man's head. It was time to turn the subject away from two men who could possibly hear them—even from fifty miles away. "Never say anything negative about the Elders. You are barely alive," he said and winked, accidentally involving both eyes. "Come back with your short-sighted opinions when you've seen three centuries pass." Adam returned a blank look and Beryl took a few deep breaths. "How many minis can a man drink?" he asked Simon in a whisper.

"A bunch."

"No more for me," Beryl mumbled and refused the next one that Simon lifted to eye-level. He lightly kicked Adam's shin. "All you need to know is that Canaan wants you to prosper."

Simon made an agreeing noise and belched into his hand. Adam snickered and Simon burped louder. "Beryl's not shitting you. Canaan is mean as hell, but he protected me when I needed it, and—"

Beryl hopped to his feet. "You're not about to bring that up!"

Adam rose as well, reading Beryl's mortified expression. He grinned and stepped forward to grab Simon's bicep, his eyes still on Beryl. "Look at those red cheeks! Bring it up! Bring it up!"

Beryl narrowed his eyes, not so drunk that he wanted Adam to have a firsthand report of his last days as a Rakum.

Simon waved in Beryl's direction. "Come on, really? I'm giving Canaan props, that's all. End of story."

"Bawk-bawk-bawk," Adam said, clucking like a chicken and flapping his elbows. Beryl gave him a sarcastic grin and cut his eyes to Simon. True to his word, the man shook his head with fervency.

"Bawk all you want, chicken-man," Simon said and got up. "Beryl's my friend. That's all you need to know."

Adam rolled his eyes and stretched his arms to the ceiling. Beryl watched the guy stroll to the curtained window and peek out. When Simon tossed him a victorious wink, he thanked him with a tiny bow. None of the details would help Adam understand. In fact, if Kilmeade's mini-me feared what he had seen in the new and gentle Elders, he would be horrified to learn what Beryl and his brethren had been capable of before 11/13.

Old Beryl, *Rakum Beryl,* had viciously seduced, cajoled, and eventually *begged* Simon to run off with him. Now that he was mortal, he could barely remember his reasons. It had to have been about the blood, but it was something more. As a human, Beryl realized early on that he leaned heterosexual, but before 11/13, they had no preference; a sensation was a sensation, no matter who or where it came from. And Beth Rider hadn't come close to describing what truly happened; her PG-13 audience could never stomach the whole truth. Beryl took one last deep breath and carefully rose to a standing position.

"Beryl the Beautiful," Simon said in a talk-show timbre, "let's take this freakshow down to the bar. Before you arrived, I parlayed my celebrity into an audience with five young ladies who recognized me at lunch." Beryl parted his lips to ask about his wife and he grinned to speak first. "Oh, not for me. For you. Let's go." Adam turned at the waist from his position at the window and Simon added, "this is Beryl's first bender. Let's tie it on right."

Adam smiled wide with the sudden mission. "Yes!" he barked and crossed to clap Beryl's back. He grasped his arm and steered him for the door.

After ninety minutes of too many fruity drinks, Beryl texted Javier that he was safe and called the two of them a cab. Later, in the taxi alongside

Adam, he received the reply, *"Tell Simon I said hi."*

Fuzzy-brained and giggling, Beryl squint his eyes to read what he had initially sent: *"@ Simon's hotel. Im fine. drank too much. Cabs here. CUsoon. Kzk"* Beryl looked at Adam, stunned he had revealed his big secret. Adam was dropped off first and Beryl hoped Javier didn't wait up; he was too sleepy and *much* too loopy to attend a lecture.

33, JULY 15

Kilmeade bid goodnight to Roman who left for the guest room as Canaan trudged to the basement. Javier had gone to bed an hour ago, having made sure Dae Kim had enough water to last him the day. Beryl's heartbeat approached the front door and Kilmeade turned to see him enter. He read the man's intoxication at a glance, the aroma of alcohol hitting moments later.

"Master," Beryl said and walked in, placing each foot carefully. "You must forgive me. I haven't been drunk before."

Kilmeade regarded him without expression. "Can you make it to your bedroom?" he asked after a quick read revealed that besides an elevated blood-alcohol content, he was healthy.

"I can sleep on the couch," he slurred and turned for the living room. "I saw Simon Miller tonight. He's my friend," Beryl said in the other room. "Goodnight, Master."

Kilmeade waited another ten seconds and Beryl was out. Back on task, he turned for the stairs. Chloe's plane left at three and Roman wanted to leave for the airport at noon. It was nearing 5 a.m. and Kilmeade stepped to Chloe's bedroom. He pulled back the covers and scooped her from bed. As he turned for the door, she opened her eyes partway and gave him a smile. She then draped her arms loosely about his neck and tucked her face into his upper chest. Kilmeade carried her downstairs, past the snoozing Beryl on the couch, and into the basement. Once there, he lay her on his twin-size daybed and spooned against her, facing the room. Canaan had kicked back on the long couch and he held Kilmeade's gaze.

"Beryl's drunk?" he asked and Kilmeade nodded. "I should go up there and hassle him," Canaan lamented quietly. "Or I could bring him down here to wake up in the dark and freak. That would be fun."

"Leave him be," Kilmeade sent silently. *"He had a nice night. They all need a break like that."* Kilmeade arranged Chloe's hair so it wouldn't pull when she moved. *"You need a break like that."*

"I need to rewind the clock is what I need to do," Canaan replied to his mind. *"You're not going to die. You'll see her again. You'll raise this little girl together. It'll*

be fun."

"It'll be great fun," Kilmeade agreed and kissed the back of Chloe's head, still holding Canaan's gaze.

Canaan huffed, seeing through his oblique response. *"Why would all the rest of them live and you die?"*

"I have guarded you from the reason for more than a hundred years and I will reveal it when the time is right," Kilmeade sent back.

"Guarded me? In the cabin? During your punishment?" Canaan's wheels were turning.

"Rest, brother," Kilmeade said aloud. "I insist."

Canaan grumbled and rolled over to face the couch. *"I'm not staying here alone—you should ponder that while you're busy guarding me from the truth."*

"Yes, you are," Kilmeade admonished telepathically. *"You will do your duty by your master and his child. I have no doubt."*

Canaan grumbled again and fell silent.

Kilmeade whispered into Chloe's sleeping ear words of the future and words she would remember when he was long gone.

《▣》

Chloe woke slowly. Her internal clock told her it was full morning, but the room was dark, save a small yellow night light. Chloe focused ahead and recognized Canaan lying across the green sofa, arms up behind his head, watching her. Coming more awake, she realized Kilmeade held her gently in both arms and he kissed her hair.

"It is 8:45, my beauty," he whispered.

Guarding her morning mouth, she rolled onto her back and met Kilmeade's liquid gaze in the dim light. "You brought me to bed with you?" He nodded and kissed her forehead and then her mouth, not concerned with whether or not she had brushed her teeth. Chloe wrapped her arms around him, ended the kiss, and held him tightly. It felt like goodbye, and not temporarily.

"Go let Dr. Canaan have one last look at the baby," he said softly when she pulled away. A lamp came on and with a sleepy nod, she walked to where Canaan reclined on the couch. He didn't sit up and regarded her with the saddest eyes she'd ever seen.

"Are you okay?" she asked him. He pat his midsection.

"We're going to miss you, that's all," he said and she allowed him to maneuver her into position. It still made her laugh, although he had now "scanned" her three times. It didn't seem necessary that she lay on top of him, but again he insisted that it was.

"Try not to get too excited," she said and lifted her nightshirt into position.

"Too late," he teased and once more encompassed her rounded tummy with both hands.

"Can ya'll put off the hunting trip and come home with me?" she asked in a small voice.

"We no longer call the shots," Canaan said softly.

Chloe sighed. He was talking about what God had for them to do. They were saving lives. *Why do I always make it about me?* Chloe shook her head at her selfishness.

"Don't be so hard on yourself, little bird," Canaan said to her telepathically and her eyes jerked to Kilmeade.

"Why is he able to do that?" she snapped unsure why she accused Kilmeade of causing it.

"Shhh, Kilmeade didn't do it," Canaan said softly, "shhhh... almost done." He moved his thumbs slightly, caressing her skin and she closed her eyes to let him finish.

"Is it the one brain thing?" she sent silently to whoever would answer.

Watching them from a few feet away, Kilmeade didn't react. Canaan took a deep breath, moved his hands slightly, and went still.

"We think its osmosis. Your mind is really open." Canaan lifted his hands and pulled the hem of her nightshirt over her exposed abdomen. "You can get off me now," he said quietly.

Chloe stayed where she was and watched Kilmeade's face. His faraway expression confused her as much as Canaan's sad face had minutes ago. They were withholding something and she wanted desperately to know what it was.

"Um, the doctor is turning into a masher, ma'am," he whispered and Chloe felt him coming awake beneath her. She giggled and scooted away to sit against Kilmeade on the edge of his mattress.

"I love you, you know," she told him.

Kilmeade stood up. "I am ready to give you your gift," he said and crossed to a shelf in the wall. When he had his purchase in hand, he presented her with a baby blue box.

Chloe tried to read more in his eyes, but he was looking at her hands. She opened it without another word and when she saw the ring, it took her breath away. A large clear diamond flanked by a dozen pink rubies had been sunk into a rose-gold carved band, and an engraved floral lattice traveled the circumference. Chloe slipped it on her left ring finger.

"Ah," Kilmeade breathed and gestured to her hand. "It is worn on the right."

"Oh..." Chloe said, assuming it was a Rakum tradition.

"It is engraved," he whispered and she held it to the light. The sentiment had been recorded in lower case letters: *"i live on because of you."*

Chloe read it twice before turning her face to Kilmeade's. "It's beautiful!" she said and allowed her tears to come finally. Kilmeade pulled her close and caressed her back.

"Wear it on the right always," he whispered.

"I promise, I will," Chloe said. She lifted her eyes to his, but he was looking at Canaan and from the concentration on his face, they were deep in conversation. Chloe turned to Canaan and his expression was one of surprise. "What's going on?" she asked, absently caressing her middle. After another moment of silent conversation, Canaan offered a tiny nod and Kilmeade put his near hand to Chloe's cheek.

"It's my decision that you will let blood for Canaan right now, a tiny bit. You will not be affected because of his rejuvenation treatment." Chloe's eyes must have been huge, because he then slow blinked in a nod, and said, "I have my reasons."

Chloe remained where she sat and flipped her gaze back to Canaan. He sent an apologetic head tip, not his usual style, and patted his leg.

"I don't understand what for..." Chloe thought and sent simultaneously, to whichever one of them caught it. Neither answered, but both waited in place for her to comply. No argument would change it, no disagreement would alter Kilmeade's decision, and so it was no use to ask her question aloud. *Either I'm his mate or I'm not,* she thought and got to her feet. It had something to do with the dread she felt inside, that Kilmeade wouldn't return from Los Angeles when it was over. When she reached Canaan, he placed his bed pillow in his lap.

"This is weird," she mumbled and looked at the floor. She made herself malleable and Canaan maneuvered her so she sat on the pillow, her back to his front. He moved her long hair aside and placed both hands on her shoulders.

"You'll be happy to discover something I do differently than Kilmeade," he said with a friendly huff. "Are you nervous?" he asked.

"No," Chloe replied and trained her eyes to the floor. In her peripheral vision, Kilmeade rose and entered the bathroom across the space. When he closed the door, she said, "He's going to die, isn't he?"

"Pfffft," Canaan sputtered. "Not if I have anything to do with it."

"I appreciate you and all you've done for him, for me, for us…"

"My pleasure, ma'am," Canaan said in a Texan drawl and placed a warm palm to her inner shoulder. "I'm going to use a knife, but I have some magic to keep it from stinging too bad."

"It's okay—I'm ready," Chloe said and exhaled. "Canaan, I consent," she whispered and his hand froze in place at the work he'd begun. "You okay?" she asked when he hadn't moved in more than a few seconds.

"I am, here we go," he said.

First, he moistened his thumb and rubbed it to her skin. Then, out of her line of vision, he pressed a point against her neck; as he promised, she felt only the pressure and no pain. Then his lips were on her skin and the odd sensation of being the cola bottle began. Her toes grew cold within the first five seconds, but before the effect traveled any further, he was done. She felt his thumb against the wound and then he wrapped his arms about her from behind and held her snugly. He moaned the tiniest sound and rest his head on her shoulder. In another few seconds, a vibration traveled across his musculature.

"You are *so* weird," she teased with a sad giggle.

A full minute passed and Chloe remained still, her eyes closed, covering his hard forearms with her own. She felt no ill effect from whatever amount he withdrew and no anger at Kilmeade's edict. He had his reasons and she trusted him.

I trust Canaan, too, so it's no biggie, she thought. *"Be nice to Canaan,"* Kilmeade had said. *"He'll be watching over you if anything happens to me."*

At that instant, Kilmeade quietly exited the bathroom and waited for her to look up. When she did, he gave her a grin and Canaan's contact dropped away. When she stood to go to him, Canaan remained bent over, palms pressed into his knees.

"I will miss you," Kilmeade said and pecked her forehead. Then he looked at the stairs moments before Roman knocked on the basement door. "There's Roman. Bye-bye, little bird."

"I'll see you later," Chloe said, holding her voice steady. He smiled and inclined his head to Canaan. Chloe turned away for the couch and repeated on the march to the other Elder, "I will see you later."

"Yes, ma'am," Canaan said slowly standing, his eyes sorrowful. He took a deep breath and put his hand on her head. "You brightened up this place." He brushed her cheek with a knuckle. "Thank you for making me pet a puppy. I'm still having nightmares." He winked and Chloe offered a tight smile.

The old Canaan had returned and she much preferred him affable. He grinned when he overheard her thoughts. *Oh, well, what else is new?*

"Weirdos," she said aloud and he nodded.

At the top of the stairs, Roman called good morning and both Elders prepared to cover their eyes before unbolting the door. They never opened the basement during the day since a single ray of sunlight could temporarily blind them. Chloe jogged up the stairs and prepared to make it quick.

"I'll see you later," she said sternly to Kilmeade who blew her a kiss. Canaan had lain back on the couch facing her and he waved his fingers. Then both Elders turned their faces away, their hands over their eyes. "I WILL SEE YOU SOON!" Chloe barked as the door clunked open and she shot through to close it again. The bolts thunking into place behind her sounded much too final. Roman greeted her, but she couldn't hear him.

"Bye-bye, little bird..."

Kilmeade's last words looped in her mind. And Canaan's melancholic wave confirming what she could not admit to herself—now or ever.

《▣》

"That was unexpected," Canaan said as they listened to the sounds of the others in the upper floors. "I understand your reasons, but *damn.*" Kilmeade grinned and closed his eyes, lying on the daybed by the wall. "It was never like that before, *shiiiit,*" he added. "Part of our evolution, ya think?"

Nodding Kilmeade sent silently, *"It was necessary for your telepathic connection. You will be able to contact her across miles if need be."*

"Sure, sure..." Canaan also lay on his back and stared at the ceiling. He stuffed his pillow under his head and punched it a few times. Chloe Bushman's distinct aroma remained behind; he had made an olfactory impression of it even before this occasion. Being in one brain with her mate gave him carbon-copy emotions and now that she was leaving, would they both return to normal or pine and ache the way he ached right now? Canaan trained his gaze on Kilmeade who opened his eyes to look back. *"What do you think?"*

After a long sigh, Kilmeade returned, *"We will pine."* Then he grinned. *"Why not? My heart of stone feels more like putty now. Yours?"*

"When I was with Marcy, I had no trouble maintaining my Rakum heart. Since the night in the storm drain, I don't care to maintain that status."

"Me either," Kilmeade replied silently. *"I decided when Chloe began pursuing me that I would let it go where it will. When I relinquished control of my melting heart, you did, too."*

"Maybe..." Canaan took a deep breath. *"I'm still a Rakum Elder with unimaginable power."*

Kilmeade nodded, his eyes closed. "Ugly, though," he jibed aloud.

"Totally," Canaan agreed, then continued in a low voice. "When she said I consent, I lost it. I think this human affection thing will eventually ruin me." Canaan chuckled inwardly, but didn't feel jovial. "Shit, I think I just prophesied."

"You did," Kilmeade offered. "But it's not a ruination, it's an evolution. You will *evolve*, be better than before. You'll see."

Canaan was quiet a long while, thinking and rethinking on his self-prophecy and Kilmeade's take on it. Then the obvious hit him and he realized Kilmeade had taken notice already, waiting for him to catch up.

"You and I can prophesy like the Fathers?" Canaan looked at Kilmeade in the dusky light. His face was turned away and he didn't need to answer; Canaan had inadvertently asked a rhetorical question. The Fathers' prophecies were 100% accurate and every Rakum knew this. Thus, Kilmeade's recent *dreams,* which were actually *visitations,* were part of it. Kilmeade *would be* leaving the flesh soon. He would accept the offer of Javier's God, knowing fully well that he would blink out of existence.

"That's not the way it works, brother," Kilmeade said in a soft, fatherly tone. "The God of the mortals breathed this world into existence. You and I came to life because He breathed into us at conception."

Canaan swung his feet to the floor and then crossed to Kilmeade's side. "Okay," he said and sat on the daybed mattress. "I misspoke. You're not being erased..."

"No, because the soul is eternal. I will return to God. The breath of God that entered this flesh at its start..." Kilmeade brought both hands to his chest. "...will re-enter the *Being of Origination*." With his palms fanning outward, the Elder lifted his arms. "That is where I will be; rejoining the One who made me."

Every word his cohort spoke rang true. Why didn't Canaan feel the same urgency?

"Because outside of your control," Kilmeade said telepathically in a wistful tone, *"you have been made a wasteland, where vain men practice vain things. But you will be made a place of glory and righteousness when Yeshua calls you to His side."*

"I've heard that three times now," Canaan grumbled.

Kilmeade chuckled and rolled to his side to see Canaan. "He will use you a little longer like this. When I'm gone, submit to His guidance. You know He'll have His way whether you listen or not." Kilmeade paused and punched his arm with muted humor. "The Puppeteer will have His way. We go along, and it is so much less difficult, much less painful."

Canaan nodded. "And Chloe?"

"I see you raising our child. I see you happy. Timelines are not my thing," he said and winked.

"I see that, too," Canaan offered with a sad nod. "Okay, then, asshole. Go join the heavenly circus. When you do, I'll hold this earthly plane together by myself."

"And romance my mate?" Kilmeade whispered with a small grin.

Canaan shrugged. "I'll want to. Who knows if she will? She's gonna be mad you left her." Canaan returned to the couch and reclined slowly. "I'll take care of her. If she wants more from me, I will oblige."

Kilmeade closed his eyes. "I'm not leaving yet. There is an event in Los Angeles. And there will be—"

"A tangle with someone or something there," Canaan finished and sighed. "It's always something."

"True," Kilmeade replied softly and fell silent.

"So..." Canaan said with a serious eye. "Which one of us will end Javie this morning? Or should it be Beryl?"

Out of necessity, both Elders had compartmentalized the boys' latest infraction, but it would need attending.

Kilmeade voiced a small, *Hmmm,* and Canaan agreed, falling into his thoughts as their guests made their exit.

34

J avier saw Roman and Chloe off without mentioning Beryl's
adventures. Beryl had slept on the couch and only the noise of their
exit woke him. Now that the house had quieted, Javier poured two
mugs of coffee and sat one before Beryl on the side table.

"How do you feel?" he asked, aware that Beryl had never been
intoxicated. Regardless of his secret meeting with Simon, Javier
commiserated with his discomfort.

"Not too bad," Beryl said quietly and sipped his brew. He moved in
slow motion, his eyes at half-mast. "I appreciate you not shouting."

Javier smiled and leaned over his knees. "I've been there."

Beryl set down his cup. "Funny thing is, I wished you were there."

"Yeah," Javier sighed. "Would've been a sight. Did you laugh a lot?"

"*Ffft,* I *giggled.* Like *a little girl,*" he stressed with a careful wink. "I've
been corresponding with Simon since the first day of our hunt."

Javier nodded thoughtfully. "How's his mind?" Beryl glared so Javier
clarified with a friendly grin. "He was a Cow, after all..."

"Oh," he huffed, returning to his relaxed posture. "You'd be
surprised; he's in a good headspace. Normal. Happy. Funny as hell."

"Good." Javier blew on his coffee. "Just so you know, I wanted you
to stay away from Simon to protect you. That's all."

"Protect me?"

Javier nodded. "He'll always be a little unbalanced, it's inevitable. But
your mind is perfect, coming out of our way of life; I was helping to
preserve that perfect mind."

Beryl considered his assertion, lips pursed. "So," he began with
suspicion, "you care more about my brain than Simon's?"

After a brief pause, Javier looked him in the eye. "Most assuredly. I
won't say this to outsiders, but we truly are a different species."

"What about all that God stuff if we're a different species?" Beryl
asked, testing Javier's logic.

"It stands. Look..." Javier leaned over his lap. "In our minds, we used
to be Rakum. Everything we learn and experience as mortals is going to be
run through a Rakum filter. I realized this distinction when Chloe was
here."

Beryl nodded. "Go ahead..."

"When I told her someone raised up a man from Kilmeade's seed, she said, 'Kilmeade has a son?'"

"A son..." Beryl nodded again. "But you and I first think, 'somebody made a man from some cells in a dish.'"

"Precisely," Javier said. "In the living room you heard her when it was announced Dae Kim and Pete went after Adam. She said—"

"Who would want to kill Kilmeade's son?" Beryl finished.

Javier tapped both knees. "Even though I corrected her twice in the car. She can only see it one way. All the mortals are like that; they can't know what it's like to be a Rakum, or how our brains work."

Beryl sighed. "So what does this mean now? To me? To us?"

Javier shrugged. "I guess it will help as we go find the last of our suffering brethren. For certain it should help us forgive ourselves. I repented to God and He erased everything I did against His law. But to the outsiders? A lion kills an antelope because he's a lion. If he suddenly became a vegetarian, he can't make amends with every antelope he ate."

Beryl chuckled softly. "Roman said essentially the same thing."

Javier nodded. "Who do you think told me this seven years ago?"

Beryl huffed. "Since we're in bro-mode, Adam met us over there."

Javier's mouth dropped. "Whoa. What did he think of the guy?"

Beryl grinned. "I used the opportunity to explain more about Rakum Cows. Simon played along." Beryl got to his feet and stretched. "I guess Adam liked him okay. Simon was loyal to the core on the who looks better game, which will sit in pretty-boy's craw all day."

Javier chuckled and stood as well. "I think your brain is in good shape and it's not likely contact with Simon will hurt you."

Beryl nodded. "I appreciate that, Pops."

Javier chuckled and followed him to the kitchen where they both set their mugs in the sink. "Are you seeing him again?"

"Might be out of time. I think we could be heading to Los Angeles tomorrow night."

"Let's both go see him today." Javier looked at the clock in the stove panel. "We can be back before dark." Javier watched Beryl's sleepy face and he nodded a few times after a big yawn. "I'll get an okay from Canaan." Javier texted the Elder and Beryl nudged his shin with his toe.

"Simon asked about you."

Before he could reply, Canaan pinged back. "Uh-oh, they want to see us down there *right now*." He turned the screen to Beryl; the Elder had used two exclamation points. "Calling us down there in the day? This can't be good." Javier rose and headed to the basement.

"I hope they don't yell," Beryl said quietly and tailed behind him.

The first floor hallway leading to the basement door was kept dark by closing every connecting room, thus reducing UV penetration when the basement opened. Aware that a single beam of sunlight would blind a Rakum, Javier and Beryl stood ready to jump in when the locks clicked no matter how well they shuttered the first floor. At the distinct *thunk!* they hopped in. One of the Elders violently pushed the door closed behind them, clipping Beryl and throwing the basement into darkness.

Heartrate elevating second-by-second, Javier headed down holding the bannister and neither Elder hit a light until they reached the bottom. Finally, a corner lamp revealed Canaan and Kilmeade standing in the center of the room, arms crossed, and their expressions grim.

"Roman and Chloe are gone thirty minutes and you're ready to abandon the mission to visit an old Cow?" It was Canaan admonishing him, his voice as stern as he'd ever heard it. "Where is your head?"

Javier searched his mind for a reply. Why were they so incensed and what made Canaan direct his fury at him *particularly*. He thought he would start with an apology, but Kilmeade spoke first.

"And don't apologize."

"Canaan, Kilmeade, help me out," Javier said quietly, his mind racing for answers. "What have I done?"

"You don't know?" Canaan looked at Kilmeade and back again. Javier stepped forward and Canaan shook his head. "No. Stay back."

Javier's breath hitched; he was in danger. Every hair on his body stood on end and he held his breath. "Read me," he whispered, barely able to speak, "I don't know what's going on."

"Look at Beryl," Canaan said softly. "What's different about him? Even a *mortal* Javier has eyes."

Javier spun to the side and examined Beryl. "He's hungover," Javier whispered and grabbed Beryl's arm; there was something odd about his hands. "What happened here..."

"Hey," Beryl complained weakly yanking his captive sleeve. Javier pulled him toward the lamp. He was missing two fingernails and all of his nail beds were rimmed brown with dried blood.

"What happened to your hands?" he asked Beryl, an urgency growing in his tone. Why hadn't he noticed upstairs? Could he possibly be *that* distracted? Beryl squinted his eyes at his fingers and Javier asked again.

"How did you do this to your hands?"

"I didn't do anything!" Beryl replied sharply and stepped away, taking his hands to himself. "I've been asleep!"

Canaan held out a palm to Beryl who stepped up without fear and looked into the Elder's face. Kilmeade gestured for Javier to come near and he did, still extremely unnerved. The Elders were enraged, Beryl's fingernails were missing, and Javier had spoken with him ten minutes *and never noticed.*

Canaan grabbed Beryl's neck. "Dae Kim has been released."

"Beryl let him out," Kilmeade added softly.

"What?" Beryl asked looking at all three of them in turn.

Kilmeade nodded, his hand grasping Javier's upper arm and holding him firmly. "Look at your phones."

Javier and Beryl simultaneously yanked out their cells. He had eleven missed calls and five unread texts from Canaan. *How did I not hear it ring? And why didn't I see these this morning?* Javier thought, and aloud he muttered, "I've been up three hours and I never noticed these."

"We have a problem," Canaan said in a rumbling voice Javier had never heard before. "Which means *you* have a bigger problem."

Kilmeade squeezed and held the contact on Javier's arm. "Canaan and I heard everything that went on in the garage. What do you think your Elders experienced?"

Helplessness. The word popped into Javier's mind, but he'd never say it aloud. *It is Daytime, someone is breaking your prisoner free, and your trusted guardians can't be roused.* The blood drained from Javier's face. "I'm s—"

Kilmeade moved his hand to grasp Javier's throat. *"Sss-ss-sss,"* he hissed and shook his head once.

"Shit, Javie—when did an Elder ever want to hear that?" Canaan whispered, real disdain in his gaze. Javier's heart shriveled and he looked back to Kilmeade standing against him.

"Your saving grace," the Elder said softly, "is that Roman was also unreachable. It was spirit interference, so not entirely your doing."

Javier's jaw dropped as his misery increased. The Elders had texted all of them and no one came to their aid. Kilmeade's contact at his throat slowly loosened without dropping away. He turned his face to Canaan and after a moment, both exhaled, crisis over. Javier sought Canaan's gaze and his stormy eyes were incrementally returning to their more familiar sky blue.

"Damn!" Javier breathed and leaned over, pressing both palms into his

thighs. Kilmeade's contact followed. "I thought you were about to end little Javie. *Shit.*"

"Oh, we were," Canaan said in a low voice, still rumbling with the unfamiliar vibrato. "...but I would have missed you a lot." When Javier looked up, he winked almost like his old self.

"Tell him," Kilmeade said then and released Javier's neck only to put his fingers in his hair cupping his scalp. Canaan touched him often, but unfamiliar with the senior Elder's tactile preferences, Javier didn't move.

"Put it together, pup," Canaan said sternly. "Beryl's vision about Adam destroying us in the sun." Canaan began with one finger upraised. "Kilmeade had a dream that *Dae Kim* would do that—today. Chloe told Kilmeade two weeks ago that she dreamed a stranger would kill us by exposing us to the sun," he said raising fingers two and three. "This is not paranoia—we don't worry about such things because you guard our day place. Think about it, before you were mortal, did you trust humans to know where you slept?"

Javier's blood again ran cold. "We grew careless," he whispered.

"Worse than that," Canaan said just as quietly, "You've been duped by demons. Not even conscious, Beryl let Dae Kim out. And looking at these hands, he didn't have a key. You said it yourself—you've been up three hours and never saw our texts? Is it as Kilmeade said—demons did that?"

The demons interfered with all of us... Javier nodded to Canaan, miserable and still panicked deep down. He and Beryl had risked the Elders' lives. A cursor in the back of his mind blinked on the question—*would they kill us?* Javier couldn't bear the answer. Then he remembered his faith; why hadn't he asked God for help just now when Canaan accused him?

"I'll get him back," Beryl said sharply and tensed to step away, but Canaan held his neck.

"Wait," Javier said and looked to each Elder in turn. "We were *both* distracted—me by trying to get to know Dr. Boone and Beryl's been spending daylight hours with Adam or Simon." Beryl inhaled to object and Javier continued. "No, it's on me. This is *my* fault. I told you to go. For the past two weeks, it hasn't even entered my mind that we were disregarding the Elders' safety leaving during the day." He turned to Canaan. "I forgot I was guarding you. We both did."

Canaan's gaze hardened, but he didn't speak.

Kilmeade rolled his eyes. "Javier..."

"With respect," Javier gently interrupted, "you count on me to lead this mission in the day because of what we accomplished in Athens." Javier draped his hand on Kilmeade's arm since the Elder's fingers had grown still on the crown of his head. "But I haven't been praying. I haven't even *thought* about praying for a while. You didn't notice because I've been going through the motions. This is going to change. Today. *Now.*"

"What are you saying?" Kilmeade asked and stared at his hand on his forearm. "And are you really holding my arm right now?"

Javier quickly opened his hand. "Canaan said it—we've been duped by demons and I'm the reason why."

"Because you're not praying," Kilmeade said as a flat statement and unconvinced.

"Yes. The way to ruin this mission is to kill the Elders. If the enemy can get me to look the other way, it can sneak in and do that. I haven't been at my post." Javier looked to Beryl. "You're in charge a few days. I'm going to get my heart in order." Javier backed toward the door and Canaan shook his head.

"Stop," the Elder said in an undertone.

"No, listen. We defeated Zahdone and Ta'avah because we leaned on Yeshua to do the work. Since our second or third hunt, I've been winging it, no prayer, no nothing. But it's not me helping our lost brethren, it never was me, and I forgot that."

"Stop," Canaan said again as Javier turned for the stairs. With a rush of air, the Elder stood in front of him and took a firm hold of his shoulders. Eye-to-eye, Javier needed a moment for his flight-response to chill. The sudden fear caused him to grin and then Canaan did, too.

"You didn't expect that, did you?" he chuckled. "Felt good. Don't get to be amazing much anymore."

"I forgot you could do that," Javier said with a short laugh. *"Shit!"* He took a deep breath and looked to Kilmeade. "Here's what I suggest. Start for Los Angeles at sundown. The itinerary is in the console of the truck. It's a three-night trip and the hotels are set up at each stop. I'll fly to join you in three days when you're arriving." He looked at Beryl, making up his plan on the fly and praying in his heart for help.

"Want me with them?" Beryl asked his tone subdued with what sounded like shame.

"I think that's best. I will need to be alone. Simon has been your main distraction. Tell him you'll catch up with him when this is over. I'll do the same with Claire."

"What about Adam?" Beryl asked.

Javier shook his head slowly. "Ya'll decide what should be done about Adam. Personally, he isn't completely vetted. I don't trust him with our lives." Javier caught both Elder's eye and said, "You didn't want him near Chloe because she's your treasure." With a gesture to Beryl he said, "You two are what we treasure right now. This is what our lives are about." In his peripheral vision, Beryl agreed with a tiny nod, which was enough.

Canaan slid his hands from Javier's shoulders to his throat and pretended to choke him. "You're so bossy," he joked and swung him back and forth. "What do you think, Kilmeade?" he asked, still grinning at Javier.

"I say go upstairs, arm yourselves, prepare everything for our departure. When the three of us hit the road, *then* you begin your sabbatical." Kilmeade exhaled and walked to the daybed and dropped onto it. "Guard my damn door. I don't want to be burned up this close to the end of our mission."

"Guard his damn door," Canaan said in Javier's ear. "Brother, don't you want to bite Javier with those fantastic teeth? Just a little nip?" Canaan called to Kilmeade's dark corner. He held Javier's gaze, his grin going to the side.

"Go guard the door," Kilmeade repeated without humor.

"Bite him first," Canaan said and Javier's smile fell. "He hasn't been praying enough. He's defenseless. Let's teach him a lesson..."

"That's not funny," Javier said working to discern if he was joking.

"Guard. My. Door," Kilmeade hissed.

Canaan grabbed Javier and yanked him close. *"You're such fun,"* he said in his ear. Then he spun him around and shoved him to the first step. "And don't forget our little B." He clicked off the lamp to force Beryl to find the steps in the dark, but Javier caught his hand and put it on the bannister.

"We're back on task," Javier said to both Elders. "Rest easy." To Beryl following behind him, he said, "Bring the extra magazine from my top dresser drawer. I'll sit by the door until sundown."

The door bolted behind them and Beryl trotted upstairs for the additional ammo. *Better safe than sorry,* Javier thought, and then he closed his eyes and reintroduced himself to God.

35

Canaan stood over Kilmeade's small bed with his arms crossed. Sundown was minutes away and from the racket the boys made upstairs, it was time to hit the road for Los Angeles. Yet his partner hadn't risen. Kilmeade lay still as the dead on his back, barely breathing, unseeing eyes open and fixed. *Another visitation.* Canaan had grown accustomed to them; this would be the fifth such occasion since they started their Rakum hunt 3½ months ago. It wasn't enough that Javier's God would remove his friend from the earth, but He constantly poked at him, too. Canaan sighed. When Kilmeade's mind returned, his visit would cascade to Canaan as they all did.

Momentarily, his friend took a big gulp of air, exhaled, and opened his eyes. When his gaze met Canaan's he grinned. "Did I miss the alarm?" he joked and put his feet to the floor.

Canaan frowned and rolled one hand. "On with it. What did your angel friend say this time?"

Kilmeade maintained his smile and stretched his arms to the low ceiling, popped his back, and twisted left and right. "Wouldn't you like to know..." he winked and stripped off his shirt, headed for the bathroom.

"Kilmeade!" Canaan followed him and stopped when the door closed in his face.

A man-shaped entity with fire for eyes places hands of light on his shoulders, he melts to the ground onto his knees... The visitation began streaming his way, so with his frown in place, Canaan dropped onto the edge of the small bed and closed his eyes. *"Because God was at your side when the enemy rose up against you, you have persevered. For the sake of your brethren, you have sacrificed all; there is no greater love than for a man to lay down his life for his brother..."* the light-being said, his voice like warm honey, drenching Canaan secondhand as the memory of the visitation replayed.

"The LORD has not given you to be prey for their teeth, nor will your soul be trapped in the fowler's snare—the snare has been broken and God who made heaven and earth has freed you..." Canaan's head bobbed at the cadence of the words of Life trickling past and he didn't notice that somewhere during the

phrasing, the being was no longer speaking to Kilmeade in the memory, but to Canaan in real-time. *"Canaan, my son, you have turned to God when you had no other salvation, when the waters overwhelmed you and the swollen waters threatened to go over your soul..."*

Canaan's eyes snapped open. The angel stood before him in the basement and he covered his face with both hands. With no clue what to do or say, Canaan remained as he was and waited for the next utterance.

"When your brother enters the light, maintain purity in your flesh until your time in the sun comes to pass," the being said, his voice vibrating throughout the basement. "Your Father in heaven loves you and is watching over you."

Canaan opened his eyes in time to see the angel fade away. Rubbing his face, he called Kilmeade. "Your blasted friend came to see me!"

Kilmeade exited the bathroom in his jeans toweling his long hair. "I see that. But it wasn't mine—you have your own now, my brother. Congratulations!" With a few violent scrubs of the towel, Kilmeade tossed it aside and grabbed a clean undershirt from a stack on the shelf. "The laundry is always so nicely folded, brother Canaan!"

Canaan growled at his partner's cheeriness and crossed angrily to stuff his keys and wallet into his pockets, Chloe's puppy memento the only thing lightening his mood. "I think it's about time you told me your 100-year-old secret."

Kilmeade hummed to himself and nodded. Arranging his damp hair behind his ears, he reached Canaan's side. "See it as I did. Begin now."

Canaan sent him a hard look and closed his eyes. "I'm ready," he muttered and magically, Kilmeade's memory became his own.

The fire died out sometime during the day so when Kilmeade awoke, the Montreal winter had thoroughly invaded his two-room forest prison. With the storm debilitating the roads, Canaan had yet to return. His comrade-warden had ridden out under saddle on the warmblood gelding; its huge round hooves better handled the balls of ice that would certainly collect there. Still, no matter how surefooted and capable the beast, little could be expected when the snow reached its chest.

"Átkizott!"[17] Kilmeade hissed; the log pile had not been replenished. Canaan used a day-man who, along with his teenaged son, kept the cabin fueled with logs and oil, stacking them nearby for Canaan to retrieve when

---

[17] (Hungarian) Expletive, curse word

he arose each night. Kilmeade rubbed his palms together and looked through the icy glass. The snow had ceased and the night sky loomed free of clouds sparkling with a million diamonds. Kilmeade scanned the clearing. He would only be a meter or so outdoors...

A curious tingle caught Kilmeade's attention deep in his mind and he pulled his gaze from the night to the ceiling of the small cabin. The Ten Fathers were watching, waiting for him to fail or succeed; either way, they were entertained. Kilmeade sent them a wink and appreciated their attention, their tests. Perhaps they delayed Canaan themselves.

"Do your worst, Masters," he sent to the Ten with respect. *"I have learned my lesson. You may throw at me the deepest freeze and I will not break your edict."*

Kilmeade's quarantine permitted him a step or two into the yard, yet he wouldn't push it. He had a mere sixty-six days left to his twenty-four-month sentence; his addiction to the blood of the dying had been defeated. The disfigurement his disobedience caused—a hunched spine, altered hair, skin, nails, eyes, and teeth—had cleared up within the first twelve months.

Well... Kilmeade grinned and ran his tongue over his teeth. During his disobedience, his canines jutted beyond his bottom lip; now they no longer protruded, yet retained a wicked point. Being a great Elder, Kilmeade willed them to remain. None of the Rakum had fangs and they came in handy when one's favorite food was trapped in a bag of skin.

CRASH!

Kilmeade didn't startle, but he turned curious toward the door. A loud thump followed the crash and the thick door shuddered.

"Monsieur Canaan! Aidez nous s'il vous plaît!"[18] a masculine voice cried through the portal. Without a thought, Kilmeade unbolted the door and watched as a man bundled in animal furs tumbled inside glittering with snow and ice. Kilmeade closed the door and backed to stand a respectful distance away while the stranger righted himself in the cold room.

When the miserable human met his eye, Kilmeade said in English, "You said help *us*. Where are your companions?"

Still on his hands and knees, the pelts giving him the appearance of an ailing bear, the man took a few deep breaths. *"Loups, Monsieur!* My boy! Help," he huffed in a mish-mash of English and French, motioning weakly with his chin toward the door.

Kilmeade regarded him with a sideways look. "What do you expect me to do? Tangle with a wolf to save your son?" Kilmeade asked in English. In the back of his mind, he realized he was not drawn to the man

---

[18] (French) Mister Canaan, please help us!

for his blood and he had no desire to end him for a Dying Buzz. This was progress!

"Please, *s'il vous plaît,*" he said mumbling and losing consciousness. It occurred to Kilmeade then to search the man for injuries. He needn't touch him; his ability to diagnose medical issues had always been outstanding. With a simple tuning-in to the man's heartbeat, his entire condition relayed before Kilmeade's inner mind. Sprained ankle, multiple contusions, frostbite on two toes, spiking blood pressure, and the early stages of hypothermia. Kilmeade had no desire to heal the man, so he stared on, hands clasped at his chest.

"*Monsieur...*" the man whispered once more and fell quiet, finally succumbing to shock.

Kilmeade returned to the wavy-glassed window. This stranger had asked for Canaan—was he the day man? *Maybe he was bringing our supplies...* Still focused on a desire for firewood, Kilmeade rolled the unconscious man away from the door with his foot and pulled it open. Cold wind lashed his face and neck before he spiraled his ragged scarf. He took two steps into the weather and listened for the wolves or the boy. Perhaps the supplies were with the son. Still searching, Kilmeade took another two steps from the cabin. The familiar tingle replayed.

"*Átkizott!*" he said with venom. Spinning on his heel, he returned to the confines of the cabin in three strides. He slammed and bolted the door facing the man on the floor and the cold, gray fireplace.

I suppose I can burn the wood box. Or the chairs...

Kilmeade didn't mind discomfort; he rather enjoyed the deep burn of a freezing appendage or the stabbing pain of a frostbitten nose tip. This notwithstanding, he could not allow his body to be overwhelmed by his environment. He could laugh at the pain all night, but if he didn't find warmth soon, he could suffer irreparable harm to his flesh. His Rakum body would repair itself a hundred times faster than a human's, but unrelenting destruction would be exhausting to keep pace with.

Kilmeade laid his hands on the wood box and broke it apart with a swift kick. The boards divided at the nails and he stacked them into the stone fireplace. Rarely had he needed to create fire in the past century, but with his partner gone and no starter flame, Kilmeade hunkered down before the broken wood and concentrated on heating a sliver of dry bark saved for kindling. As an Elder, *willing* fire into existence was not a difficult task, but the cold and wet environment made his job more challenging. After four good tries, the kindling ignited and he carefully brought the wood to life. Within another five minutes, the fire was well involved and Kilmeade sought more fuel. The two chairs were broken and added to the flames. Now the cabin became even too warm for his layers and Kilmeade shrugged off the outer furs. He allowed his flesh to be warmed and his eyes sought more flammable items to burn.

THUD!

Again, Kilmeade didn't startle at the sudden noise, but this time he grinned, thinking it might be the wolf-eaten boy. Rising to his feet, he unlocked the door and pulled it wide. In tumbled a young man, similarly bundled head-to-toe in fur, and he slithered to the plank floor to rest alongside his father.

The toasty cabin filled immediately with the aroma of fresh blood. Kilmeade's eyes widened and he carefully rolled the suffering human onto his back. Wolves had ripped at the youth's face and neck, and his lifeblood pulsed onto the floor with every beat of his heart. Kilmeade's entire body came awake. One swift swoop and the youth was cradled in his arms. The mortal would expire; why not take his blood? He didn't have to drink him to death; he would stop. He was cured. He wouldn't break the Fathers' edict...

Still deciding a course of action, the entire cabin became bathed in white light. Kilmeade had never seen the like and the essence reminded him of the sunshine he avoided since First Ritual. The bluish-white hue gave off no heat, yet was bright enough that Kilmeade shielded his eyes with his free hand. Then there was the sensation of not being alone.

Peeking through his fingers and still cradling the young man, Kilmeade lowered to one knee and called out, "Who is there?"

"Behold, Kilmeade!" a voice bellowed in the brightness, sounding very much like a violoncello bow in full vibration. "I come for the boy! He is ours! Set him down!"

Kilmeade narrowed his eyes and as he focused, a portion of the light separated out in the form of a man. It had a head, neck, a torso, arms, and legs, but no details, only beams of light emanating from its core.

"Who are you?" Kilmeade asked setting the dying man to the floor and backing away.

"I stand in the presence of the One who made you, the Creator of the Universe, the God of Abraham, Isaac, and Jacob, the God of Israel."

When the being completed its identifier, it lowered to the ground beside the youth. Hands of light touched the boy's pained face and Kilmeade watched in wonder as the being healed every wound.

"This one is ours," the being said in Kilmeade's mind. "This one has not hidden righteousness in his heart, but has spread the good news across the land for his God and King."

The youth was coming around and the white being stood to approach Kilmeade in a gliding fashion.

"Your Father in heaven loves you and wants you to prosper. I know the plans I have for you, says your Father. He loves you, Kilmeade, and He loved you first."

Kilmeade shook his head, confounded. He had a blood father—Yuri, a powerful Rakum of the Ten. High Father Abroghia was their God and King. Yet, even with such faith and knowledge of Rakum history, this light being's words did not fall on deaf ears. Contrarily, Kilmeade enjoyed a warm glow deep within at the notion of attracting the attention of a Maker he hadn't known existed.

"When the time comes, you will see me again," the being said and reached out its hand for his chest. "You will meet your *true* Father. He will come close and you will touch the face of the One who made you. At that time, you will believe in His Son and leave the flesh to join us in the light."

Kilmeade again shook his head. "I don't understand," he said and the being's hand made contact with his body. The hand pierced every layer of clothing until the beams of light rest directly on Kilmeade's skin. A rapturous and joyous feeling overcame him and he fell to his knees, such foreign mortal emotions had never before struck his black heart.

"No!" he yelped and in a flash, the being was gone.

The boy sat up on the floor and looked around. Kilmeade's mind raced and he backed to the wall. In all his years, he'd never felt alone or lost, those being pitiful weak human abstracts, but now it took all he had to not crumble to the ground, despairing the light being's departure.

"Papa! Papa!" Across the room, the young man crawled to his father's side. Kilmeade's un-Rakum-like panic grew. Unnamed terror—so unlike him, so foreign, as if possessed by an adverse entity—why was he afraid? What did he fear? Who or what could possibly harm a Rakum Elder? Unable to discern the meaning of his sudden fear, Kilmeade backed into the only other room in the cabin, the lavatory/storeroom. Since the Elders slept light-tight under the floorboards, two rooms was all they required. Kilmeade bolted the cubby, his thoughts consumed by the light being's visit.

Breathing in short gasps, he considered the tight space. A smooth hole cut into an enclosed bench provided a toilet and a hand-pump situated on the inner wall provided fresh water. Kilmeade sat upon the corner box wherein Canaan stored a supply of salted meats, all the while reciting the focusing exercises he had adopted in Elder training. For the first time, they had no effect and he was unable to compartmentalize his thoughts and impulses.

I've seen the Maker's messenger. The Maker... The Maker... The Maker...

Without intention, Kilmeade's stony heart turned to the Ten. *"Fathers, did you see? Did you see?"*

In an instant, a hand landed on his shoulder as one of the Fathers translated physically to his side. "Elder Kilmeade, rise."

The ancient voice resonated in his physical ears as well as deep in his mind. Kilmeade stood and looked into the face of Father Theophilus. Despite his current mental emergency, he bowed low and clasped his hands before him. Theophilus regarded him with a scowl and Kilmeade looked to the side.

"Explain yourself, pup," the Father said, his voice spiked with disdain. "You disgrace us with this display. A Rakum Elder does not disintegrate."

"Father, I am not myself." Kilmeade pressed his fist to his sternum, precisely where the light being had touched him. "I have seen what cannot be unseen, heard what cannot be unheard, and felt what cannot be unfelt."

"But it can," Theophilus said on top of his assertions. "Everything you have seen, heard, and felt tonight is a lie—look at me."

Kilmeade lifted his pale gray eyes into the Father's shining gaze. Theophilus placed his wrinkled but strong hands on either side of Kilmeade's head. Heat flared at the contact as Kilmeade's eyelids closed.

"Elder Kilmeade, hear me and hear me well..." Theophilus's voice echoed around the room with substance, welcome and trickling into Kilmeade's mind like sweet syrup on dry bread. "You awoke this evening to find that the cabin had gone cold. You came in to relieve yourself and when you returned, you saw the logs stacked in the wrong place. But look! There they are. Build a fire. Do it now. Your brother will return this time tomorrow. Do you understand?"

Eyes still closed, Kilmeade sighed as every last iota of confusion and disgusting mortal emotion filtered away. Taking a deep breath, he exhaled slowly, his power returning stronger than ever, his magnificence threatening to cause him to shout with joy. When he opened his eyes, he stood alone. Kilmeade chuckled. And why not? He'd just awoken and the fire had died.

Canaan will return by tomorrow night, I'm certain, Kilmeade told himself.

He pulled open the locked door and found the cabin empty. *Of course, it's empty. I need to start a fire. Merde! Why did he stack the logs over there?*

Kilmeade crossed the floor and grabbed up enough wood to bring a roaring flame. The cold fireplace was swept clean, indicating if he hadn't been delayed, Canaan would have exercised his fire duties.

Kilmeade huffed with a wry grin at the various imaginations that had occurred during his sleep period. The withdrawal symptoms of his condition included hallucinations, nausea, and flights of paranoia. It was no wonder the Fathers outlawed the Dying Buzz; Rakum who did not cease imbibing eventually went insane. Again, Kilmeade internally thanked the Fathers for finding him worthy of scrutiny and reprimand.

Wait until Canaan gets back, he thought as he warmed his hands by the fire. Looking to the floor where he had hallucinated humans blown in by the weather, he chuckled. *Oh, he will be merciless in his teasing...*

Kilmeade then glanced at the lavatory door still ajar.

A Father? Here? Never. He shook his head. *I won't tell Canaan. He would worry for my recovery...*

Fancies of a starved Rakum, was all that was. Canaan's donations kept him from succumbing to blood rage, but *human* blood is what every Rakum craved. Human blood fed their deepest, inward parts. Drinking from humans made them *in*human, the glorious state of every Rakum. No, he wouldn't tell Canaan. In sixty-six days, his sentence would end and he'd gobble up as many mortals as he could *without* drinking them to death.

"A Father in the lavatory," Kilmeade whisper-laughed and crossed to the center of the room. Canaan would return soon and he had plenty of wood and oil for cooking. Until then... Kilmeade turned a circle, taking in the entire room. Where were the chairs?

36

Kilmeade's century-old memory ended and Canaan didn't speak for several long minutes. Finally he sighed and looked to his partner leaning against the staircase. "I wondered about those chairs," he whispered shaking his head.

At the time, they both assumed Kilmeade burned them in one of his withdrawal fugues. Why not? Kilmeade believed it.

"I see more to it," Canaan said squinting his eyes at his cohort. "You think you saw this thing because you had been abstaining from human blood for so long..."

Kilmeade shrugged more or less. "Combine that with my peculiar personality and the mental training we undergo as Elders... this could have opened me up to it." He grinned then with a thought. "All of you whispered I was the greatest Elder, that I would one day be a Father. I think this visitation is what made me so advanced. I think my so-called greatness started that night."

"*Shew*...you saw something the Fathers didn't want any of us to see."

"That there is a higher Master."

His partner's gaze grew soft and Canaan exhaled. None of the grunts would have been able to process the information; he doubted the Elders could have either. Canaan chuckled; he would have gone insane if such a thing had happened to him in 1899.

"Come now, Elder Canaan," Kilmeade said with a friendly grin. "You have never given yourself enough credit. You are every bit as brilliant as Kilmeade. You know I do not lie."

"I suppose on some level..."

"No, on this level." Kilmeade pressed his palm to Canaan's forehead and continued with his thought. "That first angel visitation had been erased from my memory, but when I saw the light-being in Father Damien," Kilmeade said with reverence, "the expunged memory worked its way back. I recalled it fully after our first hunt in Jackson."

"You kept it hidden well," Canaan said with a wry grin.

"I have my reasons," Kilmeade replied, "and from this point on, my reasons are yours as well."

"Thank you," Canaan said sarcastically and then looked aside, thinking. "I find it odd that Father Theophilus is the one who came to correct you."

"Because he subverted Ta'avah at the end?" Kilmeade asked.

"I guess that's it," Canaan shrugged. "Wait, you and I are experiencing exponential increases in our abilities. What are the chances we can translate like the Fathers?"

Before Last Assembly, only the Fathers were capable of traveling by thought, the method hidden from even the Elders. Nonetheless, Kilmeade's interest mirrored Canaan's and at the same time, they both shouted for Beryl. Without delay, the little brother came to the door and tried the knob. Finding it unlocked he trotted down.

"What's going on?"

Canaan called him close, aware that at one point Beryl had been conscripted to serve Ta'avah, and the demon's proclivities nearly had them both shot by police.

"You told us that when you were trapped last year, you translated to safety."

Beryl nodded at the recollection.

"How did you do it?"

Beryl assumed a somber expression. "I was terrified. I closed my eyes and pictured the place I wanted to go." He looked between both Elders and added, "I *willed* myself there. I thought, *I will open my eyes in Mac's trailer,* and I did."

Canaan grasped Kilmeade's shoulder. "Try it. My heart is exploding to try."

With identical excitement, Kilmeade's gaze went soft as he worked through the problem. Canaan followed and the image that repeatedly came to their conjoined minds was a purple room in Kilmeade's San Francisco house.

"You left six months ago," Canaan whispered. "Who's keeping it for you with Jimmy dead?"

"Veronica is the most devoted," Kilmeade said bringing to mind the disciples at his house. "Dial the landline."

Canaan fished out his phone. As it rang, he handed it to his partner.

"What?!" a male voice barked over the line.

"I am Mr. Star. Who is this?" Kilmeade looked into Canaan's face as he spoke, mentally complaining about the man's phone etiquette. A plastic thunk emitted and distant noises filtered through the discarded unit until it was pulled to another's ear.

"Mr. Star? For real? I missed you so much! You okay?"

Kilmeade broke out in a reflexive grin. "Yes, Veronica, I'm glad to hear your voice. How are things at the house?"

"Truthfully? We just don't have the same mojo without you. The air is stale and nothing is purple."

Canaan snickered at her verbiage and Kilmeade winked.

"Have you maintained my personal space?"

"Oh, yes, sir. It's still locked from when you left."

"Excellent, I will reward you greatly for that." Kilmeade sounded giddy with relief. "You will hear from me again shortly." He disconnected the call and sank into Canaan's gaze.

"Do it," Canaan whispered.

Beryl stood nearby watching their faces, his mouth ajar.

Kilmeade's grin completed and he bit his lip. *"I will,"* he sent silently and backed two steps.

Canaan closed his eyes as Kilmeade did and watched his partner bring up the aforementioned room in his mind. Every detail popped into view, clear and three-dimensional. With a lightness in his middle that reminded him of a ride at the amusement park, the vision disappeared. Canaan opened his eyes; both of them had traveled to Kilmeade's California mansion.

"Shiiiiiittt..." Canaan breathed the word, doing a full circle. Neither expected that both of them would translate.

The first to recover from his amazement, Kilmeade crossed to the bolted door. Hand on the knob, he turned to Canaan. "Text the boys," he said with a twinkle in his eye. "Then I will introduce you to Veronica. She thinks I am a vampire," Kilmeade said with a chuckle. "She's *very* friendly."

With a matching grin, Canaan sent a short note to Beryl before gesturing for the door. "After you, Mr. Star."

With one last deep breath, Kilmeade stepped into the hallway he had deserted so long ago.

Canaan adopted a casual posture as if he'd been there a million times, using Kilmeade's thoughts as a guide. He expected dozens of people to be in residence based upon Kilmeade's memories, but heard only eight heartbeats. They navigated the long, dark hallway and the sounds of life grew more pronounced.

When Kilmeade entered the threshold of the main room, he stepped to the center of the opening and crossed his arms, surveying the occupants. Canaan stood to his right and behind, mimicking Kilmeade's posture. None of the mortals noticed them for several seconds, each deeply involved in their own interests. Two women, a boy, and five men peppered the large space filled with a dozen beanbag chairs, stools, and a long tattered sofa.

"Oh!" a woman at the back of the room exclaimed with surprise and covered her mouth. She was fortyish with a bouncy body and long bottle-blonde hair. She jogged closer stopping at a respectful distance as her name flashed to Canaan. At her exclamation, all eyes turned for the threshold and all but one stood up.

"Mr. Star!" Veronica gushed and when he extended his hand, she clasped it to kiss his fingers. "I have missed you so much!"

Kilmeade did not withdraw his hand so the woman held it with both of hers and watched his face. Kilmeade scanned the remainder and a sickly female called to them from behind the couch.

"Where's Jimmy, Mr. Star? Is he okay?"

Kilmeade shot the question to Canaan.

"Lazy ass," he sent back. To the young woman, Canaan took a step forward and responded for Kilmeade as her name popped into his head. "He killed himself in November, Missy. Don't mourn him; that's a chickenshit way to go."

The woman paled and hugged herself, likely wondering who he was and instinctively recognizing he shared Mr. Star's particular oddness.

Kilmeade addressed the group. "This is my brother, Mr. Canaan. You will treat him as if he *is* me." Kilmeade then stepped into the room, effectively pulling Veronica along with him as she still held his hand. "These men are strangers," he told her open-ended.

"Everybody you knew moved on. I don't know who these guys are," she said guarding her response from the group. Kilmeade offered a miniscule nod and inclined his head to the one who did not stand.

"What of the child?"

The one ignoring them was a boy of six or seven with a striking contrast concerning his spiky white-blond hair and mocha-colored skin. He sat leaning over his lap, sideways to their position. Canaan discerned no illness, so like Kilmeade, wondered at his behavior.

"We call him Injun," she answered in a soft voice. "He came in carrying a long feather he picked up off the ground. He don't say much."

"Go have a look," Kilmeade sent and Canaan crossed the room.

The three men backed nervously as he passed and then watched him with round eyes.

"At least their instincts work," Canaan chuckled silently.

"Squatters," he sent back ready to observe the boy's interaction with Canaan. *"I will deal with them later."*

Canaan looked down on the kid, fists on his hips. He smelled like tacos and dirt and his brown shirt had once been white. The boy's eyes remained trained to the ground so Canaan bumped his tiny sandal with the toe of his boot. Nothing.

"I'm about to be me," he sent over. *"I don't like this disrespectful shit."*

Kilmeade grinned his acquiescence and Canaan knocked the boy's sandal once more.

"Stand up and greet your host," he grumbled.

When he had no response in three seconds, he swooped down and grabbed the boy underneath his arms to hoist him over his shoulder, ready to treat him as an assigned proselyte. After all, as an Elder, Canaan had been training up youngsters the Rakum way for centuries. "Little monkey," Canaan mumbled under his breath, already heading back to Kilmeade's private quarters.

"Let's watch," Kilmeade said behind him and Veronica's hard-soled shoes clacked rapidly in his footsteps. The remaining mortals followed with their eyes, but not into the dark and shuttered east wing of the mansion.

Canaan reached the room and dropped the boy on one of two full-size beds, crossing his arms to stare the boy down. Kilmeade and Veronica entered and the door swooshed closed.

"Hey, kid, you have no sickness. Your brain is undamaged. Your tongue works. Speak now or kiss this world goodbye," Canaan said in a calm undertone. Out of the corner of his eye, Kilmeade snickered. Veronica looked petrified.

"Say sumpin', Injun! You're disrespectin'!" Veronica hissed.

Canaan pointed a finger her way. "Shut it," he said. The blood drained from her face and again, Kilmeade laughed to himself.

"No." A tiny voice floated up from the bed beside him and the child looked up. Mixed heritage had endowed him with bright hazel-green eyes and Canaan grinned after another moment at what reflected back—the boy was angry as hell.

Maintaining his wry smile, Canaan leaned in a few inches and waited for another word. When none came, he said to Kilmeade holding the boy's gaze, "Does that pitiful noise count as speech, Mr. Star?"

"I didn't hear anything except a little baby gurgling. Is that what you heard, Veronica?" Kilmeade played along. The woman by his side said nothing.

"Do it again, little baby. Did you just gurgle?" Canaan asked the boy and reached to fill his fist with the kid's filthy shirt. He pulled the boy a few inches toward him and the kid parted his lips.

"Are you a good guy or a bad guy?" the boy said in the same tiny voice. Canaan doubted Veronica even heard him.

"Depends," Canaan replied. "Why are you so angry?"

"You look like Captain Beatums. He's a good guy," the boy whispered. Canaan's eye twitched as the pro-wrestler's face came to mind—they looked *nothing* alike.

"I'll Beatums you if you ignore me again. Why are you so angry?"

The miserable boy's mouth turned up at Canaan's joke, unable to fully maintain his frown. Finally, he said, "My momma left us."

"You're better off," Canaan said and released the kid's shirt. "What else?"

"My daddy kicked me out," he said.

"Boo-hoo, *wahhhhh.*" Canaan stood to his full height, still holding the child's gaze. "What the hell are you doing *here*, at my man's house?"

The boy jerked his eyes to Kilmeade and Veronica. "I knocked and that lady let me stay here, but the man in the blue shirt hurts me." Ben pulled at the crotch of his jeans and winced.

With a disgusted huff, Kilmeade turned and left the room so quickly that Veronica was left flustered and her eyes grew wide.

"Chill out, sugar." Canaan sent her a wink and her head bobbed up and down. He returned his focus to the kid. "Where do you think Mr. Star is headed now?" he asked testing the boy's thought processes.

"The potty," the kid answered with authority.

Canaan's eye twitched again and he exhaled slowly. "Mr. Star is going to end that guy in the blue shirt. How's that sound?" Veronica gasped.

"Kill him?" the boy asked softly, his eyes hopeful.

"Oh, yeah. Gonna kill him good. We don't put up with that shit," Canaan replied. "Now, how about you shake it off and stop being so pitiful. I hate that. Makes my skin crawl." He jostled the kid's shoulder a few times and as he tried to sit up tall, Canaan helped with a hand to his forearm. "That's right. Stand up. Be a man. There you go."

The kid stood and rubbed his face. "I'm Ben."

"I'm Canaan. You ready for a piece of truth?" Canaan asked him and the youth nodded. "Your momma and daddy, if they don't want to be near you, that's on them, not you. You're not responsible for the actions of other people. Dig?"

"Uh," Ben said and paused. "I broke Daddy's mug. I'm bad."

"Shut that shit." Canaan used both hands to ruffle the boy's feathery hair. His phone chimed and he pulled it from his pocket.

"Are you coming back?"

Canaan lifted the phone to his lips and speech-to-texted his message. *"Who's the Master? You wait."* He pocketed the cell and grinned at Ben. "I keep 'em on their toes. I'll show you how to do it, too." Ben's eyes brightened.

Kilmeade's anger spiked somewhere in the house and Canaan chucked Ben's shoulder with his knuckle.

"Blue shirt is dead." Ben's eyes sparkled anew and Canaan turned to Veronica. "Show him to the shower and make sure he has everything he needs to get clean. Let him wash himself—he's big enough. Give him some clean clothes." Canaan looked back to Ben. "You smell terrible and I have a super-sensitive nose."

"Yes, sir," Ben nodded.

"When you smell nice again, Mr. Star and I are taking you on the town. You watch how we attack the world and be like us. No one will pick on Ben anymore after tonight. Got it?"

"Yes, sir," Ben said again with a tiny smile.

"Good." Canaan pushed him toward Veronica. "And you, gorgeous," he said to her and her fearful expression instantly lessened. "When you get him situated, come back and see me. Deal?"

Veronica offered a cautious grin and pulled Ben from the room.

"What?" he sent when Kilmeade snickered in his mind. His cohort had choked the molester and stuffed his body into a custom incinerator built into the basement of the enormous estate. Now he was in the kitchen listening to Missy complain about Veronica. *"Are you laughing at old Canaan?"*

"I knew you'd like her," Kilmeade returned with humor.

"We'll see." Canaan peeked into the hall. *"Thanks to you, I'm completely stove up."* Kilmeade chuckled again and Canaan leaned on the wall, drumming his fingers on the doorframe.

《回》

"Canaan and Kilmeade will meet us in Los Angeles at the planned time," Beryl said tucking his phone away. "That gives me an extra day."

"My mind is blown that they translated," Javier said with a shake of the head. "That little trip I took while fighting Isaac was scary enough." Javier said no more. Beryl had been there, still a Rakum, when the demon inside Isaac Ackaron snatched Javier to an entirely different country.

"It was awful the one time I did it, too."

For a long moment, both men remained lost in their own thoughts until Beryl's phone chimed. He looked at the screen and showed it to Javier, shaking his head.

"*Got me a mascot. 7yrO Runaway, K ended a guy who pervved on him. Adventures never end. See you in L.A.*"

Beryl gave Javier a long stare. "He's insane."

"What? That's good, right?" he asked, unsure why Beryl found it laughable. "What am I missing?" Javier pressed when Beryl was still chuckling.

"Think about it," Beryl said then, meeting Javier's eye with all seriousness. "Six months ago, Canaan killed two little boys for their blood. I was there—I brought them to him. Both kids at once, slurp-slurp—left to die."

"He changed," Javier said softly, sorry to hear about someone's children dying in such a way. "Kilmeade changed."

Beryl shrugged. "Whatever. They're not human, yet are behaving more and more human every night. They're gonna wake up mortal if they don't watch it."

"And?" Javier said with a teasing grin. Beryl didn't smile, but he saw the futility of worrying over the Elders transforming heart first. "I'm ready to get going. You cool to fly? I'm going to drive. The best quiet time is drive time."

"That's fine. I'll go see Simon and then fly to Los Angeles." Beryl pulled out his phone and scrolled to the contacts. "I have the address of the rental. I'll go there and meet you."

"Simon, eh?" Javier said, with no real opinion.

"Yeah. He makes me laugh." Beryl shouldered his single carry-on bag and then clapped Javier's arm. "When I get to L.A., I'm going to buy a Lamborghini. Midnight black with emerald green leather interior."

"Okay, hotshot," Javier laughed and made a grab for his laptop. "I'm heading out. I'll have my phone if you need me. When the Elders contact either of us, let's share, okay?"

"He'll call you first," Beryl joked. "Elder's pet."

Javier laughed. "I was never a pet, I swear."

"It's not such a bad gig." Beryl batted his eyelashes and then laughed. "I'm lying—Elders make terrible companions. *Kazak.*"

Javier shook Beryl's hand and headed for the drive. After tossing in two suitcases, his phone rang. It was Canaan.

"Beryl showed me your text. Everything okay?"

"OH, HEAVENS TO BETSY! Canaan called instead of texting! It must be the end of the world!" Canaan teased on the other end in a ridiculous impression of Javier's voice.

"Yeah-yeah-yeah," Javier said and switched on the Denali. "What?"

"It's okay, sweetheart. I know you enjoy my calls more than anything in the world. Listen up," Canaan said. "Be careful. Be safe. Watch out for bad guys. You know, all that stuff. Daddy Kilmeade and I wanted to send you off with a little cheer."

"That's weird coming from you, but thank you."

"Are you surprised? We're practically smelling roses and petting kittens over here. It's disgusting." There was a voice on Canaan's end and he returned. "What did I tell ya? There's a little turd with us; we're trying to teach him how to stop being such a Nancy. Ben... Ben..."

"I know, it's really amazing—"

"Hello? Who's this?" another voice asked, higher and probably the boy. "I'm Ben. Canaan said you were his preacher."

"No, you deaf shit. He's A preacher, not MY preacher," Canaan said in the background and Javier laughed.

"Hey, Ben," Javier said and the boy answered back. "Listen to Canaan. He is very wise and I've known him more than a hundred years," Javier said with an evil grin. "Ask him how old he is."

The phone disconnected and Javier laughed aloud. He waved at Beryl who had stepped out to check his progress and headed away from the house. Jibing Canaan first, that was fun. Now, to get his heart in order.

Deep in his thoughts, Javier did not hear Beryl shouting at him from the driveway and when he reached the end of their street, his phone chimed with a new text.

37, DALLAS

"*C*ome back. *There might be a problem.*"
Too frustrated to ask God what was up, Javier found a safe place to turn around and headed back. Beryl stood with his arms crossed at the end of the paved walkway and Javier parked the truck.

"What happened?" he asked as he reached Beryl's position.

"This." Beryl held out his hand and Javier scrutinized the item before picking it up to examine it closer. "It's a listening device. A bug. It hit the ground when you got in. You ran over it, so I doubt it's still transmitting."

Javier shook his head a fraction and turned the item over in his hand. "Who would bug our car?" he asked and Beryl had no reply. Javier's mind raced and no one came to mind. They had no enemies that he was aware of except Dae Kim, and he wouldn't have had the opportunity. He met Beryl's eyes. "Would Adam bug the car?"

"No," Beryl said on the defensive and then shrugged. "I mean, no. Why would he? We haven't withheld anything from him."

Javier studied the device again and shook his head. He wanted to ask if Simon might have done it, but didn't. How about the Cow, Stu Loudon? He had been extremely unhappy about the events of 11/13. Was he an enemy? Javier raised his eyebrows at Beryl. "What about Simon's friend, Stuart Loudon?"

"Not friends, and Simon said he went back to Australia," Beryl said and reclaimed the bug. "Is it one of the Rakum? Did Dae Kim have any confederates?"

Javier shook his head. "Canaan would have known. They both read Dae Kim very deeply."

Beryl sighed. "We don't know how long it's been listening, but just think. Every word said by you, me, Canaan and Kilmeade inside that car have been heard by someone."

"And Chloe and Roman," Javier whispered. "Could it be a police thing? Did one of us attract the authorities and not know it?"

Beryl shook his head. "You'd think the Elders would sense something if we were being surveilled. You better text Canaan."

Javier nodded and then shook his head, his mind numb. "Wait. Let me think about this. Someone one of us met felt like they needed to know what we say in private." He lifted his eyes to the house. "Our rental might be bugged, too."

Beryl turned and looked behind him at the front door. "Screw this. I'm heading out. If it's bugged, they won't hear anything else from me."

Javier agreed. "Right. Go ahead with your plan and I'll text you in a few hours. Let me be the one to tell Canaan, okay?" Javier held out his hand for the bug. When Beryl returned it to his palm, he pulled Beryl close with a hand to his shoulder. "It's going to be okay."

"Be careful," Beryl said in a soft voice.

"You, too," Javier returned and climbed into his truck. In his mind, he asked God what He was up to now.

《回》

: Rakum Elders can't make babies.

: I'm sure Kilmeade would want me to get you up to speed. So with a little detective work and the help of a geneticist your father sent to us, we picked up the trail.

: Wow, where did they go? Can we make babies from them?

: Brace yourself, but someone already did. Twenty-seven years ago to be exact.

: What? No way!

: Shh. We met him and his name is Adam.

"Adam Roberts, your secret is out..." Dr. Cary Nankin chuckled as he read over the transcripts he had been collecting since he planted listening devices in the Rakum's vehicles. Dae Kim Dawn and his retarded partner barely added anything of worth in their lame, demon-centered conversations, but the Elders and their cohorts? Every recorded word was gold. Cary had been wise to follow Roberts the Third quietly and patiently, awaiting a breakthrough as he studied the materials Cary's mother told him were left in Kilmeade's care. His mother had served Kilmeade in 1900, but was raped and disgraced by Adam Roberts's adoptive great-grandfather. It was unlikely the Elder cared that a pregnancy resulted in the rape, so Cary planned to use the element of surprise when the time presented. He would make Kilmeade suffer as he and his mother had under the brutality of Elder Yu in Beijing.

As for the brilliant-yet-clueless Kilmeade copy? Right now, he lay bound, gagged, and drugged in the trunk of Cary's car. Grabbing him had been *so easy*. After midnight scant hours ago, the man was let out by a Fort Worth cab; before he stumbled away from the curb, Cary pulled up and yanked him into his car. Thoroughly intoxicated, one blow to the head knocked the guy out for over an hour. When he came to, Cary was ready to close business at the hospital. After pulling into a quiet stretch of road to reason with the man, Roberts decided behaving was his best option. The barbiturates Cary dosed him with would wear off in another hour, so he had a little time...

He continued reading, his grin widening every second.

: It was very cool of you to rent a house for the Elders.
: Yeah, I've slept in enough bathrooms to know this is much better.
: Hah, it's easy to forget you used to be one of them. You're so normal now.

"Something happened to the Rakum... Something made all of them human except these two Elders..." Cary had pieced together a congruent timeline from his taps; November 13th, something happened to the Rakum, something that had to do with the Christian God. Cary shook his head. How could anyone—nonetheless a Rakum—put their faith in a mewling deity that offers the flesh nothing until death? Cary and his mother, rest in peace, worshiped Shangti—and because of this devotion, aside from losing his first wife and son due to Elder Yu's brutality, his entire life had been filled with reward and pleasure. Cary knew that on some level, their unexpected demise served Shangti as well, providing spiritual energy for the work he would do in Cary directly afterward.

Cary re-read the portion in his hand and pushed away thoughts of the dead. The Elders he spied upon wanted to find out if Cary's employee, Adam Roberts, was one of them—a Rakum. The man had been grown in a lab, a pairing of Dr. Penny's egg with Kilmeade's seed. Cary read on, his purpose and mission clear: Kill Kilmeade in the prescribed ritual and thus assume his Rakum might and power. With Shangti's blessing, it would be easy.

: He smells human, as normal as any man out there. But he's been consuming blood since childhood. Kilmeade's DNA combined with the ingested blood of humans did not make him a Rakum. He should smell different if he was different.

Using a red marker, Cary jotted, "ELDER CANAAN" beside the first block of conversation and "ELDER KILMEADE" at the next.

: Canaan thinks it's in his head, that he's been deluded by what he thinks he knows.

Doctor Roberts was a fool to think blood alone would turn Adam into a Rakum. When Cary's mother found him beaten and marked as a Rabbit by Elder Yu more than eighty years ago, she'd been fully aware of what it took to transform her son into a full-blooded Rakum.

"Blood and deed, idiot," Cary mumbled. "It takes *blood and deed...*" The blood was a tool, but the *ritual* put the tool to use and Cary knew the incantations by heart. Cary's mother taught him everything she knew before she passed at the ripe old age of eighty-three.

Dr. Penny served Shangti; he spoke to her daily since her teens. It was he who told her how to break the curse on the Rakum's seed in the first place. Shangti accepted her sacrifice and ceremony that night and promised if she were patient, he would raise up the perfect man from her loins.

"Well, you got me, Mom," Cary whispered and touched the small amulet he wore beneath his clothing. Inside, he kept a lock of his mother's hair. Because of her loyal and loving instruction, Cary had the knowledge required to extract power from the remaining Elders.

: I have been at the shelter. I couldn't get a job for a long time. I lived off my Cows. I was lost. How could I have known? How could any of us have known this could happen?

Another Rakum the Elders went to rescue. Cary spat on the floor. "He lived off his Cows," he mumbled and spat again. Elder Yu siphoned wages off his mother for as long as he'd been alive and making a living in Nanking had been nearly impossible. The corrupt local government paid late, if ever, and patients rarely paid with cash.

: You saw some heavy action from two indignant Elders tonight, Adam. We want you to prosper and live a long, happy life, but if you take demons into your body like Dae Kim and Pete did, we will zap you into eternity. Get it?

A different night. The two Rakum had Adam Roberts with them. They'd just murdered one of their own because he'd gone insane. Cary pondered the Elder's warning regarding demon possession, none of which jibed with what Shangti had taught him about the spirit realm. In fact, having a powerful spirit assume control of your flesh was a great honor, and as soon as he completed all of the tests, Cary expected the mighty Shangti to perform the honor unto him. Cary snickered. Javier and his bunch confused demon possession with textbook schizophrenia.

The recent transcripts fluttered into view and Cary grinned. Elder Kilmeade's weakness was as evident as the nose on Cary's face. He had a woman and she was pregnant with his child—the first child born of a Rakum that wasn't a Father. Cary shook his head and re-read his favorite parts.

: Kilmeade speaks of Chloe often. She has cheered him, I gather.

: His devotion to her is off the charts and I can tell she pleases him a lot. With very little training in how to be an Elder's wife.

: The Old Way is out the window. I doubt he has trained her at all.

: They're in one brain so you know what that means...

: Kilmeade stubs his toe and Canaan feels it?

Cary grinned and rubbed his palms together. Getting the two Elders attention wouldn't be hard. For the moment, the Elder's woman was out of reach, but Kilmeade utterly adored these men around him. Cary closed his fist. His supernatural might had only increased since Elder Yu left him half-dead that night in Beijing. He was more a Rakum than these surrounding the Elders. In fact, Cary worked *not* to cross paths with the Elders until he was ready since they would definitely detect Yu's mark.

Cary took a deep breath and thanked Shangti in his heart. Tonight, the bug he planted had been discovered, but Cary had enough information to initiate his mission. Tucking the transcripts into a folder, he stuffed the lot of them to the bottom of his briefcase. Shangti assured Cary in a vision that he would find Dae Kim in Amarillo, Texas. In addition, once there, a simple incantation accompanied with a fresh blood sacrifice would divine the Rakum's precise location. *Perfect!* Cary had become quite adept at attracting prostitutes to kill for his rituals.

Cary packed the remainder of his materials into his case and set it to the floor to erase his hard-drive. Dr. Boone had a habit of walking into his office without knocking and she was somehow involved. For now, he'd focus on the Rakum, but once they were history, he'd take care of Claire Boone. He'd leave nothing to chance. He would soon be the Perfect Man and servant to his god—and there would be no weakness found in him ever again.

"Last but not least..." Cary scooted into his private lavatory. With soap and a coarse washcloth he scrubbed the foul-smelling lotion from his exposed skin and carefully peeled the latex baldcap from his head. He was indeed bald having shaved his own head for a decade, but he had eyebrows.

The latex and oily cosmetics kept them unseen. The disguise had served him well, but he was glad to finally shed it.

Since coming to the States in 1950, he had played himself—he arrived as Cary Nankin I, procuring a position supervising the labs at Dallas Research Hospital in 1960. There, he watched Robert Roberts fiddle with cells stolen from a centuries' old Rakum Elder. From 1980 to 2000, Cary took the identity of Cary I's son and supervised labs in Manhattan, watching the fool long-distance. When Roberts finally brought the fertilized materials to life, Cary became Cary Nankin the Third and took over the labs at Baylor-Dallas.

His camouflage proved genius. The current Doctor Nankin suffered alopecia, plus a few unpleasant gastronomical ailments. His choices kept strangers aloof; women and men both avoided him due to his unhealthy visage. The lotions masked his scent if any Rakum came too near. Today, he'd stop covering the face and body Elder Yu's blood had bestowed him. With freshly washed cheeks and the padding removed from underneath his clothing, Cary was ready.

He pulled his laptop bag over his shoulder, grabbed his coffee mug and wooden-handled umbrella and headed out the door. The lock had been broken a week and he checked it to see if maintenance had filled his order. The thumb-lock held and Cary strode swiftly to the elevator to avoid his co-workers.

Covering his head with his coat, he trotted to the Lexus. Going out in the day didn't kill him, but it did make him unbearably nauseous. He'd have to hurry.

《回》

His mind consumed with avoiding the sun, holding a man captive in his trunk, catching and then coercing Dae Kim to help him, Cary Nankin did not notice he'd left behind his briefcase.

And the transcripts he'd stuffed inside.

《回》

Dae Kim leaned over the steering wheel, feeling exposed and afraid—two emotions he hated more than the circumstances that brought them on. Scant hours ago, Beryl broke him out of the Elders' truck and set him running. The famous twin did not speak as he worked the lock, and when the flap finally slammed down, Dae Kim needed no instruction. He rolled out and ran from the house as fast as his feet would carry him. Thankfully, although he had no phone, they hadn't taken his wallet. Dae Kim ran two miles to a drugstore, got cash, a phone, and called an Uber. He then had the driver drop him at a car dealership. From there in a brand new Jeep, he scooted to a gigantic shopping mall where he bought a change of clothes and miscellaneous items to hold him over while planning his next move.

For the moment, he sat in the Amarillo mall's parking garage, gathering his wits. The sun was down and the night air filtered through his partially open window, reminding him of better times when Night was the only sky he ever saw. He hadn't heard from The Master since before Beryl released him, and he surely wasn't sorry about that. Still, deep down, a hatred had been birthed. Every passing minute in the pitch blackness, a thick animosity and craving for revenge draped his spirit like a blanket. As a Rakum, his most common emotion was satisfaction—he enjoyed his life, his brethren, even his masters, the Elders, because everyone knew what was expected of them. The new way, with Elders behaving more human than Rakum, was a load of shit that Dae Kim couldn't justify.

If Kilmeade and Canaan have rejected the Old Way, shouldn't I reject them out of principle? If they're going around helping these pitiful and whiny snowflakes instead of yanking a knot in each one as they would have before 11/13—shouldn't I resist?

Dae Kim rubbed his face hard. He had respected them—all of them—but now? The Elders obviously retained their might, yet chose to pander to a pitiful ancient religion pestering their race since Last Assembly. Dae Kim hissed loudly and slammed the steering wheel with both hands.

KNOCK! KNOCK!

The sound caused Dae Kim to startle and he jerked his face to the left. Impossibly, it was Adam Roberts's boss. Unsure what to do, Dae Kim stared back, the man's empty gaze peering through the three-inch gap in his open window. When the man said nothing for a long moment, Dae Kim parted his lips to shoo him away. Roberts's boss spoke first.

"Slide over," the boss said, his voice low and eerie in Dae Kim's ears, sounding nothing like he remembered. The hair prickled on Dae Kim's arms. Roberts's boss brought two fingers within view, waved them slowly to the right, and the electronic locks on the car clicked open. Dae Kim inhaled and leaned back.

"I said, slide over," the man warned, his voice echoing in Dae Kim's mind and ears.

Dae Kim did as commanded, awkwardly working his way over the gearshift, his unease escalating. *Dr. Cary Nankin*—the name popped into his memory. Was he empowered by the demons that used to help him and Pete? Dae Kim turned sideways to keep the man in view as he slid in behind the wheel and the doctor re-locked the doors with a thought.

"First off, stop calling upon powerless invisible beings to come to your aid. I have dispersed them for good." Nankin spoke facing the cinderblock wall through the windshield. When Dae Kim only exhaled in response, he turned his head. "Show me you have the capacity for advanced thought. If you are an imbecile, you are of no use to me."

"I don't understand..." Dae Kim replied.

Dr. Nankin considered his response, exhaled, and then looked at his fingers wrapped around the steering wheel. In a cadenced voice he replied, "You were born a Rakum. Now you're turning into a mortal. You think demons will make you a Rakum again. More than anything, you want things to go back to the way they were." The doctor turned to catch his eye. "Am I close?"

"How...?" Dae Kim shook his head. Nankin's appearance differed greatly—an aristocratic and handsome face with dark blonde eyebrows had been revealed, and no longer did his skin sheen with smelly oil, his clothing flapping loose over an obviously lean physique. More confused than ever, Dae Kim uttered, "What's going on? I thought..."

"This is how it works," the doctor replied, pacing his words. "Do as I say and I will leave you alive when we accomplish our mission."

Still in a repetitive head shake, Dae Kim asked, "What?"

Dr. Nankin smiled then, chortled deep in his chest and gave Dae Kim a wink. "It's difficult pretending to be cross with you."

His gaze softened, flooding Dae Kim with a sense of relief. *This* was a look he recognized—one he knew how to deal with. *Favor.* As a Master favoring a grunt, the nerd's boss looked like an Elder. Or something close. Dae Kim's lips parted and the doctor continued in a soft tone.

"When I saw you on my hall that first time, I knew you were a Rakum. It's not fair whatever happened to steal your birthright." Nankin spoke wistfully eyeing Dae Kim up and down. "I've been seeking the Rakum for sixty years, but you hide so well."

Dae Kim closed his mouth and swallowed. With a smooth movement, Nankin removed a pocketknife from his slacks and flicked it open. He shoved up his sleeve and put the blade to his forearm.

"Look," Nankin said and pressed until the knife slipped into his flesh.

Immediately, Dae Kim saw what the doctor meant—blackish blood—*Rakum* blood—bubbled from the circular wound.

"What the shit?" Dae Kim whispered mesmerized at the sight.

Nankin raised his arm in an offering gesture and Dae Kim touched the wrist tentatively, still watching his gaze. Dae Kim put his tongue to the ooze and drew it into his mouth. Just the one pull and the doctor casually withdrew and covered the wound with his palm.

"You're still a Rakum," Dae Kim mumbled, amazed.

"I'm something else," he said with a wink. "The blood—did it pain you?"

Dae Kim touched his middle. What had probably been less than a tablespoon of blood still coated his palate and he manipulated it with his tongue to swallow it fully. Fifteen seconds passed and a peculiar heat expanded in his gut. Dae Kim placed his palm over the area of sensation. "It's growing hot..."

Nankin reached out, untucked Dae Kim's shirt with a yank and lifted it to lay his palm in the same place. "Interesting," Nankin said with a nod, not removing his hand. "When you took Roberts's blood—did it have an effect on you?" Seemingly in scientist mode, Nankin patiently awaited Dae Kim's answer.

"How'd you know? Did you see us?" he asked incredulous.

"In good time." Nankin's forensic touch morphed into a slow caress of Dae Kim's firm abdomen. "Well? Roberts's blood. Anything?"

Watching his gaze and not the contact, Dae Kim shook his head.

"Curious," Nankin said nodding. After thoughtfully withdrawing his fingers, he fixed his gaze in Dae Kim's. "In 1937, I tried to kill one of your Elders who then marked me as a Rabbit. Your brethren never came after me and within eight years, I had become a full Rakum."

Dae Kim's eyes grew wide. *"The legend of the Lost Rabbit..."* he whispered in a faraway voice.

"Adam Roberts is not a clone. He was grown in a lab from the fertilized sperm of Elder Kilmeade and my mother, Dr. Penny Chao."

Dae Kim did not hide his utter surprise. Only the Fathers were fertile, proving Kilmeade truly was greater than any of them imagined. And Adam Roberts carried his DNA...

Nankin's right hand came up and touched Dae Kim's cheek. He broke off his topic and shook his head, his blue eyes filled with emotion. "My mother told me the Rakum were perfect, beautiful, and deadly. I look at you and I see what she meant."

Instinctively, Dae Kim moved into Nankin's palm as he would have before 11/13. "Elder Yu's blood has made you beautiful, too, Doc."

Nankin lowered his hand. "I suppose so."

"Doc," Dae Kim whispered with respect, holding Nankin's eye, "you're a scientist. Is this mission to somehow use Kilmeade and Canaan's blood to increase your power?"

Nankin grinned. "I knew you would be smart." He reached across and conformed his palm to Dae Kim's near thigh.

Dae Kim glanced down reflexively and resumed eye contact. "I've been unnerved by recent events, but I'm extremely useful in many ways. I will help you; you only have to tell me what you need."

"Fantastic," the doctor replied. "I have the perfect plan to subdue the Elders. Their blood will restore you and empower me, I know it. I will help you reclaim what was stolen."

"I'm in, Master," Dae Kim said without thinking. "I will do anything to be a Rakum again. The Elders are dead to me. I want to go back."

"And you will. You will be restored." Nankin squeezed his leg. "But don't call me master; it doesn't feel right. Call me Cary, or Doc, or even Doctor Nankin, okay?"

Dae Kim agreed but had no doubt the man before him, Lost Rabbit or not, was his superior and more Rakum than the two Elders in his sights.

"Shall we proceed?"

"Your will is my will," Dae Kim answered in the Old Way and listened to the doctor's plan. Very soon, they would put it in motion and Dae Kim rejoiced. The demons that haunted and abused him were truly gone and the Lost Rabbit was going to right the wrongs in his life.

And oh, Dae Kim was thankful.

《回》

"Ready to see my catch?" Cary asked gearing to proceed. The mall garage had been deserted since they began their chat and it was time to reveal to the Rakum the other half of his plan.

"Sounds like it's a person," Dae Kim said and locked his new Jeep. They would leave it for now and the Rakum was about to learn why a sedan would work better on their long trip.

"Sort of," Cary said and after a last scan for strangers, he lifted the lid. "You know Adam Roberts."

"*Oh, shit,*" Dae Kim hissed as he locked eyes with Cary's acquisition. "Hey, handsome," Dae Kim said as Adam's gaze darted between the two of them, the thick cloth gag in his mouth preventing complaint. He reached in to touch Adam's cheek, scrubby with a three-day beard. "He and I killed a man in your building two months ago."

"I know," Cary said with a sly grin.

"Oh..." Dae Kim responded. "Can I pull him out?"

Cary nodded. "Do it."

Dae Kim yanked the man out of the trunk, exhibiting more strength than Cary expected, and propped Adam against the rear quarter panel. With a small noise, he scraped at the man's chin with his thumbnail.

"Is this your blood, Doc?"

Cary nodded. "I had to force-feed him. Didn't do anything except make him angry," he finished with a chuckle.

"Did you tap him? *Er,* take his blood?" Dae Kim asked and Cary shook his head. "Do it. If Elder Yu's blood infiltrated your system, adding Kilmeade's blood—even diluted in this kid—should make you stronger. Do the experiment on yourself."

Cary grinned, approving of Dae Kim's attitude. "In good time."

"Did you know Pete and I nabbed him a month ago?" Dae Kim asked, his eyes on their prize. "The Elders rescued him before we finished our interrogation."

Cary nodded. "Yes, and I'm happy to give you another shot."

"You know a lot," Dae Kim said, obviously impressed. He guarded his lips from Adam and whispered, "My specialty is *interrogation*...trained by the best." He wiggled his eyebrows. "Do I have permission to do whatever it takes?"

Cary read the guy's gaze and nodded slowly. "Yes, but I want him to join our cause. Make him see our perspective."

"Your will is my will," Dae Kim replied easily and turned back to Adam, stepping into his space. "Now, where were we?"

Adam made a few attempts to speak into his gag and Dae Kim touched the fabric, asking permission to remove it. Cary nodded.

"Doctor Nankin..." Adam coughed the words. "These Elders..." Adam cleared his throat. "They're unstoppable."

"Get him in the back," Cary said.

Dae Kim jerked Adam to the door and shoved him into the backseat. Still bound and hobbled, he flailed clumsily into a sitting position and Dae Kim slid in beside him.

"Talk to him. We need to get on the road," Cary instructed and pressed the ignition. They had eight hours of night remaining and a sixteen-hour drive to Los Angeles. Cary would be the worst off in the sun, but if Roberts got on board, they'd have three drivers.

"Yes, sir," Dae Kim replied and opened a half-finished bottle of water. "Here," he said to Adam who allowed him to dribble a swig into his mouth. "I'm not untying you until we know where your head is. Now, say what you wanted to say."

"Kilmeade and Canaan, you can't stop them," Adam sputtered and asked for more water. Once he'd had another slurp, he took a deep breath. "You can let me go. I'm nothing to them and I'm no good to you. I'm mortal—they ran all the tests, the *Rakum* tests."

"They didn't run *my* tests," Cary said from the driver's seat.

"I have no exceptional powers, I lost my special sight," Adam said hurriedly. "They erased a lot of my memory, too."

"Doesn't matter," Dae Kim said and moistened the cuff of his own sleeve to again, swab Adam's chin. After a moment, he jerked a napkin from a discarded food bag, poured water on it, and scrubbed Adam's cheeks and chin with vigor. "You're made of Kilmeade. That's enough."

"But he said I'm mortal... Please, let me go..."

"Roberts, I will say this only once," Cary called from the front, his tone terse. "Do not ask to be released. I have a plan and I will not deviate from it. Ask again and I will hurt you. *Badly.*"

Adam pressed his lips together and stopped speaking.

《回》

Dae Kim finished cleaning Adam's face and whistled his approval. "Damn, you look good. If you brushed your teeth and combed your hair you'd be ready for your first day of school," he said patting the top of his head. Then he scooted forward to speak between the front seats. "Doc, I don't know how well you're situated, but I have money. Tons of it. If it can help us reclaim our power, just say the word."

"Twenty million dollars," Cary said nodding. "I know and yes, that will be helpful. If Roberts signs on, he has recently inherited a fortune."

Dae Kim looked at Adam. "He'll sign on. He's already in love with me." Dae Kim winked. "Are you all comfy?"

"Can you untie my hands?" Adam asked as he shifted his weight and grimaced, his wrists bound behind him.

"Does it hurt?" Dae Kim asked with false sincerity.

"They're really burning now, please..."

"This is pitiful," Dae Kim said shaking his head. "You're definitely no

Rakum. A Rakum never complains about pain. Did you know that?"

"I just need them loosed—maybe you could tie them in front?" Adam shifted again lifting his hips a few inches before resettling.

"Let's have a lesson, shall we?" Dae Kim spun to his left and crawled in front of Adam until he straddled his lap on his knees. "Lesson one," he began and ran his hands into Adam's hair on either side of his head. "No complaining. *Ever.* What happened when you complained around Canaan or Kilmeade?"

Adam moved back, shaking his head to dislodge Dae Kim's fingers from his scalp.

Dae Kim's response was to bring one hand down and violently punch Adam in the solar plexus. Adam cried out and worked to breathe.

"You just jumped to Lesson Two. *No resisting your superiors,*" Dae Kim whispered and up front, the doctor snickered. Dae Kim grinned. "The Doc is my boss and I'm your boss. Nod if you understand?"

"Please," Adam muttered and then nodded when Dae Kim pretended to prepare another blow.

"Now, back to Lesson One," he said and returned his fingers to massaging Adam's scalp under his long hair. "Did you complain in front of the Elders?"

"Kilmeade ...wouldn't hear it," Adam said with effort, still hurting from the gut punch. "Canaan made fun of me..."

"Yep. Sounds right." Dae Kim brought his hands to rest on Adam's shoulders and looked into his face. "Rakum don't complain because for nearly twenty years, our superiors tear us down daily, physically and mentally, so every time we heal, we're stronger and more able to survive the next day."

"First Ritual," Adam gasped, still not quite recovered.

"That's right—First Ritual..."

"The Elders believed Adam would be a Rakum today if he'd been raised by your people," Doctor Cary said from the front. Dae Kim's eyebrows went up and he smiled.

"That's encouraging," Dae Kim responded and considered Adam's expression. "Are you going to complain anymore?"

"No," Adam said and shook his head.

"Nice. That makes me glad. You are a joy to observe, but when you open that beautiful mouth to whine, it ruins everything." Dae Kim paused a few seconds and Adam still breathed raggedly. "I have lots of ideas of what you can do with that mouth instead..." Dae Kim didn't grin, but it was hilarious how terrified the kid's eyes grew. In the front seat, the doctor made a noise of impatience.

Dae Kim chuckled; Adam had no pain threshold, which Dae Kim found funny. "So, you have don't complain and don't resist. Lesson Three is one you *do*, it's *pro*-active. Three is *submit*. Do you know how to submit?"

"Please don't punch me again," he whispered in lieu of a reply.

Dae Kim rolled his eyes and delivered precisely the same blow to his gut as before. This time, he pressed Adam's shoulders into the seatback so he couldn't recoil into the pain. A fat tear squeezed out of his left eye and Dae Kim swiped it off with his finger to put on his tongue.

"The tears of Kilmeade's mini-me are delicious," he said with humor, recalling Canaan's affectation for the guy.

Doctor Cary made a quiet sound of amusement. The doctor hadn't been raised among the Rakum so Dae Kim figured he would listen and get pointers without having to reveal any shortcomings. It was the least Dae Kim could do for the man who had already proven he, aside from the Elders, was the last intact Rakum on the planet.

His cheeks red with exertion, Adam's breath heaved and slowly normalized.

"Adam," Dae Kim said lowering his chin to give Adam an adoring look, "it's necessary to hurt you so you'll think before you act. Is it working?"

"Yes, yes," Adam said between gasps.

Dae Kim settled his weight fully onto Adam's lap and crossed his arms. "You've had it pretty easy, haven't you? Have you ever been abused? Have you ever been in a fight?"

"No," Adam said without hesitation.

"So when Pete and I held back questioning you, you were pretty stoked, eh?" Adam didn't answer, reading Dae Kim's gaze for a hint of the correct response. "I'm asking," Dae Kim asserted. "What ran through your head when Pete and I worked you over?"

"I... I thought your master was making you go easy on me," he answered in a hesitant voice.

Dae Kim nodded. "You're right." Taking his time, Dae Kim resituated his straddle and placed both palms flat against Adam's upper chest. "The doc said I can proceed with the interrogation *my* way, and I'm a professional. You ready to continue?" Adam nodded with wide eyes. "The doc says you spent a ton of quality time with Beryl. Tell me about that."

"He likes me and has a lot of interesting stories," Adam said in a rush, afraid to say the wrong thing, which was a sure sign of success.

"What did he tell you about me?"

Adam opened his mouth and paused as his cheeks pinked. Dae Kim grinned.

"He's blushing, Doc," Dae Kim called without looking away from Adam. "So Beryl *did* talk about me. Tell the doc what he said."

"He said you guys hung out together in New York a long time ago," Adam answered, each phrase halting as he hoped it didn't inspire Dae Kim's anger. "He said you liked sex. He said you had more sex than any Rakum they knew..."

Dae Kim laughed out loud and nodded his head. "He's right—and I did," he agreed and laughed again. "I matured early. Since my thirties, I never went without my release. Speaking of sex..." Dae Kim paused because he enjoyed the wide-eyed trepidation that reached Adam's face at the subject. When he'd waited long enough, he rubbed Adam's upper chest with one open hand. "Are you a virgin?"

Adam shook his head without offering any information.

Still massaging his pecs because it made the man squirm, Dae Kim sent him a knowing smile. "Okay. So you're not a virgin." He allowed his fingers to run up to the man's throat on both sides. "I can see that you're straight, you know. You are, right?"

Adam nodded, barely tolerating Dae Kim's roaming hands.

"The problem with humans is that they feel they need to categorize sexuality. Here's your next lesson—there is no gay or straight with Rakum. Do you have a theory why that is?"

Adam briefly closed his eyes and reopened them as Dae Kim's hands returned to massage his pecs. "Because it's about pleasure."

"Very good! You read that in the Rabbit book, didn't you?"

Adam nodded.

"Do you think I'm gay or straight?" Dae Kim asked and Adam answered without forethought.

"You're a Rakum, you're neither."

Dae Kim smiled. "Kissing up is good. Really, really good. We love that. Did you service those Elders?" Dae Kim asked and loved the look of horror that crossed the youngster's face at the question. "Well? Elders do what they want to do," Dae Kim said laughing and Adam remained ashen-faced. "Kilmeade's the one to look out for." Dae Kim lowered his chin and waited for Adam to meet his gaze. When he did, he looked horrified. "Kilmeade was always *very* affectionate."

"No, *nothing* like that happened. Not even close," Adam said jerkily.

"Then you dodged a bullet." Dae Kim paused, enjoying Adam's miserable expression. "Doc, this kid is hilarious."

"Untie him," the doctor said then from the front.

"Yes, Master," Dae Kim said stressing the second word for Adam. "See? Everyone has a master. For now, you can call me master." Dae Kim fell into Adam, chest to chest, to reach behind him and pull apart the tape at his wrists. "It's an excellent system. A zillion times better than any mortal governing system," he said as he finished, his mouth against Adam's ear. Making sure the man would feel it, he took a deep breath against Adam's throat before coming upright in his lap again.

"You need a shower," Dae Kim told him and climbed off to the guy's right to undo his ankles.

"I'll get one as soon as I can," Adam said in a monotone.

"I can't speak for the doc, but I'm a neat-freak," Dae Kim said as he popped the tape at his ankles free.

"Find out about the letter," the doc said from up front.

"Spill it." Dae Kim did not return to Adam's lap, but faced him by sitting on one leg in the middle of the bench, close enough to touch, gently or with violence—whichever might be needed.

Adam inhaled before beginning, his eyes red from stress. "When Dr. Roberts died, his lawyer gave me a package. Inside were a few trinkets from my childhood and three sheets of old paper." Adam wet his lips and Dae Kim handed him the last of the bottled water. "The first two sheets were notes about the special cells taken from Subject A—who I now know is Kilmeade. The third page is a handwritten letter from the Rakum Dr. Roberts served, addressed to Elder Kilmeade."

"Ahhh, so that's why you recognized his name when I first came to see you at your lab," Dae Kim surmised. Adam nodded.

"I couldn't read the language of the text, but his name was in English. Later, the Elders told me the letter was from another Elder named Bel who was supposed to destroy the cells and he didn't. That's all I know. Honest."

"What do you know about the woman scientist?" the doc asked.

"Only that she was a pioneer in the field."

"Learn this, Roberts," Doctor Cary continued, looking at the kid in the rearview mirror. "That woman was Dr. Penny Chao, my mother. Dr. Roberts's grandfather raped my mother. Kilmeade then sent her to China where I was born nine months later." Doctor Cary allowed the information to sink in and Dae Kim's mind raced.

"What?" Adam's voice grew softer. "But you're... You're not a hundred years old..."

"One hundred and seventeen," the doctor said. "Kilmeade did my mother no favors by giving her to another Elder. In Beijing and then in Nanking, Elder Yu abused both of us viciously, in any way he could think of. When I was thirty-seven, he raped my young wife—after which she died. She had been pregnant with my first born."

"Shit," Dae Kim whispered and looked to the rearview mirror to commiserate with the doctor.

"I tried to kill him so he marked me as a Rabbit," Doctor Cary said and paused. "Do you know what a Rabbit is, Roberts?"

"Yes," Adam said softly and then again in a normal voice.

"For eight years, my mother made sure I transformed into a Rakum, so one day I could take revenge on Kilmeade and Yu."

Dae Kim touched Adam's knee. "That means you and Doctor Cary have the same mother. You're half-brothers!" Dae Kim grinned when Adam only paled at the assertion. "Oh, boy, what a great family we have going here, Doc!"

Up front, the doctor nodded and the subject seemed closed. Dae Kim leaned back and fiddled with his phone, pulling up the map and judging how far they'd gone. In another four hours, the sun would hit the horizon and he'd take over the driving. He popped in his earbuds and started his favorite playlist. In his peripheral vision, Adam looked straight ahead with a blank stare. Dae Kim reached over and rested his hand on Adam's thigh. Until he fell in line, it was best to keep him jumpy.

38, July 16

"Adam isn't our bait," Doctor Cary said as they noshed a quick bite before returning to the road. "The Elders won't sacrifice their lives for him."

Adam had been returned to the trunk and instructed to remain quiet. They'd feed him when they were underway. For now, the rest area picnic table at dawn served just fine.

"No, Adam is for me, *for us,*" Doctor Cary quickly qualified. He finished his burger and wiped his chin. "When I came to the States, I went directly to Dr. Roberts. I watched him. I was his supervisor for twenty years; I knew what he was doing at all times."

"You hid from us very well," Dae Kim said sincerely. "All those years and none of the brethren sniffed you out?"

The doc shook his head. "I don't think I was a Rabbit by the time I moved here. And I wore disguises. My mother taught me about the Rakum's special sight, your nose, your telepathy."

"That weird smell..." Dae Kim whispered. "Your skin..."

The doc grinned. "I trained my mind, too. A Rakum Father could have come across me and not known I was different. I beat them. For decades."

"And you saw Adam brought to life?"

"No, by then, I had taken another job in a competing lab in order to perpetuate my identity as a Nankin son. I monitored Roberts from afar until 2000." Doctor Cary stood and stretched. "I went to work for Baylor-Dallas, and when Adam was old enough, I hired him at twice what his father was paying. He has worked for me ever since."

"*Shiiiiiit...*" Dae Kim shook his head. "Seventeen years, seeing this kid every day knowing he was spawned by the Elder responsible for the death of your family..."

"More than that. Every single time I laid eyes on him, I was reminded of my mother's brutal assault and the two Elders who disregarded her life. My hate has been well fed."

"You managed that hate like an Elder," Dae offered with a wry grin and added wistfully, "If Beryl knew we held Adam against his will, he'd try to rescue him."

Doctor Cary smiled. "Beryl is the one we need to grab. Your Elder Canaan is especially fond of him."

"They have history," Dae Kim said leaning forward. "Messing with Beryl is gonna be too much fun."

"I gather he was your superior."

Dae Kim nodded with a tight grin. "He and his twin brother were captains by the time we hung out." Dae Kim shrugged one shoulder.

Doctor Cary nodded. "The Elders favor the other one even more, but he's harder to get to. Javier—did you know him?" Dae Kim shook his head. "No matter. On this mission, if you see Javier before he sees you, hide. We do not want to engage him."

"You got it. May I ask why?"

Cary tucked his garbage in the paper sack. "For now, just trust me—we don't want to come against him. Maybe I can explain in more detail when you better understand the god I serve." Cary watched Dae Kim's eyes and he nodded without worry.

It would do no good to try to explain his religion and be of even less benefit to teach Dae to seek advice from Shangti. The Rakum took him at his word, and that was enough. Early on, his god had made it perfectly clear: avoid Javier D'Millier and Beth Rider-Stone at all costs. And Cary did, no questions asked.

《回》

"It's three hours to Los Angeles and you haven't convinced the doc you're on board," Dae Kim told Adam, referring to his taped wrists and ankles. "But at least you're riding up here and not in the trunk."

"This is much better," Adam agreed in what sounded to Dae Kim like a normal voice. "Am I allowed to know the plan?"

Dae Kim gave him a quick look to gauge his expression. He seemed sincere, but how could Dae Kim know for sure? Without his Rakum mental gifts, seeing into his mind was so far impossible.

"I reckon when the doc wants you to know something, he'll tell you." Dae Kim shot Adam a grin. "Hey, you know back then when I was teasing you about servicing the Elders?"

"Yeah," Adam replied almost inaudibly and again Dae Kim relished the shift in expressions. The man loved his body and feared more than anything that someone might abuse it.

"I wouldn't assault you. That's never been my thing. But it made you listen, didn't it? I mean, I *could* do it—I have the strength, the equipment, and the know-how," he said and grinned. "But I sincerely hope you'll submit and join us."

Adam made a small noise and looked out the windshield into the afternoon sun. The light didn't burn any of them; privately, Doctor Cary warned Dae Kim that when the sun sat at its zenith, he might slip into unconsciousness. Dae Kim swore to protect him if that occurred, but for now, he lay in the backseat and quietly tolerated the side effects.

After another minute of silence, Dae Kim tried again to suss out the kid's thoughts. "Doctor Cary's plan will work and both of you are geniuses." Dae Kim brought his palm to his chest. "Add me, a real Rakum, who brings that knowledge as we move forward. Think about it—Doctor Cary's spiritual aid combined with the Elders' blood, all three of us will enjoy the powerful lives we deserve."

Adam made an agreeing sound, but his gaze remained far away.

"Adam, before the Elders burst your bubble, didn't you want to be more? To discover and fulfill your destiny?" Adam only shrugged. "What did you think growing up? When Dr. Roberts fed you *blood*? When you watched Elder Bel suck his arm?" Dae Kim chortled. "What in the world did little Adam think he was?"

Adam huffed. "Our work was secret, he kept me secluded. I mean, I had fun. I had friends, toys, free time." Adam took a deep breath. "He told me I was special, different—*better*. And I had proof. I was smarter and stronger than the other kids. I had telekinetic powers. I knew there was a piece of the puzzle missing and I felt it had to do with Bel."

"You thought he was a vampire?" Dae Kim guessed.

"What else could he be? I never knew about Kilmeade and his 100-year-old science project. I thought maybe I was related to Bel and Dr. Roberts wanted me to turn into a vampire." Adam made a sad sound and shook his head. "I wanted to be special like Bel."

"Adam, take my word for it—you're much, much, much *more* than Elder Bel ever was." Dae Kim paused while Adam gathered his emotions. "Your seed donor sat just under the Fathers in power and might. *You* are a *copy* of the Rakum's greatest Elder. That's huge. In truth, you're every bit a Rakum as I am and could become stronger than us all."

Adam squeezed his eyes closed and lowered his chin. "I've wanted to believe that ever since I saw the letter." Adam swallowed hard. "I knew I was more than the man I saw in the mirror, but when I read those notes of my origins, I wanted to be like Kilmeade."

"You must have felt like a giant trapped in a tiny cage."

"Yes," Adam said with a nod and a glint in his eye. "And because of that, the Elders told me I was delusional."

"Of course, they did. They don't want you to reach your potential. Work with me and the doctor to get that power for the three of us. You like me, right? Basically? If I didn't threaten to hurt you now and then?" Dae Kim said with humor.

Adam cracked a smile and Dae Kim nodded.

"I like you a lot and I see your potential. I want to be there when you fulfill it. I want us to be brothers."

Adam's gaze fell to his hands tied in his lap. "Can I speak plainly?" Adam looked over, his eyes saying, *please don't hit me if you don't like what I say.* Dae Kim shrugged. "I *like* the idea of drawing power from my Rakum DNA, and I know Dr. Nankin is a brilliant scientist." Adam carefully chose his next words. "What I don't want to do is hurt Beryl or Javier."

"That is not up to me. I'm a killer, I'm good at it. Been killing mortals since I was eight," Dae Kim began. "But I won't do anything the doc doesn't order. That I can promise."

"Adam, Dae," Doctor Cary said from the back, his voice muffled by the jacket over his face. "I don't want to kill them. We will do our best to leave them alive."

"Okay," Adam whispered still looking at his lap.

Dae Kim had an idea. "Doc, can I pull off? I'll untie Adam and we can all stretch and take a piss. Then it's forty-five minutes to San Bernadino and a hot shower."

"I'm in no condition to chase him down if he runs."

Dae Kim chuckled throwing in an evil edge to cement the idea in Adam's mind. "He won't run, because I'll catch him. Then I'll be mad and hurt his beautiful body."

Adam looked out his window. "I'm not running. I agree with you and Dr. Nankin—I'm supposed to be more than this."

Dae Kim listened to him swallow and he seemed about to add more. When he did, it was with a stronger voice.

"I am supposed to be great like my father, even if he hates me."

Dae Kim disagreed with a low chuckle. "Understand this," Dae Kim said, his voice gentle. "You're thinking like a human. Kilmeade's emotion regarding you is *apathy*. In no shape or form does he think he's your father. To Elder Kilmeade, you're a science project that talks."

Adam regarded him blankly.

"That means you can't get all weepy and whiny, *my daddy doesn't love me,* all that shit. Got it?" Dae Kim watched his eyes for understanding.

"Roberts, listen to Dae," Dr. Cary said from the backseat. "He will teach us how to be Rakum, how to think the way he thinks and see the world the way he does. You and I are brothers already and we will learn this together."

Adam nodded with a semblance of conviction.

"Once I get us settled into the hotel, I'll get you a phone," Dae Kim said and noted a rest area sign. "The doc will need you to contact Beryl. We'll tell you what to say. Then we'll catch us some Elders."

Adam agreed and rubbed his face with the tape that bound his wrists. Dae Kim grinned and steered them onto the off-ramp. The most beautiful of the Rakum would soon be their captive and then they would nab the last two Elders and hammer them into submission. It was going to be a very great night.

《回》

The Residence Inn was the best hotel San Bernadino could offer, but it was no Waldorf Astoria. Dae Kim settled the doctor in one of the beds and closed the light-blocking double curtains. Next, he sent Adam into the shower with a pair of borrowed boxers, jeans, and clean shirt. Aware they were traveling, Dae Kim and Cary had changes of clothing, but Adam's were foul having not been changed since he was picked off the curb after a night of binge-drinking. He and Dae Kim were nearly the same height and appeared to have the same build. If nothing else, it was close enough so the man would no longer be rank. When a moment of quiet arose, Dae Kim sank onto the stiff couch in the dark and opened a browser on his phone.

Since Pete introduced him to the more obscure tabs on the Rakum website, he knew where to find the various chatroom topic threads his brethren initiated. Each entry was written in Rakum Hungarian to protect content, which Dae Kim found silly since only those with intimate knowledge of Rakum heritage could get past the Home page. What mortal could know a Rakum's name, his Elder, Father, and favorite stage of First Ritual? Dae Kim sighed with chagrin as he trolled the Los Angeles Area chatroom entries. The opening lines were simultaneously tragic and hilarious.

"Don't laugh, I sell flowers on Burbank..."

"I think there's a Father on the fourth floor..."
"Did anyone get a pet? Need advice..."
"Shit, I think I'm getting fat..."
"Has anyone seen the Elders?"

"We are all better off dead..." Dae Kim opened that one and skimmed for the Rakum's location. Ritz-Carlton, downtown L.A. *Perfect.* Dae Kim clicked the guy's profile and didn't recognize his name. Still, it was time to make contact. Any Rakum who thought it was better to be dead was one the Elders would try to save. Dae Kim punched in the guy's number and hit send. By no surprise, Mr. Depressed didn't pick up, but Dae Kim gave him a prepared message for his voicemail.

"*Kazak*, Bryson. My life is shit every day AND IT SUCKS!" he shouted. "No matter how much money they throw at us we're getting a raw deal. I'm not telling those guys on the site, but I know where the Elders are. And in case you're wondering, it's Kilmeade and Canaan—no shit. And I saw them; they're perfect—completely unchanged. Think about it..." For drama Dae Kim lowered his voice to a whisper. *"Vajon segíthet-e nekünk az idősek vére?*[19] Call me back. I'm coming into L.A. *Hurry."*

Dae Kim grinned and leaned into the couch, draping an arm to either side. Adam exited the bathroom wearing his extra clothes.

"Perfect fit—we're twins," Dae Kim said with a grin.

Adam scrubbed his long hair with a hand towel and looked down at his shirtfront. "Thanks for the loan," he said with a quiet smile and gestured to the phone sitting on Dae Kim's thigh. "Anything new?"

Dae Kim considered what he and the doctor were sharing and what they held back. Finally, he offered a tiny bone. "Figured I could find the Elders' next target by surfing our chatrooms. I'll see if he calls me back."

"Huh," Adam said with a nod, finished with the towel and tossed it back into the bathroom from where he stood. The lamps were off, but the ambient light from the small fridge inset gave the both of them enough illumination to navigate the room.

Dae Kim watched the kid drop into the armchair, his brilliant mind probably working more than his expressionless face revealed. *Or is it?* The guy was joining up, changing sides; Dae Kim had worked over enough mortals in his day to recognize a compliant personality type. Kilmeade's doppelgänger had morphed from victim to co-conspirator in a few short hours, with practically zero negative stimuli applied. With an internal

---

[19] "What if the blood of the Elders made us whole again?"

humph, Dae Kim remembered his favorite Rakum tenet—*easier is better*—and focused on the present.

"Adam, clear this up for me. You were working nights because of the sun. What was your sun sensitivity about?"

"Before I met Javier and Beryl, I had a supply of human blood that I drank on a schedule. As far back as I can remember, the sunlight made me nauseous—like the doctor. But Javier convinced me to stop."

"And now?"

"I lost weight, started feeling crappy and the sun barely bothers me."

"We need to get you some blood," Dae Kim said with a nod. "If the doc says it's okay, you can take blood off me. I don't mind."

Adam tightened his jaw.

"You've become squeamish since you met my goodie-goodie brethren," Dae Kim said. "Twenty-seven years drinking blood, seeing the benefits, and then two guys you'd never met convince you to stop?"

Adam cracked a grin. "You are very good at summing things up."

"I'm really smart," Dae Kim said and winked, more convinced of his new buddy's malleable nature.

Adam's gaze grew soft. "That night you guys came to kill me—seems like a million years ago. My life is completely turned around since then. I wonder what would have happened if you had come to *meet* me first. Tried to get me to come with you *before* you tried to kill me. I wish I knew what compelled you to kill me in the first place."

Dae Kim rolled his eyes. "You think *your* life got turned upside down... Imagine what it was like for me. *For us.* Go to sleep a prince and wake up a friggin' toad. That's a bitter pill at my age, my friend." Dae Kim shook his head. "That thing with Pete was a mistake."

Adam looked aside during Dae Kim's humble moment. Adam had been present when Canaan zapped him to sleep both times so Dae Kim dropped the topic. Adam had also heard the Elder accuse him of accepting demonic possession in exchange for a promise of power. Dae Kim hoped now, he'd finally backed the right horse.

"Dae, get Adam a phone and bring us back some dinner," Doctor Cary said in a quiet tone from the closest of the two king beds. "I want a ribeye, rare with all the fixings. And hurry back."

"I will do it," Dae Kim said and stood. To Adam, he said, "He doesn't like being called master. I don't either, not by a brother." Dae Kim shrugged. "You can guess why I put you through all that shit, right?" Adam nodded. "We respect one another, we know Doctor Cary's in charge, and everyone's happy." Dae Kim waited for Adam to agree and he turned to collect his wallet. At that moment, his phone rang with a new call. One glance at the screen and he gave Adam a thumbs-up.

"*Kazak,* Dae Kim. Elder Dawn's pack, right?"

The voice of his suicidal brother was monotone and lifeless. Dae Kim didn't recall the guy and he cursed his transformation. He played along and answered, mimicking Bryson's intonation. "Yeah, what an asshole. But at least he died a true Rakum, not like this shit we have to put up with."

"Got that right. I'm pretty much done. You probably won't get much out of meeting me..."

"I was serious about those two Elders. You've got to see them—exactly like they were before. They aren't even touched. That's gotta mean something, doesn't it? It can't be an accident..."

Bryson was quiet a moment then exhaled. "Elder Canaan liked to knock me around until I passed out. I was with Elder Roman, but at Assembly, he liked to leave us off to be babysat by that grinning shit."

Dae Kim chuckled. "He's still grinning. Give me your room number. I can be there..." Dae Kim looked over to the doc who held up his fingers. "I can be there at ten."

"Whatever. I'll be here."

"Bryson, look," Dae Kim said now more animated. "I was in Texas last week and a brother said Elder Kilmeade helped him get away from the police and directed him to the website."

"The Elder's helping us?"

"This guy said he is." Dae Kim paused. "Anyway, if they contact you before I see you, will you text or call me? I'd owe you. Big time."

"They won't call me," Bryson mumbled. "And just come on in when you get there. I'll leave my door cracked. Maybe someone will come in and end me for my iPhone," he said with a low chuckle.

"How about I slap you around a little when I get there?"

"Huh, okay. That's something," Bryson said and hung up. Dae Kim sighed and fluttered his eyebrows at Adam.

"Excellent, Dae," the doc said, his face still covered by a pillow. "Get my dinner."

Dae Kim grinned and headed for the door. When Adam reached him he clapped his shoulder. "This is going to be fun." When Adam smiled back, Dae Kim really believed it was true.

《▣》

"Look who it is," Simon said with mock surprise as he opened the door. He ushered Beryl into his hotel room fresh from the shower, evident by his still-dripping hair.

"What have you been up to that you have to shower before I get here?" Beryl asked with humor, feeling lighter as soon as Simon said hello. He pretended to peer into the bedroom across the large space. "Entertaining a lady?"

"Not on your life," Simon said with a laugh. "Lisa-Marie would punch my lights out." Simon handed Beryl a beer. "Hang on."

"Take your time," Beryl said as Simon shuffled to the bathroom. He returned after toweling his hair. He combed it with his fingers and exhaled as he stopped in front of Beryl.

"It was a day of meetings," he said and gestured for the sofa. Beryl dropped down and Simon took the soft armchair catty-corner. "Boring shit, I won't go into it." Simon held up his beer. "To friends who've never had a sports agent!"

"To friends who've not lived a hundred years!" Beryl said with a half-grin, feeling punchy and relieved the longer he sat there. Knowing their truck had been bugged for however long by whomever worried him the past two hours. Simon would make him laugh, which he needed before joining the others in California.

"Hear-hear!" Simon agreed and swigged his beer. After a quiet sigh, he yawned and stretched out his legs. "So, you're off to La-la-Land to save the world."

"Yeah," Beryl said with a wry grin.

"You look like a man with a lot on his mind. Tell me about it."

Beryl exhaled and sunk deeper in the couch, stretching his legs out as Simon had already. Beryl redirected. "What did you think of Adam?"

Simon rolled his eyes. "He's okay."

"You didn't like him," Beryl asserted.

"No, he's fine. Just..." Simon sipped his beer. "No, I don't like him," he said and giggled.

"How much have you had to drink?" Beryl asked, only just noticing his behavior.

"Oh," Simon said and looked around the room, "since lunch?"

"Oh, geez, okay." Beryl got to his feet. "Let me catch up." He crossed to the minibar and grabbed three mini vodkas.

"That's my man!" Simon said.

Beryl poured two minis into the remainder of his beer. "Okay, so

Adam. What's wrong with him?"

Simon shook his head. "I'm not the right person to ask. Be serious. Ask a Rakum, not a Cow." Simon grinned at himself. *"Rakum Cow,"* he mumbled and laughed.

"Why?" Beryl sipped his beer only to twist his face at the taste.

Simon slapped his eyes with one hand and drew his palm slowly downward. "Your friend Adam looks hungry, okay? He's hungry and I can't say it any better than that. I think Adam would eat me. Like food. Don't laugh."

Beryl didn't. He furrowed his brow and considered Simon's words. "Does he look hungry like a Rakum?"

Simon pondered, his eyes roaming the room again and then he shook his head. "No, I recall the Rakum hunger fairly well, thank you." Beryl opened his mouth and Simon held up his hand. "Present company excluded for the purposes of this conversation."

"Thank you," Beryl said and finished off his beer concoction with a disgusted snort.

"But his hunger is not for blood." Simon drew in his legs and leaned forward. "Adam looks like he wants to *consume* me. And you, too, for that matter. He wouldn't be satisfied with blood. Adam wants our *essence.* To *be* us."

Beryl shook his head. "I don't understand what you're saying." Adam was only part Rakum; what would make him appear so carnivorous? "Maybe the Elders would know what all that means."

"I can tell you one thing it means," Simon said and waited for Beryl to meet his eye. "It means *caution.* Don't trust him. Be careful. He looks unstable. That's all I have."

"But he only just found out what he is," Beryl said, deflating. He liked Adam quite a lot.

Simon reached out and touched Beryl's back. "Just watch out." Beryl nodded deep in thought. Simon withdrew his hand and finished his beer. "Call me when ya'll finish up. I'll fly out to L.A. We'll do a guy-trip. Bring Javier, but leave Canaan." Simon chuckled at the end and shook his head.

Beryl regarded him sideways. "You don't like my buddy Canaan, either?"

Simon shrugged. "Face it—he helped me that night in Stu's hotel room for Javier's sake. He and I are *not* friends."

"You took up for him with Adam."

"Only because Adam's an outsider." Simon held up his empty beer

327

can. "But between you and me? Canaan is a bully. An insidious jerk."

"He saved your life," Beryl replied watching the man's face. Isaac ripped open Simon's throat during the climax of their battle last November. If the Elder hadn't been there... "I don't think it did it for Javier that time."

"Did he do it for you?" Simon asked softly. "Did I hear you shouting, 'sew him up! sew him up!'?"

Beryl shrugged one shoulder.

"I'm grateful. I like being alive," Simon said sounding a little more whiny than before. "But I don't like Canaan. You guys don't seem to mind it, but from a human perspective—he's simply *too mean.*"

Beryl released an unexpected laugh and covered his mouth. Leaning back, he turned his shoulder to keep Simon next to him in view. "You have no idea what mean is, Simon," he said with a grin. "Okay, yes, he might appear mean to a human." Beryl still thought it was funny considering how gentle the man was compared to the rest of them.

"I wish you'd tell me what's so funny," Simon said a half-grin teasing his mouth. "It sounds like you're saying Canaan's the sweet one."

Beryl nodded. "Trust me, he is. He is the kitten of Elders, if that gives you any idea of their natures."

Simon's eyes fluttered closed and he shook his head. "How you ever stood it, I'll never know."

"Mortals *can't* know," Beryl replied, still grinning. "Was Elder Roman nice to you when you met?"

"Hah!" Simon chortled and turned sideways sitting upon one leg. "He loathed me from the get. I guess he still does." Simon chuckled as he thought back and he met Beryl's eye. "I was young, stupid, and mouthy; I can assure you that he wanted to kill me more than once."

"It wasn't all you," Beryl said laughing. "Roman had a reputation for being short-tempered with Cows."

Simon pointed to his chest with a wink.

"Back to how mean Elders are; name another that you knew."

"Just Roman," Simon said and then absently chewed his bottom lip. "I met Canaan that night you attacked me in Stu's hotel room."

"Attacked you?" Beryl repeated with a half grin and leaned back to no longer see Simon's face. "Attacked... that sounds funny now."

"I guess it would," Simon said looking to the side.

"And that night—I wasn't being *mean*; just determined. One hundred and seventeen years... I was accustomed to having my way with mortals," he finished with a chuckle. Simon didn't say anything and Beryl swiveled his head to the right. "You okay?"

"Yeah," Simon said his mood suddenly somber. He turned to lean back and face front as Beryl had. "I don't think we should reflect on those days."

"Is it embarrassing? Didn't we establish we're not to blame for our old behavior?" Simon didn't reply and Beryl sighed. "You haven't truly let it go, then."

Simon stood and walked to the mini-fridge. After he grabbed a bottle of water he sighed. "I thought I had."

Beryl stood to walk to where Simon leaned against the wall. "Does it make you regret the way things turned out?"

Simon shrugged, hemmed, and then nodded.

"And then you feel guilty for regretting it?" Beryl added, aware that Javier's teachings were getting through to him, too.

"Yeah, I guess. *Shit,*" Simon whispered and opened his bottle of water. "I have everything a man could want." He brought his shoulders to his ears and held them there several seconds. "Can you and I be friends without me wondering what would have happened if Ta'avah had won that battle?" Simon growled then and shook his body head to toe. "I'm being an idiot. I shouldn't drink so much."

"Sometimes, part of you wishes the battle went the other way," Beryl said thoughtfully. "If it had, you and I would be somewhere together, the Rabbit and the Rakum, happily ever after."

"Saying it aloud isn't helping," Simon joked weakly.

"Hear me out. When I was a Rakum," Beryl said with a friendly wink, "I would have taken care of you. I would have held you close and it would have been a great time. We would have had the world at our feet, and probably for centuries since you were a Rabbit. *But, that's never going to happen,*" Beryl stressed and took Simon's shoulders into his hands. "Look at me," he said and Simon's blue eyes locked with his own. "We can be enemies, pals, or lovers—but we will *never* be Rakum and Cow again. Those days are forever gone. That should give you peace."

"Why should it give me peace?" Simon asked dumbfounded.

"Because it is an utter impossibility, we can discuss it all we want. It'll never happen, so let's talk about it anytime we feel like it. Let's laugh about it. Let's tease each other like we did that last visit. Let's relax and not walk on eggshells. If we act like it's no big deal, maybe it won't be."

Still deep in his gaze, Simon slowly nodded. "One thing, though," he said with sudden seriousness. "I'm not gay. Then or now. We're not gonna ever be lovers."

Beryl laughed. "I know. Just testing. How about me? Am I straight? I'm still cementing my human sexuality," he said with a wink.

"You're straight, trust me. When you guys finish your mission, Lisa-Marie has this friend named Jennifer. She is gorgeous and could be Mrs. Right. I'll fix you up."

"Deal," Beryl said and clapped his back. "I gotta get a limo to the airport. But first—let's practice a tease. Go ahead."

Simon set down his water. "How about, thanks for not taking my shirt off when you came over."

Beryl grinned and wrinkled his nose. "Good one. Makes me sound like a pervert." Rakum did that to unnerve their victim, especially if he was particularly fit or good-looking. Then and now, Simon was both.

"If the shoe fits," Simon kidded. "You try it."

"Oh, it's easy for me," Beryl chided. "Rakum are better at everything. Okay," he looked around. "Here it is. Why don't you take off your shirt when I visit? Seriously, I still like that."

Simon didn't immediately laugh. "Are you kidding?"

Beryl grinned and shrugged. "Does it matter?" He pulled up the number for the car service. "Maybe I prefer looking at you half-naked, or maybe I'm ribbing you." He flipped up his eyes and winked.

"Ribbing!" Simon nodded. "Okay, shit. This will be much more fun. How long for the car?"

Beryl pressed the order and grabbed his jacket off the chair. "Walk me down."

Simon joined him and they rode down together. With a quick handshake, Beryl waved goodbye and watched him head up again. Simon was going to be a fun friend. Now, he needed to focus on the end of their mission.

Beryl set his face and watched for the car.

39, SAN FRANCISCO

"Is it past your bedtime? How old are you? Four?" Canaan asked Ben when he rubbed his eyes. It was nearing midnight and they had shut down every spot that permitted access to a seven-year-old child. He was definitely walking taller, which pleased both Elders more than they expected it would.

"*Shew,* I don't go to bed until morning," Ben said adopting Canaan's swaggering vocal style. "I'm hungry. Let's get some Wendy's."

"She's too old for you," Canaan said and got the trio walking again. "I'll give her a go, though, if she's as hot as she is on those commercials."

Kilmeade chuckled and looked up at the stars. They were strolling through a public park and plenty of well-spaced shepherd's-hook lamps provided sufficient illumination for mortal pedestrians. He and Kilmeade had searched the Elder airwaves for local lost Rakum and come up empty. The closest hit had been a fully transformed brother from Kilmeade's distant past, Lucas Poppa. The Elders didn't reveal themselves, discerning he had morphed and adjusted well to his new lifestyle. That said, he didn't know about the website or the disbursement, so Canaan hoped to contact the guy tomorrow night when they didn't have the diminutive tagalong.

A twig broke in the shadows and Ben's human ears heard nothing. Canaan and Kilmeade picked up a human heartbeat in the same vicinity. Neither Elder wanted to dance with a baddie and endanger the kid, so Canaan took the initiative. He grasped Kilmeade's wrist and plopped his hand on top of Ben's head.

"Be right back," he said and stepped off the path. Kilmeade rolled his eyes, but agreed with his decision to preempt whatever was planned in the dark. Canaan had no trouble locating the heartbeat. A young man had crouched a few yards away from the path, perhaps looking for an easy mark. He was armed with a .22 and Canaan caught a whiff of gunpowder, meaning someone had fired it recently.

"What's the world coming to?" he sent to Kilmeade who switched places with Ben so the kid would be out of the line of fire. Canaan eye-balled the gunslinger; he had approached sideways so now took in the guy's profile.

The stranger was peeking through the foliage at the man and the boy walking on the path. *"He smells clean, Kilmeade. Fancy a nibble?"*

"Just hurry up," Kilmeade returned sounding weary of the evening.

"Crabby much?" Canaan replied and in a blur, moved into the gunman and clutched him tightly; the pinned arm now aiming the pistol to the ground. Canaan covered his mouth and couldn't resist but play a little.

"Whatcha doin'?" Canaan asked in his ear, pausing only moments before he asked, "Well? Are you deaf?" Canaan didn't remove his hand and enjoyed the frantic movement of the guy's lips against his palm. "Huh? You what?" he teased.

"Tick-tock," Kilmeade sent over. He and Ben had walked on and were out of sight around the bend. *"Let's head back. Your little proselyte is after all, very little. And it's midnight."*

"I can tell time," Canaan said aloud as if speaking to the gunman. The man's lips were still moving and he hadn't yet shot his foot. For kicks, and maybe to irritate his comrade on the path, Canaan parted his fingers to see what the guy would say.

"Don't kill me, man," he whispered when allowed to speak. "I wasn't gonna hurt you. I'm hiding. Please, I got kids…"

Canaan opened his fingers a little more. "Who are you hiding from?"

"I got chased into the park, man," he said, still speaking in a whisper. "When I pulled my piece he ran that way." The man indicated with his chin the way they had been walking.

"Watch your back," Canaan sent, but at the same instant received real-time relay of a tall, thick Hispanic man charging Kilmeade and Ben.

Canaan bolted back to the path. In less than three seconds, he found Kilmeade wrestling the giant to the paved walk, the air pulsing with the aroma of Rakum blood.

"You let him stab you?" Canaan asked incredulous. One peek found Ben to the side on the grass as if shoved there. The boy sat on his rump leaning back on his palms, watching the show.

"Just make sure your tot is okay," Kilmeade sent back having pinned the man to the ground. Taking a glance around them, Kilmeade placed his palms to the man's head and he fell still. *"Miserable lout."*

"Lout. That's a pretty old word, there, grandpa," Canaan sent chuckling.

Kilmeade had ended the guy with a killing jolt so they needed to get clear of the scene. He looked down on Ben and held out his hand. When the boy looked up to grab it, Canaan grimaced.

"Uh, brother, you better hope Uncle Ta'avah is what made our blood so very

magical," he sent as Kilmeade reached their position. Ben's face was splattered with black blood and too much of the stuff smeared his lips and chin.

"*He had a knife in each hand; I didn't notice,*" Kilmeade relayed, also looking hard at the boy. "*He's fine. The Rabbits reverted 11/13...*"

"What? Am I hurt?" Ben looked up at them both without understanding their concern. Canaan pulled him to his feet and yanked him back to the path to get them moving again.

As all three walked briskly toward the perimeter of the park, Kilmeade used his jacket sleeve to wipe the kid's face. "*I remember now why I've always disliked humans,*" Kilmeade mumbled telepathically.

"*Don't blame the baddie,*" Canaan sent. "*You weren't paying attention.*"

Kilmeade didn't reply because Canaan was correct. By the time they reached the car, Ben started asking questions about the event he'd witnessed. Kilmeade was too deep in his own mind pondering imponderables to attend him. Canaan told him to shut it and Ben held his tongue until they were underway. A few miles down the road, he started up again.

"How'd you do that? How'd you pick that guy up? He was a giant!"

Behind the wheel, Canaan again told him to hold his questions for later. The youth was able to do so only a few seconds. Before long, he asked more.

"Where'd you go? Did you have to pee?" he asked Canaan, and then looked to the passenger's seat. "Are you still beedin'? I could call 9-1-1. I know how. Want me to?"

"*Pull over.*"

Canaan steered onto the wide shoulder. They were still five miles from the house and he hadn't seen yet what Kilmeade had in mind. When he put the car in park, Kilmeade turned to face him.

"*Your buddy, your responsibility.*"

Canaan remained in his partner's gaze and waited for more. Kilmeade was irritable, sure, but there was more. In the back seat, Ben stopped his questions and the car grew still. Kilmeade's frustrations floated slowly over and Canaan saw disappointment and the fringes of despair. "*I'll silence the walkie-talkie. You drive.*"

Kilmeade gave him a slow eye roll and Canaan got out to slide into the back seat. Ben watched Kilmeade exit the car and fall into the driver's seat and didn't say a word. Kilmeade pressed the ignition and Canaan turned to see Ben's upturned face.

"You have to stop talking," he told the youth. "You see this finger?" Canaan held up his pointer and waved it in Ben's face.

"Yeahhh," he replied quietly.

"I can silence you with this. Wanna try me?" Canaan lowered his chin, finger still wiggling. "Go ahead. Ask another question. I'll touch you with this and you won't be able to speak at all. You believe me?"

Ben nodded without hesitation.

"Good," Canaan said and faced front. As he leaned back to relax, Ben coughed into his hand. Once, twice, three times, each time more forcefully than before. When his heart began to race and the coughing continued, Canaan noted Kilmeade's concerned stare in the rearview. In another minute, Ben lost consciousness.

"What the f—" Canaan mumbled and jerked the kid into his lap to lay hands on his torso. No maladies presented, no imbalances, no virus, no pathogens. He shook his head.

Kilmeade pulled the car to the shoulder again, now only a mile from the house. Because his spread covered two and a half miles of frontage, at least there were no other houses around. When the car was in park, Kilmeade turned in his seat and reached out to place his hand on the boy's forehead.

"He's dying," Canaan said, incredulous. "There's nothing wrong with him. Nothing."

Kilmeade determined the same thing and shook his head.

"His heart stopped," Canaan said and moved one hand to the boy's sternum. He willed the heart to restart with no effect. Kilmeade moved his hand to the same place and tried as well.

"Did your blood do this?" Canaan asked, his mind racing.

"His brain activity has not been interrupted." Kilmeade exited the car and crawled in on Ben's opposite side. "Heart stopped, brain still going..."

Canaan fished out his small pocketknife and put it to the boy's thin forearm. With a very small movement, he opened the skin and a line of blood welled up.

"Phhheww," he grimaced and caught Kilmeade's eye. "What's that?"

Kilmeade put one hand to his nostrils. "His brain is still active."

Canaan was just as consternated as his partner. Ben's blood no longer resembled human or Rakum blood. Nor did it remind Canaan of the aroma of Javier's Anomaly blood. Something else was happening. Something new.

"We should have experimented on our blood before now," Canaan

334

said watching Kilmeade's face. Before 11/13, the tiniest drop of an Elder's blood transformed a mortal into a Rakum Rabbit, making them nearly impossible to kill. This allowed the Rakum to feed off them for as long as they were alive. After 11/13, every Rabbit reverted back to normal, so neither he nor Kilmeade thought their blood would any longer have an effect. Just then, Ben's legs kicked, his arms twitched, and he opened his eyes.

"Hey! Oops!" he yelped and scrambled out of Canaan's lap. "I fell 'sleep hard! I'm a tired old man, just like you said!" He giggled and made a big show of sitting up straight and wide-awake.

Kilmeade took a deep breath as did Canaan, and both of them exhaled slowly. Without a word, his partner exited the car. When he was behind the wheel again, Kilmeade headed for the driveway. Ben clambered over to look out the windows.

"My eyes feel weird," he said in a quiet voice.

"Anything else feel weird, little buddy?" Canaan asked subdued and catching Kilmeade's eye in the rearview.

Ben sighed and shook his head. "Nah, just my eyes. But I'm hungry," he said, still watching the night.

"Okay, we'll get something in the house," Canaan said faraway. Kilmeade didn't look up and steered them through the gate and to the front door.

Ben jumped down from the backseat and trailed Kilmeade into the house. Veronica had been waiting up and she made a big fuss over how proud she was of Ben for spending a night on the town with the big boys. Canaan listened to the banter, heard the television playing a western in the next room, heard one of Kilmeade's squatters sneezing off to the left, and he heard the squeaking of a mouse deep in the walls of the run-down mansion. Canaan heard all sorts of things, but he didn't hear Ben's heart beating. Nope. Not at all.

《回》

After valet-parking the Lexus, a snappily-dressed doorman opened the gleaming glass doors for the three men to enter. The Ritz-Carlton lobby throbbed with life at 10 P.M. and Dae Kim made way for Cary more than once. The irony hit him how only months ago, his best and last Cow Lonnie did the same for him when he went to meet Pete for the first time. Now, Lonnie and Pete were both dead. Funnily, or maybe not, he was again meeting a Rakum from the website. Maybe this time, things would end up better for everyone.

No one spoke until they exited the lift on Bryson's floor. Once the elevator swooshed away, the doc turned to Dae Kim with a grin.

"You have been brilliant and I suspect you'll be brilliant again with this Rakum." To Adam he lowered his chin. "Here is where you prove your willingness to play ball. Stick close, no wandering off." The doc gave him a steely glare. "I will only take one chance with you. Do you believe me?"

Dae Kim waited while Adam nodded, his eyes round. He was on board, but fear made for good glue.

"When the Elders come, Bryson will be read telepathically," Dae Kim offered. "It's good for ya'll to stay hidden."

"Precisely. We are nearby. Make it quick and stick to the plan. We want this guy to stay here until the Elders find him. *If* they find him."

"They will. He posted again last night about killing himself."

The doc nodded and moved out of sight.

"Bryson?" Dae Kim said through the crack in the door. As he'd promised, the brother hadn't secured the entrance. Dae Kim pushed the door open and waltzed in, feeling strong. "It's Dae Kim."

"In here," a husky voice called and Dae Kim rounded the wall to the over-sized bedroom. Sitting hunched over a laptop at the hotel-provided desk, Bryson looked up and hooked a thumb to the chair. "You don't look like I remember," he mumbled and took another careful scan of Dae Kim's entire frame. "If I wasn't so depressed, I'd put you in my lap."

"Shit... I'd end you if you tried," Dae Kim replied with a wink.

"Fun," Bryson returned and gestured to the computer screen. "Check this out..." He waited for Dae Kim to sit and then read off the screen. *"I heard the Elders were helping some of us who are having a hard time. Well, if it's true and they see this, SCREW YOU and STAY AWAY FROM ME. I hated you then and I hate you now. The rest of you, good luck. I'm out."* Bryson looked up for his guest's reaction.

"That's gonna make them come all the faster, you know," Dae Kim said with a roll of his eyes. "Don't send it unless that's what you want."

Bryson grinned. "Posted it an hour ago." He rose and passed Dae Kim for the chest of drawers. "I got this, too." In the top drawer, he shuffled around and lifted out a double-barreled shotgun. "Elder food."

Dae Kim made an approving face as Bryson shouldered the weapon and saluted like a soldier. The former Rakum was Dae Kim's height with fifty pounds more muscle around his chest and shoulders, and he was older, appearing to be about forty in human years. Being suicidal hadn't ruined his looks, he was handsome in a dark way, his jet black hair trimmed and neatly styled with dark blue eyes that pierced Dae Kim's adjoining gaze. Still, he remained unfamiliar; maybe such an admission would be endearing.

"So, we met already? This makes me nuts—I can't remember you. I can't remember hardly anything!" he said frowning and crossing his arms at his chest. Bryson offered a sympathetic shrug, tucked the weapon away, and motioned for Dae Kim to follow him to the main room.

"Don't sweat it. It was peripheral—Assembly 1969. Elder Roman dumped us with your pack for two sleeps." Bryson's voice grew hard. "Two Elder shits practiced their pummeling techniques on me until I fell unconscious."

"Canaan?" Dae Kim guessed.

"And Bel." Bryson narrowed his eyes. "Meryl took me in, got a healer to heal me up, made me *very* comfortable." Bryson rubbed his eyes. "You bunked on the end. You brought me cigarettes."

Dae Kim worked up the scene he described and the hazy memories slowly crystallized. Bryson had a beard back then, but the same scowl and angry gaze. Plus, Meryl enjoyed playing nursemaid when it would pay-off in favors later performed. Dae Kim nodded. "Camel unfiltered..."

Bryson huffed. "That was me. So where'd you see the Elders?"

"You won't believe this. I saw them at a mall in Dallas escorting a female around like frikkin' puppies. I hid from them, but I'm human—they wouldn't have picked me out anyway. Shit."

Bryson shook his head and his chuckle sounded angry. "Assholes." He clapped his hands together. "Well, I'm still offing myself. I'm-ma wait to see if they come by first. I'll give 'em a week." He shrugged. "Then you'll read about me in the paper."

"Oh? What's it gonna say?" Dae Kim said encouraging him to brag.

"Maniac Slaughters Day Campers in their Sleep. That's the headline. The sub-header will say, *"Twenty-four Children, Ages 11 to 15 Bludgeoned to Death in the Middle of the Night. Parents ask Why."* Bryson grinned and blinked with satisfaction. "You oughta come with me. I'll get you a gun. This camp up in the Hollywood hills off Canyon Drive hosts dozens of girls for these Spring sleepovers." He flickered his eyebrows rapidly. "I done the recon, located the sleeping bunker. Got the flyers for dates and times right off the website. Oh, baby!"

Dae Kim nodded slowly as he described his plan and grinned at the end. "Count me in, brother. That's the way to go out." Dae Kim's cell hummed and he fished it free. *"Nest, 24th floor."* To appear as transparent as possible, he showed the screen to Bryson.

"Who's that?" the guy asked after reading the doc's text.

Dae Kim shrugged. "He's nobody. A goofy mortal—in love with me. I let him drive me around; he's trying to cheer me up."

Bryson chortled. "Humans. I *hate* them. How do you stand it?"

"You'd like this one; he thinks I'm amazing... I guess he feeds my ego," Dae Kim admitted, picturing Adam and imagining the rest. "You wanna come meet him? He'd feed your ego, too," Dae Kim chuckled and inclined his head. It wasn't part of the plan for the guy to meet his co-conspirators, but in order to be natural, he had to invite him. As predicted, Bryson immediately shook his head.

"No, man, no." With a heavy sigh, he slumped onto the soft sofa and flicked on the giant flat-screen. "You go ahead. If you wanna go hunting with me up in the 'Hills next week, you know where I'll be."

"Oh, I'm definitely in. Don't worry about a firearm. I have my own—" he began and Bryson interrupted him.

"THAT'S why I remembered you. Meryl bragged that you were their executioner, Jack Dawn's *militia.* Ohhhhh," Bryson said thoughtfully. "Guess I'm forgetting stuff, too. Totally didn't think of that earlier." Dae Kim turned away and Bryson faced the television screen.

"Let me know if the Elders contact you or come by," he said with one foot in the hall. Bryson nodded and started switching channels. Dae Kim left the room and headed for the elevator.

"Coming down," he texted the doc. *"All good."*

"Your cake is ready for pickup," the doc texted back and Dae Kim grinned. The cake referred to his cache of weapons and tools requested for their plan. The doc used back channels and criminal enterprises he'd investigated on his own and procured everything they would need for the days ahead. Dae Kim hummed all the way to the 24th floor, everything was as it should be.

40, July 17

"The mission you launched works better when you're present," Canaan said when Javier answered the phone. It was high noon and he and Kilmeade had locked down for the day. No-heartbeat-Benny hadn't presented any medical issues up to dawn when the Elders deserted him into Veronica's questionable care. Javier hadn't responded to his comment and Canaan cleared his throat. "I remember when a grunt had a lot more respect for his Elders..."

"I was parking," Javier said quickly. "What's wrong?"

"I want you here. Now. Fly."

Javier made a low noise. "Okay..." he mumbled, as if mentally working out the logistics.

"Never mind. Forget it—we're handling it. This boy—" Canaan began and Javier interrupted.

"Is he okay? That's the little runaway, right?"

Canaan exhaled for Javier to hear. "Judas Priest, Javie. Shut it!" Canaan listened for another interruption, but the line was silent. "Good. *Shit.*" He took a deep breath. "We were out for a walk and some thug jumped Kilmeade. Protecting Ben got my man stabbed. No big deal, except his blood is on Ben's face and now Ben is mostly dead."

"What? I mean... what?" Javier said finally anxious.

"His heart stopped beating. His brain activity never slowed. Now the little guy is walking, talking, eating with no heartbeat." Canaan glanced at Kilmeade on the other bed looking as weary as he'd ever seen him. "What is your God up to now?"

"I don't know. I don't understand," Javier responded. "Where is he? With ya'll in the dark?"

"No, way. Shit, no. I'm not letting a pint-sized zombie share the day with us. He's out there with the humans."

"Have you checked on him since dawn?" Javier asked, astute as ever.

"No," Canaan said. "Shit, lemme check on the little turd. I'll call you right back and Javier—pick up the damn phone when I call." Canaan disconnected and dialed Veronica.

"Mr. Canaan? You okay?" she asked on the first ring.

"Anything different with the kid?" he asked, eyes on Kilmeade staring back at him.

"He's still asleep," she said. "Let me peek in on him."

Canaan waited and listened to the noises on her end of the phone. The TV was going and two of the men were in an argument about football. He heard Veronica saying Ben's name and then more urgently. On the fifth try, she yelled at the phone from wherever she was in the room.

"BEN! BEN! MR. CANAAN, HE'S NOT WAKING UP!" Veronica said the same words over a few more times and Canaan waited for her to come to the phone. Would she call the paramedics?

"She knows better," Kilmeade uttered morosely in the dark.

"Mr. Canaan, he won't wake up," she said into the phone now, obviously crying. "I need to call an ambulance. Where's Mr. Star?"

"Veronica," Canaan said as calmly as possible. "You will not call anyone. Carry him to our door. If any of the others follow you, I will eat them. Do you understand?" Veronica gulped an answer and was gone.

Kilmeade rose as if his veins were full of syrup and moped to the door. Shuffling steps were heard soon outside and no others had shadowed her into the forbidden wing. The bolts clunked, Kilmeade pulled the knob and took possession of the boy from Veronica's arms. She did not attempt to enter.

"Is he going to be okay? I couldn't get no pulse," she mewled from the threshold.

"He's fine. We'll see you at sundown. Bye," Canaan said and Kilmeade pushed the door with his toe. When the locks re-set, Kilmeade put Ben on the nearest bed and checked his vitals. Canaan did the same thing on the boy's opposite side.

"Same as before," Canaan mumbled and searched the area for something with which to bind the kid in case he came-to while they dozed. Canaan was a very light sleeper, but better safe than sorry—being locked in with a mysterious diminutive deadie could be risky.

"Look in that closet," Kilmeade offered, his voice solemn.

Canaan selected a belt and two ties and wrapped Ben's arms and legs. "He's probably sleeping through the day like a Rakum..."

"You said it when speaking to Javier. What is the God of the mortals doing now? What purpose could this serve?" Kilmeade shook his head. Canaan read a few more things in his partner's mind that he wouldn't voice and he agreed with them all. He fished out his phone and pressed Javier's number, who picked up during the first ring.

"Is he okay?"

"I guess. Sleeping, maybe. Heart still dead. Brain still ticking along. Kilmeade's woman brought him to us so we'll watch and see."

"Kilmeade's woman?"

"You know what I mean, idiot. This woman in the house," Canaan snapped. "Don't be difficult on purpose."

"You sound terrible. I'm flying to San Francisco. Text me the address to the house. I can be there when you get up tonight."

"Forget it..." Canaan objected weakly. He wanted Javier to come. When weird spirit shit happened, the guy was the only one equipped to deal with it.

"Text me the address," he said more firmly, "and I'll see you in a few hours." Then Javier was gone.

"'Bout time he grew some *cajones*," Canaan mumbled and lay back on his bed. Since Ben lay on the other one, Kilmeade sat in the recliner and kicked up the footrest.

"Funny we didn't foresee any of this," Canaan said mostly to himself. "What good is precognition if it doesn't prepare you for surprises?"

Kilmeade didn't answer, his mind dancing on similar paths. Canaan watched him lift his outer and under shirts and examine the place he'd been stabbed. There was no wound, of course, but Canaan watched Kilmeade press and poke the area. After another few seconds, Canaan saw what he was thinking.

"Your liver?" Canaan said and rose to walk over to Kilmeade's chair.

"We marked Rabbits with our circulatory blood. That blood on Ben's face was blacker than usual..."

Canaan nodded; Kilmeade was right. "The blood is cleansed in the liver," Canaan said and also put his fingers to the invisible wound.

"Canaan, come close," Kilmeade said before he exhaled slowly and reached out his hand. Canaan was already mere feet away. He studied the man's eyes and didn't recognize the emotion.

"What is it? Your face looks wrong." Canaan stopped talking as he realized Kilmeade was experiencing one of the more despicable human emotions: loneliness. Canaan leaned in as Kilmeade sat up and closed the recliner.

"I feel very, very poorly," Kilmeade said in a whisper, his eyes locked to Canaan's.

"I see," Canaan said just as quietly and reached out to wrap both arms around Kilmeade's upper body. Kilmeade followed suit and his long arms encircled Canaan's ribcage. The most powerful Rakum Elder he'd ever known needed a little human-style touch and Canaan had become an expert hugger after forty years with Marcy. He held him gently and wanted so badly to comment.

"Don't..." Kilmeade sent silently, and Canaan didn't.

But he wanted to.

《回》

Taking an Uber from the airport saved Beryl time and money, although only time mattered since his bank account had grown so fat. The driver arrived quickly, but when he greeted Beryl, his German accent garbled his words. For forty-five minutes as "Jugar" chauffeured him to the Lamborghini dealership, Beryl conversed in German about whatever popped into the man's head. They had covered the latest movies, to religion and politics; by the time they shared an *auf Wiedersehen*, Beryl wanted to scream. Being polite didn't come naturally, but it was getting easier thanks to Javier's leading.

Beryl found a spot beneath a shade tree situated at the door of the sales floor and watched the Uber whirl away. The beauty of Los Angeles in July caused him to pause and consider his surroundings. A cobalt blue sky over a skin-loving 70-degree temp filled Beryl with a consuming positivity he never experienced as a Rakum. He'd been mortal eight months and was still amazed at how much the sunshine delighted him. Beryl's eyes glazed as he considered the Ten Fathers, nine of whom lived to adulthood under the sun before accepting Ta'avah's demonic mantle. How did they say goodbye to such a beautiful and perfect provider of light and warmth? Now that it massaged his skin rather than searing it off, Beryl would never let it go.

Would I be a Rakum again if given the opportunity?

The unexpected internal question surprised him, but his answer did not: an unequivocal *no*.

A car zoomed with a honk and Beryl waved casually at four bikini-clad girls in a convertible saying hi the California way. Still with his back to the door, Beryl peeked at his phone before entering the dealership. He expected a text from Javier with an update, but so far nothing. Last he heard, his partner jumped schedule to fly in early at Canaan's request. He didn't get his long prayer drive and sounded worried over their elderly buds. Beryl grinned at himself for calling the Elders elderly. He shot a quick text to Javier and Canaan together saying he'd arrived in Los Angeles. He told them he'd buy a car and head for the rental. So far so good.

"Mr. Beryl?"

Beryl turned at the sound of his name and a California knock-out with long brown hair and huge hazel eyes leaned against the open glass door of the building. He offered a tiny wave and pocketed his phone.

"I'm Tina and we're going to find you the perfect car today."

"Yes, we are," Beryl replied in the same positive tone and she led him into the building.

Less than two hours later, she handed him a key fob and waved goodbye. Tina had tucked her phone number in his jacket pocket, which he found a mile down the road. Beryl grinned and set the GPS for the rental. After another mile, his cell rang and he didn't recognize the number. As was his habit with strange calls, Beryl connected without speaking. After a few seconds, Adam's voice came across.

"Beryl? Is that you? I've been trying to reach you forever. Where are you?" he asked, spikes of stress evident in his tone.

"Adam? I was on a plane. You had my itinerary." Beryl looked at the time. "Shouldn't you be at work?"

"You're not going to believe this, but I was abducted that night after Simon's. Dae Kim snatched me up right after I left you!"

Beryl's adrenaline soared and he glanced behind him for a chance to pull off the road. "What are you talking about? That was two nights ago! Where are you? Are you okay?" Beryl's mind raced as he found his chance and steered the new car to the highway shoulder. "Where's Dae Kim now?"

"I'm okay for the moment. I escaped, but I'm in Los Angeles. He brought me here because he was looking for the Elders. I need you to come get me."

"He brought you to Los Angeles? How? In the trunk?" Beryl asked meaning it as a joke.

"Yeah—I was taped up. Made me stay in there for hours. Are you in L.A. yet? Can you come get me?"

"Of course, I just left Beverly Hills. Tell me where you are."

"I'm on Melrose and..."

Beryl put his face in his hand and worked to calm his mind. In another moment, Adam gave him a cross street.

"Okay, got it." Beryl exhaled forcibly. "I'm around the corner, but with this traffic—just stay there! I'm in a black Lamborghini with gold rims, got it?"

"Beryl," Adam said, his voice suddenly small. "Can we stay on the phone..."

"Sure," Beryl said and carefully wove back into traffic. "Are you hurt? How did you get away?"

"I'm pretty embarrassed to say it, but he didn't have to hurt me much. He threatened me, but—I didn't really resist. I'm ashamed..."

"Stop it, what could you do? You're not a superhero. You did what you should do. You survived..." Beryl turned onto La Cienega, happy he knew some proper responses for his friend.

"I had no idea I could ever be that scared. How could I let him control me with *words?* I thought I was tougher than that..."

"Adam, stop blaming yourself!" Beryl raised his voice. "Dae Kim is a practiced executioner. He knows precisely what to do and what to say to scare you." Beryl spied Melrose Avenue as the cars in front crawled through the turn like turtles. "He must like you. Or more likely, he grabbed you for a reason—he needs you for something. I'm coming up on your cross street. Look for my car."

"Okay... I'm coming to the curb..."

Riding the brake and absorbing irritated honks from all sides, Beryl scoured the sidewalk for his friend. A pale arm shot up and waved him over. Beryl sighed with relief and jerked to the road edge. Adam slid into the passenger seat and took a deep breath once the door was closed and locked. He looked healthy, clean, perfect—again Beryl found himself almost ready to thank God for it.

"Thank you," he muttered and covered his face, unable to meet Beryl's eye. "What a nightmare..."

"I'm headed to the rental Javier set up for us. Is that okay?"

Adam nodded. "That sounds perfect. I jumped out of his car back on West Hollywood and ran and ran." Adam peeked over to give Beryl a glance. "You are an angel. You flew right in and rescued me."

Beryl shook his head and put the car in first. "Let's get out of here. If Dae Kim lost you downtown, he's trolling for you right now." Beryl craned his head and found his chance to merge into the flow. He concentrated on the traffic for five minutes and Adam hid his face. Once they were clear of downtown and heading into Bel-Air, Beryl reached across and squeezed Adam's shoulder.

"Man, I'm glad you're okay," he said. "Dae Kim had been locked up— I mean, while you and I were over drinking with Simon, the Elders kidnapped Dae Kim and locked him up in the truck box."

"No, really? And he got out?"

"This is what makes it my fault. I was so plastered that I let him out while I was asleep..." Beryl shook his head. "Canaan said demons got me to do it while I was intoxicated. It's my fault. I screwed up."

In his peripheral vision, Adam appeared stunned and he then looked out his window.

"I'm so sorry," Beryl said and slowed as they entered the canyon. The GPS instructed him to weave right and he drove numbly until they reached the curving climb to the house. When the California mansion came into view at the top of the hill surrounded by trees, Beryl barely noticed it, so deep in regret. He parked at the front door and switched off the car.

"You don't need to apologize," Adam said quietly. "We don't pull the strings, isn't that right?"

Beryl nodded and fished out his phone. He punched Javier's number and waited to see if he'd pick up. He didn't and Beryl readied for the voice mail.

"Dae Kim abducted Adam and brought him to L.A. I have him now and we're at the rental. Call me." Beryl ended the call and looked sideways at Adam who gave him a small grin. "Let me text Canaan." As Beryl texted Canaan the same news, Adam texted on his own phone. When they both hung up, Beryl exited first, grabbed his single bag from behind the seat, and walked Adam to the door.

"Let's get in and catch our breath. There's no way Dae Kim can know about this place so we'll sit tight and wait for the others." Beryl shoved open the door, glad Javier made all of their lodging arrangements while still in Alabama.

"Dang," Adam whispered taking in the opulence in the first room.

His face making the same expression, Beryl gestured for the staircase. "I'm going to find a shower. You good?" He waited for Adam to nod and he trotted up.

He hadn't had a chance to tell any of them what Simon said about Adam and surely didn't want the guy to overhear him when he did. After Beryl chose a bedroom, he dug out his toiletries and a change of clothes. The attached bath was huge and once closed in, he lifted his phone and hit Javier's number. He liked Adam, but in the battle between flesh and spirit, he had learned to listen to every side.

After the invisible layer of air travel funk had been erased from his skin, Beryl stepped from the rental's lavish tiled shower with an audible sigh. Invariably and without intention, his mind wandered back to the Rakum airliner his brethren had free and ready access to for decades. Unbidden, his final ride on the NCJ popped up as he scrubbed his hair with a soft towel. Elder Jack Dawn barking commands, angry at Beth Rider—at that time, an unknown power hidden in a defenseless-looking woman. Following orders, Beryl had joined his brethren violently assaulting her in an attempt to scare her senseless. She never once looked frightened.

Beryl sniffled, blinked, and discarded the towel. At the time, none of them could figure it out. He pulled on his boxers. *"At least now I know where she got all that courage,"* he thought with another sigh. *"Why don't I get some of that for myself? Javier said I only have to open the door a crack..."*

Pondering how he might do that and when, Beryl pulled on fresh jeans and shoved open the bathroom door. Remaining shirtless until the steam dissipated, he took three steps into the room and a violent shove from behind sent him to his knees. A century of combat training flooded his musculature; Beryl dropped to his side and rolled several feet from his attacker. When he stood to face off, he recognized Dae Kim.

"Come on, brother," Dae Kim said in an urgent whisper, "don't make this harder than it has to be."

Beryl dodged right when his attacker lunged with incredible speed straight for him. When Beryl spun to counter the man's move, Dae Kim faked left and leapt into Beryl from the side. His fingers dug into the waistband of Beryl's jeans, which he used as a handle to whirl him backward into a double arm grip.

"Be still, Beryl," Dae Kim said in his ear and he held him tightly, hugging him firmly enough to constrict his breathing. "I'm stronger than you. See?" he added and squeezed tighter. "Don't make me hurt you—we don't heal up like we used to."

"Dae! Stop it! Let me go!" Beryl shouted as forcefully as possible. In the old days, they had been friends and evenly matched. At the moment, Beryl grew more and more aware that somehow, Dae Kim had retained much of his Rakum strength. "Adam!" he called, hoping his friend was downstairs.

Dae Kim chuckled in his ear. "That simp is already tied up in my trunk. Settle down now..."

Beryl resisted another few seconds and attempted his last trick: dropping to the floor. Dae Kim caught on a millisecond into the move and deftly followed with his mass, thus was able to maintain his backward hold.

"Okay, buddy, here it comes," Dae Kim hissed and slid his hug into a choke hold. Beryl blocked him, but ineffectively, his strength not near enough to gain an advantage.

"Dae! Stop!" he gasped, angry and wishing he'd been more cautious. His old friend did not let up and the darkness crept closer. Beryl tried a few more counters, but none ever grew past the initial stage. One more time, he shouted for Adam and then allowed the darkness to come. Right before he blinked out, a voice deep within whispered, *"Ask God for help."* Instead, in his panic, Beryl's human heart called the one person in the flesh that cared about him the most. Then he was no more.

《回》

Nearing sundown, Canaan wanted to plan their night: Tuck Ben into someone's care and find Lucas Poppa. Maybe after that...

An errant twinge stabbed his inner eye and Canaan frowned, his hand at his temple. Did he just receive the mother of all telepathic punches? He turned to gauge Kilmeade's reaction, but there was none. Oblivious to Canaan's sudden interest in an errant telepathic relay, his partner moaned low in his throat from his lounging position in the chair. When Kilmeade covered his face with both hands, Canaan growled; his questionable mental jolt would have to be examined later.

"This shit ain't gonna fly." Canaan pulled out his cell to call Roman only to see a new text from Beryl. Growling at the interruption, he read the lead-in. *"I made it to the rental but..."*

"But, *shit!*" he barked and thumbed the icon harder than necessary. Beryl's full text opened and after the first line, every other character morphed into wingdings. "Piece of shit phone!"

"You're overly emotional..."

Putting Beryl's update aside, he flipped his gaze back to his cohort. "If I am, I'm absorbing it from you. You're gonna talk to Roman," Canaan asserted. Since Kilmeade's twin had also been an Elder, he would best know how to deal with mortal heart conditions.

"There is nothing wrong with me..."

"Bullshit," Canaan said and hung up the phone before it connected. "Kilmeade..." He awaited his cohort's eye and switched to telepathy in deference to Ben unconscious nearby.

Kilmeade regarded him with a steely glare.

"You're depressed, and goddammit, Rakum Elders do NOT suffer depression!"

347

"Be serious." Kilmeade frowned. *"If you diagnosed this human condition in me, Doc, come fix it."*

"Oh, I'll lay hands on you, but you'll be across the room in a pile," Canaan sent without humor.

"I wonder..." Kilmeade made a tiny nod. *"If I contracted a mortal mental state and you attacked me, would I respond like a Rakum or a mortal?"*

Canaan waited to see if he expected a reply. A mortal might cry if Canaan attacked him and he could not allow nor bear such an experiment performed on Kilmeade.

"I cannot believe you think I would cry," Kilmeade sent, eyes narrowed. *"Put the zombie into the hall."*

Canaan didn't move, still trying to predict Kilmeade's intentions.

"Now," he said aloud, sternly.

Canaan rose and hoisted Ben onto his shoulder to place him gently in the hall. He re-bolted the door and turned to his friend.

"Now, try to make me cry." Kilmeade got to his feet.

Canaan offered a small grin. "I will, but only because I love you," he said with a wink.

Now. *How to begin...* He had wrestled his friend over the years too many times to count and any time he won, Kilmeade had allowed it. Canaan approached slowly and had decided on a course of action by the time his partner was within arm's reach.

"The front choke is a good start," Canaan said as he wrapped both large hands around Kilmeade's throat. His partner was not a small man and his fingers only just touched around the back. At first, Kilmeade did nothing, so Canaan proceeded incrementally increasing the pressure.

Kilmeade held his gaze, his face lax. Milliseconds before Canaan's fingers would compress and crack his vertebrae, Kilmeade out-blocked Canaan's contact with enough force to fracture his forearms. Canaan leapt backward grinning and holding his arms down as they healed.

"Shit, that was *sweet,"* he whispered and circled as Kilmeade did. Barely thirty seconds later, he sensed his repair and he surged forward. Hoping to grab his friend and spin him into a chokehold, instead Kilmeade ducked and reeled him in as his mass crossed.

Kilmeade held Canaan tightly around the chest, his back to Kilmeade's front pinning both arms. Canaan thought he would try to break a few of his ribs, but surprise, surprise—Kilmeade bent at the knees and shoved upward with amazing power, sending Canaan's body in the opposite direction as he released him. Canaan landed upside-down on his upper back and slid down the drywall.

"Are you crying yet?" Canaan joked and rose to his feet, shakily at first, but recovering in a matter of seconds. He rushed Kilmeade, hands open and almost made contact with his shirt—the fabric whispered past his fingers—but the more experienced Elder again moved out of the way just in time. Canaan expected to be grabbed from behind so he spun to avoid it, but Kilmeade wasn't behind him. In the second it took to turn a circle and locate him, Kilmeade grabbed him from the opposite side in the identical hold.

"Don't throw me over there again," Canaan teased to disguise his exertion. "I wanna stay here with you..."

Kilmeade squeezed like before, but pulled him upwards to his face. Familiar fangs punctured Canaan's throat from behind. He thought to make a snide comment, but Kilmeade telepathically shushed him. Although the pummel party was in full-swing, Canaan recognized a command when he heard one. Ceasing all resistance, he hung in his superior's grip as Kilmeade pulled blood from the new wound. Taking his time, eventually his partner slowed, stopped, and exhaled over Canaan's shoulder, still holding him immoveable.

Another minute ticked by and Canaan rolled his eyes. "So, who won?" he said finally breaking the thick silence.

Kilmeade repositioned his arms so both hands filtered into Canaan's hair, still from behind. When his fingers touched on his crown, Kilmeade held them there. Canaan's arms were free so he put his fists to his hips.

"You're in love with Elder Canaan, is that it?" Canaan joked. A fraction of a second later, Kilmeade thought about Chloe and Canaan saw it, too. "No, that's not it." Canaan made a movement away and Kilmeade dropped the contact. "This is not about missing the little bird." Canaan faced him and Kilmeade's mouth turned in a crooked grin.

"No," Kilmeade responded in a low voice, "but I would not mind if she were here."

"This is something else." Canaan grasped his friend's shoulder. "You're deflecting. There is a root in there and I aim to yank it free."

Kilmeade's grin widened and Canaan's countenance also lightened.

"Why are you suddenly so happy?"

Kilmeade backed out from under Canaan's hand and covered his mouth with his fingers. His eyes smiled over his palm and he didn't reply. Canaan needn't hear him—Kilmeade was buzzing on his blood and much more than usual.

"This..." Canaan said running his finger up and down in the air toward his partner. "Tonight's demeanor has to do with your upcoming date with the Puppeteer." He stepped to the bed where he'd dropped his cell during the fight and once again dialed Kilmeade's twin.

"Hey," Roman said when he picked up.

"Roman, your brother is feeling stuff, *human* stuff, and you're going to fix him." Canaan did not wait for a response and tossed the phone to Kilmeade. "Talk to Roman."

Kilmeade lowered his hand from his lips and greeted his brother. Immediately, Roman dove in and named mortal emotions Kilmeade might experience.

Canaan collapsed onto his bed, propped his head up on his arms, and watched Kilmeade converse. So far, Kilmeade was delivering in a forthcoming manner. Canaan pointed at him and thought, *'I'm watching you.'* Kilmeade looked away, but only after his gaze assured Canaan he would do whatever it took.

Good enough.

41

"Get the door," Dae Kim grumbled as he heaved an unconscious Beryl through the kitchen to the garage. With wide eyes, Adam yanked it open and followed Dae Kim down the few steps to the parked Lexus. At least the guy had been useful enough to bring the sedan inside. Dae Kim had arrived precisely as planned, easily finding the address Adam texted. Still, when the kid texted again that Beryl was in the shower, "so come on," Adam was startled when Dae Kim actually showed up.

"He's new to this stuff. He'll be fine. I've trained up newbies plenty of times," Dae Kim had explained to the doc before sunup, lying side-by-side in the hotel bed with Adam on the other. Cary hadn't touched him much, but the longing in the Lost Rabbit's eyes was of the *mortal* kind. Dae Kim internally faced facts: when their current mission ended, he'd be expected to satisfy the doctor's need.

"Is he alive?" Adam asked as Dae Kim folded Beryl's half-naked body into the trunk of the car.

Dae Kim only glared at him and he shrunk back. He handed over supplies—rope, duct tape, a cloth gag—but was no help applying the restraints. The guy was just too soft. Dae Kim chuckled as one hand jerked the homemade hobble into place. *"They thought he'd have been a Rakum if he'd been raised by our people..."* He stole a quick glance at pretty-boy standing by with a roll of tape in each fist. *"I call bull-shit on that, Elder Kilmeade, Sir."* He laughed again, this time enough that Adam noticed.

"What? What's funny?" he asked and peered in at their captive.

Beryl had been hog-tied so his wrists and ankles met at his buttocks. Stretched taut, Beryl's torso revealed absolutely zero body fat. The guy was hitting the gym *a lot*. Dae Kim decided to use that for his excuse.

"You didn't tell me Beryl was obsessed with his physique."

Adam huffed with a half-shrug. "I never saw him with his shirt off."

"Too bad," Dae Kim joked and Adam remained quiet. "Let's get on the road. The doctor will enjoy putting the next step of our plan into place." Dae Kim took one last look at the snoozing man and closed the trunk lid. "You have his phone?"

351

Adam held up the device and slid into the passenger side.

Traffic down the canyon was light and when Dae Kim exited onto the 405, he told Adam to give the doc an update. After punching the number, the doctor's voice came over the Bluetooth.

"I know everything went perfectly."

"Yes, sir," Dae Kim answered for them both. "We're set to rendezvous in one hour and we have everything on the checklist."

"I never doubted you," Doctor Nankin replied and was gone.

《回》

"I should have trusted you, my brother," Kilmeade said softly. "I disregarded your transformation because you are so very human now." Even shooting blind, Roman had hit on Kilmeade's problem within the first minute of their conversation.

Across the miles, Roman commiserated. "I understand, really, I do. I can help you with this. It takes a little talking, which you don't like."

Kilmeade opened his mouth to reply and stopped. He looked at Canaan. Barely did he think what he was about to say and his partner jumped to finding the answer. Without a word, Canaan stepped to the door and peeked into the hall.

"He's not here." Canaan re-bolted the door and held up his finger. A quick text to Veronica found Ben had shimmied free at some point and wandered to her room. "He's in the kitchen, chowing down on pizza."

Kilmeade nodded. "You have full-dark there," he said to his brother, who answered in the affirmative. "Go now to my house. We will meet you there." Kilmeade closed the call and lobbed the cell to Canaan. "Why do we pretend we're locked down? Come, let us see Roman in person."

Canaan stepped close and his mind drifted to Javier.

Kilmeade sighed. "Can you tell where he is?"

Canaan tinkered with his cell. "He just arrived."

Kilmeade rubbed his face. "Bring him to me," he told Canaan and watched his cohort exit the room. After a quick wash-up in the lavatory, Kilmeade stepped into clean jeans and a slightly wrinkled shirt he had hanging from before.

"Here's our travelin' man," Canaan said, his demeanor muted probably for Kilmeade's sake. Javier followed him in looking as healthy and swarthy as ever. The man's enormous eyes seemed to zero in on Kilmeade's hidden despair as he approached. Anxious to get the night underway, Kilmeade greeted him with a nod and began his instructions.

"Stay with Canaan. Entertain him. I will return in a few hours." Kilmeade looked at Canaan who nodded with a slow blink. Canaan worried for him and had grown increasingly protective, as well. *Face-to-face, Roman will help. You'll see.*

"I know he will," Canaan said softly and stepped close. His old friend grasped his neck and bumped their foreheads.

Kilmeade took two steps back and closed his eyes to concentrate on his basement in Tuscaloosa. The tickling in his inner ear and a floating sensation informed him he had translated. He opened his eyes in his own home and waited for Roman.

《回》

Kilmeade dissolved from view and Canaan sighed for Javier to hear.

"Is this a mortal problem? Try to help someone weaker than you, then you're neck deep in their shit unable to dig out no matter what you do?" Canaan watched Javier resist a snicker. "Laugh it up—these needy leeches are sucking me and my man Kilmeade dry." Canaan had one hand on the doorknob as he prepared to introduce Javier to the half-dead half-wit. Javier grinned, which didn't do anything for Canaan's mood.

"If you really want an answer, I'll give it," Javier said, idiot smile in place. When Canaan glared at him, he continued. "Yes. Those of us who help others do it selflessly, which means continuously. Hardly ever does it end after one kind act."

Canaan sighed. "I'm going to hate being mortal, I know it," he mumbled and yanked open the door.

"I like the way you talk, like it'll happen."

"Oh, it will. Kilmeade and I started prophesying like the Fathers," Canaan said miserably. "We've seen some things to come." He waited for Javier to start walking.

"In your visions, have you seen who I added to the mix?" Javier asked with humorous mystery.

Canaan narrowed his eyes. "What did you do?"

"I guess the answer is no," Javier said milking the moment.

Canaan's lips parted to ask more and Kilmeade touched his mind also wondering what Javier had done. Canaan nodded his head. "Great, Kilmeade and I both need to know what you've done."

"Oh? That's fast. He's really in there," Javier said, still too jovial for Canaan's taste. Canaan took a hulking step and Javier tossed up both palms. "Trust me; I prayed over it a lot. In about two hours, Mike and Beth will be here from Alabama."

"What the *f*—" Canaan began and from two thousand miles away sensed Kilmeade shrug, uninterested, and return his attention to Roman's arrival. "What for?"

"Look, you have a heart-dead child with you. He can't be left with mortals and he can't go with us on this last leg of our mission." Javier paused and Canaan resisted agreeing right away. "He needs to be fixed. Healed. Whatever. Beth can help. She's a woman and a mother, and she'll *pray...*"

Canaan rubbed his face with one hand and sighed. "Shit. I hate Stone," he mumbled. "But you're right again." Canaan made an exaggerated toothy grin to the ceiling. "You're right, Big Guy. As always! Know-it-all..."

Javier smiled and braved to chuck Canaan's arm. "Good. God likes being called names. Makes Him really laugh."

Canaan didn't smile. "Right now, I couldn't care less what He likes." Entering the hall he waited for Javier to follow him as he added, "Now that you've ruined my night, we'll extricate ourselves from half-dead Benny so I can take you away for some me-time." Kilmeade had Roman, Javier had Beryl, Beryl had Simon—who else could Canaan garner sympathy from and commiserate with?

Javier chuckled. "That sounds lovely, sweetheart," he said in a high voice. Canaan didn't laugh and Javier jabbed the back of his shoulder. "I'm doing an impression of you, can't you tell?"

"No, you're not," Canaan spat without turning, leading them to the opposite wing of the huge house.

"Oh, yes, I am," Javier asserted. "You're just so depressed that you're deaf to my amazingness."

Canaan stopped and turned halfway. "I'm not depressed. That's a pitiful and disgusting human condition and you know it."

Javier nodded. "It used to be..."

Canaan growled and resumed walking. "Hold your tongue, pup. We'll be alone soon enough and I'll hold back a little when I punch your lights out." Javier snickered, but remained mum. "Good," Canaan said and reached the main salon.

"Mr. Canaan!" Veronica squealed. "Where's Mr. Star?"

"I talk, you listen," he barked. She paled, shrinking backward. He hooked his thumb behind. "This is Javier, he's with me. Where's Ben?"

Veronica gestured to her right and Canaan waved for Javier to follow him to the kitchen. Inside the huge grungy space, Ben sat at a chipped butcher-block counter nibbling a sandwich, his fingers flying across a gaming device. When he saw Canaan, he hopped off his stool and clambered over.

"Hey, Mr. Kay-nan! Who's dat?" Ben asked sounding much younger than seven.

"Call him Dummy," Canaan said and Javier laughed.

"I'm Javier," he said and put out his hand to shake. "We spoke on the phone last night."

"Oh, yeah!" Ben gave his hand two firm pumps and beamed at Canaan who rolled his eyes. "You said you know'd my friend Kay-nan a hundred years!"

"And I have," Javier said.

"Look-it, Benny," Canaan grumbled, "Javier and I are headed out. You stay with Veronica."

"When Mr. Star gets back, we'll 'vestigate," he said with a nod.

Canaan wrinkled his brow. What sort of knowledge was the kid coming from? He had to ask, "Investigate what?"

"Benny!" he said with a huge grin and a hand on the top of his head.

Canaan maintained a weary gaze on the boy and had to ask his other question since Kilmeade hadn't walked past the boy when he left. "What makes you think Mr. Star went somewhere?"

"I saw. He went like this..." Ben brought one hand up, palm down, hand rigid, and moved it across his body in a horizontal plane. "ZZZzzzzzzzzzzzz-BOOP!"

Canaan huffed and shot a look to Javier.

"What's the boop?" Javier asked with a cautious smile.

"That's the sound on the other end." Ben replayed the movement and this time said "boop" even louder.

"On the other end?" Canaan whispered. "Do I want to know?"

Javier did. "Is boop in this house?"

"Hah!" Ben laughed and shook his head side-to-side like a chimpanzee. "Hah-ver is funny. He's funny, right, Kaynan?"

"Hilarious," Canaan mumbled. "Come on, Hah-ver. Let's get out of here before he kills anymore of my brain cells."

"MR. STAR WILL BE BACK AND YOU'LL SEE HIM SMILE," Ben belted out and then returned to his game and sandwich.

Javier raised his eyebrows to Canaan who waved his hand.

"Zombies. Who can understand 'em?" Canaan exited the kitchen, not ready to examine the boy's strange statements. Me-time came first and they were so close to the door.

In the main room, Veronica hovered near the couch, her eyes on their movements. Canaan stepped toward her trying on a particularly gentle expression. *Gotta treat them all with such carefulness...*

"Hey, beautiful, I didn't mean to snap at you," he said when he reached her side. He spoke close to her ear as two of the other residents lounged close by watching television. "We had a rough night."

"Oh, don't worry none," she whispered and Canaan gently cupped her shoulder with one hand.

"You helped us out with the boy. Thank you. He has a medical condition that makes his heart very quiet." Canaan slowed his cadence as Veronica's gaze softened with every word. "Tonight, Mr. Star and I will find out what you need to make your life easier, okay?"

Veronica lowered her chin and her eyes fluttered out of habit. "I don't need nuthin', honest..."

"We all need something, honey," he said and tapped her chin with his knuckle. She blushed, completely forgiving him for earlier. Canaan inwardly thanked Marcy who taught him how to be nice when all he wanted to do was rip off a person's face.

"Thank you," she said softly and he sent her a wink.

"See you in a bit," he said and kissed the back of her hand. "Watch over Ben." He waited for her to nod again and he led Javier out the front door. When they reached Javier's rental, a compact *Prius,* of all things, Javier made a noise of amusement. Canaan glared at him and he held his hands up in surrender.

"I didn't get my prayer time," he said knowing Canaan didn't want an apology. "I'm not *trying* to irritate you."

"Button up, buttercup," Canaan said and opened the driver's side. "You're on my dime now." Javier turned an invisible key at his lips and fell into the passenger seat. Once on the road, Canaan took a slow lung-filling breath. "Okay, little brother," he said in the Old Way, "Kilmeade will transform after we help our last Rakum in Los Angeles."

"This is from a vision?" Javier asked turning to see Canaan's profile.

"I guess. He and I are seeing snippets of what is to come. As you might have noticed, now we see everything jointly. Every moment is shared without effort." Canaan paused and tuned in Kilmeade across the continent. "Kilmeade is with Roman right now at the island in the kitchen. Wait for it..." Canaan said, holding up one finger and steering with the opposite hand. "...'This is perfectly natural, brother,'" Canaan began in an impression of Roman's educating voice. "'The black chasm we all carried in our spirits before we knew the truth is slowly filling with light.'" Canaan stopped and took a quick glance at Javier's expression.

"That's what Roman is saying to Kilmeade?"

Canaan nodded. "Kilmeade said there was a place called Red Bird Inn down here. Pull up the address and we'll eat."

Javier worked his cell phone. "Red Bird Inn. Sweet name."

"Don't start," Canaan said and slowed as they entered downtown. Javier called out the address and he headed over. In ten minutes, they entered the lobby of the restaurant. Kilmeade recommended it because each dining area sat in a separate small room. It was pricey, but worth any cost for Canaan to have an excellent meal served in peace.

A snooty concierge with an orange mustache and shaved head showed them to their room. Canaan pressed a twenty in the guy's sweaty palm and he disappeared, promising to send over their waiter.

"This is cool," Javier said, taking in the smallish space.

Historical photographs of SanFran decorated the close walls that hugged the table so tightly that two men couldn't pass behind the chairs. Once the waiter took their order and disappeared, Canaan closed the door and was finally, deliciously away from the world. He sighed and must have made quite the expression because Javier grinned ear-to-ear.

"There he is! Hi, Elder Canaan!" Javier said.

"Har-har," Canaan replied, but smiled anyway. "The world is crushing in on your last two Elders. Speak plain to me tonight, even if you think I might punch your lights out. Deal?"

Javier nodded. "What's going on?"

"My man is breaking apart," he said and peeked in on Kilmeade again. He was still in deep discussion with Roman and when he noticed his presence, Canaan returned his focus to Javier. "When I spoke to you on the phone, Kilmeade seemed ready to crack. A few hours ago, I thought he was about *to cry*." Canaan whispered the last word, but Javier's face remained serious. "He wasn't, of course, but he's having visitations from angels and every little thing upsets him."

"You've also been touchy," Javier said and Canaan almost snapped at him. "And you told me that Kilmeade still insists he'll die soon."

"He will leave the flesh, as he put it. Return to the Father," Canaan said and then corrected himself, pointing to the ceiling. "The Father in the sky, I mean."

"God is working a number on him," Javier said softly. "I'll take a stab at why he's struggling so obviously, instead of more like I did."

"Okay. Stab." Canaan crossed his arms and leaned on his elbows. "This is why I needed you here."

Javier sipped his tea and worked on his opening line. Before he began, a knock sounded at the door and the waiter brought in their appetizers. Once they were alone again, Javier was ready.

"Before Last Assembly, I was still a kid, not even a hundred and forty years old. I had no duties, no cares." He paused and Canaan discerned he wanted to say it just right due to Canaan's short fuse. "Roman had obligations and responsibilities galore. You know—Elders dealt daily with situations and scenarios the rest of us weren't privy to. I worked out my transformation thinking only of myself. Roman resisted. He had to make sure everyone else was safe."

"That's Kilmeade." Canaan had already come to the same conclusion and Javier's input clinched it.

"Me, Beryl, David—we can't truly know what it's like to relinquish the kind of power Elders give up," Javier said with his brow furrowed.

Canaan sighed. "You see a lot, Javie. The prophecy says I will do it, too, but I don't see how." After a long moment, Canaan shook his head with a small grin. "But then again, you couldn't have told me a year ago I'd be scooping whiny-ass newly-mortal brethren from their pain and tucking them into bed."

"Heh, you mean the ones we're finding, right? Not me and Beryl."

"Oh, them, too," Canaan bantered back. "I'm very different now—my entire life I've been a loner. Besides you and Kilmeade—and of course, Marcy—I never liked anyone." Canaan scratched his head. "Don't say it." Canaan forced a laugh. "Your Puppeteer set this up from *wayyy* back. I reckon your God will change my heart even further."

"You won't believe what it says in Ezekiel 36," Javier whispered, his chin down. "Wanna see?" He began flipping around on his phone and then plopped the device in front of Canaan.

"*I will take the heart of stone out of your flesh and give you...* Aw, come on, shit," Canaan said and shoved the phone back across the table. "Subject change!"

"The next verse says then He puts His spirit inside of you," Javier said with a kind grin. "What's happening to you and Kilmeade is perfectly natural."

"*Perfectly natural,*" Canaan mocked. "Here's the question. I'm a surly, unapproachable grouch with a quick temper and a ruthless nature. Why would your God want anything to do with me?"

Javier exhaled. "He doesn't see you that way. He created you for His purposes and He knew you before you were born. Can the pot ask the potter, 'why did you make me?'"

"I'm the pot, right?" Canaan asked in a weak joke.

"The pot was formed, used, and cared for until it eventually broke and was returned to clay once more." Javier touched his chest. "That's us. He built us for His purposes. The only thing that makes it meaningful is that He loves us."

Canaan's mental block rolled upward as it always did when the subject of God came too close. "Father Damien told Kilmeade that he feared Jesus would kill him if he tried to understand this stuff."

"Are you surprised? The Fathers taught us to avoid religion, to despise the idea of a supreme God. It's the same for mortals, the voice of the enemy inside them says, 'God doesn't love you! Save yourself! Get rich and forget this crap!'"

Canaan shook his head in wonder. "I'm amazed any of us survive with all this spirit stuff going on. If I knew Ta'avah's evil voice was in me all this time, I would have gone loco already."

"Well, that comes back to the Puppeteer. He has timing for everything. He revealed Himself when the time was right."

The waiter knocked once and brought in trays of food. When he had gone, Canaan sampled his steak and pointed his fork at Javier. "Beryl texted me—he's at the rental." Javier nodded as he started in on his salad. "Of course, the rest of the text got garbled. I hate cell phones."

"Gotta stay current, old man," Javier joked.

"Speaking of B," Canaan said ignoring the jibe, "that's more crazy God shit there. Meryl and Beryl came into the world when I was 250 years old; I was gone by the time they were assigned to Jack's pack. I only saw them at Assembly and you know how it was—they were playthings, there for an Elder's pleasure. I never cared one way or another if they lived or died. But now? I *love* that guy. I mean, it's insane. A Rakum doesn't love anyone. He doesn't mourn and he doesn't brood. Since 11/13, Kilmeade and I have mourned and brooded a lot."

"I know," Javier said with a nod. "Believe me, I understand."

Canaan groaned. "My Rakum heart must be completely gooey now. It's disgusting."

"Did Chloe's visit effect you guys more than you expected?"

"Chloe..." Canaan set down his fork and knife and opened his palms against the table top. "She's become my responsibility. Kilmeade started out with her as a Rakum Elder, but within days, he wanted to know her as a mortal. When one of his visitations assured him he never would, he began turning her over to me."

Javier sighed. "Yeah, we saw that."

"Exactly. She must have seen it, too," Canaan said and returned to eating. "If I had a time machine, I'd roll it all back."

"I think we all would."

Canaan didn't reply and returned to his steak. Javier sank into silence as well and they gazed at each other a while, both in their own heads. When someone finally moved, it was Javier. He set his phone on the tabletop and glanced at the lock-screen as it lit up with a notification. Canaan read it upside down.

"Why did you make a reminder for me to call Chloe?" he asked, seriously wondering. What could he possibly have to say to her? Why would he when they said goodbye sufficiently a week ago?

"I think you should check in," Javier said softly. "She's only twenty years old and pregnant by a Rakum; she's going to need a little hello between now and whenever you go home."

Canaan turned his head partway, regarding Javier with suspicion. Marcy hadn't been that fragile. Still deciding on a course of action, Canaan pulled his phone from his jeans pocket and looked at the sleeping screen.

"Just ask her how she's feeling. It won't take long and a sentence from you will last her a long time." Javier pushed his plate aside and folded his arms on the table.

"I guess..." Canaan said and opened his contacts. His chest constricted and he pressed a closed fist into his sternum. "*Shiiiiit,* this kind of pain I can't enjoy one bit."

"Emotional pain," Javier sympathized. "When you're human, it feels exactly the same."

"Yay," Canaan said and flipped Javier a sideways bird. He covered his eyes with that hand and pressed Chloe's number. She picked up before the end of the first ring.

"OHMYGOD! Canaan? I was just thinking about you! Hello?" Chloe's happy little voice chirped in his ear and he shot a new one-finger-salute at Javier without looking up.

"How's our little bird?" he asked, picturing her in his lap the day she said goodbye.

ellen c. maze

"Did you call to check on me?" she asked.

"I did." Canaan peeked at Javier whose expression said, *I told you so.* "Javier told me young ladies pregnant with a Rakum's baby might need a phone call now and then."

"Bless him! He's right! Oh, I miss you so much!"

Canaan noticed she didn't try to separate Kilmeade out and he purposed not to analyze her omission.

"I'm using Mom's obstetrician and he's a zillion years old. It's hilarious," Chloe said and giggled. "When he puts the stethoscope on my belly it shakes all over the place." She laughed again and Canaan couldn't help but smile. "But he's competent, don't worry." Chloe lowered her voice. "I dreamed about you. Wanna hear it?"

"If I was sexy, yes. If I was boring, no."

Chloe laughed again. "You were sexy," she said, her voice muffled as if she'd guarded the phone as she spoke. "You and I were at the park in the daytime."

"And... did I do something awesome?" Canaan caught Javier's eye. Chloe's telephone voice carried in the small room so Javier heard both sides.

"Yes," Chloe said even quieter than before. "Oh, God, I'm blushing. Is Kilmeade there? He might be mad I dreamed something so—"

"Kilmeade isn't in this room with me, but he knows everything I know, little bird. Go ahead, Canaan was doing what? This is getting pretty interesting." He looked at Javier and said for Chloe to hear, "I hope I had my clothes off."

"Who's with you?" she shrieked into the phone. Canaan chuckled.

"It's only Javie. Say hi, Javie." Canaan held the phone out, but Javier didn't play along.

"Canaan! Geesh!" Chloe said and returned to her normal voice. "Okay, so what's going on with you guys?"

"Aw, now, tell me what you dreamed, little bird," Canaan begged. *"Can you read me this far away, love?"* Canaan sent a telepathic lob, unintentionally calling her a new endearment.

"Oh! Yes! I miss you so much..." Chloe's telepathic voice hitched as she cried gently on her end. *"Please hurry, I don't want to have this baby without you. It's scary... I worry about you guys every minute..."*

"Not much longer, little bird. Hang in there. You're doing great. When this is over, you'll see, everything will be wonderful for Chloe and her littler bird."

"I pray for you both every morning and night," Chloe said into the

361

phone. Then she sent silently, *"Did you see what I dreamed? I'm terrible. I'm lonely, too."*

When she mentioned it, the dream streamed past unbidden: she and Canaan on a picnic in the sunshine where they made love on a blanket.

"That was a nice dream," Canaan sent silently.

"Yeah," she said aloud, her voice still shaky from repressed tears. "I know you need to go—these stupid females and their stupid emotions..."

"It's not stupid, honey," Canaan said, another endearment popping out and he rolled his eyes when Javier noticed. "I'll call you in a few days, okay? I will keep my word."

"I know you will," she said softly. "Kilmeade heard all this, right?" Canaan grunted affirmative. "Good. I love you guys. Please, hurry home." She sounded done and added to the end, "Both of you."

When Canaan set down his cell, he looked to the side and not at Javier. He sent his mind to his brother in Tuscaloosa and found him finishing up. He seemed lighter, more like his old self. Kilmeade noticed his attention and sent him a greeting.

"Dr. Roman fixed you up, eh?" Canaan sent over, still looking at the side wall.

"Perspective is an amazing thing," Kilmeade responded. *"Your call to Chloe went perfectly. It appears we were successful, which gives me great comfort."*

Canaan shrugged more or less and Javier noted his movement. Always aware, he remained quiet and waited his turn. Kilmeade also noted all this and on his end began his goodbyes with Roman.

"You and Javier go back to the house. I will meet you there."

Canaan nodded and turned to regard his dinner date. Javier had cleaned his plate, but left half of his cheesecake. "What's wrong with that?"

"I'm full," Javier said and pushed the remaining wedge across the table. "You have it."

Canaan pulled it into place and stabbed it with his fork. As long as Javier didn't say anything about sloppy seconds, they'd be fine. Kilmeade snickered in his mind and Canaan grinned, too. It wasn't too bad sharing a brain with the guy. Now that he was feeling better, that is.

〈〈回〉〉

"Elder Canaan!" Kilmeade said as they met outside his front door. When Canaan drew close he grasped his shoulder and said in his ear, "Methinks Chloe *way* overestimated your intimate proportions..."

"Oh, she was close enough," Canaan retorted and socked Kilmeade

362

hard in the middle without warning. "That's for earlier. You don't end a pummel session by pulling rank. Not cool."

Kilmeade doubled over, the air knocked from his lungs, but he was smiling. Javier hung back as if he might become tangled in their fun, but it was over. One punch ended it for them both.

"You're absolutely right," Kilmeade huffed standing up straight and still recovering. "You didn't hold back. Nice."

Canaan raised his eyebrows a few times. "Don't talk negatively about my beautiful body and next time, I'll cut you some slack," he grinned and allowed Kilmeade to pull him toward the house.

"Oh, my brother, you know I am only jealous!" Kilmeade bellowed, now almost to the door. He felt so much like his old self that he wanted to shout forever. "I think I'm turning into you, Canaan. I can't stop being as loud as I am awesome."

"You look fantastic," Javier told him.

Kilmeade nodded and brought both men under his wing as they reached the door. It opened on its own and Kilmeade walked them through. In the main room, the squatters looked very comfortable on his couches and beanbag chairs. Besides Veronica, Missy, and Ben, the same four men watched television with sleepy eyes. Kilmeade was finished housing lazy indolent ingrates.

He touched the side of his head to Canaan's. "Take Javier into the kitchen with Ben and the girls. I'll clean house before the Stones arrive."

"Screw that," Canaan said grinning. "I like cleaning, too."

Kilmeade grinned and called Veronica over with two fingers. "I want you, Missy, and Ben in the kitchen with Javier. Go now and don't come out, no matter what you hear."

Veronica nodded with worried eyes. They watched her corral Missy and Ben into the next room. *Be careful,* Javier mouthed and entered behind them.

"These are not my people," Kilmeade sent to Canaan who got his meaning. Before he left the house to Jimmy DuPont last November, a few dozen familiars crashed there. These four were strangers and paid Kilmeade no respect.

"I'll follow your lead, boss," Canaan sent back with a nod.

Kilmeade studied the man closest. This one was fifty, if a day, with stringy white hair to his shoulders wearing a faded and grimy Rolling Stones T-shirt with tattered cargo shorts. Baddie or not, Kilmeade wanted to end him. He took in the next two men across the sofa. Both African

American, both middle-aged and yellow-eyed, wearing clothing possibly stuck to them, it was so filthy. Where did these people come from? All four of them were healthy enough to make their own wage, so why did they prefer to siphon off a stranger they had never met and eat food they didn't pay for? The last man was mid-thirties wearing a dress shirt and threadbare khakis. He looked like someone who'd gone for a job interview five years ago and was waiting to hear back.

"I'd drink that guy on the far end," Canaan said, offering to help with at least one indigent. *"He smells better than these three."*

Kilmeade sighed. Roman had given him a lesson on how to be a mortal, and murder definitely went against their God's code. *But I'm not human, yet...*

"This is true," his cohort said aloud.

"Go see if he'll come out of the room with you," Kilmeade whispered and Canaan stepped away. When he reached the man, he made a few small comments and the guy stood up to follow Canaan down the opposite hallway. *"Damn, you are good."*

"I know it," Canaan sent back and Kilmeade followed them into the dark corridor. This hall led to the solarium and two large game rooms complete with taxidermied trophy animals that had come with the mansion.

"In here," Canaan said quietly to the man who followed oblivious to any danger. He stopped in a room housing a competition pool table and three pinball machines. Canaan took hold of the man's elbow and led him to a closed door. He pushed it open, flipped on the light, and gently shoved the man into the small room. "Wash up a little, I mean, *shit.* I'll wait." His eyes as lifeless as before, the man nodded and turned for the sink. Canaan faced Kilmeade and grinned. *"Easy peasy."*

"You ever taken a Dying Buzz, my friend?" Kilmeade asked.

Canaan shook his head. *"Came close once or twice, but I'm too goodie-goodie,"* he grinned.

"Too afraid of the Fathers, you mean," Kilmeade replied with a soft chortle.

"That, too." Canaan turned to the bathroom when the man cleared his throat from the doorway.

"How's this?" he muttered and yanked down the collar of his shirt to reveal clean hands and a clean throat. "Fifty bucks, right?"

"A hundred if you're still," Canaan said and covered the transient's mouth with one hand as he pressed him against the wall. With practiced ease, he punctured the man's throat with his small knife and moved in. The stranger struggled immediately, flailing enough that Canaan had to reposition. He pulled hard and Kilmeade soon closed his eyes to the buzz cascading his way. When he sensed Canaan slowing, he leaned close.

"Don't stop. Don't," he whispered low enough the mortal wouldn't understand his words. But seconds before the man's heart went into arrhythmia, Canaan pulled away, tossing his head back for a deep breath.

"I'm... I'm..." Buzzing heavily, Canaan wrapped his hands around the squatter's throat and squeezed. "I'm too handsome... to..." he mumbled, eyes closed, his grip ending the guy moment by moment. "I can't pull off the look like you can..." His victim stopped breathing and was released to slide to the carpet.

Kilmeade laughed and leaned on the wall with both palms. "Why do you think that buzz hit you so hard, brother?" Kilmeade asked, still feeling the tingle in his middle that Canaan's mind sent. "Or did I only think it was bigger than before?"

"No," Canaan said, also leaning on the wall with both hands. "It was more than before... I don't know why..." He took a deep breath and flipped around to lean on the wall backwards. "Two things come to mind..."

"One has to do with the little bird," Kilmeade said without accusation. "The other with all these horrid changes in our hearts and spirits."

"Precisely," Canaan replied. Tonight he'd worn a round-collared Henley so he shrugged it over his head. "Take your portion, boss, and we'll finish cleaning house on a full stomach."

Kilmeade closed the distance and dug in without another word, one hand behind Canaan's neck and the other his shoulder.

"Make it last," he sent telepathically, eyes closed and head tilted up. *"You won't taste old Canaan again..."*

Kilmeade didn't reply—he'd seen the same prophecy—so he took Canaan's advice and savored the moment. When satisfied, he pulled away and joined Canaan leaning with his back against the wall. The hit he received from the blood-meal paled in comparison to Canaan's, which he'd half-expected. If Javier and Roman's God disdained the drinking of blood, it was unlikely a man so close to transforming would enjoy it as he did in the past.

"You're that close?" Canaan asked in a whisper.

Kilmeade shrugged and turned to hit Canaan with a smile. "Go see if you can entice the other three guys in here for a game of pool."

"Not a problem," Canaan said and pushed himself off the wall. He flexed his pecs to get a chuckle and then shrugged on his shirt. "Be right back."

When Canaan disappeared out the door, Kilmeade exhaled slowly and closed his eyes. His two-hour chat with Roman answered many of his questions and straightened a few kinks in his understanding of the Creator. Waiting for Canaan and Javier to return to the mansion tonight, he had another vision. This time, the angel informed him that Canaan would only see the vision if Kilmeade wished to share it. So far, this moment, he chose not to. In the vision, God's messenger shared with him how Kilmeade should conduct himself for the remainder of his time in the flesh. Tonight's celebratory delve into murder and blood stood in stark contrast to what the God of the mortals instructed him to do.

Canaan returned then and Kilmeade hadn't yet moved the body of the stranger out of sight. He also caught a glimpse of what Kilmeade had been pondering. "Did he pass out again?" Canaan asked, covering for Kilmeade's foible.

"Just now," Kilmeade played along and bent to lift the man to a chair. "I got him. He'll be okay in a minute."

"Damn fool prolly OD'd," one of the men said as he reached the pool table. The same man looked hard at Kilmeade. "Blondie said you'd pay a hundred bucks to help move stuff."

"Me, too," another man said and the third echoed in agreement.

Kilmeade nodded. "Right. But I have an even better idea," he said and gestured to the pool table. Behind them, Canaan closed the door. The first man turned, vaguely interested by the movement, but the other two focused on Kilmeade's hand as he placed several hundred dollar bills on the green felt surface.

"Are you sure about this, brother?" Canaan asked him in his mind, having seen the instruction to "behave." Kilmeade ignored him, which was an answer in itself.

Approaching the thickest of the three squatters, Kilmeade stood beside him, facing the other two men as he did. He allowed the man to wonder what he might be up to, initiate a turn his way that might have evolved into a question, but before anything materialized, Kilmeade slammed his head into the green felt. Loud and wet, the sound of his skull cracking jerked the remaining two men to attention. Both yelped, confused and terrified.

Canaan did his job, grabbing the closest man who stared on in disbelief. He was ended in a heartbeat by the flick of Canaan's wrists, his neck broken. Kilmeade's second man begged for his life only once and was similarly broken in two. Then the room fell quiet. Canaan slowed his breathing and held Kilmeade's gaze, awaiting a response. Kilmeade looked at each dead man in turn, nodding thoughtfully. Canaan chuckled and Kilmeade looked up, humor in his eye.

"You heard that, eh?" Kilmeade asked, grinning now.

"I heard it. *Not a puppet?*" Canaan said and laughed louder. *"Shiiiiit,* you are one scary son of a bitch. The Maker of All tells you to play it cool and we murder four at once." Canaan nodded. "You, my friend, have major *cajones."*

His grin to the side, Kilmeade shrugged one shoulder. "I am an Elder, we must always be learning."

Canaan shook his head, chagrin evident. "You should see your face. That is satisfaction if I ever saw it."

"It was an experiment," he said as innocently as possible.

Canaan nodded and bent down to drag his victim toward the others. "Oh, I know. A *few* experiments, Dr. Kilmeade. One, am I a puppet or can I work my own will?" Canaan dropped his guy with Kilmeade's. "Two, will the Maker still want you if you don't do what He says?"

Kilmeade snickered. "You are correct, Dr. Canaan. As always."

"I would not have dared..." Canaan shook his head still smiling and trying to hide it. "Where do you want your dead guys?"

Kilmeade looked around the room. If they left them and someone saw them in the day, they risked exposure. No, even though they were pulling out at sundown, the bodies needed to be destroyed.

"The entrance to my special dumpster is on my end of the house. Get me Javier," Kilmeade said and held out his hand for the cell. In a moment, Canaan handed it over and Javier answered the ring.

"Canaan?"

"Take Ben and the ladies for a twenty minute spin. Just go around the block and come back. Go now." Kilmeade tossed the phone back to Canaan and hopped up to sit on the pool table.

"Kilmeade, you never cease to amaze me," Canaan said his compliment coming from deep down.

"One does what one can," he responded and patted the surface beside him. "Javier will take a minute. Sit with me. Let's look at those little humans the Puppeteer didn't want me to kill."

"He's gonna call you a brat," Canaan joked hopping up beside him.

"I wonder... Does He talk or does He prefer telepathy?"

"Shewwww, I know you're not asking me," Canaan chuckled, leaning

367

over his knees.

"Serious question coming up, brother. Ready?" Kilmeade turned to catch his friend's attention. Canaan's icy blue eyes met his and Kilmeade smiled. "Have you wanted to be with Him. With their God? Have you felt yourself pulled that way?"

"No," Canaan said without hesitation, and Kilmeade saw in his mind he answered truthfully. Canaan hadn't yet felt what Kilmeade did—that if he could only be re-joined with his Maker, he would become whole, more fulfilled than he had ever been in the flesh. Canaan creased his brow at Kilmeade's stream of consciousness.

"I felt it first at Javier's condo when Isaac forced me to look into the spirit realm. Their God appeared to me and told me He loved me." Kilmeade's heart raced at the sudden memory of that night mere months ago. "At that moment, I remembered my true Father." Kilmeade lowered his voice. *"At that moment, I wanted to be with Him more than anything else in the whole world."*

"Damn," Canaan whispered. *"You're freaking me out..."*

"I tried to go to Him a few times before 11/13, and more than once afterward, brother. Each time, He sent another blasted angel to tell me to wait. That I had more to do."

Canaan's eyes widened. "I didn't see..."

"The angel blocked you from those visitations." Kilmeade slid off the table and Canaan followed suit. Outside, Javier was overheard moving his wards into the car. Kilmeade squeezed Canaan's near arm once. "That's why you're still here and will remain. You don't feel that pull. When He pulls your thread, you'll go. But you will live a mortal life and die an old man."

"Sounds great," Canaan said joking.

"For now, grab those two!" Kilmeade said loudly, his attitude refreshed. "Let's get them to the dumpster. Tomorrow, we finish this!"

Canaan helped him relocate the corpses and plan the trip to L.A. The SanFran Rakum, Lucas Poppa, went on the back burner; the time had come to save the last Rakum and call their mission a success. It was time to go home, each to their own place, and Kilmeade was ready.

42, July 17, Los Angeles

Plenty could go wrong, but so far, it hadn't. Cary chalked his success up to the training his mother instilled; developmental cognitive exercises repeated a thousand times increased Cary's critical thinking skills beyond any man alive. Now as he watched the trail opening for Dae Kim, he realized they were a mere twenty-four hours from obtaining his century's old goal: Revenge and power, attainable as soon as he had his hands on Kilmeade and his oversized partner.

The camouflage tent hidden in the copse of natural brush was invisible from the air and the primitive trail up the mountain would give even the fittest hikers a challenge. Knowing Dae Kim navigated it with a grown man over his shoulder only impressed him more. Dae Kim wouldn't be hard to revert—his earlier work to resist humanity, and now imbibing in Cary's blood, had already increased his natural advantages.

"Goin strong," a new text read from Adam's phone. Cary smirked. Roberts was a genius, but his indoors-powderpuff existence barely prepared him for what Cary had in mind. All the while his adopted father worked to imbue the kid with Rakum might, he coddled him even more. It would be funny if it wasn't so sad.

Cary regarded his extensive preparations to execute the perfect plan. The low shelter would house a broken and beaten Beryl. The Elders would be alerted of his condition with just enough time to make it up the mountain, but not enough to make it to the dark before sunup. Adam had expressed concern that Javier would come alone to rescue his pal, but Cary had planned for that. None of them would even become aware of Beryl's predicament until it was too late. And to play it safe, Cary set mechanisms in place to deter Javier from attending the rescue.

A few yards away, the brush opened and Dae Kim burst through, trotting strong as an ox under their captive's weight. Cary grinned despite himself—of all the Rakum to run into after a century of scheming, he had been gifted with the best.

In accordance with his genius, Kilmeade successfully sent Veronica and Missy away for good. With a wad of cash in hand and each with a bankbook worth half-a-million dollars, he convinced them to never return, not even for their belongings. When the women puttered away in Veronica's Towncar, Kilmeade turned to Canaan and crossed his arms.

"Tell me what you have against this Michael Stone."

Canaan grinned. "Can't get anything past you, I see," Canaan said enjoying the asinine nature of his assertion. "My memories don't speak for themselves?" Before Last Assembly, Michael Stone had been an impressive lieutenant for Jack Dawn with a reputation of ruthlessness and brutality. Being many years his senior and an Elder, Canaan conquered Stone every time Dawn pitched them together for his pummel parties. Stone was a fun sparring partner in that when he was smashed and broken, blood and snot everywhere, he didn't make a sound. He *glared,* though. Canaan laughed, and then Kilmeade did, too, following his stream of consciousness. *"He had this glare..."* Canaan shook his head.

"You squashed him—he took it like a Rakum," Kilmeade said smiling. "So why don't you like him?" Canaan only shrugged. "Because it's more fun to *dislike* him," Kilmeade said and turned for the front door. "They're here. How about you be nice to the guy? For my sake."

"Oh, I'm always *nice,* Master," Canaan said with a toothy grin.

"You like the woman, though," Kilmeade added as he led the way to the front door. "You always like the ladies..."

Canaan agreed and listened as Javier welcomed the couple into the house. When he and Kilmeade reached the living room, Beth Rider-Stone was kneeling on the tile speaking to Ben.

"You are *adorable!"* she was saying. The squirt put out his hand to shake. "Nice to meet you, Ben. My name is Beth."

"Ben and Beth!" the kid said and put his hand toward Stone who grinned down on him like a new dad.

"Hey, buddy. I'm Mike. Nice to meet you."

"Do you have a son?" Ben asked craning back his head.

"No, we have a daughter."

"Oh, that's sad," Ben said and turned to see Canaan and Kilmeade standing in the doorway. "KAY-NAN!" he shouted and grabbed Beth's hand again to pull her towards the Elders. "Beth! This is my friend Kay-nan. He's teachin' me to be a man," Ben added as he puffed out his chest. "And that's Mr. Star, Kay-nan's brother."

Canaan nodded to the woman when their eyes met. He'd barely thought about either of them since last November when they combined forces to defeat Rufus. Canaan knew he should introduce Kilmeade, but he took too long.

"Mrs. Stone," Kilmeade said stepping forward to stand beside Canaan. "Michael," he said as Stone joined his wife. "My California familiars knew me as Mr. Star. I am Elder Kilmeade," he said with a hand to his chest. "As if that matters anymore," he added.

Beth's eyebrows went up and she grinned with dimples. "That's humility and it's beautiful," she said, her gaze playfully shooting over to Canaan. "I hope you picked up some of Elder Kilmeade's habits since we last saw you."

"Come close and you tell me," Canaan said with a wink. He enjoyed teasing her maybe too much during their past association, because she ignored his flirtations entirely.

"Knock it off, Canaan," Stone said, nodding a greeting to Kilmeade.

"Oh, sweetness, please come knock it off for me. It misses you," Canaan returned and blew him a kiss. Stone was a big guy, wide and over six feet—*He'd be fun to pummel right now...* Kilmeade jabbed him mentally and Canaan made an effort to straighten up.

Ben pulled hard on Beth's hand. "Wanna see m'toys?"

"Hey, turd-butt," Canaan said to him with a stern glare, "go sit on the couch." Grinning, Ben made a fart noise and turned away. Canaan met Javier's eye and it seemed they all wondered how to begin. Michael Stone cleared his throat.

"First off, Kilmeade," he said facing the Elder, "I don't remember meeting you before now, but it's possible I forgot. If so, I apologize."

Kilmeade regally tipped his chin. "No, we never met."

"I can't stop thinking about last November when we all thought Roman's brother was dead," Stone's wife said then, addressing Kilmeade. She gave him a warm smile. "I'm very thankful you're alive. We all are."

Kilmeade bowed a few inches at the waist without speaking.

Canaan snickered inwardly. *"You sure are putting on airs for this woman,"* he sent and shook his head.

"And you are studying her much too closely," Kilmeade returned without humor.

Canaan rolled his eyes. His partner had discerned correctly—Canaan favored her. She was small-town attractive with a nice figure and dark blonde hair past her shoulders. She'd been a Rabbit seven years and still

371

looked twenty-two, not thirty. Plus, she had pluck. The woman had faced a level of brutality the Rakum reserved for the worst mortal transgressors and came out fine. In her book, she asserted her faith kept her sane. Kilmeade looked at him at that moment and prodded him to mend fences for the cause. Canaan put a hand out to Stone.

"Mike, I am a jerk," Canaan said and Stone shook his hand. "Let's start over."

"Miracle of miracles. Somebody tamed the gorilla," Stone said looking Canaan dead in the eye. In deference to his superior, Canaan only winked back.

Beth clasped her hands together with a soft sound and all four men looked her way. "It's 2 A.M. back home. You guys have coffee?" When both Elders returned blank looks, she laughed and walked away. "I'll find it. Michael, tell them about Roman's phone call."

"Sure," he said as his wife disappeared into the kitchen. "Roman caught us up on what happened with Isaac and Ta'avah in Athens and explained what happened to Javier when he took Isaac's blood." Michael glanced quickly at Ben who ignored them from the couch, playing with an action figure. "What does the kid know about what happened?"

"Only what he saw," Canaan answered. "We haven't spoken of it."

Beth returned and the coffee pot gurgled from the kitchen. "Considering everything, we need to talk to him first," she said, and when no one objected, she turned for the couch. She sat beside the boy and turned to see his profile. "Ben, it's time to talk about what happened when the mean guy attacked you and Kilmeade."

Ben looked up and set down his toy. "Mr. Star has two names. My buddy Kay-nan has one," Ben said without emotion.

Canaan grinned. *"This kid is so weird..."*

"But is he weird because of my blood or was he always weird?" Kilmeade returned with raised eyebrows.

"How about you, Ben? What's your last name?" Beth asked.

"Puddin' tain, ask me again an' I'll tell you the same," Ben said his eyes to the side.

"Ben, answer the lady," Canaan warned.

"That's okay," she said. "He can tell me later."

Canaan huffed softly. "Mrs. Stone, the kid has no heartbeat—if he can't answer the simplest questions, we're in deep shit."

"Canaan," Beth admonished and Canaan's eyes widened.

"Hey, Caveman. –Language," Kilmeade sent.

Canaan groaned. *"This is getting suckier and suckier every passing moment,"* he responded silently and crossed his arms.

"Ben, me and Michael are friends of Canaan's from a *long* time ago." Beth waved at everyone to find a seat. Canaan leaned on the armrest of the recliner Kilmeade dropped into. Stone sat in a recliner on the opposite side while Javier and Beth flanked the kid on the long tattered sofa. "We're going to treat you like a big boy. Tell you some big things."

Beth's tone was encouraging, loving, and self-esteem-building. Canaan grinned despite himself and the boy was eating it up. She asked him to describe what happened and he began without hesitation.

"Mr. Star and me was walking by ourself 'cause Kay-nan had to pee-pee. Somebody pushed me down and I got hurted." Ben yanked up his pants leg and waited until all eyes noted his abrasion. "There was a bad guy on the ground and Mr. Star made him stop moving by doing this..." Ben reached both hands to Beth's face and cupped her ears. "Dead."

Beth nodded and he dropped his hands.

"Boy, you did a great job telling us what happened," Beth said and he smiled. "When the bad guy attacked Mr. Star, he stabbed him a little. That made some of Mr. Star's blood get on your face."

"I know," Ben said interrupting. "They tol' I got it in my stomach."

"Do you feel different now that you got it in your stomach?"

Ben shrugged. "Not really, but my eyes hurt a lot and I'm hungry all the time." He put his hand to his middle and Beth looked at Canaan.

"Will you bring him something to nibble?"

Canaan looked at her blankly, prepared to ignore her request out of Elder principle, but his partner poked him mentally. *"Sh-i-i-i-i-t,"* he complained to Kilmeade alone and rose for the kitchen rolling his eyes. Understanding at least part of his complaint, Beth snickered as he left to grab the nitwit some crackers. When he came back, Beth handed Ben the box of Ritz and looked to Javier.

"Let's pray over him and see what happens."

"This part is theirs," Canaan sent silently as Javier, Stone, and Beth circled the boy. *"Let's go greet Lucas Poppa, give him the good news. He looks fun. We'll be back before sunup..."*

After a long minute, Kilmeade agreed. *"I know Poppa, he is indeed fun, but you'll find him another time. I have a better idea."* Kilmeade got to his feet.

Only Javier looked up and he gave Canaan a see-you-later wave. Canaan held out his hand and like the true bro he was, Javier tossed over the keys to the Prius. Canaan followed Kilmeade past the kumbaya and out the front door.

In the drive, Kilmeade made an abrupt right-angle turn to the side of the house. Canaan scooted behind him, a delightful idea brewing in their conjoined minds. "We aren't going to need these keys, are we, boss?"

In lieu of a reply, Kilmeade laughed into his hand. Canaan clapped his back. The night was going to be fun after all.

《 ▣ 》

Ben fell asleep on the couch, and after Beth covered him with a blanket, they stepped into the kitchen. Mike rubbed his eyes and shook his entire body.

"Here's the point I want to make," Mike said keeping his voice low, "the boy has parents. He says his father kicked him out, but he's only seven. Who knows the real story? We're walking between the worlds here and I think that's the real reason Canaan and Kilmeade need our help."

Javier nodded after considering his assertion. "What can we do with him for the next day or so?"

Beth peeked into the darkened living room. "He can't live with outsiders anymore; that's a fact as far as I'm concerned." Both Javier and Mike agreed. "I propose Michael and I take him to a hotel. We'll ask him to pretend we're his parents." She looked at her husband. "If God hasn't healed him by the time we wake up to go home, we'll take him with us."

Javier rolled in his lips and tried to imagine scenarios that could arise from such a plan. They'd be breaking mortal laws, but didn't this supernatural child's needs supersede the risk?

"It isn't ideal, but *he has no heartbeat,*" she whispered. "Put him with mortals—a shelter, his father, the police—and as soon as he's checked medically, a giant spotlight falls this way. Right on top of the Elders."

"Absolutely right, honey," Mike said to his wife rubbing her back.

"And what if he's still ...*changing?*" Beth looked at both men allowing her question to dangle.

"I know what we do," Javier said with inspiration. "Let's get Roman over here. You have celebrity and should avoid scrutiny if Ben is found out."

Beth looked at her husband and they locked eyes. Javier pulled his phone free and punched Roman's icon. It was 3 a.m. in San Francisco, but time to wake up in Alabama.

"What's the status?" he asked when he answered.

Javier put him on speaker. "Roman, I don't think the Stones should

ellen c. maze

take the risk, but what if *you* came here and got the boy, kept him until the mission is done?

Roman did not hesitate to reply. *"It's the best thing if the boy remains in his condition. My brother expects to be leaving the flesh very shortly so it won't be much longer before you come home."*

"What's this? Kilmeade will leave the flesh?" Mike asked.

"Yes," Roman replied. *"Kilmeade has foreseen his demise and it's coming soon. When they help the last Rakum in Las Angeles, he's going to go with God."*

"Wow," Beth whispered and she and her husband fell silent.

"Mike, stay over one more day. If God doesn't heal him after all four of us pray, I will assume custody. Kilmeade has friends in California that will make paperwork for Ben. Will you wait?"

After a glance to his wife, Mike agreed. "I'll text you our hotel information."

Javier took the phone off speaker and pulled up a stool. "Ben is on Day Three with no heartbeat and he still looks fine..." Mike and Beth walked out, and from his seat, Javier watched them attempt to rouse the boy in the living room. "His blood must be circulating somehow."

"Does he have blood?" Roman asked.

Javier furrowed his brow. "Canaan checked when it happened. Said his blood smelled horrible. I don't think anyone has thought about it since then."

"See if you can find out. I'm getting a plane ticket."

Javier motioned for Mike to return to the kitchen with Ben. The boy sat on his hip, head lolled on Mike's shoulder. Javier set down the phone and gestured for Mike to stand still.

"Let me look at his veins," Javier said and rotated Ben's nearest arm dangling at his side. What should have been blue and purple was flesh-colored. Javier licked his lips and caught Beth's eye.

"What's wrong?"

"I don't think he has blood anymore," Javier whispered. Beth came close and also examined his wrist.

"What are ya'll doing?" Canaan asked, entering the kitchen without a sound. All three of them jumped.

"Oh, God," Beth hissed and grinned embarrassed. "Sorry," she said with a hand over her heart.

"I'm still amazing, still gorgeous," Canaan said with half of his normal enthusiasm as he looked in on what Javier sought.

"Yeah, yeah," Stone mumbled, just as subdued. "Flirt over there."

375

"I'll put Roman back on speaker," Javier offered, meeting Canaan's eye. "Roman had the question—does he have any blood. Look..."

Canaan came closer and crowded Beth, who scooted away. Canaan sent her a kissing noise and took possession of Ben's wrist. Mike stood immobile and his wife walked to his opposite side to watch from there.

"Ben," Canaan said sharply, yanking his arm. The boy didn't awaken and Canaan yanked him again. "Ben, hey! Ben!" Not at all affected, the kid slept on. Canaan dug around in his pocket and when he presented his pocketknife and headed for the boy's arm, Beth inhaled.

"Stop!" she said and reached over Mike to cover Canaan's hand.

"Stone..." Canaan rumbled deep in his chest.

"Beth," Mike said, manually moving her hand off the Elder's. "He knows what he's doing." Frowning, Beth huffed and crossed her arms.

"Damn straight. I'm three hundred and sixty-six years old," Canaan grumbled quietly.

"She knows," Mike replied, obviously getting Canaan's meaning. "She's sorry. Go ahead."

Watching the Stones interact made Javier grin and Canaan looked up then and met his eye, his knife millimeters from Ben's arm.

"They're cute, aren't they?" he said to Javier, his humor intact. To Mike he said, "I appreciate the props. Let's see what's under the hood."

Javier was about to ask about Kilmeade, but Canaan pressed in his knife. On the phone, Roman asked what was happening. "You smell that?" Javier whispered without answering Roman.

"He's rotting," Canaan said quietly, rotating the boy's tiny arm back and forth. He pushed the edges of the wound and no fluid of any sort leaked forth.

"No blood, Roman," Javier said loudly as his heart fell. Mike and Beth matched his expression. Canaan chuckled and looked behind him.

"My kid's a zombie, Kilmeade. Nice job," he teased into the dark hallway.

Javier lifted the phone and told Roman to hurry. Once he hung up, he turned to Mike who laid Ben on the kitchen counter.

"Well?" Mike said to anyone. Beth hooked her arms around her husband's bicep, her eyes asking the same question.

Canaan pressed his palm to Ben's forehead and looked into the dark hall. After a moment, he nodded. "Brain is still active, but now he's not breathing."

Javier inhaled sharply. "Did anyone notice if he was breathing when we were questioning him earlier?" The others looked around and shook their heads. "I didn't either." Javier sighed and then huffed at Canaan who was grinning, chatting silently with an absent Kilmeade. "Canaan, what's so funny? And why isn't Kilmeade in here?"

His face the picture of mirth, Canaan looked at Javier and then at the Stones. "It's private," he said and pointed to Ben. "Half-dead's waking up. And yes, he was breathing before we left. A Rakum Elder notices everything and forgets nothing."

Javier gave Ben a grin as he awoke and sat up on the counter.

"I didn't climb up here, not my fault!" he said and looked around at the faces that encircled him. "Sumbuddy's in touble!"

Canaan backed into the hall, pointing at the child with both hands. "The zombie is now in your care," he said.

"I not a zombie!" Ben shouted trying to climb down without help.

"Benny, my boy, listen to these nice people," Canaan called to him. "Remember this?" he asked and held up one finger. Ben nodded. "Great," the Elder said with a grin. To Javier he said, "You, guard your Elders." Javier nodded, smirking at Canaan's jolly tone. "And Stone, take your wife to bed. Please. For me." Canaan winked and turned away.

Mike shook his head. "Still an idiot."

Beth held her first finger up to Ben. "What's this mean?"

Ben made a firm point and poked it into her hip. "Dead." He looked up to see her face. "My friend Kay-nan can dead you with 'is finger." Beth tittered with a tight grin.

Javier stepped into the hall in time to see Canaan shoot him a come-hither gesture. He jogged after him into the dark hallway.

"What?" he whispered at Canaan's back.

Canaan turned to face him. "My heart is so squishy tonight," he joked and crinkled his nose. "Javie, you are my favorite non-Elder person." Canaan wrapped meaty hands around Javier's throat. "You know that?"

The question was not rhetorical and Javier nodded with a smile. "Yes, I know. Ya'll rest-up. Ben is leaving with Mike and Beth to their hotel and Roman will get the kid tomorrow after we're gone. Ben is off your hands."

"Beautiful," Canaan sighed and jerked Javier close to plant a wet smooch on his forehead.

"Ugh," Javier said with a fake shudder. "Kilmeade's move. Was that from you or him?"

Canaan pushed him back to arm's length, nose still scrunched with fun. "I don't know anymore. After tonight, I don't know where he ends and I begin." Canaan laughed louder then and the Stones checked on them from the kitchen.

"Give me a minute," Javier called.

Canaan stepped further from the light of the other room pulling Javier along. "I think I might actually *be* Kilmeade now," he whispered with a mysterious grin and released Javier's neck. "And he is *meeeeeee.*"

Javier shook his head at Canaan's silliness. "You're behaving very strangely. What happened tonight?" Javier asked, his curiosity growing by the second.

Canaan winked. "Here's a hint. What makes a man smile?"

Javier paused, reading the humor in Canaan's eyes even though the Elder was nearly invisible in the dark. "A man or a Rakum?"

"A *man,*" Canaan said and lowered his chin. He began stepping backward again and Javier remained in place.

"Do you mean sex?" he asked softly. Kilmeade wouldn't step out on Chloe, even if he was about to die. Then Javier recalled the Elders could translate. "Ohhhhh... you went to Tuscaloosa," Javier said in an undertone.

Waggling his brow, Canaan tossed him the car keys and melted from view.

Javier turned for the kitchen. *Now* it made perfect sense. Both Elders loved her, one Elder could touch her, and Canaan was in Kilmeade's brain. In the kitchen Mike and Beth didn't press him to explain Canaan's behavior and he was glad. Some things didn't need to be imagined.

43, July 18

"This is it," Canaan whispered as he visualized the sun crawling slowly below the horizon outside their light-tight space in Kilmeade's California mansion. "Is tonight the night? Or tomorrow night? Or the next?"

Kilmeade hummed from his side of the room, also still reclining on his bed and staring at the dark ceiling.

"I feel like an actor who's been given the end of the scene, but not the beginning or middle." Canaan turned his face to Kilmeade several feet away. "I guess we'll start like we always do—follow our noses."

Kilmeade nodded, his gaze far away.

"Sunset 7:27; Javier has us on a jet at nine; allows two hours to set foot on the ground in L.A. and begin our hunt. Sound right?" Canaan asked, enjoying the sound of his own voice.

Again his partner only nodded slowly, facing forward.

"Then I'll ride a unicorn into McDonalds and order a Big Mac," he said in a monotone.

Kilmeade chuckled. "I love unicorns," he said without looking over.

"Me, too, especially the brisket."

"Say it again," Kilmeade whispered, finally turning to meet Canaan's gaze. Canaan nodded and prepared to be serious.

"Chloe is five-and-a-half months along and in perfect health. Your *daughter* is in perfect health and will arrive on time with absolutely no complications. I will be there for them both. I swear it."

Kilmeade grinned and came upright to put his feet to the floor. "You are one lucky man," he said to Canaan with a wink.

"Huh," Canaan managed, not yet able to be joyful that his other half would soon be leaving forever. Last night, they had indeed translated to Chloe's side and for whatever good it did, Canaan had waited across the house while they visited in private. Tonight, a brand new urgency had been born in both of them to finish what they had started.

"Ehhh…" Kilmeade made a noise that sounded like the beginning of a thought and stopped. Canaan got to his feet to stretch.

"Brother, to answer your *ehhhh...*" Canaan said with a frown, "yes, I heard you. You were praying." Canaan crossed the space and put out his hand. Kilmeade grasped it and he yanked him to his feet. "Risky, isn't it?"

"It is," Kilmeade agreed in a low voice. "I am so close, Canaan. I can almost see Him. When I close my eyes, because of our training, our specialized focus..." Kilmeade shook his head slowly. "He is my missing piece. When I go to Him, I will be home." Kilmeade sighed and finished silently. *"It's becoming much more difficult to resist the Light."*

A rush of adrenaline clouded Canaan's mind just then as he feared to the core the thought of being left without his partner. Canaan recovered quickly and held Kilmeade's gaze.

"Let me show you," Kilmeade said softly.

Canaan shook his head in slow motion, holding steady their locked eye contact. "It's not time for Canaan to see. You know it," he said, his voice somber.

Kilmeade's face broke into an easy grin and he clapped Canaan's shoulder. "Listen... quiet except for your little Javier."

"My wittle fwend," he replied and unbolted the door from where they stood.

Kilmeade touched his arm. "Take no blood tonight, brother. Not from Javier, not from anyone."

Canaan narrowed his eyes working to discern who commanded him, Kilmeade or his angelic visitor?

"For me, because of our connection," Kilmeade answered and put his hand to Canaan's cheek. "Wait until I'm gone. Will you?"

Canaan's eyes grew wide. "Shit, of course. I wasn't thinking."

"Ya'll up?" Javier called from the door. "Did you hear my heart going pitty-pat?"

"I heard you snoring," Canaan jibed. "Wipe your drooly chin and come on in." Javier entered and nodded to them both. "Kilmeade is getting ready to take that starship to the skies." He squeezed Kilmeade's bicep. Kilmeade smiled and took a deep breath.

"What of Ben?" Kilmeade asked Javier, clasping his hands at chest level. "What is your take on the boy?"

Canaan looked at Javier interested in his response. Earlier, Kilmeade had spoken internally to the Maker about the boy. Canaan resisted the worry that seized his heart; the words his partner had spoken, the sentiments, the depth of feeling and care were all so foreign. They had rescued Ben by happenstance; neither of them knew he'd be there, that he'd be an orphan, that he'd been abused. God put Ben there, and God put Kilmeade's blood in his tiny body. This evening, Kilmeade's spirit asked the God of the mortals *why?*

Canaan came back around and found Javier deep in explanation of Ben's situation. Looking briefly at Kilmeade, Canaan caught up by reading his thoughts as they formed.

"Roman used your contacts to work up a social security card for little Ben," Javier was saying to Kilmeade. "He also gave him a new last name. *Merlin,* can you believe it?"

"Merlin?" Canaan repeated loudly. "I haven't thought of him in forever." Merlin had been Kilmeade's Elder.

"I think of him every time I smell burning Cannabis," Kilmeade said grinning. "Master Merlin never put it down."

"That notwithstanding," Canaan laughed aloud, "it is an excellent name for little Ben. How's his condition?"

"No change," Javier said with a head tip. "Roman flew him back to Tuscaloosa. They touched down an hour ago. Safe and sound."

Kilmeade looked at Canaan. "I want him to live with Roman and when you get back, find a Rakum-savvy physician." Kilmeade paused thoughtfully before continuing with a grin. "You and this medical professional will investigate what he is seeing beyond his eyes."

"As in, he somehow saw you translate to Alabama," Canaan offered.

"Precisely. Look into it."

Canaan nodded. "It will be as you say."

"Good," Kilmeade said and ran his fingers through his long hair. "Let's go to Los Angeles."

《回》

Standing at the jetway, Javier's phone chimed and he checked the screen. A message from Beryl appeared, yet when opened, it had been sent the day before.

"It's from yesterday," he said and hit play. The voicemail trickled out of the speaker and noting his concerned expression, both Elders turned to listen over his shoulder.

"Hey, look, you and Canaan haven't been responding so I don't know if you got my most recent texts. I'll wrap it all up in this voicemail. Two things. First, Simon said he thinks Adam is dangerous. He said that whether or not Adam knows it, he subconsciously wants to destroy us. Sounds crazy, I know, but Elder Canaan said I shouldn't take anything for granted, no matter how stupid. The second thing is, when I

got to L.A., Adam called me on a new cell and told me Dae kidnapped him and brought him to California. I was worried so I picked him up. He's here with me at the rental. He's not acting weird and there's no sign of Dae. Anyway, if you get this, call me and I can explain better. I'm hopping in the shower, but after that, we're gonna hole up here until you guys arrive. Kazak."

Fixing Javier with his gaze, Canaan pulled out his own cell and called Beryl's number. Voicemail picked up without ringing and he turned his eyes to Kilmeade.

"He pinged me telepathically this time *yesterday,*" Canaan grumbled, his tone barely disguising his sudden anger.

"He can't do that anymore," Javier said, not sounding at all certain.

Holding his partner's eye, Kilmeade tilted his head. *"The twinge you had..."* he sent silently.

Canaan nodded and ignored Javier's continued questions. Kilmeade's eyes rolled closed and Canaan matched his movement.

"Find my B and find him now," Canaan sent, aware his inner voice had begun to shake with trepidation as much as fury at whomever threatened Beryl. In the space of a few seconds, Kilmeade opened his eyes.

"A shadow-man has joined forces with Dae Kim," he whispered so Javier could hear. "They will use Beryl to set a trap. That is all I know."

"Is he safe?" Canaan asked silently, watching Kilmeade's expression. Javier posed a few more queries, but Canaan focused on his cohort. *"Did they hurt him?"*

Kilmeade didn't know. He had no vision, no outside or divine knowledge. Nothing.

Canaan felt the blood leave his face and he grit his teeth. *"I'm not joining that asshole if He takes away my B, you hear me?"*

Kilmeade's response was to turn to Javier. "We proceed to L.A."

Javier clenched his jaw and watched for Canaan's response. It took almost a minute, but he flicked his hand in the guy's face to get him moving. Kilmeade ordered Canaan to walk ahead of him and he brought up the rear as they entered the jet for the short hop to Los Angeles.

Exactly two hours later, they had discerned their sad and needy brother had booked a room at the Ritz-Carlton. Kilmeade set the three of them out of foot traffic against a wall a block away from the luxury establishment. Canaan had tried Beryl's phone three more times since they touched down, the fear of losing his friend morphing into blind rage at those who took him. He held it inside, but only just.

"If he's in the Ritz, he has his disbursement," Javier offered.

"Who's this shadow-man? Dae Kim and who else? Is it Adam?" Canaan asked both men, his jaw as tight as a drum.

Kilmeade did not reply and his mind revealed no answers.

"We agree this visit tonight is a trap, right?" Javier asked and Kilmeade nodded.

Canaan clasped Kilmeade's forearm in his fingers. "Dammit, Kilmeade, are you blocking me? *I can't see shit in your head right now!*" he hissed, falling silent at the end.

"No, I hold nothing back. This Rakum—he knows you. Quiet your mind and listen," Kilmeade admonished. Canaan didn't comply right away, but Kilmeade was right—he was overreacting. It occurred to Canaan that when he became mortal, his temper would be hard to master.

A stranger passed their position too closely and Javier pulled both Elders by their sleeves down the wall a few more feet toward the alley.

Canaan closed his eyes and leaned against the brick. Sorting through his mental garbage like the Rakum he still was, he began to receive images of their target. *Bryson—Roman's pup.* His cohort was correct—he knew this one. The man's name opened the gate on every memory he had of the guy and Kilmeade telepathically followed along.

"Fill me in," Javier said quietly, watching around them for anything or anyone suspicious. Canaan held up his hand and Javier fell silent.

"His spirit is calling us, I hear him, his despair is deep," Kilmeade sent over, and then whispered, "Did you see that?"

Canaan nodded. His partner had a clear glimpse of an impending danger. Right alongside that was a mandate to proceed to the man's room. He held Kilmeade's gaze a moment longer and turned to Javier.

"Your God, again," Canaan growled and took a deep breath. "We have to go up even though one of us is going to get hurt."

Javier nodded, ready to proceed.

Canaan narrowed his eyes and dropped a hand on his shoulder. "What the hell is wrong with you?"

"What?" Javier asked. "Let's go to it."

"Your God just told Kilmeade one of us will get hurt, maybe killed, and you're just *la-dee-dah,* let's go play!" Canaan barked.

Javier's expression grew somber. "God has this under control. Whatever He wants to happen will happen. We can trust Him 100%."

Canaan looked at Kilmeade who gave a tiny nod. "He's right."

"Well, halleluiah! Let's go to it!" Canaan spun toward the hotel.

Once through the glass doors, sniffing the guy out was as easy as ever and Canaan led the way. When he and Kilmeade had narrowed it down to the man's actual room, he asked Javier to hang back. After he called into the room with their Rakum greeting, Bryson asked them inside. Kilmeade entered first with Canaan two steps behind; both Elders recognized the furtive movement dead ahead.

"Javie, hit the ground!" Canaan shouted as he and Kilmeade whirled for opposite sides of the large salon. Quantities of leadshot peppered the air, blasting through the partially closed door into the hall. Without predicated communication, Canaan and Kilmeade chose tasks and got to them. Canaan zoomed into the hallway to check Javier and Kilmeade used the same speed to disarm Bryson.

Javier had ducked, but now lay on his side with both hands to his face. He made barely a sound, but Canaan sensed multiple penetrations of the scattered shot in his friend's face. As Kilmeade dealt with Bryson, Canaan scooped Javier into his arms and jogged quickly to the stairwell. Before a single soul had opened their doors to the noise, he had descended three floors. A custodian's closet lay on the fourth descent and he pressed in. Canaan sat against the closed door, legs crossed, and pulled Javier into his lap. Still not complaining, but in immense pain, Javier's eyes were swelling shut.

"*Shitshitshit,*" Canaan whispered shaking his head.

"*Bryson is deceased. How is Javier?*" Kilmeade sent over.

Canaan could see in their connection that, because of the commotion raised, Kilmeade had been forced to flee out the window fifteen floors up.

"*Stop worrying about me. How is our boy?*"

"*He needs eye surgery to remove the shot. Dammit!*" Canaan cursed a few more times and concentrated on the wounds not in his eyes.

"*Get him to an ambulance and meet me outside.*"

Canaan nodded in the dark closet and finished removing the shot he could reach. Pulling the material free by sheer will and closing the wounds was no problem. The eyes, though...

"How bad?" Javier whispered, gritting his teeth against the pain.

"You need surgery," Canaan whispered and ripped a portion of Javier's shirt from the bottom. He wrapped the strip around the crown of his friend's head as a blindfold and carefully got him to his feet.

"I'm going to lose my eyesight," he said under his breath.

"No, I see the pieces, there's only seven—five embedded in your lids, two in your sclera. A surgeon can reach them." Canaan opened the closet door and stepped him toward the door to the floor they'd reached. "I could get them with the right instruments so I know a doctor will. You're gonna be fine."

In the hallway, he dialed 911 and the operator directed personnel already en-route to Bryson's room to their location. Outside, Kilmeade had reached their rendezvous point and telepathically attended all of Canaan's movements. Medics bandaged Javier's eyes and bundled him onto a gurney while a uniformed policeman questioned Canaan as a potential witness. He slipped away from the scene as soon as the officers became distracted with the mess Kilmeade made in Bryson's hotel room.

Using the stairs to the main floor and then going through the dining room and kitchen, Canaan exited the building in the rear and Kilmeade met him before he reached the street.

"It's not my preferred way of doing things," Kilmeade told him silently with a slight grin, *"but when I had Bryson in my grip, I realized why we'd been sent."*

Canaan nodded, understanding and commiserating simultaneously as he saw everything his partner had. Bryson and Dae Kim had planned an extravagant killing spree and the Elder's visit tonight saved the lives of at least twenty-four little girls.

"And Javier needed to be incapacitated," Canaan said and had meant to ask. When Kilmeade only shrugged, Canaan added, *"I might be figuring something out about this Puppeteer. Whatever is required from us next, whatever makes you transform and leave the flesh, and whatever brings Beryl back was going to be too dangerous for Javie."* Canaan watched his friend's eyes. *"What do you think? Did his God just move him out of the way?"*

Kilmeade seemed thoughtful and Canaan watched ideas and postulations cascade across his mind. A satisfactory conclusion had just formed when Canaan's cell buzzed with a new call. Canaan pulled it free of his pocket and Beryl's phone number showed on the screen. Canaan swallowed hard and answered. "Beryl?"

"Elder Canaan, you gigantic ass! Look who's in control now," Dae Kim said on the other end. "I'll make this short. I have Beryl and Adam. Shortly, I'm going to hurt them both really bad. But, oh no! I can't heal anymore! Dang!" Dae Kim chuckled at himself. "But *you* can. I'll send a video with instructions on getting your boys back."

Click.

Canaan searched Kilmeade's impressions, but he had moved on already to finding a light-tight place to spend the night. Canaan shook his head. "Focus, brother. We don't need a place to sleep. We need to find

Beryl."

Kilmeade walked along the wall toward the street. "We will head for the rental. Come," he ordered and continued away. Canaan followed after a halting moment, realizing his partner's plan was the same, only more forward-thinking. Sit in the rental where they have guaranteed light-tight space and await Dae Kim's instructions.

Canaan trotted behind Kilmeade, now walking at a good clip. They reached Olympic Boulevard and the crowds of night folks enjoying life. Catching the upcoming cross street, Canaan hit the Uber app and stomped his heart into submission.

44, July 19

The campsite disappeared into the night as a starless sky consumed the lights of the city below the hills. Not a soul had approached and with mere hours until sunup, Dae Kim sensed the doctor's excitement growing every passing minute.

Beryl had come-to, but only after Dae Kim had him securely taped to the stake. Tied beside him, Adam played his part, seeming to be genuinely terrified whenever he was threatened. Doctor Nankin had already exited the area, lest he be seen by Beryl or the Elders. The plan only worked if they remained unaware of the Lost Rabbit, leaving the doc with his secret until the last moment. Dae Kim grinned; time to get back in the tent and put a hurtin' on his old pal.

When he lifted the flap of the low structure, Beryl growled struggling furiously to be free. His stake had been mechanically driven three feet into the ground so he would never be able to bring it up. Taking his cue from Beryl, Adam flailed, too.

"Hush now," Dae Kim said switching on a battery-powered lantern. "We're making a little movie for your friends." Dae Kim had positioned his tripod earlier, so he fixed his iPhone in place and set it to record.

"Kazak, Masters!" He looked directly into the lens as he crossed to Beryl still thrashing against his bonds. "I guess you're sorry you abused little Dae Kim these past couple of months..."

Dae Kim drew back his hiking boot and kicked Beryl in the side of the head. As an expert, he knew precisely what would bruise, injure, maim, or kill, and for now, he wanted the man's injuries to look much worse than they were. With his back to the camera, he slapped Adam's cheek with an open hand. He held back for the wimp's sake and Beryl jerked his gaze over at the violent sound. As expected, Adam cried out and Beryl voiced his violent opposition through his gag. Dae Kim returned to the lens.

"I'm going to beat them *almost* to death. *Almost*, you see? You know I'm an expert. Hell, Master Canaan—you showed me most of this stuff yourself!" Dae Kim lowered his gaze for the Elders and grinned. "After these guys are busted up, I'm gonna give you the coordinates to our location so you can get here and heal them." He shrugged for the camera. "See? That's fair. Oh! And I got my own giant Rakum box!"

Dae Kim walked back to the tripod and swiveled the camera an inch to take in the shadowy corner of the tent.

"There it is! Just like the one you shoved me into. It will hold you both and keep you safe from the sun." He looked back into the lens and got in closer, making an expression of surprise.

"Oh, dang, did I forget to tell you that by the time you get here to heal your pals, it'll be nearly sunup?" Dae Kim giggled in a high voice and covered his lips with his fingers. "Masters, my Rakum box holds two Elders. One. Two. And I will make sure it takes two Elders to save these boys' lives." He leaned in closer than ever. "I will bring them to the edge of death—just like Elder Canaan taught me."

Behind him, Beryl renewed his efforts to escape. Dae Kim peeked at him reflexively and returned his focus to the video.

"The way I see it—if only *one* of you comes, one of these guys will die. If *two* of you come, both morons are saved. Then you both get in my box and I'll keep you for my pets." Dae Kim lifted the phone off the tripod, keeping his face in the lens and he walked it closer to Beryl. He extended his arm so the phone would look down on him and pick up Beryl in the background. Bright red blood ran from the man's broken nose and bruising puddled under his eyes.

"Isn't this crazy?" Dae Kim shook his head. He was about to go off script and he hoped Doctor Nankin, who was streaming the entire evening, wouldn't fault him for it.

"IT IS CRAZY!" he shouted. "No Rakum would give his life for another. If you do this, if you risk your lives to rescue these imbeciles, then you're not RAKUM AT ALL! You're not worthy of the Ten, not worthy of the hundred-thousand, not worthy of the title Elder!"

Dae Kim hawked back and spit a generous loogie at the camera. Taking a deep breath, he calmed his sudden flare of disgust.

"You'll get the coordinates by text." Dae Kim put the phone inches from his face. "*Assholes...* Don't do it. Don't lower yourselves. If you do, you deserve everything I have planned for you."

Dae Kim shut off the video and left the shelter to preview his work. Deep down, his anger simmered. *Dammit! Why did they have to be so weak?* Never in a million years would any of their Elders display such human behavior. The video rolled in the viewer and Dae Kim watched, his mind still seething against two men he had once served as gods. When the clip ended, he shut down his thoughts with a snort. The Elders would comply or die. Not his fault they became such pansies.

Now to the plan...

Timing was everything. The only way to their location on short notice would be on foot; helicopters and beasts of burden took time to hire. The route had been timed to the minute, allowing a mere sixty seconds leeway. Translating mystically to the site would be impossible, as he had happily explained to his cohorts, a Rakum Father could translate his physical body from one location to the next only if he had been there before. The doctor's plan hinged on the assertion that Los Angeles was too foreign to the Elders for them to have visited their random hillside campsite in the past.

To prevent the Elders from translating to safety between healing the boys and sunup, Dae Kim had his sniper rifle camouflaged, set and ready; a .300 Win Mag caused a dramatic hole, big enough to prevent the concentration necessary to think oneself to another place. The Elders would run to the box if they wanted to live another day.

Kilmeade and Canaan would receive the video and be instructed to wait for the precise coordinates. It would take the Elders sixty-five minutes to reach the campsite with only five minutes of healing time before the first beams of UV crossed the horizon. Rakum eyes blinded easily and Dae Kim chuckled with excitement.

And if the unthinkable happened? If the plan failed on any level? Adam would resume his friendship with the group and Doctor Cary's confederate would wait in the wings until called. The plan was foolproof and more evidence of Doctor Cary's genius.

At that moment, Dae Kim's timer alarmed and he sent the video. Watching remotely, Doctor Nankin, sent him a text with a thumbs-up. His face set, Dae Kim re-entered the tent; it was time to *nearly kill* Beryl and catch them some Elders.

《回》

Canaan tried, but he couldn't stop cursing. Even before the video ended, the fury he'd been barely suppressing bubbled up and out, leaving it to Kilmeade's stream of consciousness to fill him in on the evil little shit's final threats. At the moment, his other half held him to the ground employing a method of restraint Canaan hadn't learned in his training. *Hell,* Canaan thought as the red haze slowly filtered away, *Kilmeade probably made it up himself.*

"Has it located it's sanity? If it has, I will allow it to rise and play with the team," Kilmeade relayed, using Canaan's favorite teases against him.

"I am back," Canaan grunted, his words garbled through a cheek compressed firmly to the ceramic tile floor. "Thank you." The last was gratitude, glad that Kilmeade allowed him to remain conscious when he could have easily put him out and been done with his foolishness. Kilmeade's weight disappeared and Canaan pushed to his feet.

The outburst had been building for weeks, which Kilmeade also recognized. *"Since that night the boys couldn't find Adam,"* his partner sent now leaning against the kitchen island.

Canaan nodded, cracked his neck both ways and then his back at the waist. "Well, Boss...what can you say to cheer your old friend?" Canaan wasn't joking. He didn't have the faith of Javier, nor the sure knowledge of Kilmeade. All he had was blind rage and a despicable helplessness regarding the avalanche of pain surrounding his heart.

"I have much to say, my brother, but now is not the time." Kilmeade flicked his gaze to the cell phone face up on the counter surface. "Dae Kim will send us the coordinates soon and you are not going to like my orders."

Canaan shook his head in tiny increments. "No, the hell, no. There is no way..."

Kilmeade held up one hand. "You're working yourself up again."

"Kilmeade," Canaan murmured, taking slow deliberate breaths. His friend was planning to go alone, heal both men, and then do his final trick—transform into a mortal and leave the flesh. "You can do all that, I want you to—but not alone. I will be there. I'll get in DK's damn box. If both men are near death, you heard him—you won't be able to save them both. He's right—I taught him well."

"I will heal them both," Kilmeade countered holding Canaan's gaze. "Your place is here, for Javier, little Ben, and Chloe."

Canaan's eye twitched at Chloe's name. Yes, if he allowed Dae to hold him as some sort of torture toy, who'd take care of Chloe and the baby? Hadn't Kilmeade had a vision that *Canaan* would be the one in that position? The red fog rolled in again and Canaan shook his head. Javier's God too much enjoyed yanking them to and fro, giving and taking, petting and abusing—

"No more," Canaan whispered. "DK's no match for me. Let him open that box once. I have tricks even *you* don't know of. We are in this together, big brother. The end."

Kilmeade's mouth developed a slow smile and he nodded in half-time. He stood off the island, stretched, and stepped up.

"Come close," he said, his smile to the side. He pulled Canaan into his strong arms and kissed his cheek. "Ask me how I know the Puppeteer loves me," he said into Canaan's ear.

"How?" Canaan asked with a cautious grin.

"Because He gave me you as a companion."

Canaan nodded and the embrace did not end. Kilmeade held him tightly and an odd hitch sounded in his old friend's chest. Canaan braced to move away and check on him, and the world went black.

《◉》

The house was unfamiliar, but because of Javier's excellent forethought, the basement had been made deliciously light-tight before their arrival. Kilmeade placed Canaan on the oversized leather couch in the basement gameroom. Heavy-duty bolts had been installed on the access, so with one last look around to ensure his partner was safe, he returned to the first floor and locked the door on Canaan's side.

So far the cell phone hadn't chimed. Kilmeade sprinted to the garage and slipped into the car Javier arranged. In three minutes, he was picking his way out of the canyon and he paused at the bottom. Left or right? He had to choose.

"If You wish it, You could tell me which way to go to have a jump on Dae's plan..." Speaking directly to the Creator—as a Rakum Elder—Kilmeade awaited a prod. Either He would help or leave Kilmeade to flounder along. Waiting only ten seconds, Kilmeade touched the gas and turned right, heading away from the city and into the dark hills. Was it common sense or had he been nudged? Taking a card from Javier's deck, Kilmeade decided to *go and do,* and trust the Creator's plans would come to pass.

Fifteen minutes later, the cell alerted with a text from Dae Kim. Slowing only slightly and driving with one eye on the winding road, he memorized the coordinates and copied them into the phone's GPS. The route popped up and Kilmeade grinned. He was half-way there.

"Someone was listening," he said to himself in the quiet car. Daring one more communication, Kilmeade stared at the black road zipping underneath his wheels and asked Javier's God to have His way tonight. Javier had told them that asking for God's will to be done was 100% safe, all the time. *"Because you can trust Him,"* Javier had said. Kilmeade nodded to no one and increased his speed.

In ten minutes, he reached a trailhead and exited the car, the predawn sky slowly purpling. Allowing only a split-second to imagine himself in the sunshine, Kilmeade re-focused and his heart pulled him toward the captive Rakum. He had already sensed Beryl's thread, the same one they used when he was a Rakum. Kilmeade tugged it as he jogged urgently across the rough terrain, ignoring brambles that grabbed his clothing and skeletal tree branches reaching for his face and neck. Canaan's little brother was unconscious, Kilmeade discerned, but he continued to poke at him, hoping to diagnose his injuries even before he reached the site.

Kilmeade stopped suddenly and dropped to his knees. Ahead twenty yards, he heard heartbeats and the sigh of masculine breathing. As he concentrated on the identities, he searched any others and found none. To be certain he wouldn't be ambushed as he healed the men, he sent his mind out a mile and sensed no one else close. As assured as he was going to be, Kilmeade leapt up and ran for the tent, bursting in with only the sound of the canvas flap pushed aside. A tickle deep inside alerted Kilmeade he was being watched. Unsure if the Maker sent the warning, an angel, or his own Rakum intuition, Kilmeade's face jerked left to peer directly into the lens of a hidden camera. With barely a thought, he burned its circuits and returned to his task.

As Dae Kim promised, Beryl was near death. Kilmeade disregarded Adam entirely and expertly loosed the former Rakum to draw him into his lap. Multiple facial contusions were ignored as Kilmeade lay both palms open on Beryl's bare torso. Under the skin, his spleen had been ruptured and leaked its fluids into his body cavity. One kidney had been badly bruised, threatening to shut down, and a rib fracture penetrated his lower lung three full centimeters. With Kilmeade's calm and even concentration, every soft-tissue injury responded and stepped up the repair and replacement of destroyed cells.

Beryl groaned once and was still as Kilmeade moved to phase two—bone regeneration. An ugly wound at his temple hid a skull fracture that closed with little effort and so Kilmeade cupped the man's neck in both hands and carefully adjusted the misaligned vertebrae. One tender palm to Beryl's nose and the healing was complete and the patient opened his eyes.

"Master," he breathed, not immediately recognizing he'd fallen into the habits of his past life.

"Rise up and free Adam. Canaan needs you." Kilmeade helped him stand with Beryl nodding and focusing his eyes. When he shivered, Kilmeade shrugged off his shirt and Beryl slipped it over his nakedness.

To their left, Adam muttered to himself, more asleep than unconscious. Kilmeade studied his injuries as Beryl untethered him from the stake. Besides a bloody nose and split lip, the kid pretending to be a Rakum had nothing to attend. Kilmeade huffed in disgust. Either Dae Kim was in love with the kid or there was a new subterfuge in play. Kilmeade pulled the man to his feet as he awoke and took in his surroundings.

"Where's Dae Kim?" he said catching Beryl's eye to his right.

"Shut up and listen," Kilmeade hissed in his face jerking him close. "Beryl was beaten nearly to death and you're not even broken." Kilmeade yanked him outside the shelter and into the waning nighttime, Adam following on strong legs.

"What? I don't know what's going on!" Adam whined.

Kilmeade shook him. "Be quiet!" he snapped and closed his eyes. Now inside his search radius, a heartbeat had entered from the west. He released Adam and stepped back.

"Beryl, Canaan needs you. *Right now.*" He tossed Beryl the phone and car keys. "Go back down the mountain through there," he said pointing behind them, "and you'll find the car. And Beryl... *run.*"

Obedient to the core, Canaan's little brother turned and was gone, dragging Adam behind him. The first blinding rays of the sun were four minutes away. He'd bought himself a little time, but not much.

"Translate back. Do it now."

Canaan had come-to.

Kilmeade made note of the horizon and with a small grin stepped into the open away from the shelter. *"Watch for Beryl, he is completely restored."* Kilmeade listened for the heartbeat growing closer, imagining it was Dae Kim.

"Come back. You have time. We'll get that little shit later..."

In another five seconds, he recognized the heart-sounds assigned to the traitorous brother.

"Brother, you know I—" An explosion sounded as a projectile knocked Kilmeade back. He did not lose his feet, but looked down at a large through-and-through bullet wound in his chest.

"DAMMIT, KILMEADE, COME BACK!" Canaan's telepathic voice shouted as Kilmeade touched his wound and tried to pinpoint the shooter's vantage spot. By the approaching noise, Dae Kim would jog into view in less than sixty seconds. Canaan also felt the blast and his mental voice grew weary.

"Kilmeade, please..."

"Brother, when I put you out, I left you a deposit. Use it as needed," Kilmeade said kindly, referring to a collection of memories and instructions he thought his co-Elder might need in the future.

"I sensed it. Now, brother..." Canaan began and, finally out of time, Kilmeade interrupted him.

"Listen closely and hear me well. I perished that day at the cabin, in the cold, when you were impeded by the blizzard. Whether the visitation occurred as you and I recalled, I can't be sure, but I left the flesh. The Maker returned me to my station to fulfill the purpose He set for me from the beginning of the world. Do you see what that means? Do you see the mercy of our Creator? The Maker of all things stooped down to ensure that one insignificant half-demon found his way Home." Kilmeade paused and went on with urgency, sensing his final moments had arrived. *"The deposit that awaits in your subconscious contains a special word for when your time to receive His Spirit arrives. Until then, remember how He rearranged the laws of nature to save your beloved Kilmeade. I am proud of you. I love you. But He loves you more."* Kilmeade finished and peeked again at the western edge of the site.

Stunned and unable to reply, Canaan's mind sent only an evenly-split measure of joy and sadness.

"Hah! This wound has closed already," Kilmeade sent over with chagrin. *"Dae Kim will die. Watch Adam. I didn't have time to read him. Determine if he is the shadow-man."*

"I will do it," Canaan responded, his telepathic voice soft. *"Kazak, brother. You will be greatly missed."*

"Take care of our Chloe," Kilmeade sent and disconnected, cutting his tether entirely.

Then, three things happened at once. Dae Kim emerged from the treeline, readying his rifle for another shot; the morning sun peeked over the horizon just enough to blind a Rakum; and in his mind's eye Kilmeade watched as the familiar angel walked toward him, arms wide.

"Leave Dae Kim to us," the angel said in his mind. *"Are you ready?"*

Dearly desiring to know the details, Kilmeade hesitated. Would he end the man? Kilmeade had comforted himself since the receipt of the video that before the sun rose, Beryl's abductor would be dead. Not offering any reply, the angel remained as he was, shining as brightly as the sun that had already removed Kilmeade's eyesight.

Kilmeade dropped to his knees as warmth slowly kissed the skin of his face and neck. How many years since The Ritual of the Stinging Sun, the last time Kilmeade faced the ultra-violet light that slowly peeled away Rakum skin and melted aged tissues?

The angel again prompted him to proceed. Kilmeade turned his heart to the Creator of all.

"I confess I know You, Yeshua ben Elohim[20], Immanuel[21], the God of Israel, and I know You have loved me from the beginning of the world. I receive You as my Father, my God, and King. I have sinned against You and eaten Your people as one eats bread. Wash me clean by Your sacrifice on the cross. Thank You for this life, for my friends, and for the child I never expected, nor deserve. I am ready to come home if You will have me. I discard my flesh into dust and into Your hands I commit my spirit."

The blinding white light emanating from the messenger of God dimmed in Kilmeade's vision and the landscape of the campsite slowly filtered into view. The California sun looked back at him, a ball radiating yellow beams and sitting on the far hills as a stool. With no pain in his eyes or elsewhere Kilmeade took a deep breath. What he expected to be white and excruciating was velvety and hued blue as the morning light crept along the topography. Second by second, the light morphed to a pale violet and he lifted his hand to look at his fingers, rotating his palm. The light did not burn his flesh. On the contrary, it massaged every atom in his body. The thoughts that slammed to the forefront of his mind—"I am mortal," and, "the sun was never a cursed thing after all"—gave him peace as he turned full circle to watch the azure light on the ground transition seamlessly to yellows and golds.

As if from a million miles away, Dae Kim shouted, but Kilmeade couldn't make out the words. Riding both worlds and sensing his impending departure, Kilmeade watched the angel approach Dae Kim across the site and touch his shoulder. The former Rakum crumbled to the ground as the messenger turned to Kilmeade and put out one shining hand.

"Your Father awaits."

Kilmeade nodded and with a smile, went Home.

---

[20] (Hebrew) Jesus, Son of God
[21] (Hebrew) "God with us"

45

Maybe it had been a mistake planting only one camera at the campsite. Cary thought the action would take place near the Rakum box and never did he foresee the Elder would realize he was being filmed. So... *what happened after Kilmeade terminated the feed?*

Cary flipped the switch and the CCTV camera hidden across from their L.A. rental's front door popped open its view. He allowed it to remain, streaming in real-time as he texted and attempted to call Dae Kim. After trying for twenty minutes, a black sedan pulled into the rental's drive and Beryl and Adam emerged. He still had no answers to his main two questions: Where was Dae and had Canaan come, too?

Cary watched the two men enter the house and he closed the laptop with a growl. If Kilmeade went into the sun, he was dead. If he was dead, why hadn't Dae Kim checked in? Cary tossed the computer to the backseat and started up the car. All the way to the trailhead, he ran through possible scenarios of what occurred. In another fifteen minutes, he exited at the small parking lot and began the laborious hike upward.

By the time he reached the site, the sun had found a comfortable spot mid-sky. Cary didn't have to look inside the structure; Dae Kim lay a few yards away. He jogged to the man's side and turned him over. Deceased, rifle in reach with no visible wounds.

"Where are the Elders?" he asked the air and walked in concentric circles from the spot Dae Kim lay. On the fourth pass, his shoe slid with a liquid noise and he looked down. Measuring approximately two feet square and with the appearance of melted candlewax, Cary stared unbelieving at what he surmised were Elder Kilmeade's remains. In the purplish-red mix, the Rakum's clothing shimmered in the new day as the effluence of a four-hundred-year-old creature leached into the earth. No remnants of Elder Canaan presented and Cary backed away.

"Time to initiate Plan C," he told himself and turned to make haste. He grabbed up anything in the shelter that might bear his fingerprints and hoofed it to the car. There hadn't been a Plan C, so his keen mind would have to cook one up. For now, the sun pierced his eyes and a swiftly-

396

expanding migraine threatened to cripple his escape. Cary made it to the car and crawled into the backseat. If the cops should come by and suspect him, he'd be helpless...

Plan C. Why didn't I make a Plan C?

With his last bit of energy, Cary pushed the auto-locks and curled into a ball, covering his head with the bag he had used to tote his camera.

I'll be fine. I've broken no laws; my name is on none of Dae Kim's accoutrements.

Cary had been so very careful to do all of his business in the Rakum's name. To top it off, Dae Kim had signed over his fortune hours before they abducted Beryl, the funds securely tucked away in foreign accounts under one of Cary's Chinese aliases.

It's fine... he said to himself and the memory of his mother. *I'm rich enough to beat any rap. It's fine. This is not over...*

A fresh wave of nausea flowed over him and Cary took a deep breath. *I can still get Canaan... Roberts won't talk. I'll move him in with me; we'll experiment on each other... yes, there's my Plan C. Continue my research with Adam at my side.* Despite the pain, a tiny grin hit Cary's mouth.

"Mother's two sons," he gasped, for the first time thinking on his connection to Kilmeade's doppelganger in a familial way. With renewed hope, Cary turned his heart to Shangti for guidance. His god didn't speak with words, but the confidence and pride that infiltrated his being made him aware he had been heard.

When the time is right, I'll pick up Elder Canaan to add his power to our blood.

Cary's phone chimed with a new text and with every ounce of concentration he could muster, he peeked at the illuminated lockscreen. It was Adam sending a joint text to Dae Kim and Cary both.

"What happened?"

Cary mentally huffed, not having the energy to scoff at the youngster's naiveté. What if they saw him texting? What if they confiscated his phone? Cary forced himself to trust the guy would at least lay low until he was contacted. Surely, Dae Kim explained how the escape plan worked. Of course, Cary expected Dae to survive and he was mad and angry to lose such a perfect specimen.

I have Dae Kim's log-in for their website...

Cary pressed the bag harder over his eyes and grimaced at a new stab of pain.

Yeah, Cary, stop crying. There are other Rakum resisting the change, pining for their former glory. Some of them hate the Elders out of simple jealousy. Adam and I will make new friends...

The sound of a motor reached Cary's keen hearing and within another minute, a four-wheel-drive pick-up parked close. A high-pitched screech of joy and a parent's admonishing reply filled the air. Cary squeezed his eyes tighter. A baby wailed from the same direction and a woman shouted for the picnic basket.

Babies!

As a full-blown Rakum Elder, Kilmeade bred a baby in that girl's womb!

More than that, Cary's pained mind brought forth, *this child is a daughter with a womb of her own...* He and Adam were expert geneticists, and both of them were full of Rakum DNA.

Cary was falling asleep, forced by the sun to succumb once and for all, but he had a new idea. One that held the greatest promise of all. He relinquished control of his consciousness and faded away. But when he awoke, he'd go back to work. He had a lot to do and even more to plan.

EPILOGUE, TUSCALOOSA

Weary and bedraggled by the events of the past thirty-six hours, Javier and Beryl declined Canaan's offer of rejuvenation and all three rode in weary silence from the airport in a hastily-ordered Lyft. Two mornings ago, healed to perfection, Beryl returned to the rental with Adam in tow. By the time Canaan came up top at sunset, Adam was gone. Had he been complicit in the plot? With no direct evidence to accuse the man, Canaan chose to get his boys home and deal with Roberts later. By sunset the following evening, Beryl brought Javier home from the hospital; he'd keep his sight and was otherwise no worse for wear. The three of them flew home over two nights, arriving in Birmingham, Alabama by midnight.

Canaan flicked his gaze to the driver's profile; the youngster was Indian and hadn't spoken a word since they gave him their addresses. *Kilmeade would have liked that,* Canaan thought miserably. His other half had been gone only a few days and the wound in his spirit remained open, raw, and oozing. How long would he ache in the deep places his fellow occupied the past several months? Canaan resisted turning to see his friends in the back, and instead invested his energy in alleviating the human pain cleaving his spirit.

The driver turned onto Oppenheim as he had been directed. Canaan was relieved he didn't need to instruct the bearded child twice; he was in no mood to coddle university tots. Javier needed to be dropped first and then the driver would take Canaan and Beryl home where he'd collect his truck to get Chloe from her mother's.

Chloe... Because of a gentle phone call from Javier, she knew Kilmeade had left the flesh. Still, knowing a thing and then seeing his friends return without him was an entirely different animal. The car pulled into Roman's driveway and two seatbelts unbuckled in the rear. Canaan didn't turn, guessing what Beryl had in mind.

"I'm crashing with Javier," he said in a monotone.

Canaan nodded once and the back doors closed. He didn't need to speak; everyone knew the score. Chloe would cry and it was up to Canaan to absorb her pain. His duty to Kilmeade had everything now to do with his mate and the baby she carried.

In less than five minutes, the driver pulled in behind Canaan's still-new black Ford and he exited the car. With a heavy sigh, he unlocked his truck and climbed in. The Bushmans lived ten miles away so he sent Chloe a short text message, which she answered with a capital letter K.

When he reached the Bushman home, he stared at the front door a few long moments, gathering his thoughts. His telepathic connection to Chloe informed him she knew he had arrived and was watching from a curtained window, as nervous about facing him as facing the reality that she was now a widow and her baby fatherless. The last two thoughts had been hers, not his, and he sighed.

"Oh, little bird," he sent over and stepped out of the truck. *"I'm bringing Kilmeade with me. You'll see..."* Canaan trudged toward the house under a full moon and when he stepped onto the porch, the door pulled open. Kilmeade's widow stood in the doorway holding firmly to her lax expression. She didn't want to speak, lest she lose control of her emotions. Canaan had practiced the proper greeting, but his mind went blank. "Hey, little bird," he whispered.

"Canaan!" she yelped as the dam broke in her spirit. She lurched into his arms, ferociously grabbing him about the neck until he stood and brought her off the ground. "Please, take me home," she mewled into his neck, her tears wetting his shirt.

"Come on, baby," he whispered and repositioned to carry her properly before him with her still holding on tightly. Mrs. Bushman stepped into the doorway as he turned and he paid her no mind. Focusing on Chloe, he carried her to the passenger side of the pickup and put her gently in. Chloe looked into his face as he stood away to close the door and he gave her a smile.

"Everything's gonna be okay," he sent silently; she responded with a tiny nod. Once behind the wheel, Chloe scooted over and belted herself in the middle of the bench seat. She wrapped around his near bicep and he kissed the top of her head before pulling off. The fifteen minute ride to the house was only interrupted by a chime on her cell phone, which she ignored. When he pulled into the garage and switched off the truck, the wide door mechanically rolled down, sending the room into gloom.

"Want me to carry the bird inside?" he asked softly. The corner of her mouth turned up the tiniest bit and she nodded. "Sit tight."

Canaan came around and gathered her up to take the four steps to the door. Inside, he set her feet to the tile and they exhaled in unison. Chloe giggled a sad sound.

"What now?" she asked in a soft voice, looking into the dark house.

"Wanna make out?" Canaan weakly joked.

Subdued, she popped his arm with a forced laugh. "Let's sit down."

Chloe stepped to the living room and wiped her cheeks with her sleeve before falling into the couch. Canaan sat across from her in the recliner. She regarded him in the low light and he stared back, his mind blank. Finally she broke the silence.

"What did you mean you brought Kilmeade with you?" Chloe crossed her legs Indian-style and cupped her knees with both hands.

Canaan remained forward resting his elbows on his thighs. "At the end," Canaan paused to work up the correct word. "He downloaded everything of importance."

"Downloaded?" Chloe asked, holding her tears at bay.

"Yes," Canaan said, dragging out the word. "Rakum prefer isolation. We socialize with each other, but don't share ourselves as mortals do..." Canaan's telling tapered off as he realized the idiocy of continuing. The Rakum were over. Why give lessons now?

"Don't stop," Chloe said quietly. She unfolded her legs and scooted closer. "So Kilmeade shared his memories with you before he left?"

Canaan held her gaze a few long seconds and rolled in his lips. With a slow nod he took a deep breath. "In one brain all this time, I read his consciousness, but to recall something with him, he'd have to bring it to his mind." When she blinked with understanding, he continued. "Before he left, he did the best he could to remember everything meaningful. Everything you or I might need or enjoy in the days and years to come."

"That's wonderful," Chloe said and her eyes landed on the ring Kilmeade gave her. After a minute, she scooted closer still. "Anything come to mind? Anything to comfort us now?"

Canaan stood and crossed to the fireplace. He leaned on the mantel seeking a proper reply. Chloe rose and stood by the couch.

"It's okay," she whispered.

Canaan caught her gaze, apologizing with his eyes. "I want to comfort you, but I don't know what to say."

"Listen," she said, "it's not about words." Her voice broke at the end and she stepped closer. "From the beginning, you always made me feel better. I saw your devotion to Kilmeade, to Javier and Beryl." Chloe wiped her eyes. "To me," she said and closed the distance between them to embrace his middle. *You always comforted me,* she sent silently.

401

Canaan enveloped her, her cheek against his chest. He stroked her long hair and waited for something more to say. Again, she spoke first.

"Kelly Meade is due Oct 23rd," she said softly.

"That's a beautiful name, little bird."

"Yeah," she whispered, the sound causing one of Kilmeade's transmitted memories to pop into his mind. She had said the word in that same manner moments before they consummated their mate-up. Canaan kept it to himself, unwilling to bring up possible futures for the two of them. Would she even want him for a mate after all she'd been through? He kissed her head tenderly and then rest his chin on her hair.

"I am here for you for the duration. You only have to ask—or *think* it," he said and leaned over to see her face, "and I will do it."

Chloe squeezed him tight and remained. "Kilmeade ordered all sorts of new security for the house," she continued with her eyes closed. "Cameras and monitors, and I overheard they're even building us a wall." She leaned out to see his face. "It'll be a compound like in *The Godfather.*"

"The security fulfills one of Kilmeade's final visions—a fortress of stone built around his child. You'll have security like the Secret Service." Canaan's expression grew somber as he recalled why Kilmeade felt such measures necessary. What had they told Chloe? Canaan asked her what she knew of the past several hours.

"Nothing except Kilmeade is gone," she said and released Canaan. Her shoulders slumped as she looked into his face. "So it's not over?"

"I have no more visions of the future. Dae Kim is dead, your friends are alive. Will you hear the rest of it?" Canaan watched her eyes; an Elder's mate should never be guarded from hard truths. Even if the Rakum were over forever.

"Canaan," she said with seriousness, "I've proven my hardiness. From this day on, I always want to know *everything* concerning our safety—mine, the baby, *and you.*"

Canaan agreed and touched her cheek. "There is an unknown danger remaining. The shadow-man from your dream is a real person. Neither Kilmeade nor I know if it is Adam. *Whoever* it is set up an extremely elaborate plan and used Dae Kim as a means to an end. Adam is a genius, but when I looked inside him, I saw nothing that indicated he was capable of this level of subterfuge."

Chloe's expression held and she covered his fingers still on her face. "So what does this mean?"

"This means I will fulfill my promises to Kilmeade. You will get your fortress; you will be happy and safe."

"And you'll be looking for Adam?"

Canaan shrugged. "He'll remain on my radar, but I want to concentrate on you, your baby, and our friends. Over time, the truth will come out. You know that's how the Puppeteer operates." Chloe's eyes sparkled with humor at how he referred to her God. "Like that, do ya?"

She nodded and at the same time, a familiar internal nudge warned Canaan the sun neared the horizon. He came to attention with a tiny jerk.

"Time for me to go below, little bird."

Chloe looked at her phone screen for the time and caught a peek at the text she'd received from her mother. She flashed it to Canaan.

Tell that Canaan he better take good care of our baby."

Canaan grinned and Chloe moved to stand in front of him. "Let me come with you. I don't want to be alone." Canaan hemmed and Chloe shifted to his side to clutch his arm close to her body. "I'll fall right to sleep and when I wake up, I'll leave you in peace. Deal?"

Canaan began walking from the room and she kept up with him. "I don't mind," he said with a chuckle, "but no funny business. This right here—" he said moving his hand in the air around himself, "is extremely difficult to resist. Ask anyone."

Chloe giggled. "I know. I'll do my best."

"I'll count on it," he said as they reached the basement. "Ladies first." Chloe grabbed the handrail and stepped down.

At the bottom, he nodded with approval at the changes Chloe had made. A queen bed hugged the far wall, with a pool table and pinball machine across the room. Canaan snickered when his eye landed on the blue pillow-top comforter where his and hers flannel pajamas sat folded.

"I don't wear jammies, sweetheart," he chuckled.

"Wear the pants, at least," she said with a teasing glare. She reached for the women's set and scooted to the attached bathroom.

Canaan shook his head. "Kilmeade, you should have stuck around..." he said to the air.

Only One was listening anymore and Canaan sent the Puppeteer a wink. He'd sign up soon.

Soon, but not yet.

End *Anomaly*

Watch for Book Five in the Rabbit Saga

CONUNDRUM
The Lost Rabbit
Little Roni Publishers (Winter 2018)

Conundrum [kuh-**nuhn**-druh m] noun. Anything that puzzles, a riddle.

Out of 100,000, **Canaan is the last of his kind.** Over the course of eight years, the God of the mortals deftly decimated his people, deploying a myriad of methods, including using Canaan's closest companions toward that end. Yet, Elder Canaan isn't angry with the Maker; **he believes the prophecy** that he, too, will one day walk in the Light after shedding his supernatural and bloodthirsty nature.

But first… **One more romp in glory.**

Living among his now-human brethren, Canaan wrestles with his desire to please the Maker and the visceral draw of his birthright: unfathomable power, limitless strength, and as much human blood as he can consume.

Canaan promises he will answer.
Soon.
But not yet.

The Rabbit Trilogy

The Rabbit Saga includes 6 novels. The first 3 involve the Rakum becoming aware of a Creator, and the last 3 bring every last one to choose sides.

Sneak Peek

Conundrum
The Lost Rabbit

The Rakum were anti-man, demonic, & self-preserving. Can a Rakum Elder remain sane in an all-mortal world or will he strike the ones he loves as his flesh resists the Light?

Roman scanned the backyard, seeking his pint-sized, half-dead ward. More than a century ago, another little boy had been dropped into Roman's care, and as before, he addressed the challenge head-on. In 1885, at eight years old, Javier arrived on his doorstep ready to be proselytized into a powerful example of their race.[i] He had succeeded in spades—then and now, Javier could not make him prouder. Now, in 2018, there was Benny.

"RUNNN, GRAC-IEEE!" Ben bellowed, encouraging Mike and Beth's daughter Grace Louise to follow him as he streaked across the sunny yard.

Roman grinned and stepped away from the window. The Stones were on the back patio and at any moment, Beryl would arrive from his apartment, with or without his constant companion (*and Javier's former Cow*, Roman recalled with an eye-twitch), Simon Miller. Javier had invited any of Chloe's guests who arrived before sundown to stay over until the party began at Canaan's house.

Which was Kilmeade's house and Kilmeade's bride not too long ago...

Roman huffed at himself for bringing up the memory of his brother in such a way. Kilmeade knew months in advance that he would be leaving the flesh. What courage and strength of character it took to continue doing the job God had for him, even though he had seen Yeshua[22] and knew he would join God in paradise as soon as his time arrived. Kilmeade had been the greatest Elder of their people, but never would Roman have guessed he would also become a tool of Almighty God.

'Look and see! Be utterly astounded! For I will work a work in your days which you would not believe, even if you were told!'[23]

Roman's lips parted as he repeated the Bible verse in his mind. Across

---

[22] "Yeshua," Jesus' Hebrew name, literally means, "Salvation."
[23] Habakkuk 1:5

the space, Beryl entered with an easy nod, saving him from thinking too hard upon any of it. Beryl tipped his chin toward the stairs seeking Javier and he held up his cell. "The master has commanded me to bring him on over," he said with gentle snark.

"Everything okay?"

"As far as I know. I don't know what he wants Javier for, but he thinks I'm not happy." Beryl chuckled and his unique fawn-colored eyes shined across the distance.

"Are you?" Roman asked. "Happy?"

"Supremely, *Master,*" he answered and winked to erase any offense before he started away. Roman didn't mind, even though the surprise utterance of his former title caused snippets of his past to flood his consciousness. All who turned to the Maker were expected to purposefully forget their past; Javier was doing it. David, too. So far, Roman only pretended to forget. In reality, too often he woke from a fit of dreams where his body was not human, and it craved blood.

THUD!

Roman startled out of his thoughts and faced forward. Benny had run into the sliding glass door face first and seconds later, remained flat against the glass, his head to the side.

"Mr. Roman, guess what I am. Guess," he said through the closed door. Roman didn't reply and he answered anyway. "BUG ON-NA WINN-SHIELD!" he shouted and peeled himself off to crazily guffaw his way into the yard. The Stones looked in grinning at the boy's antics. What was God doing with the tiny zombie?

From the foyer, Javier called goodbye. Mike and Beth entered to see him close the door and Mike chuckled.

"The old gorilla got bored," he joked referring to Canaan.

Roman responded with a courtesy huff. He had been an Elder for two hundred years and commiserated with Canaan's aversion to idle time. Michael was brighter than many of his Rakum peers, but he could never know what it was like inside an Elder's mind.

"The kids are right behind us," Beth said as she found a seat. "I want to tell you what Gracie told me about Ben."

Roman also took a seat and Mike sat on the arm of Beth's chair.

"I was trying to explain who Benny was using broad terms. I mean, she's only seven; she doesn't need to know the science of it." Beth glanced at Mike who nodded. "I told her that you adopted Benny from California and that he had a medical condition no one can figure out. I was preparing her, you know, in case he dies."

"Sure," Roman said. He had grown incredibly attached to the boy—they all had—but Benny was technically dead. It made sense that when God was finished with him, the boy would be brought to Jesus instead of miraculously returned to normal.

"She explained who Benny really was," Beth continued with wide eyes. "She said, and I quote, 'Benny had a mean daddy, and lots of mean people used to hurt him in his room. But one night, he met Uncle Canaan and all those people disappeared.'" Beth paused and Roman made a sound of surprise. "I know," Beth agreed. "But it gets weirder…" She looked to her husband. "Tell Roman what she told you."

With a half-shake of his head, Mike sighed. "She said Billy told her that Ben is already with Jesus. I said he wasn't, that he was at Uncle Roman's house. But she stood firm. Here they come," Mike said looking up. "I'll ask her again."

The children marched inside after an overly dramatic pull on the door. Mike called his daughter close and whispered in her ear.

Ben crossed his arms. "No secrets!" he asserted and Roman pulled him close by his sleeve. Ben allowed it and leaned against Roman's knees watching Mike and Gracie, mumbling, "Rude-frood-in-a-loose-mood."

Mike sat up and his daughter turned to meet Roman's eye.

"Billy knows lots of things that are hard for grown-ups to believe," the little girl said speaking more like a twelve-year-old. Or maybe, Roman realized, he had spent too much time with Ben, who did not sound more than five most of the time.

"Sometimes it's hard for grown-ups to *understand,*" Roman explained in elementary-teacher mode. "I *believe* you, but how can Benny be with Jesus if I'm looking at him right now?"

Grace Louise giggled and held out her fingers. When Ben trotted over and clasped her hand, she continued with them both facing Roman. "Two Benny's, Uncle Roman. One-two. Show him," she said then, shaking the boy's hand.

With a wide grin, Ben closed his eyes and mimicked holding hands on his empty side. "HEY, 'SHUA!" he shouted.

Roman's lips parted to ask another question, but the boy began speaking in a new tongue. Roman concentrated on the phrases since he spoke more than fifty mortal languages, but only a few words rang familiar. Mike was listening, too, and shaking his head. After thirty seconds, Ben opened his eyes and dropped his empty hand.

"I back!" he said with glee and wiggled Grace's fingers.

"What did you and Yeshua talk about?" Beth asked, leaning forward.

Ben smiled showing his teeth. "We like to talk about Kay-nan. I asked Shua, when are we gon' to see Kay-nan. I wanna go now!"

Roman chuckled, amazed to think the boy with no heartbeat had spoken to the Creator and asked only about tonight's schedule.

"What'd He say?" Mike asked thumping Ben's head.

"Tole me be patient..." The boy's shoulders drooped.

"Can we play the piano until time to go?" Grace Louise asked then, first to her mother's face and then to Roman's. He nodded and Beth told them to be careful.

"Yes, ma'am!" the children sang in tandem and wound their way to the front room where Roman had set up a baby grand. When tentative notes filtered from their direction, Mike exhaled.

"What is God doing with this?" he asked. "I can't imagine what purpose his condition could serve."

Roman sighed. "I hope it's to somehow help Canaan finally believe." Both guests nodded at his statement. "He spends his evenings consoling Chloe and visiting with us, but that's no life for a Rakum Elder. He won't be able to keep that up."

"What are you saying?" Beth asked, hearing more in his words than he let on. "You are afraid he'll what?"

Roman looked aside and wondered how much to reveal. He was projecting onto Canaan what he felt, what Kilmeade felt when it was nearing his time to go. Finally, he met the woman's eye.

"Unless God intervenes in some way, Canaan will eventually crack. He's not taking enough blood and he's not being stimulated." Beth appeared clueless and Roman added, "Kilmeade kept him busy *being* an Elder. But now?" Roman shrugged.

Her eyes widening, Beth asked, "He'll crack?"

From the arm of her chair, Mike rubbed her upper back. "Flip out." He looked to Roman. "How do we help him?"

"Remain available," Roman said in his most serious tone. "All of us. We can drag it out longer by being available when he calls. If he ever starts getting busy signals, he could withdraw. Regress."

Beth shook her head. "You sound certain. This is going to happen?"

"If he doesn't take enough blood, yes. If he doesn't stretch his mind, yes. If he doesn't get enough exercise. He needs stimulation." Roman removed his glasses and rubbed his face with one hand. "Elders are cognitively advanced, exponentially more contemplative than any mortal." He waited to let his words sink in, recalling the sensations from his own transformation eight years ago. "He sleeps three hours out of twenty-four, which leaves plenty of time to be aware of what's missing."

"*Can* he be stimulated?" Beth asked. "Legally? *Safely?*"

Roman caught her drift. "He can take blood off Javie and Beryl—he knows that. But he has no release for the violence he's so fond of. He jokes with Mike constantly about wanting to wrestle." Roman smiled with chagrin. "Maybe you should let him pummel you. He'll be careful."

"You're joking," Mike said not as a question and Roman laughed.

"Just keep this in mind until God seals the deal."

"We'll keep praying for him to believe," Beth said.

"And that he doesn't crack before then," Mike added without a smile.

"Roman," Beth said, "is Chloe in danger?"

Roman hemmed. The possibility was there, but he hated to guess what another Elder was capable of when out of his mind. "Javier and I will tell him what to look for. We'll warn Chloe, too. If he gets that close, Javier and I will be able to help him."

Mike and Beth said they would trust him and Roman changed the subject to the party. In another hour, they'd head over for Chloe to show them all she could go on without his brother. Deep down, Roman still grieved, but it had nothing to do with Chloe or Canaan. Deep down, he ran a continuing complaint against God for not allowing him and Kilmeade more time.

"*He's a big God; he can take it,*" Roman told himself and mostly believed it.

Connect with the author on Twitter: @authorellenmaze
Follow the author on Amazon to receive email alerts of all new releases: http://tinyurl.com/yyatd6xm

Conundrum available 12/24/2019
from Run Rabbit Books,
an Imprint of Little Roni Publishers
www.LittleRoniPublishers.com

Author Beth Rider wrote a vampire novel that caused the Rakum to think about God...
Read the Book that Started it All...

The Judging
The Corescu Chronicles Book One
"How do you perform the will of God when you've become a monster?"
With the sharp stab of the demon's fangs, village priest Markus Corescu finds his world turned upside-down, coming to the realization that he has been transformed into an abomination— a vampire. Immediately, the newly-undead clergyman assigns a divine calling to his bloodthirsty nature and satisfies his despicable hunger on the humans around him without remorse. Fast forward to the present, and the priest begins to recall (and is forced to deal with) his suppressed past. Can he make amends with God in such accursed flesh?

About the Author

Raised on Bram Stoker and Stephen King, Ellen read Frank Peretti's *This Present Darkness* in 2000, and has never been the same. Now she takes the horror/paranormal/vampire genre directly into the heart of spiritual matters, pitting good against evil within the confines of biblical truth. Scripture is often bloody and the struggle to escape the claws of evil is real and personal. With writing as her passion and her main hobby, Ellen lives in Alabama with her family and does NOT have holes in her neck.

ELLEN'S LINKS:
www.ellencmaze.com
Emails welcome: ellenmaze@aol.com
Twitter: @authorellenmaze
Facebook: www.facebook.com/ellencmaze
Ellen writes and illustrates children's books and nonfiction under the pen name Ellen Sallas.

---

[i] As anchoring characters, Elder Roman's relationship with Javier is woven into the plot-points of *Rabbit: Chasing Beth Rider* and forward.

www.ingramcontent.com/pod-product-compliance
Lightning Source LLC
Chambersburg PA
CBHW060140260626
47160CB00001B/54